The Keys of the Kingdom

Books in the Loyola Classics Series

Catholics by Brian Moore

Cosmas or the Love of God by Pierre de Calan

Dear James by Jon Hassler

The Devil's Advocate by Morris L. West

Do Black Patent Leather Shoes Really Reflect Up?
by John R. Powers

The Edge of Sadness by Edwin O'Connor

Helena by Evelyn Waugh

In This House of Brede by Rumer Godden

The Keys of the Kingdom by A. J. Cronin

The Last Catholic in America by John R. Powers

Mr. Blue by Myles Connolly

North of Hope by Jon Hassler

Saint Francis by Nikos Kazantzakis

The Silver Chalice by Thomas B. Costain

Things As They Are by Paul Horgan

The Unoriginal Sinner and the Ice-Cream God by John R. Powers

Vipers' Tangle by François Mauriac

The Keys of the Kingdom

A. J. CRONIN

Introduction by Joseph Bottum

CHICAGO

LOYOLAPRESS.
3441 N. Ashland Avenue
Chicago, Illinois 60657
(800) 621-1008
www.loyolapress.com/loyola-classics

Series art direction: Adam Moroschan
Series design: Adam Moroschan and Erin VanWerden
Cover design: Erin VanWerden
Interior design: Erin VanWerden

Library of Congress Cataloging-in-Publication Data
Cronin, A. J. (Archibald Joseph), 1896-1981.
The keys of the kingdom / A.J. Cronin.
p. cm. — (Loyola classics series)
ISBN-13: 978-0-8294-2334-1
ISBN-10: 0-8294-2334-6
I. Title. II. Series.
PR6005.R68K4 2006
823'.912—dc22

2006008350

Printed in the United States of America
09 10 11 12 Bang 10 9 8 7 6 5 4 3 2

Contents

Introduction

Joseph Bottum

The problem is that A. J. Cronin was a hack—a popular hack, as it happens, and a skillful one, whose unhappy attempts to practice medicine produced a successful writing career. Beginning to write in his thirties, he quickly discovered he could pen a readable story in nice, clean prose, with a fast-stepping plot, a sharp dramatic turn, and a set of generally stock but well-turned characters. Filmmakers loved him. They snapped up nearly everything he wrote, from the novels *The Stars Look Down* (1935) and *The Citadel* (1937) to the stories that formed the television series *Dr. Finlay's Casebook* in the 1960s. On and on, the list of his filmed novels runs—*The Keys of the Kingdom* (1942), *The Green Years* (1944), *The Spanish Gardener* (1950)—each vastly successful at the time, each mostly forgotten now.

Except, perhaps, *The Keys of the Kingdom*. Something a little extra—something a little beyond ready and popular hackery—seems to have slipped unexpectedly into this tale of a Catholic missionary to China named Father Francis Chisholm. Cronin clearly felt an affinity for his hero. As his 1964 memoir *A Song of Sixpence* reveals, his own childhood in Scotland was similar to the early life he gives Chisholm. Cronin used *The Keys of the*

Kingdom to express his thoughts about the embattled West as it struggled in the Second World War, the Christian faith as it was carried out to a distant and hostile culture, and the shape that a good man's life could take if he gave himself to God.

That's not to say that they were particularly deep thoughts. When Cronin sets down what he clearly imagines are the profound spiritual revelations of his novel, they turn out to be little more than pious uplift, along the lines of "Why can't we all just get along?" and "Aren't all religions really saying the same thing?" Thus, for example, the elderly Father Chisholm, back in Scotland after a lifetime of preaching and ministering to the poorest of the poor in China, carefully explains: "If we have the fundamentals—love for God and our neighbor—surely we're all right? And isn't it time for the religions of the world to cease hating one another . . . and unite? The world is one living, breathing body, dependent for its health on the billions of cells which comprise it."

To which one wants to say, as a matter of fact, no. Not at a moment when the neo-pagan Nazis and the Japanese militarists were at the peak of their power. Not in an era when the mandarin Confucianism so admired by Father Chisholm had broken down into a China brutally divided among cynical warlords. Not at a time when Christian missionaries like Father Chisholm, sent off to convert the Far East, were being martyred from Singapore to Seoul. Then, if ever, was an occasion in which to draw a distinction—an era in which to realize that Jesus Christ brought something *different* into the world.

Curiously, that's one of the things that the novel actually does reveal. The unique Christian faith that produced a unique culture shines through *The Keys of the Kingdom*. A. J. Cronin really could write, and it is in the background to his story—in all that he probably took for granted—that a thick and interesting moment of Catholic culture is documented and preserved.

At the time Cronin was writing *The Keys of the Kingdom*, that culture seemed solid and unlikely ever to change, but he describes it with precision and intensity. The antagonism of Protestants and Catholics in Scotland. The priest-run school system that knew how to sharpen the bright, serious young boys and loose them like arrows on the world. The great movement of Christian missions in Asia that for three generations had captivated the imagination of Christians—Protestant and Catholic alike. It's a little-remarked-upon story, but the real origins of modern Christian unity are found in the mission fields of China and Burma and Indonesia—where much of the ancient feud of European Protestantism and Catholicism was set aside in a kind of ecumenism of the trenches.

All this is what Cronin knows and his novel captures. Surely that makes a world still worth recalling. Surely that makes *The Keys of the Kingdom* a novel still worth reading.

The number of medical doctors who end up as writers is surprisingly large. There's the poet William Carlos Williams, of course, and the essayist Oliver Wendell Holmes Sr., and the novelist Walker Percy. The work of doctor authors runs from the genre-creating mystery stories of Dr. Arthur Conan Doyle, to the genuine literary achievements of Dr. Anton Chekhov, and on to the immensely popular thrillers of Dr. Michael Crichton.

The early and mid-twentieth century seemed particularly flooded with novelizing doctors. Francis Brett Young and W. Somerset Maugham were probably the ones with the highest literary aim, but there was a kind of middle run of enormously popular medical writers. Published in 1929, Axel Munthe's now-unread *Story of San Michele*, for instance, may have been the best-selling book of its time. Warwick Deeping sold books like hotcakes, though there is probably no one alive who remembers the plot of his 1935 novel *Sorrell and Son*. Frank G. Slaughter's medical potboilers and Richard Gordon's *Doctor in the House* comedies reached large audiences, though their works are so faded they have disappeared even from the used-book tables.

And then there was Archibald Joseph Cronin. Born in 1896 in the Scottish town of Cardross, he lost his father at an early age and suffered badly from the ensuing poverty. Like his character Francis Chisholm, Cronin was brought up a Catholic, and he suffered as well from the taunts and bullying of the Protestant schoolboys who had learned from their parents to hate Scotland's Catholic minority.

A wealthy uncle paid his way through school, and in 1919 he finished his medical training at Glasgow University, where he met his wife Agnes Mary Gibson. There followed the usual succession of doctor's jobs in those days: a stint as a surgeon in the Royal Navy, residencies in various London and Welsh hospitals, and a cruise as the onboard doctor for a passenger ship. In 1924, he was appointed a medical inspector of mines in

Wales—the origin of his angry, 1935 social-commentary novel *The Stars Look Down*.

Health problems drove him back to Scotland in 1930. During his convalescence, he penned his first book, *Hatter's Castle*, the story of a Scottish hatmaker who longs to join the upper class. Though critics noted that the story borrowed heavily from other authors' works, the novel did well enough that Cronin decided to transfer all his energy to writing. One success after another quickly followed: in the 1930s, *The Stars Look Down*, *The Citadel*, and *Lady with Carnations*; in the 1940s, *The Keys of The Kingdom*, *The Green Years*, and *Shannon's Way*; in the 1950s, *Adventures in Two Worlds*, *The Spanish Gardener*, and *Beyond This Place*. By the mid-1960s, however, the string was running out. Though he continued writing until his death in 1981, the audience for his books was declining steadily, and few of his books remain in print.

Though his specialty was always medical stories—his most famous character still is probably Dr. Finlay Hyslop, the hero of the long-running British television series *Dr. Finlay's Casebook*—A. J. Cronin had an enduring interest in religious themes. Often the medical and the religious overlapped. His 1961 novel *The Judas Tree*, for example, tells the story of a wealthy physician named David Moray who betrays a woman on her way to a Christian mission in Africa. A disturbing chapter—quite possibly Cronin's best piece of writing—in *Adventures in Two Worlds* tells the story of a doctor who is gradually drawn into complicity with a woman's illegal abortion. And *The Minstrel Boy*, published in 1975 and one of his final books, features a spoiled priest whose successful career after leaving the priesthood gradually reveals the emptiness of his life—and he sets off at last for the Christian missions of India.

The religious theme in Cronin's work is at its clearest and best in this book, *The Keys of the Kingdom*. Almost without noticing what he was doing, A. J. Cronin caught in enduring detail the harsh boyhood Scotland of Francis Chisholm. Almost as an incidental feature of his story, he photographs the faith of a Catholic world now lost forever. Almost in asides, he documents the great sacrifice of the Christian missionaries to the Far East in the early twentieth century. And almost through indirection, he teaches the joy of that sacrifice—the wonder of that faith.

Joseph Bottum is the editor of First Things.

The Keys of the Kingdom

To my friend F. M.,
for twenty years a missionary in China

"And I will give to thee the keys of the kingdom of heaven."

—Christ to Peter

PART I

Beginning of the End

1

Late one afternoon in September 1938 old Father Francis Chisholm limped up the steep path from the church of St. Columba to his house upon the hill. He preferred this way, despite his infirmities, to the less arduous ascent of Mercat Wynd; and, having reached the narrow door of his walled-in garden, he paused with a kind of naive triumph—recovering his breath, contemplating the view he had always loved.

Beneath him was the river Tweed, a great wide sweep of placid silver, tinted by the low saffron smudge of autumn sunset. Down the slope of the northern Scottish bank tumbled the town of Tweedside, its tiled roofs a crazy quilt of pink and yellow, masking the maze of cobbled streets. High stone ramparts still ringed this Border burgh, with captured Crimean cannon making perches for the gulls as they pecked at partan crabs. At the river's mouth a wraith lay upon the sandbar, misting the lines of drying nets, the masts of smacks inside the harbor pointing upward, brittle and motionless. Inland, dusk was already creeping upon the still bronze woods of Derham, toward which, as he gazed, a lonely heron made labored flight. The air was thin and clear, stringent with woodsmoke and the tang of fallen apples, sharp with the hint of early frost.

With a contented sigh, Father Chisholm turned into his garden: a patch beside his pleasance upon the Hill of Brilliant Green Jade, but a pretty one, and, like all Scots gardens, productive, with a few fine fruit trees splayed on the mellow wall. The Jargonelle espalier in the south corner was at its best. Since there was no sign of the tyrant Dougal, with a cautious glance toward the kitchen window he stole the finest pear from his own tree, slid it under his soutane. His yellow, wrinkled cheek was ripe with triumph as he hobbled—dot and carry—down the graveled drive, leaning on his one indulgence, the new umbrella of Chisholm tartan that replaced his battered favorite of Pai-tan. And there, standing at the front porch, was the car.

His face puckered slowly. Though his memory was bad and his fits of absentmindedness a perpetual embarrassment, he now recollected the vexation of the bishop's letter, proposing, or rather announcing, this visit of his secretary Monsignor Sleeth. He hastened forward to welcome his guest.

Monsignor Sleeth was in the parlor, standing, dark, thin, distinguished, and not quite at ease, with his back to the empty fireplace—his youthful impatience heightened, his clerical dignity repelled, by the mean surroundings in which he found himself. He had looked for a note of individuality: some piece of porcelain perhaps, or lacquer, a souvenir from the East. But the apartment was bare and nondescript, with poor linoleum, horsehair chairs, and a chipped mantelpiece on which, out of the corner of a disapproving eye, he had already noted a spinning top beside an uncounted litter of collection pennies. Yet he was resolved to be pleasant. Smoothing his frown, he stifled Father Chisholm's apology with a gracious gesture.

"Your housekeeper has already shown me my room. I trust it will not disturb you to have me here for a few days. What a superb afternoon it has been. The colorings!—as I drove up from Tynecastle I almost fancied myself in dear San Morales." He gazed away, through the darkening window, with a studied air.

The old man nearly smiled at the imprint of Father Tarrant and the seminary—Sleeth's elegance, that bladelike look, even the hint of hardness in the nostril, made him a perfect replica.

"I hope you'll be comfortable," he murmured. "We'll have our bite presently. I'm sorry I can't offer you dinner. Somehow we've just fallen to the habit of a Scots high tea!"

Sleeth, head half-averted, nodded noncommittally. Indeed, at that moment, Miss Moffat entered and, having drawn the drab chenille curtains, stealthily began to set the table. He could not but reflect, ironically, how the neutral creature, darting him one frightened glance, matched the room. Though it caused him a passing asperity to observe her lay places for three, her presence enabled him to lead the conversation safely into generalities.

As the two priests sat down at table he was eulogizing the special marble which the bishop had brought from Carrara for the transept of the new Tynecastle procathedral. Helping himself with good appetite from the ashet of ham, eggs, and kidneys before him, he accepted a cup of tea poured from the Britannia metal teapot. Then, busy buttering brown toast, he heard his host remark mildly:

"You won't mind if Andrew sups his porridge with us. Andrew—this is Monsignor Sleeth!"

Sleeth raised his head abruptly. A boy about nine years of age had come silently into the room and now, after an instant's indecision, when he stood tugging at his blue jersey, his long pale face intense with nervousness, slipped into his place, reaching mechanically for the milk jug. As he bent over his plate a lock of dank brown hair—tribute to Miss Moffat's sponge—fell over his ugly bony forehead. His eyes, of a remarkable blue, held a childish prescience of crisis—they were so uneasy he dared not lift them up.

The bishop's secretary relaxed his attitude, slowly resumed his meal. After all, the moment was not opportune. Yet from time to time his stare traveled covertly toward the boy.

"So you are Andrew!" Decency demanded speech, even a hint of benignity. "And you go to school here?"

"Yes . . ."

"Come then! Let us see how much you know." Amiably enough, he propounded a few simple questions. The boy, flushed and inarticulate, too confused to think, betrayed humiliating ignorance.

Monsignor Sleeth's eyebrows lifted. *Dreadful*, he thought. *Quite a gutter brat!*

He helped himself to another kidney—then suddenly became aware that while he trifled with the rich meats of the table the other two kept soberly to porridge. He flushed: this show of asceticism on the old man's part was insufferable affectation.

Perhaps Father Chisholm had a wry perception of that thought. He shook his head: "I went without good Scots oatmeal so many years I never miss it now I have the chance."

Sleeth received the remark in silence. Presently, with a hurried glance, out of his downcast muteness, Andrew begged permission to depart. Rising to say his grace, he knocked a spoon spinning with his elbow. His stiff boots made an uncouth scuffling toward the door.

Another pause. Then, having concluded his meal, Monsignor Sleeth rose easily and repossessed, without apparent purpose, the fleshless hearth rug. With feet apart and hands clasped behind his back he considered, without seeming to do so, his aged colleague, who, still seated, had the curious air of waiting. *Dear God,* thought Sleeth, *what a pitiable presentation of the priesthood—this shabby old man, with a stained soutane, soiled collar, and sallow, desiccated skin!* On one cheek was an ugly weal, a kind of cicatrix that everted the lower eyelid, seemed to tug the head down and sideways. The impression was that of a permanent wry neck, counterpoising the lame and shortened leg. His eyes, usually lowered, took thus—on the rare occasions that he raised them—a penetrating obliqueness, which was strangely disconcerting.

Sleeth cleared his throat. He judged it time for him to speak and, forcing a note of cordiality, he inquired: "How long have you been here, Father Chisholm?"

"Twelve months."

"Ah, yes. It was a kindly gesture of His Grace to send you—on your return—to your native parish."

"And his!"

Sleeth inclined his head suavely. "I was aware that His Grace shared with you the distinction of having been born here. Let me see . . . what age are you, Father? Nearly seventy is it not?"

Father Chisholm nodded, adding with gentle senile pride: "I am no older than Anselm Mealey."

Sleeth's frown at the familiarity melted into a half-pitying smile. "No doubt—but life has treated you rather differently. To be brief"—he gathered himself up, firm, but not unkind—"the bishop and I both have the feeling that your long and faithful years should now be recompensed; that you should, in short, retire!"

There was a moment of strange quiet.

"But I have no wish to retire."

"It is a painful duty for me to come here"—Sleeth kept his gaze discreetly on the ceiling—"to investigate . . . and report to His Grace. But there are certain things that cannot be overlooked."

"What things?"

Sleeth moved irritably. "Six—ten—a dozen things! It isn't my place to enumerate your—your Oriental eccentricities!"

"I'm sorry." A slow spark kindled in the old man's eyes. "You must remember that I spent thirty-five years in China."

"Your parish affairs are in a hopeless muddle."

"Am I in debt?"

"How are we to know? No returns on your quarterly collections for six months." Sleeth's voice rose; he spoke a little faster. "Everything so . . . so unbusinesslike. . . . For instance when

Bland's traveler presented his bill last month—three pounds for candles, and so forth—you paid him entirely in coppers!"

"That's how it comes to me." Father Chisholm viewed his visitor thoughtfully, as though he looked straight through him. "I've always been stupid about money. I've never had any, you see. . . . But after all . . . do you think money so dreadfully important?"

To his annoyance Monsignor Sleeth found himself reddening. "It makes talk, Father." He rushed on. "And there is other talk. Some of your sermons . . . the advice you give . . . certain points of doctrine." He consulted a morocco-covered notebook already in his palm. "They seem dangerously peculiar."

"Impossible!"

"On Whitsunday you told your congregation, 'Don't think heaven is in the sky . . . it's in the hollow of your hand . . . it's everywhere and anywhere.'" Sleeth frowned censoriously as he turned the pages. "And again . . . here is an incredible remark you made during Holy Week. 'Atheists may not all go to hell. I knew one who didn't. Hell is only for those who spit in the face of God!' And, good gracious, this atrocity: 'Christ was a perfect man, but Confucius had a better sense of humor!'" Another page was turned indignantly. "And this incredible incident . . . when one of your best parishioners, Mrs. Glendenning, who cannot of course help her extreme stoutness, came to you for spiritual guidance you looked at her and replied, 'Eat less. The gates of paradise are narrow.' But why should I continue?" Decisively, Monsignor Sleeth closed the gilt-edged book. "To say the least, you seem to have lost your command of souls."

"But . . ." Calmly: "I don't want to command anyone's soul."

Sleeth's color heightened disagreeably. He did not see himself in theological discussion with this shambling dotard.

"There remains the matter of this boy whom you have so misguidedly adopted."

"Who is to look after him—if I don't?"

"Our own sisters at Ralstone. It is the finest orphanage in the diocese."

Again Father Chisholm raised his disconcerting eyes. "Would you have wished to spend your own childhood at that orphanage?"

"Need we be personal, Father? I've told you . . . even conceding the circumstances . . . the situation is highly irregular and must be ended. Besides . . ." He threw out his hands. "If you are going away—we must find some place for him."

"You seem determined to be rid of us. Am I to be entrusted to the sisters too?"

"Of course not. You can go to the aged priests' home at Clinton. It is a perfect haven of rest."

The old man actually laughed—a dry short laugh. "I'll have enough perfect rest when I'm dead. While I'm alive I don't want to be mixed up with a lot of aged priests. You may think it strange—but I never have been able to stand the clergy in bulk."

Sleeth's smile was pained and flustered. "I think nothing strange from you, Father. Forgive me, but to say the least of it . . . your reputation, even before you went to China . . . your whole life has been peculiar!"

There was a pause. Father Chisholm said in a quiet voice: "I shall render an account of my life to God."

The younger man dropped his eyelids with an unhappy sense of indiscretion. He had gone too far. Though his nature was cold he strove always to be just, even considerate. He had the grace to look uncomfortable. "Naturally I don't presume to be your judge—or your inquisitor. Nothing is decided yet. That is why I am here. We must see what the next few days bring forth." He stepped toward the door. "I am going to the church now. Please don't trouble. I know my way." His mouth creased into an unwilling smile. He went out.

Father Chisholm remained seated, motionless, at the table, his hand shading his eyes, as though thinking deeply. He felt crushed by this threat that had gathered, so suddenly, above the quiet of his hard-won retreat. His sense of resignation, long overtaxed, refused acceptance of it. All at once he felt empty and used up, unwanted by God or man. A burning desolation filled his breast. Such a little thing, and yet so much. He wanted to cry out: *My God, my God, why hast thou forsaken me?* He rose heavily, and went upstairs.

In his attic above the spare room the boy Andrew was already in bed and asleep. He lay upon his side, one skinny arm crooked before him on the pillow, defensively. Watching him, Father Chisholm took the pear from his pocket and placed it on the clothes folded upon the cane-bottomed chair beside the bed. There seemed nothing more for him to do.

A faint breeze swayed the muslin curtains. He moved to the window and parted them. Stars were quivering in the frosty sky.

Under these stars the span of his years reached out in all its ineptitude, built of his puny strivings, without form or nobility. It seemed such a short time since he had been a boy himself, running and laughing in this same town of Tweedside. His thoughts flew back. If there were any pattern in his life at all the first fateful stroke was surely drawn on that April Saturday sixty years ago when, out of untroubled happiness, so deep it passed unrecognized . . .

PART II

Strange Vocation

1

That spring morning, at early breakfast in the snug dark kitchen, with the fire warm to his stockinged feet and the smell of kindling wood and hot oatcakes making him hungry, he was happy, despite the rain, because it was Saturday and the tide was right for salmon.

His mother finished her brisk stirring with the wooden spurtle, and placed the blue-ringed bowl of pease brose on the scrubbed table between his father and himself. He reached for his horn spoon, dipped in the bowl, then in the cup of buttermilk before him. He rolled his tongue over the smooth golden brose, made perfectly, without lumps or gritty unmixed meal.

His father, in worn blue jersey and darned fishing stockings, sat opposite, his big frame bowed, supping in silence, with quiet slow movements of his red hands. His mother shook the last batch of oatcakes from the griddle, set them on their ends against the bowl, and sat down to her cup of tea. The yellow butter melted on the broken oatcake that she took. There was silence and comradeship in the little kitchen, with the flames leaping across the bright fender and the pipe-clayed hearth. He was nine years of age, and he was going to the bothy with his father.

There, he was known—he was Alex Chisholm's laddie, accepted by the men in their woolen jerseys and leather hip boots with a quiet nod or, better still, a friendly silence. He had a dark secret glow of pride as he went out with them, the big flat cobble sweeping wide round the butt, the rowlocks creaking, the seine skillfully payed out by his father in the stern. Back on the butt, their tackets rasping the wet stones, the men huddled themselves low against the wind, some squatting with a yellowed sailcloth across their shoulders, others sucking warmth from a blackened inch-long clay. He stood with his father, apart. Alex Chisholm was the headman, the watcher of Tweed Fisheries Station No. 3. Together, not speaking, cut by the wind, they stood watching the far circle of corks dancing in the choppy backlash where the river met the sea. Often the glare of sun upon the ripples made his head swim. But he would not, he could not, blink. Missing even a single second might mean the missing of a dozen fish—so hard to come by, these days, that in distant Billingsgate they brought the fisheries company a good half crown a pound. His father's tall figure, the head sunk a little on the shoulders, the profile keen beneath the old peaked cap, a fine blood whipped into the high cheekbones, had the same still unswerving tensity. At times, mingled exquisitely in his consciousness with the smell of wrack, the distant strike of the Burgess Clock, the cawing of the Derham rooks, the sense of this unspeaking comradeship drew moisture to the boy's already smarting eyes.

Suddenly his father shouted. Try as he might Francis could never win first sight of the dipping cork: not that tidal bobbing, which sometimes caused him foolishly to start, but the slow downward tug, which to long experience denoted the thrusting of a fish. At the quick high shout there was an instant clatter as the crew jumped to the windlass that hauled the net. Usage never staled that moment: though the men drew a poundage bonus on their catch, the thought of money did not stir them; this deep excitement sprang from far primeval roots. In came the net, slowly, dripping, flaked with kelp, the guide ropes squeaking on the wooden drum. A final heave, then, in the purse of the billowing seine, a molten flash, powerful, exquisite—salmon.

One memorable Saturday they had taken forty at a cast. The great shining things arched and fought, bursting through the net, slithering back to the river from the slippery butt. Francis flung himself forward with the others, desperately clutching at the precious escaping fish. They had picked him up, sequined with scales and soaked to the bone, a perfect monster locked in his embrace. Going home that evening, his hand inside his father's, their footfalls echoing in the smoky twilight, they had stopped, without comment, at Burley's in the High Street, to buy a pennyworth of cockles, the peppermint ones that were his special choice.

Their fellowship went further still. On Sundays, after Mass, they took their rods and slipped secretly—lest they shock finer sensibilities—through the back ways of the Sabbath-stricken town, out into the verdant valley of the Whitadder. In his tin, packed with sawdust, were luscious maggots, picked the night before from Mealey's boneyard. Thereafter the day was heady with the sound of the stream, the scent of meadowsweet—his father showing him the likely eddies, the crimson-speckled trout wriggling on bleached shingle, his father bent over a twig fire, the crisp sweet goodness of the frizzled fish . . .

At other seasons they would go to gather blueberries, wood strawberries, or the wild yellow rasps that made good jam. It was a gala day when his mother accompanied them. His father knew all the best places and would take them deep into devious woods, to untouched canebrakes of the juicy fruit.

When snow came and the ground was clamped by winter, they stalked between the frozen trees of Derham "policies," his breath a rime before him, his skin pricking for the keeper's whistle. He could hear his own heart beating as they cleared their snares, under the windows, almost, of the great house itself—then home, home with the heavy game bag, his eyes smiling, his marrow melting to the thought of rabbit pie. His mother was a grand cook, a woman who earned—with her thrift, her knack of management and homely skill—the grudging panegyric of a Scots community: "Elizabeth Chisholm is a well-doing woman!"

Now, as he finished his brose, he became conscious that she was speaking, with a look across the breakfast table toward his father.

"You'll mind to be home early tonight, Alex, for the Burgess."

There was a pause. He could see that his father, preoccupied—perhaps by the flooded river and the indifferent salmon season—was caught unawares, recalled to the annual formality of the Burgess Concert, which they must sustain that evening.

"You're set on going, woman?" with a faint smile.

She flushed slightly; Francis wondered why she should seem so queer. "It's one of the few things I look forward to in the year. After all, you are a burgess of the town. It's . . . it's right for you to take your seat on the platform with your family and your friends."

His smile deepened, setting lines of kindness about his eyes—it was a smile Francis would have died to win. "Then it looks like we maun gang, Lisbeth." He had always disliked the Burgess, as he disliked teacups, stiff collars, and his squeaky Sunday boots. But he did not dislike this woman who wanted him to go.

"I'm relying on you, Alex. You see," her voice, striving to be casual, sounded an odd note of relief, "I have asked Polly and Nora up from Tynecastle—unfortunately it seems Ned cannot get away." She paused. "You'll have to send someone else to Ettal with the tallies."

He straightened with a quick look which seemed to see through her, right to the bottom of her tender subterfuge. At first, in his delight, Francis noticed nothing. His father's sister, now dead, had married Ned Bannon, proprietor of the Union Tavern in Tynecastle, a bustling city some sixty miles due south. Polly, Ned's sister, and Nora, his ten-year-old orphan niece, were not exactly close relations. Yet their visits could always be counted occasions of joy.

Suddenly he heard his father say in a quiet voice: "I'll have to go to Ettal all the same."

A sharp and throbbing silence. Francis saw that his mother had turned white.

"It isn't as if you had to. . . . Sam Mirlees, any of the men, would be glad to row up for you."

He did not answer, still gazing at her quietly, touched on his pride, his proud exclusiveness of race. Her agitation increased. She dropped all pretense of concealment, bent forward, placed nervous fingers upon his sleeve.

"To please me, Alex. You know what happened last time. Things are bad again there—awful bad, I hear."

He put his big hand over hers, warmly, reassuringly.

"You wouldn't have me run away, would you, woman?" He smiled and rose abruptly. "I'll go early and be back early . . . in plenty time for you, our daft friends, and your precious concert to the bargain."

Defeated, that strained look fixed upon her face, she watched him pull on his hip boots. Francis, chilled and downcast, had a dreadful premonition of what must come. And indeed, when his father straightened it was toward him he turned, mildly, and with rare compunction.

"Come to think of it, boy, you'd better bide home today. Your mother could do with you about the house. There'll be plenty to see to before our visitors arrive."

Blind with disappointment, Francis made no protest. He felt his mother's arm tensely, detainingly, about his shoulders.

His father stood a moment at the door, with that deep contained affection in his eyes, then he silently went out.

Though the rain ceased at noon the hours dragged dismally for Francis. While pretending not to see his mother's worried frown, he was racked by the full awareness of their situation. Here in this quiet burgh they were known for what they were—unmolested, even warily esteemed. But in Ettal, the market town four miles away where, at the fisheries head office, his father, every month, was obliged to check the record of the catches, a different attitude prevailed. A hundred years before the Ettal moors had blossomed with the blood of Covenanters; and now the pendulum of oppression had relentlessly swung back. Under the leadership of the new provost a furious religious persecution had recently arisen. Conventicles were formed, mass gatherings held in the square, popular feelings whipped to frenzy. When the violence of the mob broke loose the few Catholics in the town were hounded from their homes, while all others in the district received solemn warning not to show themselves upon the Ettal streets. His father's calm disregard of this threat had singled him for special execration. Last month there had been a fight in which the sturdy salmon watcher had given good account of himself. Now, despite renewed menaces, and the careful plan to stay him, he was going again. . . . Francis flinched at his own thoughts, and his small fists clenched violently. Why could not people let one another be? His father and his mother had not the same belief, yet they lived together, respecting each other, in perfect peace. His father was a good man, the best in the world . . . why should they want to do him harm? Like a blade thrust into the warmth of his life came a dread, a shrinking from that word *religion,* a chill bewilderment that men could hate one another for worshiping the same god with different words.

Returning from the station at four o'clock, somberly leaping the puddles to which Nora, his half cousin, gaily dared him—his mother walking with Aunt Polly, who came, dressed up and sedate, behind—he felt the day oppressive with disaster. Nora's friskiness, the neatness of her new brown braided dress, her manifest delight in seeing him, proved but a wan diversion.

Stoically, he approached his home, the low neat gray-stone cottage, fronting the Cannelgate, behind a trim little green where in summer his father grew asters and begonias. There was evidence of his mother's passionate cleanliness in the shining brass knocker and the spotless doorstep. Behind the immaculately curtained windows three potted geraniums made a scarlet splash.

By this time, Nora was flushed, out of breath, her blue eyes sparkling with fun, in one of her moods of daring, impish gaiety. As they went round the side of the house to the back garden where, through his mother's arrangement, they were to play with Anselm Mealey until teatime, she bent close to Francis's ear so that her hair fell across her thin laughing face, and whispered in his ear. The puddles they had barely missed, the sappy moisture of the earth, prompted her ingenuity.

At first Francis would not listen—strangely, for Nora's presence stirred him usually to a shy swift eagerness. Standing small and reticent, he viewed her doubtfully.

"I know he will," she urged. "He always wants to play at being holy. Come on, Francis. Let's do it. Let's!"

A slow smile barely touched his somber lips. Half-unwilling, he fetched a spade, a watering can, an old news sheet from the little toolshed at the garden end. Led by Nora, he dug a two-foot hole between the laurel bushes, watered it, then spread the paper over it. Nora artistically sprinkled the sheet with a coating of dry soil. They had barely replaced the spade when Anselm Mealey arrived, wearing a beautiful white sailor suit. Nora threw Francis a look of terrible joy.

"Hello, Anselm!" she welcomed brilliantly. "What a lovely new suit. We were waiting on you. What shall we play at?"

Anselm Mealey considered the question with agreeable condescension. He was a large boy for eleven, well padded, with pink and white checks. His hair was fair and curly; his eyes were soulful. The only child of rich and devoted parents—his father owned the profitable bonemeal works across the river—he was already destined, by his own election and that of his pious mother, to enter Holywell, the famous Catholic college in northern Scotland, to study for the priesthood. With Francis he served the altar at St. Columba's. Frequently he was to be found kneeling in church, his big eyes fervent with tears. Visiting nuns patted him on the head. He was acknowledged, with good reason, as a truly saintly boy.

"We'll have a procession," he said. "In honor of St. Julia. This is her feast day."

Nora clapped her hands. "Let's pretend her shrine is by the laurel bushes. Shall we dress up?"

"No." Anselm shook his head. "We're praying more than playing. But imagine I'm wearing a cope and bearing a jeweled monstrance. You're a white Carthusian sister. And Francis, you're my acolyte. Now, are we all ready?"

A sudden qualm swept over Francis. He was not of the age to analyze his relationships; he only knew that, though Anselm claimed him fervently as his best friend, the other's gushing piety evoked in him a curious painful shame. Toward God he had a desperate reserve. It was a feeling he protected without knowing why, or what it was, like a tender nerve, deep within his body. When Anselm burningly declared in the Christian doctrine class "I love and adore our Savior from the bottom of my heart," Francis, fingering the marbles in his pocket, flushed a deep dark red, went home sullenly from school, and broke a window.

Next morning when Anselm, already a seasoned sick visitor, arrived at school with a cooked chicken, loftily proclaiming the object of his charity as Mother Paxton—the old fishwife, sere with hypocrisy and cirrhosis of the liver, whose Saturday-night brawls made the Cannelgate a bedlam—Francis, possessed, visited the cloakroom during class and opened the package, substituting for the delicious bird, which he consumed with his companions, the decayed head of a cod. Anselm's tears, and the curses of Meg Paxton, had later stirred in him a deep dark satisfaction.

Now, however, he hesitated, as if to offer the other boy an opportunity of escape. He said slowly: "Who'll go first?"

"Me, of course," Anselm gushed. He took up his position as leader. "Sing, Nora: *Tantum Ergo.*"

In single file, at Nora's shrill pipe, the procession moved off. As they neared the laurel bushes, Anselm raised his clasped hands to heaven. The next instant he stepped through the paper and squelched full-length in the mud.

For ten seconds no one moved. It was Anselm's howl as he struggled to get up that set Nora off. While Mealey blubbered clammily, "It's a sin; it's a sin!" she hopped about laughing, taunting wildly, "Fight, Anselm; fight. Why don't you hit Francis?"

"I won't; I won't," Anselm bawled. "I'll turn the other cheek."

He started to run home. Nora clung deliriously to Francis—helpless, choking, tears of laughter running down her cheeks. But Francis did not laugh. He stared in moody silence at the ground. Why had he stooped to such inanity while his father walked those hostile Ettal causeways? He was still silent as they went in to tea.

In the cozy front room, where the table was already set for the supreme rite of Scots hospitality, with the best china and all the electroplate the little household could muster, Francis's mother sat with Aunt Polly, her open rather earnest face a trifle flushed from the fire, her stocky figure showing an occasional stiffening toward the clock.

Now, after an uneasy day, shot equally with doubt and reassurance—when she told herself how stupid were her fears—her ears were tuned acutely for her husband's step: she was conscious of an overwhelming longing for him. The daughter of Daniel Glennie, a small and unsuccessful baker by profession, and by election an open-air preacher, leader of his own singular Christian brotherhood in Darrow, that shipbuilding town of incomparable drabness which lies some twenty miles from the city of Tynecastle, she had, at eighteen, during a week's holiday from the parental cake counter, fallen wildly in love with the young Tweedside fisher, Alexander Chisholm, and promptly married him.

In theory, the utter incompatibility of such a union foredoomed it. Reality had proved it a rare success. Chisholm was no fanatic: a quiet, easygoing type, he had no desire to influence his wife's belief. And she, on her side, sated with early piety, grounded by her peculiar father in a strange doctrine of universal tolerance, was not contentious.

Even when the first transports had subsided she knew a glowing happiness. He was, in her phrase, such a comfort about the place; neat, willing, never at a loss when it came to mending her wringer, drawing a fowl, clearing the bee skeps of their honey. His asters were the best in Tweedside; his bantams never failed to take prizes at the show; the dovecote he had finished recently for Francis was a wonder of patient craftsmanship. There were moments, in the winter evenings when she sat knitting by the hearth, with Francis snug in bed, the wind whistling cozily around the little house, the kettle hissing on the hob, while her long raw-boned Alex padded the kitchen in his stocking feet, silently intent upon some handiwork, when she would turn to him with an odd, tender smile: "Man, I'm fond of you."

Nervously she glanced at the clock: yes, it was late, well past his usual time of homecoming. Outside a gathering of clouds was precipitating the darkness and again heavy raindrops splashed against the windowpanes. Almost immediately Nora and Francis came in. She found herself avoiding her son's troubled eye.

"Well, children!" Aunt Polly summoned them to her chair and wisely apostrophized the air above their heads. "Did you have a good play? That's right. Have you washed your hands, Nora? You'll be looking forward to the concert tonight, Francis. I love a tune myself. God save us, girl, stand still. And don't forget your company manners, either, my lady—we're going to get our tea."

There was no disregarding this suggestion. With a hollow sensation of distress, intensified because she concealed it, Elizabeth rose.

"We won't wait on Alex any longer. We'll just begin." She forced a justifying smile. "He'll be in any moment now."

The tea was delicious, the scones and bannocks homemade, the preserves jelled by Elizabeth's own hands. But an air of strain lay heavily about the table. Aunt Polly made none of those dry remarks which usually gave Francis such secret joy, but sat erect, elbows drawn in, one finger crooked for her cup. A spinster, under forty, with a long, worn, agreeable face, somewhat odd in her attire, stately, composed, abstracted in her manner, she looked a model of conscious gentility, her lace handkerchief upon her lap, her nose humanly red from the hot tea, the bird in her hat brooding warmly over all.

"Come to think, Elizabeth—" She tactfully filled a pause. "They might have brought in the Mealey boy—Ned knows his father. A wonderful vocation, Anselm has." Without moving her head she touched Francis with her kindly omniscient eye. "We'll need to send you to Holywell too, young man. Elizabeth, you'd like to see your boy wag his head in a pulpit?"

"Not my only one."

"The Almighty likes the only ones." Aunt Polly spoke profoundly.

Elizabeth did not smile. Her son would be a great man, she was resolved, a famous lawyer, perhaps a surgeon; she could not bear to think of him as suffering the obscurity, the sorry hardships of the clerical life. Torn by her growing agitation she exclaimed: "I do wish Alex would come. It's . . . it's most inconsiderate. He'll keep us all late if he doesn't look sharp."

"Maybe he's not through with the tallies," Aunt Polly reflected considerately.

Elizabeth flushed painfully, out of all control. "He must be back at the bothy by now . . . he always goes there after Ettal." Desperately she tried to stem her fears. "I wouldn't wonder if he'd forgotten all about us. He's the most heedless man." She paused. "We'll give him five minutes. Another cup, Aunt Polly?"

But tea was over and could not be prolonged. There was an unhappy silence. What had happened to him? . . . Would he never, never come? Sick with anxiety, Elizabeth could restrain herself no longer. With a last glance, charged with open foreboding, toward the marble timepiece, she rose. "You'll excuse me, Aunt Polly; I'll have to run down and see what's keeping him. I'll not be long."

Francis had suffered through these moments of suspense—haunted by the terror of a narrow wynd, heavy with darkness and surging faces and confusion, his father penned . . . fighting . . . falling under the crowd . . . the sickening crunch of his head upon the cobblestones. Unaccountably he found himself trembling. "Let me go, Mother," he said.

"Nonsense, boy." She smiled palely. "You stay and entertain our visitors."

Surprisingly, Aunt Polly shook her head. Hitherto she had betrayed no perception of the growing stress. Nor did she now. But with a penetrating staidness she remarked: "Take the boy with you, Elizabeth. Nora and I can manage fine."

There was a pause during which Francis pleaded with his eyes.

"All right . . . you can come."

His mother wrapped him in his thick coat; then, bundling into her plaid cape, she took his hand and stepped out of the warm bright room.

It was a streaming, pitch-dark night. The rain lathered the cobblestones, foamed down the gutters of the deserted streets. As they struggled up the Mercat Wynd past the distant square and the blurred illumination of the Burgess Hall, new fear reached at Francis from the gusty blackness. He tried to combat it, setting his lips, matching his mother's increased pace with quivering determination.

Ten minutes later they crossed the river by the Border bridge and picked their way along the waterlogged quay to Bothy No. 3. Here his mother halted, dismayed. The bothy was locked, deserted. She turned indecisively, then suddenly observed a faint beacon, vaporous in the rainy darkness, a mile upriver: Bothy No. 5, where Sam Mirlees, the underwatcher, made his lodging. Though Mirlees was an aimless, tippling fellow, he could surely give them news. She started off again, firmly, plodding across the sodden meadows, stumbling over unseen tussocks, fences, ditches. Francis, close at her side, could sense her apprehension, mounting with every step.

At last they reached the other bothy, a wooden shanty of tarred boards, stoutly planted on the riverbank, behind the high stone butt and a swathe of hanging nets. Francis could bear it no longer. Darting forward with throbbing breast, he threw open the door. Then, at the consummation of his daylong fear, he cried aloud in choking anguish, his pupils wide with shock. His father was there with Sam Mirlees, stretched on a bench, his face pale and bloodied, one arm bound up roughly in a sling, a great purple weal across his brow. Both men were in their jerseys and hip boots, glasses and a mutchkin jar on the nearby table, a dirty crimsoned sponge beside the turbid water dipper, the hurricane swing lamp throwing a haggard yellow beam upon them, while beyond the indigo shadows crept, wavered in the mysterious corners and under the drumming roof.

His mother rushed forward, flung herself on her knees beside the bench. "Alex . . . Alex . . . are ye hurt?"

Though his eyes were muddled he smiled, or tried to, with his blenched and battered lips.

"No worse nor some that tried to hurt me, woman."

Tears sprang to her eyes, born of his willfulness and her love for him, tears of rage against those who had brought him to this pass.

"When he came in he was near done," Mirlees interposed with a hazy gesture. "But I've stiffened him up with a dram or two."

She threw a blazing look at the other man: fuddled, as usual on Saturday night. She felt weak with anger that this sottish fool should have filled Alex up with drink on top of the dreadful hurt he had sustained. She saw that he had lost a great quantity of blood . . . she had nothing here to treat him with . . . she must get him away at once . . . at once. She murmured, tensely:

"Could you manage home with me, Alex?"

"I think so, woman . . . if we take it slow."

She thought feverishly, battling her panic, her confusion. All her instinct was to move him to warmth, light, and safety. She saw that his worst wound, a gash to the temple bone, had ceased to bleed. She swung round toward her son.

"Run back quick, Francis. Tell Polly to get ready for us. Then fetch the doctor to the house at once."

Francis, shivering as with ague, made a blind, convulsive gesture of understanding. With a last glance at his father he bent his head and set off frantically along the quay.

"Try, then, Alex . . . let me give you a hand." Bitterly dismissing Mirlees's offer of assistance, which she knew to be worse than none, she helped her husband up. He swayed slowly, obediently to his feet. He was dreadfully shaky, hardly knew what he was doing. "I'll away then, Sam," he muttered, dizzily. "Good night to ye."

She bit her lip in a torment of uncertainty, yet persisted, led him out, met by the stinging sheets of rain. As the door shut behind them and he stood, unsteady, heedless of the weather, she was daunted by the prospect of that devious return, back through the mire of the fields with a helpless man in tow. But suddenly, as she hesitated, a thought illuminated her. Why had it not occurred to her before? If she took the shortcut by the tile-works bridge she could save a mile at least, have him home and safe in bed within half an hour. She took his arm with fresh resolution. Pressing into the downpour, supporting him, she pointed their course upriver toward the bridge.

At first he did not apparently suspect her purpose, but suddenly, as the sound of rushing water struck his ear, he halted.

"Whatna way's this to come, Lisbeth? We cannot cross by the tile works with Tweed in such a spate."

"Hush, Alex . . . don't waste your strength by talking." She soothed him, helped him forward.

They came to the bridge, a narrow hanging span, fashioned of planks with a wire rope handrail, crossing the river at its narrowest, quite sound, though rarely used, since the tile works that it served had long ago shut down. As Elizabeth placed her foot upon the bridge, the blackness, the deafening nearness of the water, caused a vague doubt, perhaps a premonition, to cross her mind. She paused, since there was not room for them to go abreast, peering back at his subdued and sodden figure, swept by a rush of strange maternal tenderness.

"Have ye got the handrail?"

"Ay, I have the handrail."

She saw plainly that the thick wire rope was in his big fist. Distracted, breathless, and obsessed, she could not reason further. "Keep close to me, then." She turned and led on.

They began to cross the bridge. Halfway across his foot slid off a rain-slimed board. It would have mattered little another night. Tonight it mattered more, for the Tweed, in flood, had risen to the planking of the bridge. At once the racing current filled his thigh boot. He struggled against the pull, the overpowering weight. But they had beaten the strength from him at Ettal. His other leg slipped, both boots were waterlogged, loaded as with lead.

At his cry she spun round with a scream and caught at him. As the river tore the handrail from his grip her arms enfolded him; she fought closely, desperately, for a deathless instant to sustain him. Then the sound and the darkness of the waters sucked them down.

All that night Francis waited for them. But they did not come. Next morning they were found, clasped together, at low tide, in the quiet water near the sandbar.

2

One Thursday evening in September four years later, when Francis Chisholm ended his nightly tramp from Darrow Shipyard by veering wearily toward the blistered double headboard of Glennie's Bakery, he had reached a great decision. As he trudged down the floury passage dividing the bake house from the shop—his smallish figure oddly suppressed by an outsize suit of dungarees, his face grimy beneath a man's cloth cap worn back to front—and went through the back door, placing his empty lunch pail on the scullery sink, his dark young eyes were smoldering with this purpose.

In the kitchen Malcom Glennie occupied the table—its soiled cover now, as always, littered with crockery—lolling on his elbow over *Locke's Conveyancing,* a lumpish pallid youth of seventeen, one hand massaging his oily black hair, sending showers of dandruff to his collar, the other attacking the sweetbread cooked for him by his mother on his return from the Armstrong College. As Francis took his supper from the oven—a twopenny pie and potatoes cremated there since noon—and cleared a place for himself, aware, through the torn opaque paper on the half-glazed partition door, of Mrs. Glennie serving a customer in the front shop, the son of the house threw him a glance of peevish disapproval. "Can't you make less noise when I'm studying? And God! What hands! Don't you ever wash before you eat?"

In stolid silence—his best defense—Francis picked up a knife and fork in his calloused, rivet-burned fingers.

The partition door clicked open and Mrs. Glennie solicitously scuffled in. "Are you done yet, Malcom dear? I have the nicest baked custard—just fresh eggs and milk—it won't do your indigestion a mite of harm."

He grumbled: "I've been gastric all day." Swallowing a deep bellyful of wind, he brought it back with an air of virtuous injury. "Listen to that!"

"It's the study, son, that does it." She hurried to the range. "But this'll keep your strength up . . . just try it . . . to please me."

He suffered her to remove his empty plate and to place a large dish of custard before him. As he slobbered it down she watched him tenderly, enjoying every mouthful he took, her raddled figure, in broken corsets and dowdy, gaping skirt, inclined toward him, her shrewish face with its long thin nose and pinched-in lips doting with maternal fondness.

She murmured, presently: "I'm glad you're back early tonight, son. Your father has a meeting."

"Oh, no!" Malcom reared himself, in startled annoyance. "At the mission hall?"

She shook her narrow head. "Open air. On the green."

"We're not going?"

She answered with a strange, embittered vanity: "It's the only position your father ever gave us, Malcom. Until he fails at the preaching too, we'd better take it."

He protested heatedly. "You may like it, Mother. But it's damned awful for me, standing there, with Father Bible-banging, and the kids yelling 'Holy Dan.' It wasn't so bad when I was young, but now when I'm coming out for a solicitor!" He stopped short, sulkily, as the outer door opened and his father, Daniel Glennie, came gently into the room.

Holy Dan advanced to the table, absently cut himself a slice of cheese, poured a glass of milk, and, still standing, began his simple meal. Changed from his working singlet, slacks, and burst carpet slippers, he was still an insignificant and drooping figure in shiny black trousers, an old cutaway coat too tight and short for him, a celluloid dickey, and a stringy black tie. His cuffs were of celluloid too, to save the washing; they were cracked; and his boots might have done with mending. He stooped slightly. His gaze, usually harassed, often ecstatically remote, was now thoughtful, kind, behind his steel-rimmed spectacles. As he chewed, he let it dwell in quiet consideration on Francis.

"You look tired, grandson. Have you had your dinner?"

Francis nodded. The room was brighter since the baker's entry. The eyes upon him now were like his mother's.

"There's a batch of cherry cakes I've just drawn. You can have one, if you've a mind to—on the oven rack."

At the senseless prodigality Mrs. Glennie sniffed: casting his goods about like this had made him twice a bankrupt, a failure. Her head inclined in greater resignation.

"When do you want to start? If we're going now I'll shut the shop."

He consulted his big silver watch with the yellow bone guard. "Ay, close up now, Mother, the Lord's work comes first. And besides"—sadly—"we'll have no more customers tonight."

While she pulled down the blinds on the fly-blown pastries he stood, detached, considering his address for tonight. Then he stirred. "Come, Malcom!" And to Francis: "Take care of yourself, grandson. Don't be late out your bed!"

Malcom, muttering beneath his breath, shut his book and picked up his hat. He sulkily followed his father out. Mrs. Glennie, pulling on tight black kid gloves, assumed her martyred "meeting" face. "Don't forget the dishes, now." She threw a meaning sickly smile at Francis. "It's a pity you're not coming with us!"

When they had gone he fought the inclination to lay his head upon the table. His new heroic resolution inflamed him; the thought of Willie Tulloch galvanized his tired limbs. Piling the greasy dishes into the scullery he began to wash them, rapidly probing his position, his brows tense, resentful.

The blight of enforced benefactions had lain upon him since that moment, before the funeral, when Daniel had raptly told Polly Bannon: "I'll take Elizabeth's boy. We are his only blood relations. He must come to us!"

Such rash benevolence alone would not have uprooted him. It took that later hateful scene when Mrs. Glennie, grasping at the small estate, money from his father's insurance and the sale of the furniture, had beaten down Polly's offer of guardianship, with intimidating invocations of the law.

This final acrimony had severed all contact with the Bannons—abruptly, painfully, as though he, indirectly, had been to blame: Polly, hurt and offended, yet with the air of having done her best, had undoubtedly erased him from her memory.

On his arrival at the baker's household, with all the attraction of a novelty, he was sent, a new satchel on his back, to the Darrow Academy: escorted by Malcom; straightened and brushed by Mrs. Glennie, who watched the departing scholars from the shop door with a vague proprietary air.

Alas! The philanthropic flush soon faded. Daniel Glennie was a saint, a gentle noble derided soul who passed out tracts of his own composition with his pies and every Saturday night paraded his van horse through the town with a big printed text on the beast's rump: "Love thy neighbor as thyself." But he lived in a heavenly dream, from which he periodically emerged, careworn, damp with sweat, to meet his creditors. Working unsparingly, with his head on Abraham's bosom and his feet in a tub of dough, he could not but forget his grandson's presence. When he remembered he would take the small boy by the hand to the backyard, with a bag of crumbs, to feed the sparrows.

Mean, shiftless yet avaricious, viewing with a self-commiserating eye her husband's progressive failure—the sacking of the van man, of the shopgirl, the closing of one oven after another, the gradual decline to a meager output of twopenny pies and farthing pastries—Mrs. Glennie soon discovered in Francis an insufferable incubus. The attraction of the sum of seventy pounds she had acquired with him quickly faded, seemed dearly bought. Already wrung by a desperate economy, to her the cost of his clothing, his food, his schooling became a perpetual calvary. She counted his mouthfuls resignedly. When his trousers wore out she "made down" an old green suit of Daniel's, a relic of her husband's youth, of such outlandish pattern and color it provided derisive outcry in the streets, shrouded the boy's life in misery. Though Malcom's fees at the academy were paid upon the nail she usually succeeded in forgetting Francis's until, trembling, pale with humiliation, having publicly been called as a defaulter before the class, he was forced to approach her. Then she would gasp, feign a heart attack by fumbling at her withered bosom, count out the shillings as though he drew away her very blood.

Though he bore it with stoic endurance the sense of being alone . . . alone . . . was terrible for the little boy. Demented with sorrow, he took long solitary walks, combing the sick country vainly for a stream in which to guddle trout. He would scan the outgoing ships, consumed with longing, stuffing his cap between his teeth to stifle his despair. Caught between conflicting creeds, he knew not where he stood; his bright and eager mind was dulled, his face turned sullen. His only happiness came on the nights that Malcom and Mrs. Glennie were from home, when he sat opposite Daniel by the kitchen fire watching the little baker turning the pages of his Bible, in perfect silence, with a look of ineffable joy.

Daniel's quiet but inflexible resolve not to interfere with the boy's religion—how could he, when he preached universal tolerance!—was an added, ever-present goad to Mrs. Glennie. To a "Christian" like herself, who was saved, this reminder of her daughter's folly was anathema. It made the neighbors talk.

The climax came at the end of eighteen months when Francis, with ungrateful cleverness, had the bad taste to beat Malcom in an essay competition open to the school. It was not to be endured. Weeks of nagging wore the baker down. He was on the verge of another failure. It was agreed that Francis's education was complete. Smiling archly for the first time in months, Mrs. Glennie assured him that now he was a little man, fit to contribute to the household, to take his coat off and prove the nobility of toil. He went to work in Darrow Shipyard as a rivet boy, twelve years old, at three and six a week.

By quarter past seven he had finished the dishes. With greater alacrity, he spruced himself before the inch of mirror and went out. It was still light, but the night air made him cough and turn up his jacket as he hurried into High Street, past the livery stable and the Darrow Spirit Vaults, reaching at length the doctor's shop on the corner, with its two bulbous red and green vials and its square brass plate: "Dr. Sutherland Tulloch: Physician and Surgeon." Francis's lips were parted, faintly, as he entered.

The shop was dim and aromatic with the smell of aloes, asafetida, and licorice root. Shelves of dark green bottles filled one side and at the end three wooden steps gave access to the small back surgery where Dr. Tulloch held his consultations. Behind the long counter, wrapping physic on a marble slab spattered with red sealing wax, stood the doctor's eldest son, a sturdy freckled boy of sixteen with big hands, sandy coloring, and a slow taciturn smile.

He smiled now, staunchly, as he greeted Francis. Then the two boys looked away, avoiding one another, each reluctant to view the affection in the other's eyes.

"I'm late, Willie!" Francis kept his gaze intently on the skirting of the counter.

"I was late myself . . . and I've to deliver these medicines for Father, bless him." Now that Willie had begun his medical curriculum at the Armstrong College, Dr. Tulloch had, with solemn facetiousness, accredited him his assistant.

There was a pause. Then the older boy threw a secret glance toward his friend.

"Have you decided?"

Francis's gaze was still downcast. He nodded broodingly, his lips set. "Yes."

"You're right, Francis." Approval flooded Willie's plain and stolid features. "I wouldn't have stood it so long."

"I wouldn't . . . either . . ." Francis mumbled, "except for . . . well . . . my grandfather and you." His thin young face, concealed and somber, reddened deeply as the last words came out with a rush.

Flushing in sympathy, Willie muttered: "I found out the train for you. There's a through leaves Alstead every Saturday at six thirty-five . . . Quiet. Here's Dad." He broke off, with a warning glance, when the surgery door opened and Dr. Tulloch appeared, showing his last patient out. As the doctor returned toward the boys, a brusque, bristling dark-skinned figure in pepper-and-salt tweeds, his bushy hair and glossy whiskers seemed to spark with sheer vitality. For one who bore the awful reputation of the town's professed freethinker, open adherent of Robert Ingersoll and Professor Darwin, he had a most disarming charm, and the look of one who would be useful in a sickroom. Because the hollows in Francis's cheeks made him grave, he cracked a frightful joke. "Well, my lad—that's another one killed off! Oh, he's not dead yet! Soon will be! Such a nice man too, leaves a large family." The boy's smile was too drawn to please him. He cocked his clear, challenging eye, mindful of his own troubled boyhood: "Cheer up, young housemaid's knee—it'll all be the same in a hundred years." Before Francis could reply the doctor laughed briefly, thrust his hard square hat on the back of his head, and began pulling on his driving gloves. On his way out to his gig he called back: "Don't fail to bring him for supper, Will. Hot prussic acid served at nine!"

An hour later, with the physic delivered, the two boys made their way in unspeaking comradeship toward Willie's house, a large dilapidated villa facing the green. As they talked in low voices of the daring promise of the day beyond tomorrow, Francis's spirits lifted. Life never seemed so hostile in Willie Tulloch's company. And yet, perversely, their friendship had begun in strife. After school, one day, larking down Castle Street with a dozen classmates, Willie's gaze had strayed to the Catholic church, ugly but inoffensive, beside the gasworks. "Come on," he shouted, in animal spirits. "I've got sixpence. Let's go in and get our sins forgiven!" Then, glancing round, he saw Francis in the group. He reddened with healthy shame. He had not meant the stupid jibe, which would have passed unheeded if Malcom Glennie had not pounced on it and fanned it skillfully into the occasion for a fight.

Incited by the rest, Francis and Willie fought a bloody indecisive battle on the green. It was a good fight, rich in uncomplaining courage, and when the darkness stopped it, though neither was the victor, each had clearly had enough. But the spectators, with the cruelty of youth, refused to let the quarrel rest. On the next night, after school, the contestants were brought together, whetted with the taunt of cowardice, and set to batter each other's already battered heads. Again, bloody, spent, yet dogged, neither would concede the victory. Thus for a dreadful week they were matched, like gamecocks, to make sport for their baser fellows. The inhuman conflict, motiveless and endless, became, for each, a nightmare. Then, on the Saturday, the two met unexpectedly, face-to-face, alone. An agonizing moment followed, then the earth opened, the sky melted, and each had an arm round the other's neck, Willie blubbering: "I don't want to fight you, I like ye, man!"—while Francis, knuckling his purple eyes, wept back: "Willie, I like you best in the whole of Darrow!"

They were halfway across the green, a public open space carpeted by dingy grass, with a forlorn bandstand in the center, a rusty iron urinal at the far end, and a few benches, mostly without backs, where pale-faced children played and loafers smoked and argued noisily, when suddenly Francis saw, with a tightening of his skin, that they must pass his grandfather's meeting. At the end farthest from the urinal a small red banner had been planted bearing the words in tarnished gilt: "Peace on Earth to Men of Goodwill." Opposite the banner stood a portable harmonium furnished with a camp stool on which Mrs. Glennie sat, wearing her victim's air, with Malcom, glumly clasping a hymnbook, beside her. Between the banner and the harmonium on a low wooden stand, surrounded by some thirty people, was Holy Dan.

As the boys drew up on the fringe of the gathering Daniel had finished his opening prayer and, with his uncovered head thrown back, was beginning his address. It was a gentle and beautiful plea. It expressed Daniel's burning conviction, bared his simple soul. His doctrine was based on brotherhood, the love of one another and of God. Man should help his fellow man, bring peace and goodwill to earth. If only he could lead humanity to that ideal! He had no quarrel with the churches but chastised them mildly: it was not the form that mattered but the fundamentals, humility and charity. Yes, and tolerance! It was worthless to voice these sentiments if one did not practice them.

Francis had heard his grandfather speak before, and felt a throb of dogged sympathy for these views which made Holy Dan the laughingstock of half the town. Now, edged by his wild intention, his heart swelled in understanding and affection, in longing for a world free of cruelty and hate. Suddenly, as he stood listening, he saw Joe Moir, the skip of his riveting squad at the shipyard, sidle up the outskirts of the meeting. Accompanying Joe was the gang that hung about the Darrow Vaults, with an armament of bricks, decayed fruit, and oily waste thrown out from the boiler works. Moir was a ribald likable giant, who, when drunk, gleefully pursued salvation rallies and other outdoor conclaves. He fingered a fistful of dripping waste and shouted: "Hey! Dan! Give us a song and dance!"

Francis's eyes dilated in his pale face. They were going to break up the meeting! He had a vision of Mrs. Glennie, clawing a ripe tomato from her splattered hair, of Malcom, with a greasy rag plastering his hateful face. His being exulted with a wild ecstatic joy.

Then he saw Daniel's face: still unconscious of the danger, lit by a strange intensity, every word throbbing, born of unquenchable sincerity, from the depths of his soul.

He started forward. Without knowing how, or why, he found himself at Moir's side, restraining his elbow, pleading breathlessly: "Don't Joe! Please don't. We're friends, aren't we?"

"Hell!" Moir glanced down, his boozy scowl melting to friendly recognition. "For Christ's sake, Francis!" Then, slowly, "I forgot he was your grandpa." A desperate pause. Then, commandingly, to his followers: "Come on lads, we'll go up to the square and take it out on the Hallelujahs!"

As they moved off, the harmonium wheezed with life. No one but Willie Tulloch knew why the thunderbolt had not fallen.

A minute later, entering his house, he asked, baffled yet impressed: "Why did you, Francis?"

Francis answered shakily: "I don't know. . . . There's something in what he says. . . . I've had enough hating these last four years. My father and mother wouldn't have got drowned if people hadn't hated him . . ." He broke off, inarticulate, ashamed.

Silently, Willie led the way to the living room, which, after the outer dusk, glowed with light and sound and a prodigal untidy comfort. It was a long, high, maroon-papered chamber, asprawl with broken red plush furniture; the chairs castorless; the vases cracked and glued together; the bellpull tugged out; a litter of vials, labels, pillboxes on the mantelpiece, and of toys, books, and children upon the worn ink-stained Axminster. Though it was shockingly near nine o'clock none of the Tulloch family was abed. Willie's seven young brothers and sisters, Jean, Tom, Richard—a list so complex even their father admitted to forgetting it—were diversely occupied in reading, writing, drawing, scuffling, and swallowing their supper of hot bread and milk while their mother Agnes Tulloch, a dreamy voluptuous woman with her hair half down and her bosom open, had picked the baby from his crib upon the hearth and, having removed its steaming napkin, now placidly refreshed the nuzzling bare-bottomed infant at her creamy, fire-lit breast.

She smiled her welcome, unperturbed, to Francis. "Here you are then, boys. Jean, set out more plates and spoons. Richard, leave Sophia alone. And Jean, dear, a fresh diaper for Sutherland from the line! Also see that the kettle's boiling for your father's toddy. What lovely weather we are having. Dr. Tulloch says there is much inflammation about though. Be seated, Francis. Thomas, didn't your father tell you to keep away from the others!" The doctor was always bringing home some disorder: measles one month, chicken pox the next. Now Thomas, aged six, was the victim. His poll shorn and smelling of carbolic, he was happily disseminating ringworm through the tribe.

Squeezed on the crowded twanging sofa beside Jean, at fourteen the image of her mother, with the same creamy skin, the same placid smile, Francis supped his bread and milk flavored with cinnamon. He was still upset from his recent outburst; there was an enormous lump inside his chest; his mind was a maze of confusion. Here was another problem for his aching brain. Why were these people so kind, happy, and contented? Reared by an impious rationalist to deny, or rather to ignore, the existence of their God, they were damned, hellfire already licked their feet.

At quarter past nine the crunch of the dogcart's wheels was heard on the gravel. Dr. Tulloch strode in; a shout went up; he was at once the center of an attacking mob. When the tumult stilled, the doctor had bussed his wife heartily, was in his chair, a glass of toddy in his hand, slippers on his feet, the infant Sutherland goggling on his knee.

Catching Francis's eye, he raised his steaming tumbler in friendly satire.

"Didn't I tell you there was poison going! Strong drink is raging—eh, Francis?"

Seeing his father in high humor, Willie was tempted to relate the story of the prayer meeting. The doctor slapped his thigh, smiling at Francis. "Good for you, my wee Roman Voltaire. I will disagree to the death with what you say and defend with my life your right to say it! Jean, stop making sheep's eyes at the poor laddie. I thought ye wanted to be a nurse! Ye'll have me a grandfather before I'm forty. Eh, well—" He sighed suddenly, toasting his wife. "We'll never get to heaven, woman—but at least we get our meat and drink."

Later, at the front door, Willie gripped Francis by the hand. "Good luck. . . . Write to me when you're there."

At five next morning, while all was still dark, the shipyard hooter sounded, long and dolorous, over the cowering dreariness of Darrow. Half-senseless with sleep, Francis tumbled out of bed and into his dungarees, stumbled downstairs. The frigid morning, pale yet murky, met him like a blow as he joined the march of silent shivering figures, hurrying with bent head and huddled shoulders toward the shipyard gates.

Over the weigh bridge, past the checker's window, inside the gates . . . Gaunt specters of ships rose dimly in their stocks around him. Beside the half-formed skeleton of a new ironclad, Joe Moir's squad was mustering: Joe and the assistant plater, the holders-on, the two other rivet boys, and himself.

He lit the charcoal fire, blew the bellows beneath the forge. Silently, unwillingly, as in a dream, the squad set itself to work. Moir lifted his sledge, the hammers rang, swelled and strengthened, throughout the shipyard.

Holding the rivets, white-hot from the brazier, Francis shinned up the ladder and thrust them quickly through the bolt holes in the frame, where they were hammered flat and tight, annealing the great sheets of metal that formed the ship's hull. The work was fierce: blistering by the brazier, freezing on the ladders. The men were paid by piecework. They wanted rivets fast, faster than the boys could give them. And the rivets must be heated to the proper incandescence. If they were not malleable the men threw them back at the boys. Up and down the ladder, to and from the fires, scorched, smoky, with inflamed eyes, panting, perspiring, Francis fed the platers all day long.

In afternoon the work went faster: the men seemed careless, straining every nerve, unsparing of their bodies. The closing hour passed in a swimming daze with eardrums tense for the final hooter.

At last, at last it sounded. What blessed relief! Francis stood still, moistening his cracked lips, deafened by the cessation of all sound. On the way home, grimed and sweaty, through his tiredness, he thought: *Tomorrow . . . tomorrow.* That strange glitter returned to his eye; he squared his shoulders.

That night he took the wooden box down from its hiding place in the disused oven and changed his hoard of silver and coppers, saved with agonizing slowness, into half a sovereign. The golden coin, clutched deep in his trouser pocket, fevered him. With a queer, exalted flush he asked Mrs. Glennie for a needle and thread. She snubbed him, then threw him suddenly a veiled appraising glance.

"Wait! There's a reel in the top drawer—by that card of needles. You can take it." She watched him go out.

In the privacy of his bare and wretched room above the bake house he folded the coin in a square of paper, sewed it firm and tight inside the lining of his coat. He had a sense of glad security as he came down to give her back the thread.

The following day, Saturday, the shipyard closed at twelve. The thought that he would never enter these gates again so elated him that at dinner he could scarcely eat; he felt his flushed restlessness more than enough to raise some sharp inquiry from

Mrs. Glennie. To his relief she made no comment. As soon as he left the table, he edged out of the house, slipped down East Street, then fairly took to his heels.

Outside the town, he slipped into a brisk walk. His heart was singing within him. It was pathetic commonplace: the timeworn flight of all unhappy childhood. Yet for him it was the road to freedom. Once he was in Manchester he could find work at the cotton mills; he was sure, doubly sure. He covered the fifteen miles to the railway junction in four hours. It was striking six o'clock as he entered Alstead Station.

Seated under an oil lamp on the drafty deserted platform, he opened his penknife, cut the sewing on his jacket, removed the folded paper, took the shining coin from within. A porter appeared on the platform, some other passengers, then the booking office opened.

He took his place at the grille, demanded his ticket.

"Nine and six," the clerk said, punching the green cardboard slip into the machine.

Francis gasped with relief: he had not, after all, miscalculated the fare. He pushed his money through the grille.

There was a pause. "What's the game? I said nine and six."

"I gave you half a sovereign."

"Oh, you did! Try that again young feller and I'll have you run in!" The clerk indignantly flung the coin back at him.

It was not a half sovereign but a bright new farthing.

In anguished stupor, Francis saw the train tear in, take up its freight, and go whistling into the night. Then his mind, groping dully, struck the heart of the enigma. The sewing, when he ripped it open, was not his own clumsy stitching but a close firm seam. In a withering flash he knew who had taken his money: Mrs. Glennie.

At half past nine, outside the colliery village of Sanderston, in the dank wet mist that blurred his gig lamps, a man in a dogcart almost ran down the solitary figure keeping the middle of the road. Only one person was likely to be driving in such a place on such a night. Dr. Tulloch, holding in his startled beast, peered downward through the fog, his masterly invective suddenly cut short.

"Great Lord Hippocrates! It's you. Get in. Quick, will you—before the mare pulls my arms from their sockets." Tulloch wrapped the rug about his passenger, proceeded without questions; he knew the virtue of a healing silence.

By half past ten Francis was drinking hot broth before the fire in the doctor's living room, now bereft of its occupants and so unnaturally still the cat slept peacefully on the hearth rug. A moment later Mrs. Tulloch came in, her hair in plaits, her quilted dressing gown open above her nightgown. She stood with her husband studying the deadbeat boy, who seemed unconscious of their presence, their murmured converse, wrapped in a curious apathy. Though he tried to smile, he could not when the doctor came forward, producing his stethoscope with a jocular air: "I'll bet my boots that cough of yours is a put-up job." But he submitted, opening his shirt, letting the doctor tap, and listen to, his chest.

Tulloch's saturnine face wore a queer expression as he straightened himself. His fund of humor had surprisingly dried up. He darted a look at his wife, bit his full lip, and suddenly kicked the cat.

"Damn it to hell!" he cried. "We use our children to build our battleships. We sweat them in our coal mines and our cotton mills. We're a Christian country. Well! I'm proud to be a pagan." He turned brusquely, quite fiercely, to Francis. "Look here, boy, who are these folks you knew in Tynecastle? What's that—Bannon, eh? The Union Tavern. Get away home now and into bed unless you want treble pneumonia."

Francis went home, resistance crushed in him. All the next week Mrs. Glennie wore a martyred frown and Malcom a new checked waistcoat: price half a sovereign at the stores.

It was a dire week for Francis. His left side hurt him, especially when he coughed; he had to drag himself to work. He was aware, dimly, that his grandfather fought a battle for him. But Daniel was beaten down, defeated. All the little baker could do was to offer, humbly, some cherry cakes that Francis could not eat.

When Saturday afternoon came round he had not the strength to go out. He lay upstairs in his bedroom gazing in hopeless lethargy through the window.

Suddenly he started; his heart gave a great and unbelieving bound. In the street below, slowly approaching, like a bark navigating strange and dangerous waters, was a hat, a thing of memory, unique, unmistakable. Yes, yes: and the gold-handled umbrella, tightly rolled, the short sealskin jacket with the braided buttons. He cried out weakly, with pale lips: "Aunt Polly."

The shop door pinged below. Dithering to his feet, he crept downstairs, poised himself, trembling, behind the half-glazed door.

Polly was standing, very erect, in the center of the floor, her lips pursed, her gaze sweeping the shop, as though amusedly inspecting it. Mrs. Glennie had half-risen to confront her. Lounging against the counter, his mouth half-open, gaping from one to the other, was Malcom.

Aunt Polly's vision came to rest above the baker's wife. "Mrs. Glennie, if I remember right!"

Mrs. Glennie was at her worst: still unchanged, wearing her dirty forenoon wrapper, her blouse open at the neck, a loose tape hanging from her waist.

"What do you want?"

Aunt Polly raised her eyebrows. "I have come to see Francis Chisholm."

"He's out."

"Indeed! Then I'll wait till he comes in." Polly arranged herself on the chair by the counter as though prepared to remain all day.

There was a pause. Mrs. Glennie's face had turned a dirty red. She remarked, aside: "Malcom! Run round to the bake house and fetch your father."

Malcom answered shortly: "He went to the hall five minutes ago. He won't be back till tea."

Polly removed her gaze from the ceiling, brought it critically to bear on Malcom. She smiled slightly when he flushed, then, entertained, she glanced away.

For the first time Mrs. Glennie showed signs of uneasiness. She burst out angrily: "We're busy people here; we can't sit about all day. I've told you the boy is out. Like enough he won't be back till all hours—with the company he keeps. He's a regular worry with his late hours and bad habits. Isn't that so, Malcom?"

Malcom nodded sulkily.

"You see!" Mrs. Glennie rushed on. "If I was to tell you everything you'd be amazed. But it makes no difference; we're Christian people here; we look after him. You have my word for it—he's perfectly well and happy."

"I'm glad to hear it," Polly spoke primly, politely stifling a slight yawn with her glove, "for I've come to take him away."

"What!" Taken aback, Mrs. Glennie fumbled at the neck of her blouse, the color flooding, then fading from, her face.

"I have a doctor's certificate," Aunt Polly enunciated, almost masticated, the formidable phrase with a deadly relish, "that the boy is underfed, overworked, and threatened with a pleurisy."

"It's not true."

Polly pulled a letter from her muff and tapped it significantly with the head of her umbrella. "Can you read the Queen's English?"

"It's a lie, a wicked lie. He's as fat and well fed as my own son!"

There was an interruption. Francis, flat against the door, following the scene in an agony of suspense, leaned too heavily against the rickety catch. The door flew open; he shot into the middle of the shop. There was a silence.

Aunt Polly's preternatural calm had deepened. "Come over, boy. And stop shaking. Do you want to stay here?"

"No, I don't."

Polly threw a look of justification toward the ceiling. "Then go and pack your things."

"I haven't anything to pack."

Polly stood up slowly, pulling on her gloves. "There's nothing to keep us."

Mrs. Glennie took a step forward, white with fury. "You can't walk over me. I'll have the law on you."

"Go ahead, my woman." Polly meaningly restored the letter to her muff. "Then maybe we'll find out how much of the money that came from the sale of poor Elizabeth's furniture has been spent on her son and how much on yours."

Again there was a shattered silence. The baker's wife stood, pale, malignant, and defeated, one hand clutching at her bosom.

"Oh, let him go, Mother," Malcom whined. "It'll be good riddance."

Aunt Polly, cradling her umbrella, examined him from top to toe. "Young man, you're a fool!" She swung round toward Mrs. Glennie. "As for you, woman," looking straight over her head, "you're another!"

Taking Francis triumphantly by the shoulder, she propelled him, bareheaded, from the shop.

They proceeded in this fashion toward the station, her glove grasping the fabric of his jacket firmly, as though he were some rare and captive creature who might at any moment escape. Outside the station she bought him, without comment, a bag of Abernethy biscuits, some cough drops, and a brand-new bowler hat. Seated opposite him in the train, serene, singular, erect, observing him moisten the dry biscuits with tears of thankfulness, extinguished almost by his new hat which enveloped him to the ears, she remarked with half-closed, judicial eyes:

"I always knew that creature was no lady; I could see it in her face. You made an awful mistake letting her get hold of you, Francis dear. The next thing we'll do is get your hair cut!"

3

It was wonderful these frosty mornings to lie warm in bed until Aunt Polly brought his breakfast, a great plate of bacon and eggs still sizzling, boiling black tea and a pile of hot toast, all on an oval metal tray stamped "Allgood's Old Ale." Sometimes he woke early, in an agony of apprehension; then came the blessed knowledge that he need no longer fear the hooter. With a sob of relief he burrowed more deeply into his thick yellow blankets, in his cozy bedroom with its paper of climbing sweet peas, its stained boards and wool-work rug, a lithograph of Allgood's prize brewery dray horse on one wall, of Pope Gregory on another, and a little china holy-water font with a sprig of Easter palm stuck sideways in it by the door. The pain in his side was gone; he seldom coughed; his cheeks were filling out. The novelty of leisure was like a strange caress and, though the uncertainty of his future still troubled him, he received it gratefully.

On this fine morning of the last day of October, Aunt Polly sat on the edge of his bed exhorting him to eat. "Lay in, boy! That'll stick to your ribs!" There were three eggs on the plate; the bacon was crisp and streaky; he had forgotten that food could taste so good.

As he balanced the tray on his knees, he sensed an unusual festivity in her manner. And soon she gave him one of her profound nods.

"I've news for you today, young man—if you can stand it."

"News, Aunt Polly?"

"A little excitement to cheer you up—after your dull month with Ned and me." She smiled dryly at the quick protest in his warm brown eyes. "Can't you guess what it is?"

He studied her with the deep affection that her unceasing kindness had awakened in him. The homely angular face—poor complexioned, the long upper lip downed with hair, a tufted blemish at the angle of the cheek—was now familiar and beautiful.

"I can't think, Aunt Polly."

She was moved to her short rare laugh, a little snort of satisfaction at her success in provoking his curiosity.

"What's happened to your wits, boy? I believe too much sleep has addled them."

He smiled happily in sympathy. It was true that the routine of his convalescence had hitherto been tranquil. Encouraged by Polly, who had feared for his lungs—she had a dread of "consumption," which "ran" in her family—he had usually lain abed until ten. Dressed, he accompanied her on her shopping, a stately progress through the main streets of Tynecastle, which, since Ned ate largely and nothing but the best, demanded great prodding of poultry and sniffing of steak. These excursions were revealing. He could see that it pleased Aunt Polly to be "known," deferred to, in the best stores. She would wait, aloof and prim, until her favorite shop man was free to serve her. Above all, she was ladylike. That word was her touchstone, the criterion of her actions, even of her dresses, made by the local milliner in such dreadful taste they sometimes evoked a covert snigger from the vulgar. In the street she had a graduated series of bows. To be recognized, greeted by some local personage—the surveyor, the sanitary inspector, or the chief constable—afforded her a joy that, though sternly concealed, was very great. Erect, the bird in her hat atwitter, she would murmur to Francis: "That was Mr. Austin, the tramway manager . . . a friend of your uncle's . . . a fine man." The height of her gratification was reached when Father Gerald Fitzgerald, the handsome portly priest of St. Dominic's, gave her in passing his gracious and slightly condescending smile. Every forenoon they would stop in at the church and, kneeling, Francis would be conscious of Polly's intent profile, the lips moving silently, above her rough, chapped, reverent hands. Afterward she bought him something for himself, a stout pair of shoes, a book, a bag of aniseed drops. When he protested, often with tears in his eyes, as she opened her worn purse, she would simply press his arm and shake her head. "Your uncle won't take 'no.'" She was touchingly proud of her relationship with Ned, her association with the Union Tavern.

The Union stood near the docks at the corner of Canal and Dyke streets, with an excellent view of the adjacent tenements, of coal barges, and the terminus of the new horse tramway. The brown painted stucco building was of two stories, and the

Bannons lived above the tavern. Every morning at half past seven Maggie Magoon, the scrubwoman, opened the saloon and began, talking to herself, to clean it. At eight precisely Ned Bannon came down, in his braces, but closely shaved, with his forelock oiled, and strewed the floor with fresh sawdust from the box behind the bar. It was unnecessary: a kind of ritual. Next, he inspected the morning, took in the milk, and crossed the backyard to feed his whippets. He kept thirteen—to prove that he was not superstitious.

Soon the first of the regulars began to drop in; Scanty Magoon always in the van, hobbling on his leather-padded stumps to his favorite corner, followed by a few dockers, a tram driver or two, returning from the night shift. These workmen did not stop: only long enough to down their half of spirits and chase it with a glass, a schooner, or a pint of beer. But Scanty was a permanent, a kind of faithful watchdog, gazing propitiatingly at Ned as he stood bland, unconscious, behind the bar with its somber woodwork and the framed notice: "Gentlemen Behave Others Must."

Ned, at fifty, was a big thick figure of a man. His face was full and yellowish, with prominent eyes, very solemn in repose, matching his dark clothes. He was neither genial nor flashy, the qualities popularly attributed to a publican. He had a kind of solemn, bilious dignity. He was proud of his reputation, his establishment. His parents had been driven out of Ireland by the potato famine; he had known poverty and starvation as a boy, but he had succeeded against inconceivable odds. He had a "free" house, stood well with the licensing authorities and the brewers, had many influential friends. He said, in effect, "The drink trade is respectable, and I prove it." He set his face against young men drinking and refused rudely to serve any woman under forty: there was no family department in the Union Tavern. He hated disorder; at the first sound of it he would rap crossly with an old shoe—maintained handy for that purpose—on the bar, and keep rapping till the discord ceased. Though a heavy drinker himself he was never seen the worse for it. Perhaps his grin was loose, his eye inclined to wander on those rare evenings which he deemed "an occasion," such as St. Patrick's Night, Halloween, Hogmanay, or after a day's dog racing when one of his whippets had added another medal to the galaxy on the heavy watch chain that spanned his stomach. At any rate, on the following day he would wear a sheepish air and send Scanty up for Father Clancy, the curate at St. Dominic's. When he had made his confession he rose heavily, dusting his knees, from the boards of the back room and pressed a sovereign for the poor box into the young priest's hand. He had a healthy respect for the clergy. For Father Fitzgerald, the parish priest, he had, indeed, considerable awe.

Ned was reputed "comfortable"; he ate well, gave freely, and, distrusting stocks and shares, had money invested in "bricks and mortar." Since Polly had a competence of her own, inherited from Michael, the dead brother, he had no anxiety on her account.

Though slow to form an affection, Ned was, in his own cautious word, "taken" with Francis. He liked the boy's unobtrusiveness, the sparseness of his speech, the quiet way he held himself, his silent gratitude. The somberness of the young face, caught unguarded, in repose, made him frown dumbly, and scratch his head.

In the afternoon Francis would sit with him in the half-empty bar, drowsy with food, the sunlight slanting churchwise through the musty air, listening with Scanty to Ned's genial talk. Scanty Magoon, husband and encumbrance of the worthy witless Maggie, was so named because there was not enough of him, only in fact a torso. He had lost his legs from gangrene caused by some obscure disorder of the circulation. Capitalizing on his complaint, he had promptly "sold himself to the doctors," signing a document that would deliver his body to the dissecting slab on his demise. Once the purchase price was drunk, a sinister aura settled on the bleary, loquacious, wily, unfortunate old scamp. An object now of popular awe, in his cups he indignantly declared himself defrauded. "I never got enough for myself. Them bloody scalpers! But they'll never get a hold of me poor old Adam! God damn the fear! I'll enlist for a sailor and drown myself."

Occasionally Ned would let Francis draw a beer for Scanty, partly for charity, partly to give the boy the thrill of the "engine." As the ivory-handled pull came back, filling the mug—Scanty prompting anxiously, "Get a head on her, boy!"—the foamy brew smelled so nutty and good Francis wanted to taste it. Ned nodded permission, then smiled in slow delight at the wryness of his nephew's face. "It's a acquired taste," he gravely asserted. He had a number of such clichés, from "Women and beer don't mix," to "A man's best friend is his own pound note," which, through frequency and profundity of utterance, had been hallowed into epigrams.

Ned's gravest, most tender affection was reserved for Nora, daughter of Michael Bannon. He was devoted to his niece who, when three, had lost her brother from tuberculosis, and her father through that same murderous malady, so fatal to the Celtic race, two years later. Ned had brought her up, sent her off at the age of thirteen to St. Elizabeth's, the best convent boarding school in Northumberland. It was a genuine pleasure for him to pay the heavy fees. He watched her progress with a fond indulgent eye. When she came home for the holidays he was a new man: spryer, never seen in braces, ponderously devising excursions and amusements and, lest anything should offend her, much stricter in the bar.

"Well—" Aunt Polly was gazing half-reproachfully across the breakfast tray at Francis. "I see I'll have to tell you what it's all about. In the first place your uncle's decided to give a party tonight to celebrate Halloween . . . and"—momentarily she dropped her eyes—"for another reason. We'll have a goose, a four-pound black bun, raisins for the snapdragon, and of course the apples—your uncle gets special ones at Lang's market garden in Gosforth. Maybe you'll go over for them this afternoon. It's a nice walk."

"Certainly, Aunt Polly. Only, I'm not quite sure of where it is."

"Someone'll show you the way." Polly composedly produced her main surprise. "Someone who's coming home from her school to spend a long weekend with us."

"Nora!" he exclaimed abruptly.

"The same." She nodded, took up his tray and rose. "Your uncle's pleased as punch she's got leave. Hurry up and dress now, like a good boy. We're all going to the station to meet the little monkey at eleven."

When she had gone Francis lay staring in front of him with a queer perplexity. This unexpected announcement of Nora's arrival had taken him aback, and strangely thrilled him. He had always liked her, of course. But now he faced the prospect of meeting her again with an odd new feeling, between diffidence and eagerness. To his surprise and confusion he suddenly found himself reddening to the roots of his hair. He jumped up hurriedly and began to pull on his clothes.

Francis and Nora started off, at two o'clock, on their excursion, taking the tram across the city to the suburb of Clermont, then walking across country toward Gosforth, each with a hand on the big wicker basket, swinging it between them.

It was four years since Francis had seen Nora and, stupidly tongue-tied all through lunch, when Ned had surpassed himself in massive playfulness, he was still painfully shy of her. He remembered her as a child. Now she was nearly fifteen and, in her modestly long navy-blue skirt and bodice, she seemed quite grown-up, more elusive and unreadable than ever before. She had small hands and feet and a small, alert, provoking face, which could be brave or suddenly timid. Though she was tall and awkward from her growth, her bones were fine and slender. Her eyes were teasing, darkly blue against her pale skin. The cold made them sparkle, made her little nostrils pink.

Occasionally, across the basket handle, his fingers touched Nora's. The sensation was remarkable: sweet, and warmly confusing. Her hands were the nicest things to touch that he had ever known. He could not speak, did not dare look at her, though from time to time he felt her looking at him and smiling. Though the golden blaze of the autumn was past, the woods still glowed with bright red embers. To Francis the colors of the trees, of the fields and sky, had never appeared more vivid. They were like a singing in his ears.

Suddenly she laughed outright and, tossing back her hair, began to run. Attached to her by the basket he raced like the wind alongside until she drew up, gasping, her eyes sparkling like frost on a sunny morning.

"Don't mind me, Francis. I get wild sometimes. I can't help it. It's being out of school, perhaps."

"Don't you like it there?"

"I do and I don't. It's funny and strict. Could you believe it?" She laughed, with a little rush of disconcerting innocence. "They make us wear our nightgowns when we take a bath! Tell me, did you ever think of me all the time you were away?"

"Yes." He stumbled out the answer.

"I'm glad . . . I thought of you." She threw him a swift glance, made as though to speak, and was silent.

Presently they reached the Gosforth market garden. Geordie Lang, Ned's good friend and the owner of the garden, was in the orchard, among the half-denuded trees, burning leaves. He gave them a friendly nod, an invitation to join him. They raked the crackling brown and yellow leaves toward the great smoldering cone he had already built, until the smell of the leaf smoke impregnated their clothing. It was not work but glorious sport. They forgot their earlier embarrassment, competed as to who should rake the most. When he had raked a great pile for himself, Nora mischievously despoiled it. Their laughter rang in the high clear air. Geordie Lang grinned in broad sympathy. "That's women, lad. Take your pile and laugh at ye."

At last Lang waved them toward the apple shed, a wooden erection at the end of the orchard.

"You've earned your keep. Go and help yourself!" he called after them. "And give my best respects to Mr. Bannon. Tell him I'll look in for my drop spirits sometime this week."

The apple shed was soft with crepuscular twilight. They climbed the ladder to the loft where, spaced out on straw, not touching, were rows and rows of the Ribston pippins for which the garden was renowned. While Francis filled the basket, crouching under the low roof, Nora sat cross-legged on the straw, picked an apple, shone it on her bony hip, and began to eat.

"Oh, my, it's good," she said. "Have one, Francis?"

He sat down opposite, took the apple she held out to him. The taste was delicious. They watched each other eating. When her small teeth bit through the amber skin into the crisp white flesh, little spurts of juice ran down her chin. He did not feel so shy in the dark little loft, but dreamy and warm, suffused with the joy of living. He had never liked anything so much as being here, in the garden, eating the apple she had given him. Their eyes, meeting frequently, smiled; but she had a half smile, strange and inward, that seemed entirely for herself.

"I dare you to eat the seeds," she teased suddenly; then added quickly: "No, don't, Francis! Sister Margaret Mary says they give you colic. Besides a new apple tree will grow from each of those seeds. Isn't it funny! Listen, Francis . . . you're fond of Polly and Ned?"

"Very." He stared. "Aren't you?"

"Of course . . . except when Polly coddles me every time I get a cough . . . and when Ned pets me on his knee—I hate that."

She hesitated, lowered her gaze for the first time. "Oh, it's nothing; I shouldn't; Sister Margaret Mary thinks I'm impudent, do you?"

He glanced away awkwardly, his passionate repudiation of the charge condensed in a clumsy: "No!"

She smiled almost timidly. "We're friends, Francis, so I will say it, and spite old Margaret Mary. When you're a man what are you going to be?"

Startled, he stared at her. "I don't know. Why?"

She picked with sudden nervousness at the serge of her dress. "Oh, nothing . . . only, well . . . I like you. I've always liked you. All those years I've thought of you a lot, and it wouldn't be nice if you . . . sort of disappeared again."

"Why should I disappear?" He laughed.

"You'd be surprised!" Her eyes, still childish, were wide and wise. "I know Aunt Polly . . . I heard her again today. She'd give anything to see you made a priest. Then you'd have to give up everything, even me." Before he could reply she jumped up, shaking herself, with a great show of animation. "Come on, don't be silly, sitting here all day. It's ridiculous with the sun shining outside, and the party tonight." He made to rise. "No, wait a minute. Shut your eyes, and you might get a present."

Even before he thought of complying she darted over and gave him a hurried little kiss on the cheek. The quick warm contact, the touch of her breath, the closeness of her thin face with the tiny brown mole on the cheekbone, stunned him. Blushing deeply, unexpectedly she slipped down the ladder and ran out of the shed. He followed slowly, darkly red, rubbing the small moist spot upon his cheek as though it were a wound. His heart was pounding.

That night the Halloween party began at seven o'clock. Ned, with a sultan's privilege, closed the bar at five minutes to the hour. All but a few favored patrons were politely asked to leave. The guests assembled upstairs, in the parlor, with its glass cases of wax fruit, the picture of Parnell above the blue-glass lusters, the velvet-framed photograph of Ned and Polly at the Giant's Causeway, the bog-oak jaunting car—a present from Killarney—the aspidistra, the varnished shillelagh hung on the wall with green ribbon, the heavy padded furniture, which emitted a puff of dust when heavily sat upon. The mahogany table was fully extended, with legs like a dropsical woman, and set for twenty. The coal fire, banked halfway up the chimney, would have prostrated an African explorer. The smell, off, was of rich basting birds. Maggie Magoon, in cap and apron, ran about like a maniac. In the crowded room were the young curate, Father Clancy, Thaddeus Gilfoyle, several of the neighboring tradesmen, Mr. Austin—the manager of the tramways—his wife and three children, and, of course, Ned, Polly, Nora, and Francis.

Amid the din, with beaming benevolence and a sixpenny cigar, Ned stood laying down the law to his friend Gilfoyle. A pale, prosaic, and slightly catarrhal young man of thirty was Thaddeus Gilfoyle, clerk at the gasworks—who in his spare time collected the rents of Ned's property in Varrell Street, was a sidesman at St. Dominic's, a steady-going chap who could always be relied on to do an odd job, to fill the breach, to "come forward," as Ned phrased it—who never had two words to rub against one another nor a single idea that might be called his own, yet who somehow managed to be there, hanging around, on the spot when he was wanted, dull and dependable, nodding in agreement, blowing his nose, fingering his confraternity badge, fish eyed, flat-footed, solemn, safe.

"You'll be for making a speech tonight?" he now inquired of Ned, in a tone which implied that if Ned did not make a speech the world would be desolate.

"Ah, I don't know now." Modestly yet profoundly, Ned considered the end of his cigar.

"Ah, you will now, Ned!"

"They'll not expect it."

"Pardon me, Ned, if I beg to differ."

"Ye think I should?"

With solemnity, "Ned, ye both should and would!"

"Ye mean . . . I ought to?"

"You must, Ned, and you will."

Delighted, Ned rolled the cigar across his mouth. "As a matter of fact, Thad," he cocked his eye, significantly, "I have a announcement . . . a important announcement I want to make. I'll say a few words later, since you press me."

Led by Polly as a kind of overture to the main event, the children began to play Halloween games—first snapdragon, scrambling for the flat blue raisins, ablaze with spirit, on a big china dish, then duck apple, dropping a fork from between the teeth over the back of a chair into a tub of swimming apples.

At seven o'clock the "gowks" came in: working lads from the neighborhood, with soot-blackened faces and grotesque attire, mumming their way around the district, singing for sixpences, in the strange tradition of All Hallows' Eve. They knew how to please Ned. They sang "Dear Little Shamrock," "Kathleen Mavourneen," and "Maggie Murphy's Home." Largesse was distributed. They clattered out. "Thank you, Mr. Bannon! Up the Union! Good night, Ned!"

"Good lads. Good lads all of them!" Ned rubbed his hands, his eye still moist with Celtic sentiment. "Now, Polly, our friends' stomachs will be thinking their throats is cut."

The company sat down at table, Father Clancy said grace, and Maggie Magoon staggered in with the largest goose in Tynecastle. Francis had never tasted such a goose—it dissolved, in rich flavors, upon the tongue. His body glowed from the long excursion in the keen air and from a strange interior joy. Now and then his eyes met Nora's across the table, shyly, with exquisite understanding. Though he was so quiet, her gaiety thrilled him. The wonder of this happy day, of the secret bond that lay between them, was like a pain.

When the repast was over Ned got up slowly, amid applause. He struck an oratorical attitude, one thumb in his armpit. He was absurdly nervous.

"Your Reverence, ladies and gentlemen, I thank you one and all. I'm a man of a few words"—a cry of "No, No," from Thaddeus Gilfoyle—"I say what I mean, and I mean what I say!" A short pause while Ned struggled for more confidence. "I like to see my friends happy and contented round about me—good company and good beer never hurt any man." Interruption at the doorway from Scanty Magoon, who had sneaked in with the gowks and contrived to remain. "God save you, Mr. Bannon!" brandishing a drumstick of the goose. "You're a fine man!" Ned remained unperturbable—every great man has his sycophants. "As I was remarkin' when Mrs. Magoon's husband flung a brick at me . . ." Laughter. ". . . I favor the social occasion. I'm sure we're proud and pleased, every mother's son of us—and daughter—to welcome into our midst my poor wife's brother's boy!" Loud applause and Polly's voice: "Take a bow, Francis." "I'm not going into recent history. Let the past bury its dead, I say. But I say and say it I will, look at him now, I say, and when he came!" Applause and Scanty's voice in the corridor: "Maggie, for the love of God, will ye bring some more of the goose!" "Now, I'm not one to blow my own trumpet! I try to do fair between God and man and beast. Look at my whippets if ye don't believe me." Gilfoyle's voice: "The best dogs in Tynecastle!" A longer pause, during which Ned lost the thread of his speech. "Where am I?" "Francis!" Polly prompted quickly. "Ah, yes." Ned raised his voice. "When Francis came, I said to myself, says I, here's a boy that might be useful. Shove him behind the bar and let him earn his keep? No, by God—saving your presence, Father Clancy—that's not us. We talk it over, Polly and me. The boy's young; the boy's been ill treated; the boy has a future before him; the boy's my poor dead wife's brother's boy. Let's send him to college, we say; we can manage it between us." Ned paused. "Your Reverence, ladies and gentlemen, I'm pleased and proud to announce that next month Francis starts off for Holywell!" Making the name the triumphant keystone of his peroration, Ned sat down, perspiring, amid loud applause.

4

Though the elm shadows were long upon the cropped lawns of Holywell, the northern June evening was still light as noon. The darkness would come late, so close to dawn the aurora borealis would but briefly glitter across the high pale heavens. As Francis sat at the open window of the high little study which he shared, since his election to the "Philosophers," with Laurence Hudson and Anselm Mealey, he felt his attention wander from the note-book, drawn, almost sadly, with a sense of the transience of beauty, to the lovely scene before him.

From the steep angle of his vision he could see the school, a noble gray granite baronial mansion, built for Sir Archibald Frazer in 1609, and endowed, this century, as a Catholic college. The chapel, styled in the same severity, lay at right angles, linked by a cloister, to the library, enclosing a quadrangle of historic turf. Beyond were the fives and handball courts, the playing fields, the end of a game still in progress, wide reaches of pasture threaded by the Stinchar River with stumpy black polled Angus cattle grazing stolidly, woods of beech and oak and rowan clustering the lodge, and in the ultimate distance the backdrop, blue, faintly serrated, of the Aberdeenshire Grampians.

Without knowing, Francis sighed. It seemed only yesterday that he had landed at Doune, the drafty northern junction, a new boy, scared out of his wits, facing the unknown and that first frightful interview with the headmaster, Father Hamish MacNabb. He remembered how "Rusty Mac," great little Highland gentleman, blood cousin to MacNabb of the isles, had crouched at his desk beneath his tartan cape, peering from bushy red eyebrows, dreadfully formidable.

"Well, boy, what can you do?"

"Please, sir . . . nothing."

"Nothing! Can't you dance the Highland fling?"

"No, sir."

"What! With a grand name like Chisholm?"

"I'm sorry, sir."

"Humph! There's not much profit in you, is there boy?"

"No, sir, except sir . . ." Trembling: ". . . Maybe I can fish."

"Maybe, eh?" A slow dry smile. "Then maybe we'll be friends." The smile deepened. "The clans of Chisholm and MacNabb fished together, ay, and fought together, before you or I were thought of. Run now, before I cane ye."

And now, in one more term, he would be leaving Holywell. Again his gaze slanted down to the little groups promenading to and fro on the graveled terraces beside the fountain. A seminary custom! Well, what of it? Most of them would go from here to the seminary of San Morales in Spain. He discerned his roommates walking together: Anselm, as usual, extrovert in his affections, one arm tenderly linking his companion's, the other gesticulating, but nicely, as befitted the outright winner of the

Frazer Good Fellowship Prize! Behind the two, surrounded by his coterie, paced Father Tarrant—tall, dark, thin . . . intense yet sardonic . . . classically remote.

At the sight of the youngish priest, Francis's expression tightened oddly. He viewed the open notebook before him on the window ledge with distaste, picked up his pen, and began, after a moment, his imposition. His frown of resolution did not mar the clean brown molding of his cheek or the somber clearness of his hazel eyes. Now, at eighteen, his body had a wiry grace. The chaste light heightened absurdly his physical attractiveness, that air, unspoiled and touching, which—inescapable—so often humiliated him.

"*June 14th, 1887.* Today there occurred an incident of such phenomenal and thrilling impropriety I must revenge myself on this beastly diary, and Father Tarrant, by recording it. I oughtn't really to waste this hour before Vespers—afterward I shall be dutifully cornered by Anselm to play handball—I should jot down *Ascension Thursday: Fine day; memorable adventure with Rusty Mac,* and leave it. But even our incisive administrator of studies admitted the virtue of my breed—conscientiousness—when he said to me, after his lecture: 'Chisholm! I suggest you keep a diary. Not of course for publication'—his confounded satire flashed out—'as a form of *examen.* You suffer, Chisholm, inordinately, from a kind of spiritual obstinacy. By writing your inmost heart out . . . if you could . . . you might possibly reduce it.'

"I blushed, of course, like a fool, as my wretched temper flared. 'Do you mean I don't do what I'm told, Father Tarrant?'

"He barely looked at me, hands tucked away in the sleeves of his habit, thin, dark, pinched in at the nostrils, and oh, so unanswerably clever. As he tried to conceal his dislike of me, I had a sharp awareness of his hard shirt, of the iron discipline I know he uses unsparingly upon himself. He said vaguely: 'There is a mental disobedience . . .' and walked away.

"Is it conceit to imagine he has his knife in me because I do not model myself upon him? Most of us do. Since he came here two years ago he has led quite a cult of which Anselm is deacon. Perhaps he cannot forget the occasion when, at his instruction to us upon the 'one, true, and apostolic religion' I suddenly remarked: 'Surely, sir, creed is such an accident of birth God can't set an exclusive value on it.' In the shocked hush that followed he stood nonplussed, but icy cold. 'What an admirable heretic you would have made, my good Chisholm.'

"At least we have one point in common: agreement that I shall never have a vocation.

"I'm writing ridiculously pompously for a callow youth of eighteen. Perhaps it is what is named the affectation of my age. But I'm worried . . . about several things. Firstly, I'm terribly, probably absurdly, worried about Tynecastle. I suppose it's inevitable that one should lose touch, when one's "home leave" is limited to four short summer weeks. This brief annual vacation, Holywell's only rigor, may serve its purpose of keeping vocations firm, but it also strains the imagination. Ned never writes. His correspondence during my three years at Holywell has been effected through the medium of sudden and fantastic gifts of food: that colossal sack of walnuts for instance, from the docks, in my first winter, and last spring, the crate of bananas, three quarters of which were overripe and created an undignified epidemic among the 'clergy and laity' here.

"But even in Ned's silence there's something queer. And Aunt Polly's letters make me more apprehensive. Her dear inimitable gossip about parochial events has been replaced by a meager catalog of, mainly, meteorological facts. And this change in tone arrived so suddenly. Naturally Nora hasn't helped me. She is the original postcard girl, who scribbles off her obligations in five minutes, once a year, at the seaside. It seems, however, centuries since her last brilliant 'Sunset from Scarborough Pier' and two letters of mine have failed even to produce a 'Moon over Whitley Bay.' Dear Nora! I shall never forget your Eve-like gesture in the apple loft. It's because of you that I anticipate these coming holidays so eagerly. Shall we walk again, I wonder, to Gosforth? I have watched you grow, holding my breath, seen your character—by which I mean your contradictions—develop. I know you as someone quick, shy, bold, sensitive, and gay, a little spoiled by flattery, full of innocence and fun. Even now, I see your impudent sharp little face, lit up from within, as you indulge your amazing gift of mimicry—'taking off' Aunt Polly . . . or me—your skinny arms akimbo, blue eyes provoking, reckless, ending by flinging yourself into a dance of gleeful malice. Everything about you is so—human and alive, and—even those flashes of petulance and fits of temper that shake your delicate physique and end in such tremendous weepings. And I know, despite your faults, how warm and impulsive is your nature, making you run, with a quick and shamefaced blush, toward someone you have hurt . . . unconsciously. I lie awake thinking of you, of the look in your eyes, the tender pathos of your collarbones above your small round breasts . . ."

Francis broke off here, and with a sudden flush scored out the last line he had written. Then, conscientiously, he resumed.

"Secondly, I am selfishly concerned about my future. I'm now educated above—here again Father Tarrant would agree—my station. I've only another term at Holywell. Am I to return gracefully to the beer pulls of the Union? I can't continue to be a charge on Ned—or more justly Polly, since I recently ascertained quite by accident that my fees have been discharged, out of her modest income, by that wonderful woman! My ambitions are so muddled. My fondness for Aunt Polly, my overbrimming gratitude, make me long to repay her. And it is her dearest wish to see me ordained. Again, in a place like this, where three-quarters of the students and most of one's friends are predestined for the priesthood, it is hard to escape the inevitable pull of sympathy. One wants to line up in the ranks. Tarrant apart, Father MacNabb thinks I should make a good priest—I can feel it in his shrewd, friendly provocativeness, his almost godlike sense of waiting. And as principal of this college he should know something about vocations.

"Naturally I'm impetuous and hot tempered; and my mixed upbringing has left me with a schismatic quirk. I can't pretend to be one of these consecrated youths—our college library teems with them—who lisp prayers throughout their infancy, make boyish shrines in the woods, and sweetly rebuke the little girls who jostle them at the village fair. 'Keep away, Thérèse and Annabelle, I am not for thee.'

"Yet who can describe those moments that come to one suddenly: alone upon the back road to Doune, waking in the darkness in one's silent room, remaining behind, quite solitary, when the scraping, coughing, whispering mob has gone in the empty yet breathing church. Moments of strange apprehension, of intuition. Not that sentimental ecstasy which is as loathsome to me as ever—query: why do I want to vomit when I see rapture on the master of novices' face?—but a sense of consolation, of hope.

"I'm distressed to find myself writing like this—though it is for no other eye than mine. One's private ardors make chilling stuff on paper. Yet I must record this inescapable sense of belonging to God, which strikes at me through the darkness, the deep conviction, under the measured, arranged, implacable movement of the universe, that man does not emerge from, or vanish into, nothing. And here—is it not strange?—I feel the influence of Daniel Glennie, dear, cracked Holy Dan, feel his warm unearthly gaze upon me. . . .

"Confound it! And Tarrant! I *am* literally pouring out my heart. If I am such a Holy Willie why don't I set out and do something for God, attack the great mass of indifference, of sneering materialism in the world today . . . in short, become a priest? Well . . . I must be honest. I think it is because of Nora. The beauty and tenderness of my feeling for her overfills my heart. The vision of her face, with its light and sweetness, is before me even when I am praying to our Lady in church. Dear, dear Nora. You are the real reason why I don't take my ticket on the celestial express for San Morales!"

He stopped writing and let his gaze travel into the distance, a faint frown on his brow, but his lips smiling. With an effort, he again collected himself.

"I must, I must get back to this morning and Rusty Mac. This being a holiday of obligation, I had the forenoon on my hands. On my way down to post a letter at the lodge I ran into the headmaster coming up from the Stinchar with his rod and without fish. He stopped, supporting his short burly form on the gaff, his ruddy face screwed up, rather put out, beneath his blaze of red hair. I do love Rusty Mac. I think he has some fondness for me and perhaps the simplest explanation is that we are so dourly Scottish and both of us fishers . . . the only two in the school. When Lady Frazer endowed the College from her Stinchar properties, Rusty claimed the river as his own. The jingo in the *Holywell Monitor* beginning

> I'll not have my pools
> Whipped to ribbons by fools . . .

neatly takes off his attitude—for he's a mad fisher. There's a story of him, in the middle of Mass at Frazer Castle, which Holywell serves, when his staunch friend, the Presbyterian Gillie, stuck his head through the window of the oratory, bursting with suppressed excitement. 'Your Reverence! They're rising like fury in Lochaber Pool!' Never was a Mass more quickly completed. The stupefied congregation, including Her Ladyship, was pattered over, blessed at breakneck speed; then a dark streak, not unlike the local concept of the devil, was seen flying from the sacristy. 'Jock! Jock! What flee are they taking?'

"Now, he looked at me disgustedly. 'Not a fish in sight. Just when I wanted one for the notables!' The bishop of the diocese and the retiring principal of our English seminary at San Morales were coming to lunch at Holywell that day.

"I said, 'There's a fish in the Glebe Pool, sir.'

"'There's no fish in the river at all, not even a grilse. . . . I've been out since six.'

"'It's a big one.'

"'Imaginary!'

"'I saw it there yesterday, under the weir, but of course I didn't dare try for it.'

"From beneath his sandy brows he gave me his dour smile. 'You're a perverse demon, Chisholm. If you want to waste your time—you've my dispensation.' He handed me his rod and walked off.

"I went down to the Glebe Pool, my heart leaping as it always does at the sound of running water. The fly on the leader was a Silver Doctor, perfect for the size and color of the river. I began to fish the pool. I fished it for an hour. Salmon are painfully scarce this season. Once I thought I saw the movement of a dark fin in the shadows of the opposite bank. But I touched nothing. Suddenly I heard a discreet cough. I swung round. Rusty Mac, dressed in his best blacks, wearing gloves and his ceremonial top hat, had stopped, on his way to meet his guests at Doune Station, to condole with me.

" 'It's these large ones, Chisholm,' he said with a sepulchral grin, 'they're always the hardest!'

"As he spoke, I made a final cast thirty yards across the pool. The fly fell exactly on the spume eddying beneath the far edge of the weir. The next instant I felt the fish, struck, and was fast in it.

" 'Ye have one!' Rusty cried. Then the salmon jumped—four feet in the air. Though for my own part I nearly dropped, the effect on Rusty was stupendous. I could feel him stiffen beside me. 'In the name of God!' he muttered in stricken awe. The salmon was the biggest I had ever seen, here, in the Stinchar, or in my father's Tweedside bothy. 'Keep his head up!' Rusty suddenly shouted. 'Man, man—give him the butt!'

"I was doing my best. But now the fish was in control. It set off, downstream, in a mad tearing rush. I followed. And Rusty followed me.

"The Stinchar, at Holywell, is not like the Tweed. It runs in a brown torrent through pines and gorges, making not inconsiderable somersaults over slippery boulders and high shaley ledges. At the end of ten minutes, Rusty Mac and I were half a mile downstream, somewhat the worse for wear. But we still stayed with the fish.

" 'Hold him, hold him!' Mac was hoarse from shouting. 'You fool, you fool, don't let him get in that slack!' The brute, of course, was already in the slack, sulking in a deep hole, with the leader ensnared in a mess of sunken roots.

"'Ease him, ease him!' Mac hopped in anguish. 'Just ease him while I give him a stone.'

"Gingerly, breathlessly, he began flipping stones, trying to start out the fish without snapping the cast. The game continued for an agony of time. Then *whirr!*—off went the fish, to the scream of the reel. And off again went Rusty and I.

"An hour later, or thereabouts, in the slow wide flats opposite Doune village, the salmon at last showed signs of defeat. Exhausted, panting, torn by a hundred agonizing and entrancing hazards, Rusty gave a final command.

"'Now, now! On this sand!' He croaked: 'We've no gaff. If he takes you down farther, he's gone for good.'

"My mouth was gulpy and dry. Nervously, I stood the fish close. It came, quiet, then suddenly made a last frantic scuttle. Rusty let out a hollow groan. 'Lightly . . . lightly! If you lose him now I'll never forgive you!'

"In the shallows the fish seemed incredible. I could see the frayed gut of the leader. *If I lost him!*—an icy lump came under my shirt. I slid him gently to the little flat of sand. In an absolute tense silence Mac bent over, whipped his hand in the gills, and heaved the fish, monstrous, onto the grass.

"It made a noble sight on the green meadow, a fish of over forty pounds, run so freshly the sea lice still were on its arching back.

"'A record, a record!' Mac chanted, swept, as was I, by a wave of heavenly joy. We had joined hands and were dancing the fandango. 'Forty-two pounds if it's an ounce . . . we'll put it in the book.' He actually embraced me. 'Man, man—you're a bonny, bonny fisher.'

"At that moment, from the single railway line across the river, came the faint whistle of an engine. Rusty paused, gazed in bewildered fashion at the plume of smoke, at the toylike red-and-white signal which had suddenly dipped over Doune village station. Recollection flooded him. He dug in consternation for his watch. 'Good Heavens, Chisholm!' His tone was that of the Holywell headmaster. 'That's the bishop's train.'

"His dilemma was apparent: he had five minutes to meet his distinguished visitors and five miles of roundabout road to reach the station—visible, only two fields away, across the Stinchar.

"I could see him slowly make up his mind. 'Take the fish back, Chisholm, and have them boil it whole for luncheon. Go quickly now. And remember Lot's wife and the pillar of salt. Whatever you do, *don't look back!*'

"I couldn't help it. Once I reached the first bend of the stream, from behind a bush, I risked a salty ending. Father Mac had already stripped to the buff and tied his clothing in a bundle. Wearing his top hat firmly on his head, with the bundle uplifted like a crozier, he stepped stark naked into the river. Wading and swimming, he reached the other side, scrambled into his suit, and sprinted manfully toward the approaching train.

"I lay on the grass, rolling, in a kind of ecstasy. It was not the vision—which would live with me forever—of the top hat planted dauntlessly upon the nubile brow, but the moral pluck that lay behind the escapade. I thought: *he too must hate our pious prudery, which shudders at the sight of human flesh, and cloaks the female form as though it were an infamy.*"

⊕

A sound outside made Francis pause, and he ceased writing as the door opened. Hudson and Anselm Mealey came into the room. Hudson, a dark quiet youth, sat down and began to change his shoes. Anselm had the evening mail in his hand.

"Letter for you, Francis," he said effusively.

Mealey had grown into a fine pink-and-white young man. His cheek had the smoothness of perfect health. His eye was soft and limpid, his smile ready. Always eager, busy, smiling: without question he was the most popular student in the school. Though his work was never brilliant, the masters liked him—his name was usually on the prize list. He was good at fives and racquets and all the less rough games. And he had a genius for procedure. He ran half a dozen clubs—from the Philatelists to the Philosophers. He knew, and glibly employed, such words as *quorum, minutes,* and *Mr. Chair.* Whenever a new society was proposed, Anselm's advice was sure to be invoked—automatically he became its president. In praise of the clerical life he was lyrical. His only cross was this singular paradox: the headmaster and a few odd lonely souls cordially disliked him. To the rest he was a hero, and he bore his successes with open smiling modesty.

Now, as he handed Francis the letter, he gave him that warm disarming smile. "Hope it's full of good news, dear fellow."

Francis opened the letter. Undated, it was written in pencil upon an invoice headed:

Dr. to Edward Bannon
Union Tavern,
Corner Dyke and Canal streets,
Tynecastle.

Dear Francis,

I hope this finds you well as it leaves me. Also please excuse pencil. We are all upset. It grieves me to tell you Francis you won't be able to come home this holiday. No one is more sick and sorry than me about it not having seen you since last summer and all. But believe me it is impossible and we must bow to the will of God. I know you are not one to take no for an answer but this time you must the BVM be my witness. I won't disguise we have trouble as you must guess but it is nothing you can help or hinder. It is not money nor sickness so do not worry. And it will all pass by the help of God and be forgotten. You can easy arrange to stay the holidays at the college. Ned will pay all extras. You'll have your books and your nice surroundings and all. Maybe we'll fix for you to come down at Christmas, so don't fret. Ned has sold his whippets but not for the money. Mr. Gilfoyle is a comfort to all. You are not missing much in the weather, it has been terrible wet. Now don't forget Francis we have people in the house, there isn't no room, you are not to come.

Bless you my dear boy and excuse haste.

Yours affectionately,

Polly Bannon

At the window, Francis read the letter several times: though its purpose was plain, its meaning remained troubling and inscrutable. With a strained look he folded the sheet and placed it in his pocket.

"Nothing wrong I hope?" Mealey had been studying his face solicitously.

Francis, uncomfortably silent, hardly knew what to say.

"My dear fellow, I am sorry." Anselm took a step forward, placed his arm lightly, comfortingly, around the other's shoulders. "If there's anything I can do for mercy's sake let me know. Perhaps," he paused earnestly, "perhaps you don't feel like handball tonight?"

"No," Francis mumbled. "I believe I'd rather not."

"Quite all right, my dear Francis!" The Vespers bell rang. "I can see there is something bothering you. I'll remember you tonight in my prayers."

All through Vespers Francis worried about Polly's incomprehensible letter. When the service was over he had a sudden impulse to take his trouble to Rusty Mac. He went slowly up the wide staircase.

As he entered the study he became aware that the headmaster was not alone; Father Tarrant sat with him, behind a pile of papers; and from the odd sudden silence his appearance provoked, Francis had the extraordinary feeling that the two had been discussing him.

"I'm sorry, sir." He cast an embarrassed glance toward Rusty Mac. "I didn't know you were engaged."

"That's all right, Chisholm. Sit down."

The quick warmth of the tone compelled Francis, already half-turned toward the door, into the wicker chair beside the desk. With slow movements of his stubby fingers Rusty went on stuffing shag into his corroded briar pipe. "Well! What can we do for you, my good man?"

Francis colored. "I . . . I rather thought you'd be alone."

For some queer reason the headmaster avoided his appealing gaze. "You don't mind Father Tarrant? What is it?"

There was no escape. Without guile to invent further excuse Francis stumbled out: "It's a letter I've had . . . from home." He had meant to show Polly's note to Rusty Mac but, in Tarrant's presence, his pride restrained him. "For some obscure reason they don't seem to want me back for the vacation."

"Oh!" Was he mistaken: was there again swift interchange between the two? "That must be something of a disappointment."

"It is, sir. And I feel worried. I was wondering . . . in fact I came to ask you what I should do."

Silence. Father MacNabb himself sank more deeply into his old cape, still fumbling at his pipe. He had known many boys, known them inside out; yet there was about this youth who sat beside him a fineness, beauty, and dogged honesty, which lit a fire in his heart. "We all have our disappointments, Francis." His meditative voice was sad, more than unusually mild. "Father Tarrant and I have suffered one today. Retirements are the order of the day at our seminary in Spain." He paused. "We are appointed there, I as rector, Father Tarrant as my administrator of studies."

Francis stammered a reply. San Morales was, indeed, a coveted advancement, next step to a bishopric; but whatever Tarrant's reaction—Francis shot a quick glance at the expressionless profile—MacNabb would not so regard it. The dry Aragon plains would be alien for a man who loved the green woods and rushing waters of Holywell with all his soul. Rusty Mac smiled gently. "I had my heart set on staying here. You had set yours on going away. What d'you say? Shall we both agree to take a beating from Almighty God?"

Francis strove to pluck the proper phrase from his confusion. "It's just . . . being anxious . . . I wondered if I shouldn't find out what's wrong and try to help?"

"I question if I should." Father MacNabb answered quickly. "What would you say, Father Tarrant?"

In the shadow, the younger master stirred. "Troubles resolve themselves best, in my experience, without outside interference."

There appeared nothing more to be said. The headmaster turned up his desk lamp which, while it brightened the dark study, seemed to terminate the interview. Francis got up. Though he faced them both, haltingly, from his heart, he spoke to Rusty Mac.

"I can't say how sorry I am that you are leaving for Spain. The school . . . I . . . I shall miss you."

"Perhaps we shall see you there?" There was hope, quiet affection in the voice.

Francis did not answer. As he stood there, indecisively, hardly knowing what to say, torn by conflicting difficulties, his downcast gaze struck suddenly upon a letter, lying open on the desk. It was not so much the letter—illegible at that distance—as the letter's bright blue-stamped heading that caught his eye. Quickly he glanced away. But not before he had read "St. Dominic's Presbytery, Tynecastle."

A shiver went through him. Something was wrong at home. Now he was sure. His face revealed nothing, remained impassive. Neither of the two masters was aware of his discovery. But as he moved toward the door he knew, despite all persuasion to the contrary, that one course at least was clear before him.

5

The train arrived at two o'clock that sultry June afternoon. Carrying his handbag, Francis walked rapidly from the station, his heart beating faster as he approached the familiar quarter of the city.

A queer air of quiet hung outside the tavern. Thinking to take Aunt Polly by surprise, he ran lightly up the side stairs and entered the house. Here, too, it was quiet and oddly dim after the glare of the dusty pavements; no one in the lobby or the kitchen, no sound but the thunderous ticking of a clock. He went into the parlor.

Ned was seated at the table, both elbows on the red drugget cover, gazing endlessly at the opposite blank wall. Not the attitude alone, but the alteration in the man himself, drew from Francis a stifled exclamation. Ned had lost three stones in weight; his clothes hung upon him; the rotund beaming face had turned dreary and cadaverous.

"Ned!" Francis held out his hand.

There was a pause, then Ned sluggishly slewed round, perception slowly dawning through his settled wretchedness.

"It's you, Francis." His smile was bewitching, evasive. "I'd no idea you were expected."

"I'm not really, Ned." Through his anxiety Francis essayed a laugh. "But the minute we broke up I simply couldn't wait. Where's Aunt Polly?"

"She's away. . . . Yes . . . Polly's away for a couple of days to Whitley Bay."

"When'll she be back?"

"Like enough . . . tomorrow."

"And where's Nora?"

"Nora!" Ned's tone was flat. "She's away with Aunt Polly."

"I see." Francis was conscious of a throb of relief. "That's why she didn't answer my wire. But Ned . . . you . . . you're well yourself, I hope?"

"I'm all right, Francis. A trifle under the weather maybe . . . but the like of me'll come to no harm." His chest took a sudden grotesque heave. Francis was horrified to see tears run down the egg-shaped face. "Away now and get yourself a bite. There'll be plenty in the cupboard. Thad'll get you anything you want. He's below in the bar. A great help he's been to us, has Thad." Ned's gaze wavered, then wandered back to the opposite wall.

In a daze, Francis turned, put his bag in his own small room. As he came along the passage the door of Nora's room was open: the neat white privacy caused him to withdraw his eyes in sudden confusion. He hastened downstairs.

The saloon was empty, even Scanty vanished, his vacant corner arresting, unbelievable, like a gap blown through the solid structure of the wall. But behind the bar, in his shirtsleeves, smugly drying glasses, was Thaddeus Gilfoyle.

Thad stopped his silent whistle as Francis entered. Slightly taken aback, an instant elapsed before he offered a welcome with his limp and dampish hand.

"Well, well!" he exclaimed. "Here's a sight for sore eyes."

Gilfoyle's air of proprietorship was hateful. But Francis, now thoroughly alarmed, succeeded in affecting indifference. He said lightly: "I'm surprised to see you here, Thad? What's happened to the gasworks?"

"I've give up the office," Thad answered composedly.

"What for?"

"To be here. Permanent." He picked up a glass and eyed it professionally, breathed on it softly, and began to polish. "When they asked me to come forward . . . I couldn't do more!"

Francis felt his nerves tighten beyond endurance. "In the name of heaven, what's all this about, Gilfoyle?"

"*Mister* Gilfoyle, if you don't mind, Francis!" Thad rolled his tongue smugly around the reproach. "It heartbreaks Ned not to see me get my place. He's not the same man, Francis. I doubt he'll ever be himself again."

"What's happened to him? You talk as if he were out of his mind!"

"He was, Francis, he was . . ." Gilfoyle groaned, "but he's come to senses now, poor man." His eye watchful, he stopped Francis's angry interruption with a whine. "Now don't take on that way with me. I'm the one that's doin' right. Ask Father

Fitzgerald if you disbelieve me. I know you've never liked me much. I've seen ye on vacations making sport of me as you growed up. I've the best intentions toward you, Francis. We ought to pull together . . . now, especially."

"Why now especially?" Francis gritted his teeth.

"Oh, yes, yes . . . you wouldn't know . . . to be sure." Thad darted a fearful smirk. "The banns was only put up for the first time last Sunday. You see, Francis, me and Nora's going to be wed!"

Aunt Polly and Nora returned late the following evening. Francis, sick with apprehension, with his failure to penetrate Gilfoyle's fishlike secrecy, had awaited their arrival in an agony of impatience. He tried immediately to corner Polly.

But Polly, after her first start, her wail of recognition—"Francis, I told you not to come"—had fled upstairs with Nora, her ears closed to his importunities, reiterating the formula, "Nora's not well . . . she's sick I tell you . . . get out of my road . . . I've got to tend to her."

Rebuffed, he climbed somberly to his room, chilled by the mounting premonitions of this unknown dread. Nora, having scarcely given him a look, had gone immediately to bed. And for an hour he heard Polly, scurrying with trays and hot-water bottles, entreating Nora in a low voice, persecuting her with agitated attentions. Nora, thin as a wand, and pale, somehow had the air of sickrooms. Polly, worn and harassed, even more negligent in her dress, had acquired a new gesture—a quick pressing of her hand against her brow. Late into the night, from her adjoining room, he heard the mutter of her prayers. Torn by the enigma, Francis bit his lip, turning restlessly between his sheets.

Next morning dawned clear. He rose and, according to his habit, went out to early Mass. When he returned he found Nora seated outside on the backyard steps warming herself in a patch of sunshine while at her feet some chickens cheeped and scuttled. She made no move to let him pass, but when he had stood a moment, she raised her head contemplatively.

"It's the holy man . . . been out already, saving his soul!"

He reddened at her tone, so unexpected, so quietly bitter.

"Did the Very Reverend Fitzgerald officiate?"

"No. It was the curate."

"The dumb ox in the stall! Ah, well, at least he's harmless."

Her head drooped, she stared at the chickens, propping her thin chin upon a thinner wrist. Though she had always been slight he was startled to discover this almost childish fragility, which matched so ill the sullen maturity in her eyes, and the new gray dress, womanly and costly, which stiffly adorned her. His heart melted, his breast was filled with a white fire, an unsupportable pain. Her hurt plucked at the chords of his soul. He hesitated, his gaze averted. His voice was low.

"Have you had breakfast?"

She nodded. "Polly shoved it down my throat. God! If she'd only leave me be!"

"What are you doing today?"

"Nothing."

He paused again, then blurted out, all his feeling for her flooding through the anxiety in his eyes, "Why don't we go for a walk, Nora? Like we used to. It's so glorious a day!"

She did not move. Yet a faint tinge of animation seemed to penetrate her hollow, shadowed cheek.

"I can't be bothered," she said heavily. "I'm tired!"

"Oh, come on, Nora . . . please."

A dull pause. "All right."

His heart gave another great painful thud. He hurried into the kitchen and cut, with nervous haste, some sandwiches and cake, wrapped them clumsily into a packet. There was no sign of Polly and now, indeed, he was eager to avoid her. In ten minutes Nora and he sat in the red tram, clanging across the city. Within the hour, they tramped side by side, unspeaking, toward the Gosforth Hills.

He wondered at the impulse which had sent him to this familiar stretch. Today the burgeoning countryside was lovely; but its very loveliness was tremulous, unbearable. As they came upon Lang's orchard, now foamy with blossom, he paused, tried to break the steely silence that lay between them.

"Look, Nora! Let's take a stroll round. And have a word with Lang."

She threw one glance at the orchard, the trees standing spaced and stiff, like chessmen, around the apple shed. She said rudely, bitterly: "I don't want to. I hate that place!"

He did not answer. Dimly he knew her bitterness was not toward him.

By one o'clock they reached the summit of Gosforth Beacon. He could see that she was tired and, without consulting her, stopped under a tall beech, for lunch. The day was unusually warm and clear. In the flat distance beneath them, sparkling with golden light, lay the city, domed and spired, and from afar, ineffably beautiful.

She scarcely touched the sandwiches he produced and, remembering Polly's demonstrative tyranny, he did not press her. The shade was soothing. Overhead the new green flickering leaves sent quiet patterns chasing across the moss, carpeted with dry beechnuts, on which they sat. There was a smell of flowing sap; the throaty call of a thrush came from a high twig overhead.

After a few moments she leaned back against the bole of the tree, tilted her head, and closed her eyes.

Her relaxation seemed somehow the greatest tribute she could pay him. He considered her with a deeper surge of tenderness, stirred to undreamed-of compassion by the arch of her neck, so thin and unprotected. The welling tenderness within him made him strangely protective. When her head slipped a little from the tree he scarcely dared touch her. Yet, fancying her asleep, he moved his arm instinctively to support her. The next instant she wrenched herself free, struck him repeatedly on the face and chest with her clenched knuckles, hysterically breathless.

"Leave me alone! You brute! You beast!"

"Nora, Nora! What's the matter?"

Panting, she drew back, her face quivering, distorted. "Don't try to get round me that way. You're all the same. Every one of you!"

"Nora!" He pleaded with her desperately. "For pity's sake . . . let's get this straight."

"Get what straight?"

"Everything . . . why you're going on like this . . . why you're marrying Gilfoyle."

"Why shouldn't I marry him?" She threw the question at him, with a bitter defensiveness.

His lips were dry; he could scarcely speak. "But Nora, he's such a poor creature. . . . He's not your sort."

"He's as good as anybody. Haven't I said you're all the same? At least I'll keep him in his place."

Confounded, he stared at her with a pale and stricken face. And there was that in his unbelieving eyes that cut her so cruelly, she more cruelly cut back.

"Perhaps you think I should be marrying you . . . the bright-eyed altar boy . . . the half-baked carpet priest!" Her lip twitched with the bitterness of her sneer. "Let me tell you this. I think you're a joke . . . a sanctimonious scream. Go on, turn up your blessed eyes. You don't know how funny you are . . . you holy paternoster. Why if you were the last man in the world I wouldn't . . ." She choked and shuddered violently, tried, painfully, uselessly, to check her tears with the back of her hand and then, sobbing, flung her head upon his breast. "Oh, Francis, Francis, dear, I'm sorry! You know I've always loved you. Kill me if you want to . . . I don't care."

While he quieted her, clumsily, stroking her brow, he felt himself trembling as much as she. The racking violence of her sobs diminished gradually. She was like a wounded bird in his arms. She lay, spent and passive, her face hidden against his coat. Then slowly she straightened herself. With averted eyes, she took her handkerchief, rubbed her ravaged, tear-stained face, straightened her hat, then said, in an exhausted neutral tone: "We'd better get home."

"Look at me, Nora?"

But she would not, only remarking in that same odd monotone: "Say what you want to say."

"I will then, Nora." His youthful vehemence overcame him. "I'm not going to stand this! I can see there's something behind it. But I'll get to the bottom of it. You're not going to marry that fool Gilfoyle. I love you, Nora. I'll stand by you."

There was a pitiful stillness.

"Dear Francis," she said, with an oddly hollow smile. "You make me feel as though I'd lived a million years." And rising, she bent and kissed him, as she had kissed him once before, upon the cheek. As they went down the hill the thrush had ceased its singing in the high tree.

That evening, with fixed intention, Francis set out for the dockside tenement inhabited by the Magoons. He found the banished Scanty alone, since Maggie was still out charring, squatting by a spark of fire in the single back-to-back apartment, glumly working a wool-rug shuttle by the light of a tallow dip. As he recognized his visitor there was no mistaking the pleasure in the exile's bleary eye, a gleam that heightened when Francis uncovered the gill bottle of spirits he had privily removed from the bar. Quickly, Scanty produced a chipped delft cup, solemnly toasted his benefactor.

"Ah, that's the stuff!" he muttered, across the back of his ragged sleeve. "Devil the sup have I had since that skinflint Gilfoyle took over the bar."

Francis drew up the backless wooden chair. He spoke with dark intensity, the shadows heavy beneath his eyes.

"Scanty! What's happened at the Union—to Nora, Polly, Ned? I've been back three days, and I'm still no wiser. You've got to tell me!"

A look of alarm invaded Scanty's expression. He glanced from Francis to the bottle—from the bottle to Francis.

"Ah! How would I know?"

"You do know! I can see it in your face."

"Didn't Ned say nothing?"

"Ned! He's like a deaf-mute these days!"

"Poor ould Ned!" Scanty groaned, blessed himself, and poured out more whiskey. "God save us! Who would ever have dreamed it. Sure there's bad in the best of us." With a sudden hoarse emphasis: "I couldn't tell ye, Francis; it's a shame to remember; it don't do no good."

"It will do good, Scanty," Francis urged. "If I know, I can do something."

"Ye mean, Gilfoyle . . ." With head cocked, Scanty considered, then he nodded slowly. He took another tot to stiffen himself, his battered face oddly sober, his tone subdued. "I'll tell you then, Francis, if you swear to keep it dark. The truth of it is . . . God pity us . . . that Nora's had a baby."

Silence: long enough for Scanty to take another drink. Francis said: "When?"

"Six weeks ago. She went down to Whitley Bay. The woman there has the child . . . a daughter. . . . Nora can't bear the sight of it."

Cold, rigid, Francis struggled with the tumult in his breast. He made himself ask: "Then Gilfoyle is the father?"

"That gutless fish!" Hatred overcame Scanty's caution. "No, no, he's the one that came forward, as he's pleased to call it, to give the little one a name, and get his foot in the Union to the bargain, the bla'g'ard! Father Fitzgerald's behind him, Francis. It's all settin' pretty as a pictur', the way they've pulled it. Marriage lines in the drawer, not a soul the wiser, and the daughter brought here later on, as it were, at the end of a long vacation. God strike me down dead if it don't turn the stomach of a pig!"

A band, an insupportable constriction, girded Francis's heart. He fought to keep his voice from breaking.

"I never knew Nora was in love with anyone? Scanty . . . Do you know who it was . . . I mean . . . the father of her child?"

"Before God I don't!" The blood rushed to Scanty's forehead as he thumped the floorboards in vociferous denial. "I don't know nothing about that at all. How should a poor creature like me! And Ned don't either, that's gospel truth! Ned always treated me right, a fine generous upstanding man, except for occasions, like when Polly was away, and the drink took hold of him. No, no. Francis, take it from me, there's not a hope of findin' the man!"

Again a silence, frozen, prolonged. A film clouded Francis's eyes. He felt deathly sick. At last, with a great effort he got up.

"Thank you, Scanty, for telling me."

He quit the room, went giddily down the bare flights of tenement stairs. His brow, the palms of his hands, were bedewed with icy sweat. A vision haunted, tormented him: the trim neatness of Nora's bedroom, white and undisturbed. He had no hatred, only a searing pity, a dreadful convulsion of his soul. Outside in the squalid courtyard he leaned, suddenly overcome, against the single lamppost and retched his heart out, into the gutter.

Now he felt cold, but firmer in his intention. He set out resolutely in the direction of St. Dominic's.

The housekeeper at St. Dominic's admitted him with that noiseless discretion that typified the presbytery. In a minute, she glided back to the half-lit hall, where she had left him, and for the first time faintly smiled at him. "You're fortunate, Francis. His Reverence is free to see you."

Snuffbox in hand, Father Gerald Fitzgerald rose as Francis entered, his manner a mixture of cordiality and inquiry, his fine handsome presence matching the French furniture, the antique prie-dieu, the choice copies of Italian primitives upon the walls, the vase of lilies on the escritoire, scenting the tasteful room.

"Well young man, I thought you were up north? Sit down! How are all my good friends in Holywell?" As he paused to take snuff, his eye touched upon the college tie, which Francis wore, with affectionate approval. "I was there myself, you know, before I went to the Holy City . . . a grand gentlemanly place. Dear old MacNabb. And Father Tarrant. A classmate of mine at the English College in Rome. There's a fine, a coming man! Well now, Francis." He paused, his needled glance sheathed by a courtier's suavity. "What can we do for you?"

Painfully distressed, breathing quickly, Francis kept his eyes down. "I came to see you about Nora."

The stammered remark rent the room's serenity, its note of mannered ease.

"And what about Nora, pray?"

"Her marriage with Gilfoyle . . . She doesn't want to go through with it. . . . She's miserable. . . . It seems so stupid and unjust . . . such a needless and horrible affair."

"What do you know about the horrible affair?"

"Well . . . everything . . . that she wasn't to blame."

There was a pause. Fitzgerald's fine brow expressed annoyance, yet he gazed at the distraught youth before him with a kind of stately pity.

"My dear young man, if you enter the priesthood, as I trust you will, and gain even half the experience that unhappily is mine, you will comprehend that certain social disorders demand equally specific remedies. You are staggered by this . . . ," he returned the phrase with an inclination of his head, ". . . horrible affair. I am not. I even anticipated it. I know and abominate the whiskey trade for its effect upon the brute mentality of the clods who constitute this parish. You and I may sit down and quietly enjoy our Lacryma Christi, like gentlemen. Not so Mr. Edward Bannon. Enough! I make no allegations. I merely say, we have a problem, unhappily not unique to those of us who spend drab hours in the confessional." Fitzgerald paused to take snuff, with a distinguished wrist. "What are we to do with it? I will tell you. First, legitimize and baptize the offspring. Second, marry the mother if we can, to as decent a man as will have her. We must regularize, regularize. Make a good Catholic home out of the mess. Weave the loose ends into our sound social fabric. Believe me, Nora Bannon is highly fortunate to get Gilfoyle. He's not so bright, but he's steady. In a couple of years you'll see her at Mass with her husband and family . . . perfectly happy."

"No, no." The interruption was wrenched from Francis's shut lips. "She'll never be happy—only broken and miserable."

Fitzgerald's head was a trifle higher. "And is happiness the ultimate objective of our earthly life?"

"She'll do something desperate. You can't compel Nora. I know her better than you."

"You seem to know her intimately." Fitzgerald smiled with withering suavity. "I hope you have no physical interest in the lady yourself."

A dark red spot burned on Francis's pale cheek. He muttered: "I am very fond of Nora. But if I love her—it's nothing that would make your confessional more drab. I beg you—" His voice held a low, desperate entreaty. "Don't force her into this marriage. She's not common clay. . . . She's a bright sweet spirit. You can't thrust a child upon her bosom and a husband into her arms—because—in her innocence, she's been . . ."

Stung to the quick, Fitzgerald banged his snuffbox on the table.

"Don't preach at me, sir!"

"I'm sorry. You can see I don't know what I'm saying. I'm trying to beg you to use your power." Francis mustered his flagging forces in a final effort. "At least give her a little time."

"That is enough, Francis!"

The parish priest, too much master of himself, and of others, to lose his temper or his countenance for long, rose abruptly from his chair and looked at his flat gold watch. "I have a confraternity meeting at eight. You must excuse me." As Francis got up, he patted him reproachfully on the back. "My dear boy, you are very immature. Might I even say a little foolish? But thank God you have a wise old mother in Holy Church. Don't run your head against the walls, Francis. They've stood for generations—against stronger batterings than yours. But there now—I know you're a good lad. Come up and have a chat about Holywell when the wedding's over. And meanwhile—as a little act of reparation for your rudeness will you say the Salve Regina for my intention?"

A pause. It was useless, quite useless. "Yes, Father."

"Good night then, my son . . . and God bless you!"

The night air was raw and chill. Defeated, crushed by the impotence of his youth, Francis dragged himself away from the presbytery. His footsteps echoed dully on the paved pathway. As he passed the chapel steps, the sacristan was closing the side doors. When the last chink of light was gone, Francis stood, hatless, in the darkness, his eyes fixed on the wraithlike windows of the clerestory. He blurted out, in a kind of final desperation: "Oh, God! Do what's best for all of us."

As the wedding day approached, consuming Francis with a deadly, sleepless fever, the atmosphere of the tavern seemed insensibly to settle, like a stagnant pool. Nora was quiet, Polly vaguely hopeful; and though Ned still cringed in solitude, the muddled terror in his eyes was less. The ceremony would, of course, be private. But no restraint need operate upon the trousseau, the dowry, the elaborate honeymoon to Killarney. The house was littered with robes and rich materials. Polly, beseeching another try-on, with a mouthful of pins, waded through bales of cloth and linen, enveloped in merciful fog.

Gilfoyle, smugly observant, smoking the Union's best cigars, would occasionally hold conference, upon matters of finance, with Ned. There was a deed of partnership, duly signed, and great talk of building, to accommodate the new ménage. Already Thad's numerous poor relatives hung about the house, sycophantic yet assertive. His married sister, Mrs. Neily, and her daughter Charlotte, were perhaps the worst.

Nora had little enough to say. Once, meeting Francis in the passage, she stopped.

"You know . . . don't you?"

His heart was breaking; he dared not meet her eye. "Yes, I know."

There was a suffocating pause. He could not sustain the torture in his breast. Incoherently he burst out, boyish tears starting in his eyes: "Nora . . . We can't let this happen. If you knew how I've felt for you . . . I could look after you—work for you. Nora . . . let me take you away."

She considered him with that strange and pitying tenderness. "Where would we go?"

"Anywhere." He spoke wildly, his cheek wet and shining.

She did not answer. She pressed his hand without speaking, then went on, quickly, to be fitted for a dress.

On the day before the wedding, she unbent a little, losing something of her marble acquiescence. Suddenly, over one of those cups of tea which Polly inflicted upon her, she declared: "I believe I'd like to go to Whitley Bay today."

Astounded, Polly echoed: "Whitley Bay?" then added in a flutter, "I'll come with you."

"There's no need." Nora paused, gently stirring her cup. "But of course if you want to . . ."

"I do indeed, my dear!"

Reassured by that lightness in Nora's manner—as though a bar of that old mischievous gaiety reechoed, like distant music, in her being—Polly came to view the excursion without disfavor. She had a gratified, bewildered idea that Nora was coming round. As she finished her tea she discoursed upon the beautiful Lake of Killarney, which she had once visited as a girl. The boatmen there had been most amusing.

The two women, dressed for the expedition, left for the station after the dinner hour. As she turned the corner, Nora looked up toward the window where Francis stood. She seemed to linger for a second, smiled gravely, and waved her hand. Then she was gone.

News of the accident reached the district even before Aunt Polly was brought home, in a state of collapse, in a cab. The sensation throughout the city was impressive. Popular interest could never have been so stirred by the mere stupidity of a young woman stumbling between a platform and a moving train. It was the prenuptial timing that made the thing so exquisite. Around the docks women ran out of their doorways, gathering in groups, beshawled, arms akimbo. Blame for the tragedy was finally pinned upon the victim's new shoes. There was enormous sympathy for Thaddeus Gilfoyle, for the family, for all young women about to be married and under the necessity of traveling by train. There was talk of a public funeral—with the confraternity band—for the mangled remains.

Late that night, how he knew not, Francis found himself in St. Dominic's church. It was quite deserted. The flickering wick of the sanctuary lamp drew his haggard eyes, a feeble beacon. Kneeling, stiff and pale, he felt, like an embrace, the remorseless foreclosure of his destiny. Never had he known such a moment of desolation, of abandonment. He could not weep. His lips, cold and stricken, could not move in prayer. But from his tortured mind there soared an offering of anguished thought. First his parents; and now Nora. He could no longer ignore these testaments from above. He would go away . . . he must go . . . to Father MacNabb . . . to San Morales. He would give himself entirely to God. He must become a priest.

6

During Easter, in the year 1892, an event occurred in the English seminary of San Morales that set the place humming with a note of consternation. One of the students, in the subdiaconate, disappeared completely for the space of four entire days.

Naturally the seminary had witnessed other seditions since its foundation in these Aragon uplands fifty years before. Students had mutinied for an hour or so, skulking to the *posada* outside the walls, hurriedly deranging conscience and digestion with long *cigarros* and the local *aguardiente.* Once or twice it had been necessary to drag some tottering recusant by the ears from the dingy parlors of the *via amorosa* in the town. But this—for a student to march out through the open gates in broad daylight and, half a week later, by the same gates, in even brighter light of day, to limp in again, dusty, unshaven, disheveled, offering every evidence of horrible dissipation, and then, with no other excuse than "I've been for a walk!" to fling himself upon his bed and sleep the clock round—it was apostasy.

At the recreation the students discussed it in awed tones—little groups of dark figures on the sunny slopes, between the bright green copperas-sprayed vineyards, with the seminary, white and gleaming against the pale pink earth, beneath them.

It was agreed that Chisholm would undoubtedly be expelled.

The Committee of Examination had immediately been constituted. According to precedent, as in all grave breaches of discipline it was composed of the rector, the administrator, the director of novices, and the head seminarian. After some preliminary discussion, the tribunal opened its proceedings, in the theological atrium, on the day following the runagate's return.

Outside the *solano* was blowing. The ripe black olives fell from the blade-leafed trees and burst beneath the sun. A scent of orange flowers swept across from the grove above the infirmary. The baked earth crackled with the heat. As Francis entered the white and lofty-pillared room, its polished empty benches cool and dark, he had a quiet air. The black alpaca soutane stressed the thinness of his figure. His hair, cropped and tonsured, gave tautness to his face bones, intensified the darkness of his eyes, his dark contained reserve. There was an odd tranquility about his hands.

Before him, on the platform reserved for protagonists in debate, were four desks, already occupied by Father Tarrant, Monsignor MacNabb, Father Gomez, and Deacon Mealey. Conscious of a mingling of displeasure and concern in the united gaze now upon him, Francis hung his head, while in a rapid voice Gomez, director of novices, read out the accusation.

There was a silence. Then Father Tarrant spoke.

"What is your explanation?"

Despite the quietness that enclosed him Francis suddenly began to flush. He kept his head down.

"I went for a walk!" The words resounded lamely.

"That is sufficiently apparent. We use our legs whether our intentions are good or bad. Apart from the obvious sin of leaving the seminary without permission, were your intentions bad?"

"No."

"During your absence did you indulge in alcoholic liquor?"

"No."

"Did you visit the bullfight, the fair, the casino?"

"No."

"Did you consort with women of ill fame?"

"No."

"Then what did you do?"

Silence again, then the muttered inarticulate reply. "I've told you. You wouldn't understand. I . . . I went for a walk!"

Father Tarrant smiled thinly. "Do you wish us to believe that you spent these entire four days ceaselessly perambulating the countryside?"

"Well . . . practically."

"What destination did you reach eventually?"

"I—I got to Cossa!"

"Cossa! But that is fifty miles away!"

"Yes, I suppose so."

"You were there for some specific purpose?"

"No."

Father Tarrant bit his thin lip. He could not brook obstruction. He had a sudden wild longing for the rack, the boot, the wheel. Small wonder the medievalists had recourse to such instruments! There were circumstances that fully justified them.

"I believe you are lying, Chisholm."

"Why should I lie—to you?"

A muffled exclamation came from Deacon Mealey. His presence was purely formal. As the chief prefect he sat there as a symbol, perhaps a cipher, expressive of the student body. Yet he could not restrain his earnest pleading.

"Please, Francis! For the sake of all of the students . . . all of us who love you . . . I . . . I implore you to own up."

As Francis remained silent, Father Gomez, the young Spanish novice master, inclined his head and murmured to Tarrant: "I've had no evidence . . . none whatever, from the town. But we might write to the priest at Cossa."

Tarrant shot a swift glance at the Spaniard's subtle face.

"Yes. That is decidedly an idea."

Meanwhile the rector had taken advantage of the lull. Older, slower than at Holywell, he leaned forward. He spoke slowly and kindly.

"Of course, you must realize, Francis, that in the circumstances, so general an explanation is barely adequate. After all, it is a serious matter to play truant—not merely the breaking of the seminary rule, the disobedience—but rather the underlying motive which prompted you. Tell me! Are you not happy here?"

"Yes, I am happy."

"Good! And you've no reason to doubt your vocation?"

"No! I want more than ever to try to do some good in the world."

"That pleases me greatly. You don't wish to be sent away?"

"No!"

"Then tell us in your own words how you came to—to take your remarkable adventure."

At the quiet encouragement, Francis raised his head. He made a great effort, his eyes remote, his face troubled.

"I . . . I had just been to the chapel. But I couldn't pray, I couldn't seem to settle. I was restless. The *solano* was blowing—the hot wind seemed to make me more restless, the routine of the seminary suddenly seemed petty and vexatious. Suddenly, I saw the road outside the gates, white and soft with dust. I couldn't help myself. I was on the road, walking. I walked all night, miles and miles. I walked—"

"All the next day." Father Tarrant bit out the satiric interruption. "And the next!"

"That's what I did."

"I never heard such a pack of rubbish in my life! It is an insult to the intelligence of the committee."

The rector, with frowning resolution, suddenly straightened himself in his chair.

"I propose that we temporarily adjourn." While the two priests stared at him in surprise, he said decisively to Francis: "You may go for the present. If we think it necessary we will recall you."

Francis left the room in a dead silence. Only then did the rector turn to the others. He declared coldly: "I assure you that bullying will do no good. We must go carefully. There is more in this than meets the eye."

Smarting under the interference, Father Tarrant moved fretfully.

"It is the culmination of an unruly career."

"Not at all." The rector demurred. "He's been eager and persevering ever since he came here. There is nothing damaging in his record, Father Gomez?"

Gomez turned the pages, on the desk, before him.

"No." He spoke slowly, reading from the record. "A few practical jokes. Last winter he set fire to the English newspaper when Father Despard was perusing it in the common room. Asked why . . . he laughed and answered, 'The devil finds work for idle hands!'"

"Never mind that." The rector spoke sharply. "We all know Father Despard corners every paper that comes into this seminary."

"Then," Gomez resumed, "when deputed to read aloud in the refectory he smuggled in and substituted for *The Life of St. Peter of Alcantara* a CRS tract entitled *When Eva Stole the Sugar* which—until he was stopped—induced much unseemly hilarity."

"Harmless mischief."

"Again . . ." Gomez turned another page. "In the comical procession the students got up, representing the sacraments—you may remember, one dressed up as a baby representing baptism, two others were got up as matrimony, and so on—it was all done with permission of course. But," Gomez shot a dubious glance at Tarrant, "on the back of the corpse carried in for extreme unction, Chisholm pinned a card:

Here lies Father Tarrant
I've gladly signed his warrant.
If ever—"

"That's enough." Tarrant broke in sharply. "We've more to concern us than these absurd lampoons."

The rector nodded. "Absurd, yes. But not malicious. I like a young man who can knock some fun out of life. We cannot ignore the fact that Chisholm is an unusual character—most unusual. He has great depth and fire. He's sensitive, inclined to fits of melancholy. He conceals it behind these high spirits. You see, he's a fighter; he'll never give in. He's a queer mixture of childlike simplicity and logical directness. And, above all, he's a complete individualist!"

"Individualism is rather a dangerous quality in a theologian," Tarrant interposed acidly. "It gave us the Reformation."

"And the Reformation gave us a better-behaved Catholic Church." The rector smiled mildly at the ceiling. "But we're getting from the point. I don't deny there's been a gross breach of discipline. It must be punished. But the punishment cannot be rushed. I can't expel a student of Chisholm's quality without first knowing positively that he deserves expulsion. Therefore, let us wait a few days." He rose, innocently. "I'm sure you all agree."

As the three priests left the platform, Gomez and Tarrant went off together.

During the next two days an air of suspended doom overhung the unhappy Francis. He was not restrained. No apparent ban was placed upon his studies. But wherever he went—to the library, refectory, or common room—an unnatural silence struck his fellows, followed swiftly by an exaggerated casualness, which deceived no one. The knowledge that he was the universal topic gave him a guilty look. His Holywell companion, Hudson, also in the subdiaconate, pursued him with affectionate attentions and a worried frown. Anselm Mealey led another faction, which clearly felt itself outraged. At recreation they consulted, approached the solitary figure. Mealey was the spokesman.

"We don't want to hit you when you're down, Francis. But this touches all of us. It's a slur upon the student body as a whole. We feel that it would be so much finer and manlier if you would make a clean breast and own up to it."

"Own up to what?"

Mealey shrugged his shoulders. There was a silence. What more could he do? As he turned away with the others he said:

"We've decided to make a novena for you. I feel it worse than the others. I hoped you were my best friend."

Francis found it harder to maintain his pretense of normality. He would start off to walk in the seminary grounds, then stop, sharply, recollecting that walking had been his ruin. He drifted about, aware that for Tarrant and the other professors he had ceased to exist. At the lectures he found he was not listening. The summons to the rector he half hoped for did not come.

His sense of personal stress increased. He failed to understand himself. He was a purposeless enigma. He brooded over the justification of those who had predicted that he had no vocation. He had wild conceptions of setting out as a lay brother to some dangerous and distant mission. He began to haunt the church—but secretly. Above all there existed the necessity of putting on a face to meet his little world.

It was on the morning of the third day, Wednesday, that Father Gomez received the letter. Shocked but deeply gratified, his resourcefulness confirmed, he ran with it to the administrator's office. He stood, while Father Tarrant read the note, like an intelligent dog awaiting its reward, a kind word or a bone.

Mi Amigo,

In reply to your honored communication of Whitsunday, I deeply regret to inform you that inquiries have elicited the fact that a seminarian, of such bearing, height, and color as you define, was observed in Cossa on April 14th. He was seen to enter the house of one Rosa Oyarzabal late that evening and to leave early the following morning. The woman in question lives alone, is of a known character, and has not frequented the altar rails for seven years.

I have the honor to remain, dear padre,
Your devoted brother in Jesus Christus,
Salvador Bolas
P. P. Cossa

Gomez murmured: "Don't you agree it was good strategy?"

"Yes, yes!" With a brow of thunder Tarrant brushed the Spaniard aside. Bearing the letter like something obscene, he strode into the rector's room at the end of the corridor. But the rector was saying his Mass. He would be occupied for half an hour.

Father Tarrant could not wait. He crossed the courtyard like a whirlwind and, without knocking, burst into Francis's room. It was empty.

Checked, realizing that Francis must also be at Mass, he struggled with his fury as an ungovernable horse might fight its bit. He sat down, abruptly, forcing himself to wait, his dark thin figure charged with lightning.

The cell was barer even than others of its kind, its inventory a bed, a chest, a table, the chair he occupied. Upon the chest stood one faded photograph, an angular woman in a frightful hat holding the hand of a white-clad little girl: "Love from Aunt Polly and Nora."

Tarrant repressed his sneer. But his lip curled at the single picture on the whitewashed walls, a tiny replica of the Sistine Madonna, Our Lady of Chastity.

Suddenly, upon the table, he saw an open notebook: a diary. Again he started, like a nervous horse, his nostrils dilated, a dark red fire in his eye. For a moment he sat, battling his scruples, then rose and went slowly toward the book. He was a gentleman. It was repugnant to pry like a vulgar chambermaid, into another's privacy. But it was his duty. Who could guess what further iniquities this scroll contained? With relentless austerity upon his face, he picked up the written page.

". . . was it St. Anthony who spoke of his 'ill-judged, obstinate, and perverse behavior'? I must console myself in the greatest despondency I have ever known, with that single thought! If they send me away from here my life will be broken. I'm a miserable crooked character; I don't think straight like the others; I cannot train myself to run with the pack. But with my whole soul I desire passionately to work for God. In our Father's house there are many mansions! There was room for such diversities as Joan of Arc and . . . well, Blessed Benedict Labre who let even the lice run over him. Surely there is room for me!

"They ask me to explain to them. How can one explain nothing—or what is so obvious as to be shameful? Francis de Sales said: 'I will be ground to powder rather than break a rule.' But when I walked out of the seminary I did not think of rules, or of breaking them. Certain impulses are unconscious.

"It helps me to write this down: it gives my transgression the semblance of reason.

"For weeks I had been sleeping badly, tossing through these hot nights in a fever of unrest. Perhaps it is harder for me here than for the others—judged at least by the voluminous literature on the subject, wherein the steps to the priesthood are represented as sweet untroubled joys, piled one upon another. If our beloved laity knew how one has to fight!

"Here my greatest difficulty has been the sense of confinement, of physical inaction—what a bad mystic I should make!—always aggravated by echoes, stray sounds, penetrating inward from the outer world. Then I realize that I am twenty-three, that I have done nothing yet to help a single living soul, and I am fevered with unrest.

"Willie Tulloch's letters provide—in Father Gomez's phrase—the most pernicious stimuli. Now that Willie is a qualified doctor and his sister Jean a certified nurse, both working for the Tynecastle Poor Law Board and enjoying many thrilling, if verminous adventures, in the slums, I feel that I should be out and fighting too.

"Of course I shall, one day. . . . I must be patient. But my present ferment seems heightened by the news of Ned and Polly. I was happy when they decided to remove from above the tavern and have Judy, the child, to live with them in the little flat that Polly had taken at Clermont, on the outskirts of the city. But Ned has been ill, Judy troublesome, and Gilfoyle—left to manage Union Tavern—a most unsatisfactory business partner. Ned, in fact, has gone to pieces, refuses to go out, sees no one. That one impulse of blind unthinkable stupidity has finished him. A baser man would have survived it.

"The pattern of life sometimes demands great faith. Dear Nora! That tender platitude conceals a thousand avenues of thought and feeling. When Father Tarrant gave us that practical talk—*agendo contra*—he said most truly: 'Some temptations cannot be fought—one must close one's mind and fly from them!' My excursion to Cossa must have been that kind of flight.

"At first, though walking fast, I did not mean to go far when I passed through the seminary gates. But the relief, the sense of escape from myself that the violent exercise afforded, drove me on. I sweated gloriously, like a peasant in the fields—that salty running sweat that seems to purge one of human dross. My mind lifted; my heart began to sing. I wanted to go on and on until I dropped!

"I walked all day without food or drink. I covered a great distance, for, when evening drew near, I could smell the sea. And as the stars broke out in the pale sky, I came over the hill and found Cossa at my feet. The village, harbored on a sheltered creek where the sea barely lapped, with blossoming acacia trees lining its single street, had an almost heavenly beauty. I was dead with tiredness. There was an enormous blister on my heel. But as I came down the hill the place welcomed me with its quiet pulse of life.

"In the little square the villagers were enjoying the cool air, scented with acacia flowers, the dusk made dimmer by the lamps of the little inn, where at an open doorway stood two pine benches. Before the benches in the soft dust some old men were playing bowls with wooden balls. From the creek came the booming of frogs. Children laughed and ran. It was simple and beautiful. Though I now realized that I had not a peseta in my pocket, I seated myself on one of the benches outside the door. How good it was to rest. I was stupid with fatigue. Suddenly, in the quiet darkness beneath the trees, the sound of Catalan pipes rang out. Not loud—low, attuned to the night. If one has not heard these reeds, or the shrill, sweet native tunes, one cannot fully estimate the gladness of that moment. I was enchanted. I suppose, as a Scot, I've the lilt of the pipes in my blood. I sat as though drugged by the music, the darkness, the beauty of the night, my utter weakness.

"I had resolved to sleep out on the beach. But presently, as I thought to move there, a mist rolled in from the sea. It fell like a mystery upon the village. In five minutes the square was choked with twisting vapor, the trees dripping, and everybody going home. I had reached the conclusion, unwillingly, that I must go to the local priest, 'give myself up,' and get a bed, when a woman seated on the other bench suddenly spoke to me. For some time I had felt her gazing at me with that mixture of pity and contempt which the mere sight of a religious seems to provoke in Christian countries. Now, as if she read my thoughts, she said: 'They are tight people there. They will not take you in.'

"She was about thirty years of age, dressed quietly in black, with a pale face, dark eyes, and a thickened figure. She continued indifferently:

" 'There is a bed in my house if you wish to sleep in it.'

" 'I have no money to pay for a lodging.'

"She laughed scornfully. 'You can pay me with your prayers.'

"It had now begun to rain. They had closed the *fonda*. We both sat on the wet benches under the dripping acacia trees in the deserted square. The absurdity of this seemed to strike her. She rose.

" 'I am going home. If you are not a fool you will accept my hospitality.'

"My thin soutane was soaked. I had begun to shiver. I reflected that I could send her money for my room on my return to the seminary. I got up and walked with her down the narrow street.

"Her house was halfway down the row. We descended two steps into the kitchen. When she had lit the lamp, she threw off the black shawl, put a pot of chocolate on the fire, and took a new loaf from the oven. She spread a red-checked tablecloth. Bubbling chocolate and hot bread made a good smell in the small clean room.

"As she poured the chocolate into thick cups she looked at me across the table. 'You had better say grace. That improves the flavor!' Though now there was no mistaking the irony in her voice, I said grace. We began to eat and drink. The flavor needed no improvement.

"She kept watching me. She had once been a very pretty woman, but the remnants of her beauty made her dark-eyed olive face seem hard. Her small ears were close to her head and pierced with heavy gold rings. Her hands were plump like the hands of a Rubens Madonna.

"'Well, little padre, you are lucky to be here. I have no liking for the priests. In Barcelona, when I pass them I break into open laughter!'

"I couldn't help smiling. 'You don't surprise me. It's the first thing we learn—to be laughed at. The best man I ever knew used to preach in the open air. The whole town turned out to laugh at him. They named him, in mockery, Holy Daniel. You see, there's so little doubt nowadays that anyone who believes in God is a hypocrite or a fool!'

"She took a slow drink of chocolate, watching me over her cup. 'You are no fool. Tell me, do I please you?'

"'I think you are charming and kind.'

"'It is my nature to be kind. I've had a sad life. My father was a Castilian noble who was dispossessed by the Madrid government. My husband commanded a great ship in the navy. He was lost at sea. I myself am an actress—living quietly here at present until my father's estate is recovered. Of course you understand that I am lying.'

"'Perfectly!'

"She didn't take this as a joke as I had hoped. She reddened slightly. 'You are too clever. But I know why you are here, my run-away priestling; you are all the same.' She got over her fit of pique, and mocked: 'You forsake Mother Church for Mother Eve.'

"I was puzzled, then her meaning dawned on me. It was so absurd I wanted to laugh. But it was annoying too—I supposed I'd have to clear out. I had finished my bread and chocolate. I rose and took my hat. 'Thank you exceedingly for my supper. It was excellent.'

"Her expression changed, all the malice driven out of it by surprise. 'So you are a hypocrite then.' She bit her lip sulkily. As I went to the door she said suddenly: 'Don't go!'

"A silence. She said defiantly:

"'Don't look at me like that. I'm entitled to do as I choose. I enjoy myself. You should see me Saturday evenings, sitting in the Cava at Barcelona—more fun than ever you'll have in your miserable little life. Go upstairs and sleep.'

"There was a pause. Her attitude now seemed reasonable; and I could hear the rain outside. I hesitated, then moved toward the narrow stairs. My feet were swollen and smarting. I must have limped badly, for she exclaimed suddenly, coldly: 'What is the matter with your precious foot?'

"'It's nothing . . . only blistered.'

"She studied me with those strange unfathomable eyes.

"'I will bathe it for you.'

"In spite of all my protests she made me sit down. When she had filled a basin with warm water she kneeled and took off my boot. My sock was sticking to the raw flesh. She softened it with water and drew it off. Her unexpected kindness embarrassed me. She bathed both my feet and put some ointment on them. Then she stood up.

"'That should feel better. Your socks will be ready for you in the morning.'

"'How can I thank you?'

"She said unexpectedly in an odd dull tone: 'What does one do with a life like mine!' Before I could answer she raised the pitcher in her right hand. 'Do not preach at me or I will break your head. Your bed is on the second landing. Good night.'

"She turned away toward the fire. I went upstairs, found a small room beneath the skylight. I slept as though stunned.

"Next morning when I came down, she was moving about the kitchen, making coffee. She gave me breakfast. As I took my leave I tried to express my gratitude. But she cut me short. She gave me her sad peculiar smile. 'You are too innocent to be a priest. You will be a great failure.'

"I started back for San Morales. I was lame and rather scared of my reception. I was afraid. I took my time."

Father Tarrant remained motionless at the window for a long moment, then quietly replaced the diary upon the table, reminded by a glint of recollection that it was he who had first asked Francis to keep it. Methodically he tore the Spanish priest's letter into fragments. The expression on his face was quite remarkable. For once it lacked its bleakness, that iron austerity seared into every feature by pitiless self-mortification. It became a young face, flooded with generosity and thoughtfulness. With his clenched hand still holding the pieces of the letter, slowly, almost unconsciously, he struck his breast three times. Then he spun round and left the room.

As he descended the broad staircase Anselm Mealey's solid head came up and around the spiral balustrade. Observing Father Tarrant, the model seminarian dared to pause. He admired the administrator to excess. To be noticed by him was a heavenly joy. He ventured modestly:

"Excuse me, sir. We are all very anxious. I am wondering if there is any more news . . . concerning Chisholm?"

"What news?"

"Well . . . of his leaving."

Tarrant contemplated his creature with remote distaste. "Chisholm is not leaving." He added, with sudden violence, "You fool!"

That evening as Francis sat in his study, dizzy and unbelieving under the miracle of his redemption, one of the college servants silently handed in a packet. It contained a superb figure of the Virgin of Montserrat carved in ebony, a tiny masterpiece of fifteenth-century Spanish craftsmanship. No message accompanied the exquisite thing. Not a word of explanation. Suddenly, with a wild consuming thought, Francis remembered he had seen it above the prie-dieu in Father Tarrant's room.

It was the rector, meeting Francis at the end of the week, who put his finger on the manifest inconsistency. "It strikes me, young sir, that you have escaped gey lightly, through a sinister screen of sanctity. In my young days playing truant—'plunking' we called it—was a punishable crime." He fixed on Francis his shrewd and twinkling gaze. "As a penance you might write me an essay—two thousand words—on the virtue of walking."

In the small universe of a seminary the very walls have ears, the keyholes diabolic vision. The story of Francis's escapade came gradually to light, was fitted, piece by piece, together. It grew, gained indeed, as it passed from lip to ear. Assuming the facets of the finished gem, it seemed likely to descend—a classic in the seminary's history. When Father Gomez had the final details, he wrote fully to his friend the parish priest of Cossa. Father Bolas was much impressed. He wrote back, a glowing five-page letter, of which, perhaps, the final paragraph merits quotation:

> Naturally, the pinnacle of achievement would have been the conversion of the woman, Rosa Oyarzabal. How wonderful it would have been had she come to me and wept, on her knees, in true contrition, as the result of our young apostle's visitation! But alas! She has gone into partnership with another madam and opened a brothel in Barcelona, which I grieve to report is flourishing.

PART III

An Unsuccessful Curate

1

It was raining steadily, early that Saturday evening in January when Francis arrived at Shalesley, on the branch line, some forty miles from Tynecastle. But nothing could damp the eagerness, the burning of his spirit. While the train disappeared into the mist, he stood expectantly on the wet open platform, his alert eyes sweeping its dreary vacancy. No one had come to meet him. Undismayed, he picked up his bag and swung into the main street of the colliery village. The Church of the Redeemer should not be hard to find.

It was his first appointment, his first curacy. He could scarcely believe it. His heart sang . . . at last, at last, newly ordained, he had his chance to get into the battle and fight for human souls.

Though he had been forewarned, Francis had never seen greater ugliness than that which now surrounded him. Shalesley consisted of long gray rows of houses and poor cheap shops, interspaced with plots of wasteland, slag heaps—smoking even in the rain—a refuse dump, several taverns and chapels, all dominated by the high black headstocks of the Renshaw colliery. But he told himself gaily that his interest lay in the people, not the place.

The Catholic church stood on the east side of the village, adjacent to the colliery, harmonizing with the scene. It was a big erection of raw red brick with Gothic blue-stained windows, a dark red corrugated-iron roof, and a sawed-off rusty spire. The school lay on one side; the presbytery, fronted by a weedy plot and girded by a broken-toothed fence, upon the other.

With a deep, excited breath, Francis approached the small, ramshackle house and pulled the bell. After some delay, when he was about to ring again, the door was opened by a stout woman in a blue striped apron. Inspecting him, she nodded.

"It'll be yourself, Father! His Reverence is expecting you. In there!" She pointed with privileged good nature to the parlor door. "What weather to be sure. I'll away and put on the kippers."

Francis sturdily entered the room. Already seated at a table covered with a white cloth and laid for a repast, a thickset priest of about fifty stopped his impatient knife tapping to greet his new curate.

"You're here at last. Come in."

Francis extended his hand. "Father Kezer, I imagine?"

"That's right. Who did you expect? King William of Orange? Well, you're just in time for supper. Trust you!" Tilting back, he called to the adjoining kitchen. "Miss Cafferty! Are you going to be all night?" Then, to Francis: "Sit down and stop looking like the lost chord. I hope you play cribbage. I like a game of an evening."

Francis took a chair at the table, and soon Miss Cafferty hurried in with a large covered dish of kippers and poached eggs. As Father Kezer helped himself to two eggs and a brace of kippers she laid another place for Francis. Then Father Kezer passed over the dish, his mouth full.

"Go ahead and help yourself. Don't stint. You'll have to work hard here so you'd better eat."

He himself ate rapidly, his strong crunching jaws and capable hands, felted with black hairs, never at rest. He was burly, with a round cropped head, and a tight mouth. His nose was flat, with wide nostrils out of which sprouted two dark snuff-stained tufts. He conveyed the impression of strength, of authority. Every movement was a masterpiece of unconscious self-assertion. As he cut an egg in two and slipped one half into his mouth his little eyes watched, formed an opinion of Francis, as a butcher might weigh the merits of a steer.

"You don't look too hardy. Under eleven stone, eh? I don't know what you curates are coming to. My last was a weak-kneed effort! Should have called himself flea—not Lee—he hadn't the guts of one. It's this Continental la-di-da that ruins you. In my time—well, the fellows that came out of Maynooth with me were men."

"I think you'll find me sound in wind and limb." Francis smiled.

"We'll soon see." Father Kezer grunted. "Go in and hear confessions when you've finished. I'll be in later. There won't be many tonight though . . . seeing it's wet. Give them an excuse! They're bone lazy—my beautiful lot!"

Upstairs, in his thin-walled room, massively furnished with a heavy bed and an enormous Victorian wardrobe, Francis washed his hands and face at the stained washstand. Then he hastened down toward the church. The impression Father Kezer had given him was not favorable, but he told himself he must be fair: immediate judgments were so often unjust. He sat for a long time in the cold confessional box—still marked with the name of his predecessor, "Fr. Lee"—hearing the drumming of the rain on the tin roof. At last he came out and wandered round the empty church. It was a depressing spectacle—bare as a barn and not very clean. An unhappy attempt had been made to marble the nave with dark green paint. The statue of St. Joseph had lost a hand and been clumsily repaired. The stations of the cross were sad little daubs. On the altar some gaudy paper flowers, in vases of tarnished brass, hit the eye like an affront. But these little shortcomings only made his opportunity the greater. The tabernacle was there. And Francis knelt before it, with throbbing fervor, dedicating his life anew.

Habituated to the cultured atmosphere of San Morales, a halfway house for scholars and preachers, men of breeding and distinction moving between London, Madrid, and Rome, Francis found the next few days increasingly difficult. Father Kezer was not an easy man. Naturally irascible and inclined to surliness, age, experience, and failure to win affection from his flock had made him hard as nails.

At one time he had held an excellent parish in the seaside resort of Eastcliffe. He had proved himself so disagreeable that important people in the town had petitioned the bishop to remove him. The incident, at first bitterly resented, had been hallowed by time into an act of personal sacrifice. He would remark, soulfully: "Of my own free will I stepped from the throne to the footstool . . . but, ah! . . . those were the days."

Miss Cafferty, his cook and housekeeper combined, alone stood by him. She had been with him for years. She understood him; she was of his own kidney; she could take his slangings and heartily slang him back. The two respected each other. When he departed on his annual six weeks' holiday to Harrogate he allowed her to go home for her own vacation.

In his personal habits he had scant refinement. He stamped around his bedroom, opened and slammed the single bathroom door. The matchboard house reverberated with his wind.

Unwittingly, he had reduced his religion to a formula—with no conception of interior meanings, of the unsubstantial, no elasticity of outlook. "Do this or be damned" was imprinted on his heart. There were certain things to be accomplished with words, water, oil, and salt. Without them, hell was ready, hot and gaping. He was deeply prejudiced, loudly voicing his detestation of every other denomination in the village—an attitude which did little to gain him friends.

Even in his relations with his own congregation he was not at peace. The parish was a poor one with a heavy debt upon the church, and despite a stringent economy he was often desperately pressed to make ends meet. He had a legitimate case to place before his people. But his natural ire was a poor substitute for tact. In his sermons, planted solidly on his feet, head thrust aggressively forward, he lashed the sparse congregation for its neglect.

"How do you expect me to pay the rent and the taxes and the insurance? And keep the church roof over your heads?

You're not giving it to me; you're giving it to Almighty God. Now listen to me, every man and woman of ye. It's silver I want to see in the plate, not your miserable brass farthings. You're most of you in work you men, thanks to the generosity of Sir George Renshaw. You've no excuse! As for the wimmen of the parish—if they'd put more in the offertory and less on their backs it would fit them better." He thundered on, then took up the collection himself, glaring accusingly at each of his parishioners as he shoved the plate beneath their noses.

His demands had provoked a feud, a bitter vendetta between himself and his parishioners. The more he berated them the less they gave. Enraged, he devised schemes, took to distributing little buff envelopes. When they left the empty envelopes behind he went round the church after the service, gathering up the litter and muttering furiously: "That's how they treat Almighty God!"

In this gloomy financial sky there was one bright sun.

Sir George Renshaw, who owned the Shalesley colliery, with, indeed, fifteen other coal mines in the county, was not only a man of immense resources and a Catholic but an inveterate philanthropist. Though his country seat, Renshaw Hall, was seventy miles away, on the other side of the shire, the Church of the Redeemer had somehow gained a place upon his list. Every Christmas, with the utmost regularity, a check for one hundred guineas reached the parish priest. "Guineas, mind ye!" Father Kezer anointed the word. "Not just measly pounds. Ah! There's a gentleman for ye!" He had seen Sir George only twice, at public gatherings in Tynecastle many years before, but he spoke of him with reverence and awe. He had a lurking fear that, through no fault of his, the magnate might discontinue the charity.

By the end of his first month at Shalesley, close association with Father Kezer began to take effect on Francis. He was continually on edge. No wonder young Father Lee had had such a bad nervous breakdown. His spiritual life became overcast, his sense of values confused. He found himself regarding Father Kezer with growing hostility. Then he would recollect himself with an inward groan, and strive wildly for obedience, for humility.

His parochial work was desperately hard, particularly in this wintry weather. Three times a week he had to bicycle to Broughton and Glenburn, two distant wretched hamlets, to say Mass, hear confessions, and take the catechism class in the local town hall. The lack of response among his people increased his difficulties. The very children were lethargic, shuffling. There was much poverty, heartrending destitution; the whole parish seemed steeped in apathy, savorless and stale. Passionately he told himself he would not surrender to routine. Conscious of his clumsiness and inefficiency, he had a burning desire to reach these poor hearts, to succor and revive them. He would kindle a spark, blaze the dead ashes into life, if it were the last thing he did.

What made it worse was the fact that the parish priest, astute and watchful, seemed to sense, with a kind of grim humor, the difficulties his curate was experiencing, and to anticipate slyly a readjustment of the other's idealism to his own practical common sense. Once when Francis came in, tired and wet, having bicycled ten miles through wind and rain to an outlying sick call at Broughton, Father Kezer compressed his attitude into a single gibe. "Handing out halos isn't what you thought it was—eh?" He added, naturally: "A good-for-nothing lot."

Francis flushed hotly. "Christ died for a good-for-nothing lot."

Deeply upset, Francis began to mortify himself. At meals he ate sparingly, often only a cup of tea and some toast. Frequently, when he woke up in the middle of the night, tortured by misgivings, he would steal down to the church. Shadowed and silent, washed in pale moonlight, the bare edifice lost its distracting crudity. He flung himself down on his knees, begging for courage to embrace the tribulations of this beginning, praying with impetuous violence. At last, as he gazed at the wounded figure on the cross, patient, gentle, suffering, peace would fill his soul.

One night, shortly after midnight, when he had made a visit of this nature and was tiptoeing upstairs, he found Father Kezer waiting on him. Wearing his nightshirt and an overcoat, a candle in his hand, the parish priest planted his thick hairy legs on the top landing, angrily barred the way.

"What d'you think you're doing?"

"Going to my room."

"Where have you been?"

"To the church."

"What! At this time of night!"

"Why not?" Francis forced a smile. "Do you think I might wake our Lord up?"

"No, but you might wake me up." Father Kezer lost his temper. "I won't have it. I never heard such nonsense in my life. I'm running a parish, not a religious order. You can pray all you want in the day, but while you're under my orders you'll sleep at night."

Francis suppressed the hot answer on his tongue. He walked to his bedroom in silence. He must curb himself, make a great effort to get on with his superior, if he were to do any good in the parish at all. He tried to concentrate on Father Kezer's good points: his frankness and courage, his odd jocularity, his adamantine chastity.

A few days later, choosing a moment that he thought propitious, he diplomatically approached the older priest.

"I've been wondering, Father . . . we've such a scattered district, so out of the way, with no proper places of amusement . . . wondering if we couldn't have a club for the youngsters of the parish."

"Aha!" Father Kezer was in his jocular mood. "So you're out for popularity, my lad!"

"Good gracious, no." Francis took up an equal heartiness, so intent was he on winning his point. "I don't want to presume. But a club might take the young people off the streets—and the older ones out of the pubs. Develop them physically and socially." He smiled. "Even make them want to come to church."

"Ho, ho!" Father Kezer guffawed. "It's well you're young. I believe you're worse than Lee. Well, go ahead if you want to. But you'll get all your thanks in one basket from the good-for-nothing crowd that hangs out here."

"Thank you, thank you. I only wanted your permission."

With thrilling eagerness Francis immediately began to carry out his plan. Donald Kyle, the manager at Renshaw Colliery, was a Scot and a steady Catholic who had showed signs of goodwill. Two other officials at the pit, Morrison the checkweigher, whose wife occasionally came in to help at the presbytery, and Creeden, the head shot-firer, were also members of the church. Through the manager, Francis received permission to use the colliery first-aid hall three nights a week. With the help of the other two he set out to stir up interest in the proposed club. His own money, added up, made less than two pounds, and he would have died sooner than ask assistance from the parish. But he wrote to Willie Tulloch—whose work brought him into touch with the Tynecastle Corporation Recreation Centers—begging him to send along some old and cast-off athletic gear.

Puzzling how he might best launch the venture, he decided that nothing could draw the young people better than a dance. There was a piano in the room, and Creeden was a first-rate performer on the fiddle. He posted up a notice on the Red Cross door, and when Thursday arrived, he expended his capital on a buffet of cakes, fruit, and lemonade.

The success of the evening, after a stiff start, surpassed his wildest expectations: so many turned out they managed eight sets of lancers. Most of the lads had no shoes; they danced in their pit boots. Between the dances they sat on the benches round the room, red faced and happy, while the girls went to the buffet to find them refreshment. When they waltzed they all sang the words of the refrain. A little group of pitmen going off shift gathered at the entrance, the gaslight showing their teeth white against their grimed faces. Toward the end they joined in the singing, and one or two of the brighter sparks among them nipped in and stole a dance. It was a merry evening.

As he stood at the door, with their good nights ringing in his ears, Francis thought with a surge of trembling joy: "They've begun to come alive. Dear God, I've made a start."

Next morning Father Kezer came in to breakfast in a towering rage.

"What's this I hear? A fine to-do! A right royal example. You ought to be ashamed of yourself."

Francis looked up in amazement. "What on earth do you mean?"

"You know what I mean! That infernal stew you put on last night."

"You gave me permission—only a week ago."

Father Kezer snarled: "I didn't give you permission to start a promiscuous rigadoon on the very doorstep of my church. I've had trouble enough to keep my young girls pure without your introducin' your immodest pawing and prancing!"

"The entire evening was perfectly innocent."

"Innocent!—As God is above us!" Father Kezer was dark red with anger. "Don't you know what that sort of gallantry leads to—you poor dolt—clutching and clasping and bodies and legs together? It starts bad thoughts working in these young folks' minds. It leads to concupiscence, carnality, and lusts of the flesh."

Francis was very pale; his eyes were blazing with indignation. "Aren't you confusing lust with sex?"

"Holy St. Joseph! What's the difference?"

"As much as there is between disease and health."

Father Kezer's hands made a convulsive gesture. "What in the foul fiend's name are you talking about?"

The pent-up bitterness of the past two months broke over Francis in a tempestuous wave. "You can't suppress nature. If you do it'll turn on you and rend you. It's perfectly natural and good for young men and women to mix together, to dance together. It's a natural prelude to courtship and marriage. You can't keep sex under a dirty sheet like a stinking corpse. That's what starts the sly laugh, the prurient sneer. We must learn to educate and transmute sex, not choke it as though it were an adder. If you try that you'll fail, besides making something filthy out of what is clean and fine!"

A horrible silence. The veins in Father Kezer's neck were swollen, purple. "You blasphemous pup! I'll not have my young folks couplin' in your dance halls!"

"Then you'll drive them to couple—as you call it—in the dark lanes and fields."

"You lie," Father Kezer stuttered. "I'll keep the maidenhood of this parish undeflowered. I know what I'm about."

"No doubt," Francis answered bitterly. "But the fact remains that statistics show the Shalesley illegitimacy rate to be the highest in the diocese."

For a moment it seemed as though the parish priest must have a fit. His hands clenched and unclenched, as though seeking something to strangle. Rocking slightly on his feet, he raised his finger and leveled it at Francis.

"Statistics'll show another thing. And that is there's no club within five miles of this spot I'm standing on. Your fine plan is finished, smashed, done for. I say that! And in this case *my* word is final!" He flung himself down at the table and furiously began his breakfast.

Francis finished quickly and went upstairs to his room, pale and shaken. Through the dusty panes he could see the first-aid room, with the packing case of boxing gloves and Indian clubs outside, which had arrived yesterday from Tulloch, all useless now, forbidden. A terrible emotion rose up in him. He thought rigidly: *I cannot continue to submit; God cannot demand such subservience; I must fight, fight, on Father Kezer's level, fight, not for myself, but for this pitiful, broken-winded parish.* He was rent by an overflowing love, an undreamed-of longing to help these poor people, his first charge from God.

During the next few days, as he went through the routine of the parish, he sought feverishly for some means of lifting the ban upon his club. Somehow the club had become the symbol of the parish's emancipation. But the more he dwelt upon it the more unassailable Father Kezer's position appeared.

Drawing his own conclusions from Francis's quietness the older priest showed an ill-concealed jubilation. He was the one to tame them, to bring these young pups to heel. The bishop must know how good he was to send him so many, one after the other. His sour grin broadened.

Quite suddenly, Francis had an idea. It struck him with overwhelming force, a slender chance, perhaps, yet one which might succeed. His pale face colored slightly; he almost cried out loud. With a great effort, he calmed himself. He thought: *I'll try; I must try . . . whenever Aunt Polly's visit is over.*

He had arranged for Aunt Polly and Judy to come to Shalesley for a holiday during the last week in June. Shalesley, it is true, was not a health resort. But it stood high; the air was good. The fresh green of spring had touched its bleakness with a transient beauty. And Francis was particularly anxious that Polly should have the rest she so richly deserved.

The winter had been hard for her, physically and financially. Thaddeus Gilfoyle was, in her own phrase, "ruining" the Union, drinking more than he sold, failing to show receipts, trying to get the remnants of the business into his own hands. Ned's chronic illness had taken a peculiar turn, for twelve months now he had lost the power of his legs and was quite beyond business. Confined to a wheeled chair, he had lately become irresponsible and irrational. He had absurd delusions, spoke to the smirking, toadying Thaddeus of his steam yacht, his private brewery in Dublin. One day he had escaped her care and attended by Scanty—a grotesque spectacle of motion—had propelled himself to the Clermont shops and ordered himself two dozen hats. Dr. Tulloch, called in at Francis's request, had pronounced Ned's condition no stroke, but a tumor of the brain. It was he who had procured the male nurse who was now relieving Polly.

Francis would have greatly preferred Judy and Aunt Polly to occupy the guest room at the presbytery—indeed, one of his dreams was a parish of his own where Polly would be his housekeeper and Judy his particular charge. But Father Kezer's attitude made a request for hospitality out of the question. Francis found a comfortable lodging for them at Mrs. Morrison's. And on June 21, Aunt Polly and Judy arrived.

Welcoming them at the station, he felt a sudden pain in his heart. Polly, a stiff valiant figure, advanced from the train, leading by the hand, as she had led Nora, the small, dark, glossy-haired child.

"Polly. Dear Polly." He spoke as to himself. She was little changed, a trifle shabbier perhaps, her gaunt cheeks more drawn. She had the same short coat, gloves, and hat. She never spent a penny on herself, always on others. She had cared for Nora and himself, for Ned, and now for Judy. She was so utterly selfless, his breast filled. He stepped forward and hugged her.

"Polly, I'm so glad to see you . . . you're . . . you're eternal."

"Oh, dear." She fumbled in her bag for her handkerchief. "It's windy here. And there's something in my eye."

He took her arm and Judy's, and escorted them to their rooms.

He did his utmost to give them a happy time. In the evenings he had long talks with Polly. Her pride in him, in what he had become, was touching. She made light of her troubles.

But she admitted one anxiety—Judy was a problem.

The child, now ten years of age and attending the day school at Clermont, was a queer mixture. Superficially she had an engaging frankness, but beneath she was suspicious and secretive. She hoarded all sorts of odds and ends in her bedroom, and would shake with temper if they were disturbed. She had wild enthusiasms which quickly faded. In other moods she was timid and uncertain. She could not bear to admit a fault and would wander glibly from the truth to hide it. The hint that she was lying brought floods of indignant tears.

With this before him Francis made every effort to win her confidence. He had her frequently to the presbytery where, with the complete unconsciousness of the young, she made herself at home, often wandering off into Father Kezer's room, climbing on his sofa, fingering his pipes and paperweights. It was embarrassing, but since the parish priest made no protest, Francis did not restrain the child.

On the last day of their short holiday, when Aunt Polly had gone for a final walk and Judy had at length come to rest with a picture book in the corner of Francis's room, a knock sounded on the door. It was Miss Cafferty. She addressed Francis.

"His Reverence wants to see you immediately."

Francis's brows lifted at the unexpected request. There was something ominous in the housekeeper's words. He rose, slowly.

Father Kezer stood waiting in his own room. For the first time in weeks he looked straight at Francis.

"That child is a thief."

Francis said nothing. But he felt a sudden hollow in his stomach.

"I trusted her. I let her play about the place. I thought she was a nice little thing even though—" Kezer broke off angrily.

"What has she taken?" Francis said. His lips were stiff.

"What do thieves usually take?" Father Kezer swung round to the mantelpiece where a row of little pillars stood, each made up of twelve pennies, wrapped in white paper by his own careful hands. He picked one up. “She’s stolen from the collection money. It’s worse than thievery. It’s simony. Look at this.”

Francis examined the packet. It had been opened and clumsily retwisted at the top. Three of the pennies were missing.

“What makes you think Judy did this?”

“I’m not a fool,” Father Kezer snapped. “I’ve been missing pennies all week. Every copper in these packets is marked.”

Without a word Francis turned toward his own room. The parish priest followed him.

“Judy. Show me your purse.”

Judy looked as though she had been struck. But she recovered quickly. She smiled innocently.

“I left it at Mrs. Morrison’s.”

“No, here it is.” Francis bent forward and took the purse from the outside patch pocket of her dress. It was a new little strap purse, which Aunt Polly had given her before the holiday. Francis opened it with a sinking heart. There were three pennies inside. Each had a cross scratched on the back.

Father Kezer’s scowl was both outraged and triumphant. “What did I tell you? Ah! You wicked little brat, stealing from God!” He glared at Francis. “She ought to be prosecuted for this. If she were my responsibility I’d march her straight down to the police.”

“No, no.” Judy burst into tears. “I meant to put it back, truly, I did.”

Francis was very pale. The situation was horrible for him. He took his courage in both hands.

“Very well,” he said quietly. “We’ll go down to the police station and charge her before Sergeant Hamilton.

Judy's grief became hysterical. Father Kezer, taken aback, sneered: "I'd like to see you."

Francis picked up his hat and took Judy's hand.

"Come along, Judy. You must be brave. We're going down to Sergeant Hamilton to tell him Father Kezer charges you with stealing three pennies."

As Francis led the child toward the door, confusion, then positive apprehension, flared up in Father Kezer's eyes. He had let his tongue run away with him. Sergeant Hamilton, an Orangeman, was no friend of his: they had often clashed bitterly in the past. And now . . . this trivial charge . . . he saw himself jeered at all over the village. He mumbled suddenly:

"Ye needn't go!"

Francis did not seem to hear.

"Stop!" Father Kezer shouted. He fought down his temper, choked out: "We'll . . . we'll forget about it. Talk to her yourself."

He walked out of the room seething with rage.

When Aunt Polly and Judy returned to Tynecastle, Francis had a quick revulsion: he wanted to explain, to express his regret for Judy's petty pilfering. But Father Kezer froze him. A sense of being balked had further embittered the older man. Besides, he was shortly leaving on his vacation. He wanted to put the curate thoroughly in his place before he left.

He ignored Francis with tight-mouthed surliness. By arrangement with Miss Cafferty he took his meals alone, before the junior priest was served. On the Sunday before his departure, he preached a violent sermon, every word aimed at Francis, on the seventh commandment: "Thou shalt not steal."

The sermon decided Francis. Immediately the service was over he went direct to Donald Kyle's house, took the manager aside, and talked to him with restrained intensity. Gradually a light broke over Kyle's face, still dubious perhaps, but hopeful, aroused. He muttered, finally: "I doubt if we can do it! But I'm with ye all the way." The two men shook hands.

On Monday morning Father Kezer left for Harrogate where, for the next six weeks, he would drink the waters. That evening Miss Cafferty went off to her native Rossiare. And on Tuesday, early, Francis met Donald Kyle by appointment at the station. Kyle carried a portfolio of papers and a glossy new brochure recently issued by a large rival coal combine in Nottingham. He wore his best clothes and an air only slightly less resolved than Francis's. They took the eleven o'clock train from Shalesley.

The long day passed slowly, they did not return until late evening. They came up the road together in silence; each looked straight ahead. Francis seemed tired, his expression revealed nothing. It was perhaps significant that the colliery manager smiled with grim solemnity as they said good night.

The next four days passed normally. Then, without warning, there began a period of strange activity.

The activity seemed centered upon the colliery, not unnaturally, since the colliery was the center of the district. Francis was there a good deal between the works of the parish, consulting with Donald Kyle, studying the architect's blueprints, watching the squads of men at work. It was remarkable how quickly the new building grew. In a fortnight it had risen above the adjoining aid room, in a month the structure was complete. Then the carpenters and plasterers came in. The sound of hammering fell exquisitely on Francis's ears. He sniffed the aroma of fresh wood shavings. Occasionally he set to and did a job with the men. They liked him. He had inherited from his father a fondness for working with his hands.

Alone in the presbytery, except for the unobtrusive daily visits of Mrs. Morrison, his temporary housekeeper, free of the nagging of his superior, his fervor knew no limits, a pure white glow pervaded him. He felt himself getting close to the people, breaking down suspicion, gradually entering their dulled lives, bringing to hidden stolid eyes a sudden startled gleam. It was a glorious sensation, a mingling of purpose and achievement, as though, embracing the poverty and wretchedness about him, he drew near in pity and soaring tenderness to the threshold of the unseen God.

Five days before Father Kezer's return, Francis sat down and wrote a letter. It ran as follows:

Shalesley,
September 15th, 1897.
Dear Sir George,

The new recreation center which you have so generously donated to Shalesley Village is now practically complete. It should prove a tremendous boon, not only to your own colliery workers and their families, but to everyone else in this scattered industrial district, irrespective of class or creed. A nonpartisan committee has already been formed and a syllabus drawn up on the lines we discussed. From the copy I enclose you will see how comprehensive is our winter program: boxing and singlestick classes, physical culture, first-aid instruction, and a weekly dance every Thursday.

When I consider the unhesitating liberality with which you met the diffident and perhaps unwarranted approach of Mr. Kyle and myself I am quite overwhelmed. Any words of gratitude that I might use would be hopelessly inadequate. Your real thanks will come from the happiness that you bring to the working people of Shalesley and from the good that must undoubtedly result from their increased social unity.

We propose holding a gala opening night on September 21. If you would consent to honor us with your presence our gratification would be complete.

Believe me,

Yours most sincerely,

Francis Chisholm

Curate of the Church of the Redeemer

He posted the letter with a strange taut smile. His words were heartfelt, burningly sincere. But his legs were trembling.

At midday on the nineteenth, one day after his housekeeper's return, Father Kezer reappeared. Fortified by the saline waters, he was bursting with energy—in his own phrase: fair itching to get his fingers on the reins. Reinfusing the presbytery with his loud, black, hairy essence, with his shouted greeting to Miss Cafferty, his demand for substantial food, he ran through his correspondence. Then he bustled into lunch, rubbing his hands. On his plate lay an envelope. He ripped it open, drew out the printed card.

"What's this?"

Francis moistened his dry lips, mustered all his courage. "It appears to be an invitation to the opening night of the new Shalesley Athletic and Recreation Club. I've had one too."

"Recreation club. What's that to us!" Holding it at arm's length, he glared redly at the card. "What is it?"

"A fine new center. You can see it from the window." Francis added, with a tremor: "The gift of Sir George Renshaw."

"Sir George . . ." Kezer broke off, stupefied, then stamped to the window. He gazed through the window, a long time, at the impressive proportions of the new erection. Then he returned, sat down, and slowly began his lunch. His appetite was scarcely that of a man with a purified liver. He kept darting glances at Francis out of his small, lowering eyes. His silence blasted the room.

At length Francis spoke—awkwardly, with tense simplicity. "You must decide, Father. You've put a ban on dancing and all mixed recreation. On the other hand if our people don't co-operate, ostracize the club, and stop away from the dances, Sir George will feel himself mortally insulted." Francis kept his eyes on his plate. "He's coming down, in person, on Thursday, for the opening."

Father Kezer could eat no more. The thick and juicy beef-steak on his plate might have been dishcloth. He rose abruptly, crushing the card in his hairy fist with sudden, dreadful violence. "We'll not go to the foul fiends' opening! We'll not. Do you hear me? Once and for all, I've said it!" He rampaged out of the room.

On the Thursday evening, freshly shaved, in clean linen and his best black, his face a dreadful compromise of gaiety and gloom, Father Kezer stalked over to the ceremony. Francis followed behind him.

The new hall was warm with lights and excitement, filled to capacity with the working people of the community. On the raised platform a number of the local notables were seated, Donald Kyle and his wife, the colliery doctor, the council schoolmaster, and two other ministers of religion. As Francis and Father Kezer took their seats there was prolonged cheering, then a few catcalls and loud laughter. Father Kezer's jaws snapped sourly together.

The sound of a car arriving outside heightened the expectation, and a minute later, amid a great ovation, Sir George appeared on the platform. He was a medium-sized man of about sixty with a shining bald head fringed with white hair. His moustache was silvery also, and his cheeks were brightly colored. He had that remarkably fresh pink-and-whiteness achieved by some fair-haired persons in their declining years. It seemed preposterous that one so quiet in his dress and manner should command such enormous power.

He listened agreeably while the ceremony proceeded, sustained the address of welcome from Mr. Kyle, then delivered a few remarks himself. He concluded amiably:

"I should like in fairness to state that the first suggestion of this very worthy project came directly from the vision and broadmindedness of Father Francis Chisholm."

The applause was deafening and Francis flushed, his eyes, pleading and remorseful, bent on his superior.

Father Kezer raised his hands automatically, brought them soundlessly together twice, with a grin of sickly martyrdom. Later, when the impromptu dance started, he stood watching Sir George swing round the hall with young Nancy Kyle. Then he faded into the night. The music of the fiddlers followed him.

When Francis returned, late, he found the parish priest sitting up in the parlor, with no fire, his hands on his knees.

Father Kezer seemed oddly inert. All the fight had gone out of him. In the last ten years he had knocked out more curates than Henry VIII had wives. And now a curate had knocked him out. He said tonelessly:

"I'll have to report you to the bishop!"

Francis felt his heart turn over in his breast. But he did not flinch. No matter what happened to him, Father Kezer's authority was shaken. The older priest continued glumly: "Perhaps you'd be the better of a change. The bishop can decide. Dean Fitzgerald needs another curate in Tynecastle . . . your friend Mealey's there, isn't he?"

Francis was silent. He did not wish to leave this now faintly stirring parish. Yet even if he were forced to do so, things would be easier for his successor. The club would continue. It was a beginning. Other changes would come. He had no personal exultation, but a quiet, almost visionary, hope. He said in a low voice: "I'm sorry if I have upset you, Father. Believe me, I was only trying to help . . . our good-for-nothing lot."

The eyes of the two priests met. Father Kezer's fell first.

2

One Friday toward the end of Lent, in the dining room of St. Dominic's presbytery, Francis and Father Slukas were already seated at the meager midday repast of boiled stockfish and butterless brown toast served on Victorian silver and fine blue Worcester china, when Father Mealey returned from an early sick call. From the suppression of his manner, his indifferent mode of helping himself, Francis was immediately aware that Anselm had something on his mind. Dean Fitzgerald dined upstairs at this season of the church, and the three junior priests were alone. But Father Mealey, munching without taste, a faint color beneath his skin, kept silence till the end of the meal. Only when the Lithuanian had brushed the crumbs from his beard, risen, bowed, and departed, did his tension relax. He drew a long pressing breath.

"Francis! I want you to come with me this afternoon. You've no engagements?"

"No . . . I'm free till four o'clock."

"Then you must come. I'd like you as my friend, as my fellow priest, to be the first . . ." He broke off, would say no more to lift the heavy mystery of his words.

For two years Francis had been the second curate at St. Dominic's, where Gerald Fitzgerald, now Dean Fitzgerald, still remained, with Anselm his senior assistant and Slukas, the Lithuanian father, a necessary encumbrance on account of the many Polish immigrants who kept crowding into Tynecastle.

The change from the backwoods of Shalesley to this familiar city parish where the services went like clockwork and the church was elegantly perfect had left a curious mark on Francis. He was happy to be near Aunt Polly, to maintain an eye on Ned and Judy, to see the Tullochs, Willie and his sister, once or twice a week. He had a queer consolation, a sense of indefinable support, in the recent elevation of Monsignor MacNabb from San Morales to be bishop of the diocese. Yet his new air of maturity, the lines about his steady eyes, the spareness of his frame, gave silent indications that the transition had not been easy.

Dean Fitzgerald, refined and fastidious, priding himself on being a gentleman, stood at the opposite pole from Father Kezer. Yet, though he strove to be impartial, the dean was not without a certain lofty prejudice. While he warmly approved Anselm, now his prime favorite, and blankly ignored Father Slukas—whose broken English and table habits, a napkin tucked beneath the beard at every meal, coupled with a strange predilection for wearing a derby hat with his soutane, placed him far beyond the pale—toward his other curate he had a strange wariness. Francis soon realized that his humble birth, his association with the Union Tavern, with, indeed, the whole stark Bannon tragedy, must prove a handicap he could not lightly overcome.

And he had made such a bad beginning! Tired of the shop-worn platitudes, the same old parrot sermons that came, almost by rote, on the appointed Sundays of the year, Francis had ventured, soon after his arrival, to preach a simple homily, fresh and original, his own thoughts, on the subject of personal integrity. Alas, Dean Fitzgerald had cuttingly condemned the dangerous innovation. Next Sunday, at his behest, Anselm had mounted the pulpit and given forth the antidote: a magnificent peroration on the Star of the Sea, in which harts panted for the water and barks came safe across the bar; ending dramatically with arms outstretched, a handsome suppliant for love, on the admonition: "Come!" All the women of the congregation were in tears, and afterward, as Anselm ate a hearty breakfast of mutton chops, the dean pointedly congratulated him. "That!—Father Mealey—was eloquent. I heard our late bishop deliver practically the same sermon twenty years ago."

Perhaps these opposite orations set their courses: as the months passed Francis could not but dejectedly compare his own indifferent showing with Anselm's remarkable success. Father Mealey was a figure in the parish, always cheerful, even gay, with a ready laugh and a comforting pat on the back for anyone in trouble. He worked hard and with great earnestness, carrying a little book full of his engagements in his waistcoat pocket, never refusing an invitation to address a meeting or make an after-dinner speech. He edited the *St. Dominic's Gazette:* a newsy and often humorous little sheet. He went out a good deal and, though no one could call him a snob, took tea at all the best houses. Whenever an eminent cleric came to preach in the city, Anselm was sure to meet him and to sit admiringly at his feet. Later he would send a letter, beautifully composed, expressing ardently the spiritual benefit he had derived from the encounter. He had made many influential friends through this sincerity.

Naturally there were limits to his capacity for work. While he vigorously assumed the post of secretary to the new Diocesan Foreign Missionary Center in Tynecastle—a cherished project of the bishop—and worked unremittingly to please His Grace, he had been obliged reluctantly to decline, and depute to Francis, the management of the Working Boy's Club in Shand Street.

The property round Shand Street was the worst in the city, tall tenements and lodging houses, a network of slums, and this, properly enough, had come to be regarded as Francis's district. Here, though his results seemed trivial and meaningless, he found plenty to do. He had to train himself to look destitution in the eye, to view without shrinking the sorrow and the shame of life, the eternal irony of poverty. It was not a communion of saints that grew about him but a communion of sinners, rousing such pity in him it brought him sometimes to the brink of tears.

"Don't say you're taking forty winks," said Anselm reproachfully.

Almost with a start Francis came out of his reverie to find Father Mealey, waiting on him, hat and stick in hand, beside the lunch table. He smiled and rose in acquiescence.

Outside, the afternoon was fresh and fine, with a rousing, bustling breeze, and Anselm strode along with a brisk swing—clean, honest, and healthy—greeting his parishioners bluffly. His popularity at St. Dominic's had not spoiled him. To his many admirers his most engaging characteristic was the way in which he deprecated his achievements.

Soon Francis saw that they were making for the new suburb recently added to the parish. Beyond the city boundary, a housing development was in progress, on the parklands of an old country property. Workmen were moving with hods and barrows. Francis subconsciously noted a big white board: "Hollis Estate, Apply Malcom Glennie, Solicitor." But Anselm was pushing on, over the hill, past some green fields, then down a wooded pathway to the left. It was a pleasant rural stretch to be so near the chimney pots.

Suddenly Father Mealey halted, with the still excitement of a pointing hound.

"You know where we are, Francis? You've heard of this place?"

"Of course."

Francis had often passed it: a little hollow of lichened rocks, screened with yellow broom and enclosed by an oval copse of copper beeches. It was the prettiest spot for miles around. He had often wondered why it was known as "the well" and sometimes, indeed, as "Marywell." The basin had been dry for fifty years.

"Look!" Clutching his arm, Father Mealey led him forward. From the dry rocks gushed a crystal spring. There was an odd silence, then, stooping with cupped hands, Mealey took an almost sacramental drink.

"Taste it, Francis. We ought to be grateful for the privilege of being among the first."

Francis bent and drank. The water was sweet and cold. He smiled. "It tastes good."

Mealey regarded him with wise indulgence, not without its tinge of patronage. "My dear fellow, I could call it a heavenly taste."

"Has it been flowing long?"

"It began yesterday afternoon at sundown."

Francis laughed. "Really, Anselm, you're a Delphic oracle today—full of signs and portents. Come on, give me the whole story. Who told you about this?"

Father Mealey shook his head. "I can't . . . yet."

"But you've made me so confoundedly curious."

Pleased, Anselm smiled. Then his expression regained its solemnity. "I can't break the seal yet, Francis. I must go to Dean Fitzgerald. He's the one who must deal with this. Meantime, of course, I trust you . . . I know you will respect my confidence."

Francis knew his companion too well to press him further.

On their return to Tynecastle, Francis parted from his fellow curate and went on to Glanville Street to make a sick call. One of his club members, a boy named Owen Warren, had been kicked on the leg in a football game some weeks before. The youngster was poor and undernourished and heedless of the injury. When the poor-law doctor was eventually called in, the condition had developed into an ugly ulcer of the shin.

The affair had upset Francis—the more so since Dr. Tulloch seemed dubious of the prognosis. And this evening, in his endeavor to bring some comfort to Owen and his worried mother, the peculiar and inconclusive excursion of the afternoon was driven completely from his mind.

Next morning, however, loud and minatory sounds emerging from Dean Gerald Fitzgerald's room brought it back before him.

Lent was a deadly penance for the dean. He was a just man, and he fasted. But fasting did not suit his full elegant body, well habituated to the stimuli of rich and nourishing juices. Sorely tried in health and temper, he kept to himself, walked the presbytery with no recognition in his hooded eye, and each night marked another cross upon the calendar.

Although Father Mealey stood so high in Fitzgerald's favor, it demanded considerable resourcefulness to approach him at such a time, and Francis heard Anselm's voice fall, persuasive and pleading, across the dean's irascible abruptness. In the end the softer voice triumphed—like drops of water, Francis reflected, wearing out granite through sheer persistence.

An hour later, with a very bad grace, the dean came out of his room. Father Mealey was waiting on him in the vestibule. They departed together in a cab in the direction of the center of the town. They were absent three hours. It was lunchtime when they returned, and for once the dean broke his rule. He sat down at the curate's table. Though he would eat nothing he ordered a large pot of French coffee, his one luxury in a desert of self-denial. Sitting sideways, his legs crossed, a handsome elegant figure, sipping the black and aromatic brew, he diffused an air of warmth, almost of comradeship, as though a little taken out of himself by an inner, thrilling exaltation. He said, meditatively, to Francis and the Polish priest—it was notable that he included Slukas in his friendly glance:

"Well, we may thank Father Mealey for his persistence . . . in the face of my somewhat violent disbelief. Naturally it is my duty to maintain the utmost skepticism toward certain . . . phenomena. But I have never seen, I had never hoped to see, such a manifestation, in my own parish—" He broke off and, taking up his coffee cup, made a generous gesture of renunciation toward the senior curate. "Let it be your privilege to tell them, Father."

That faint excited color persisted in Father Mealey's cheek. He cleared his throat and began, readily and earnestly, as though the incident he related demanded his most formal eloquence:

"One of our parishioners, a young woman, who has been delicate for a considerable time, was out walking on Monday of this week. The date, since we wish above everything to be precise, was March 15, and the time, half past three in the afternoon. The reason for her excursion was no idle one—this girl is a devout and fervent soul not given to giddiness or loitering. She was walking in accordance with her doctor's instructions—to get some fresh air—the medical man being Dr. William Brine of 42 Boyle Crescent, whom we all know as a physician of unimpeachable, I might say, of the highest, integrity. Well!" Father Mealey took a tense gulp of water and went on. "As she was returning from her walk, murmuring a prayer, she chanced to pass the place that we know as Mary's Well. It was twilight, the last rays of the sun lingering in pure radiance upon the lovely scene. This young girl stopped to gaze and admire when suddenly to her wonder and surprise she saw standing before her a lady in a white robe and a blue cape with a diadem of stars upon her forehead. Guided by holy instinct our Catholic girl immediately fell upon her knees. The lady smiled to her with ineffable tenderness and said: 'My child, sickly though you are, you are the one to be chosen!' Then, half-turning, still addressing the awestruck yet comprehending girl: 'Is it not sad that this well that bears my name is dry? Remember! It is for you and those like you that this shall happen.' With a last beautiful smile she disappeared. At that instant a fount of exquisite water sprang from the barren rock."

There was a silence when Father Mealey concluded.

Then the dean resumed: "As I have said, our approach to this delicate matter was made in the frankest incredulity. We don't expect miracles to grow on every gooseberry bush. Young girls are notoriously romantic. And the starting of the spring might have been a sheer coincidence. However—" His tone took on a deeper gratification. "I've just completed a long interrogation of the girl in question with Father Mealey and Dr. Brine. As you may imagine, the solemn experience of her vision was a great shock to her. She went to bed immediately after it and has remained there ever since." The voice became slower, fraught with immense significance. "Though she is happy, normal, and physically well nourished, in these five days she has touched neither food nor drink." He gave the amazing fact its due weight in silence. "Moreover . . . moreover, I say, she shows plainly, unmistakably, and irrefutably, the blessed stigmata!" He went on triumphantly: "While it is too early to speak yet, while final evidence must be collected, I have the strongest premonition, amounting almost to conviction, that we in this parish have been privileged by Almighty God to participate in a miracle comparable to, and perhaps far-reaching as, those that gave our holy religion the newfound grotto at Digby and the older and more historic shrine at Lourdes."

It was impossible not to be affected by the nobility of his peroration.

"Who is the girl?" Francis asked.

"She is Charlotte Neily!"

Francis stared at the dean. He opened his lips and closed them again. The silence remained impressive.

The next few days brought a growing excitement to the presbytery. No one could have been better equipped to deal with the crisis than Dean Gerald Fitzgerald. A man of sincere devotion, he was wise also in worldly ways. Long and hard-won experience on the local school board and urban councils gave him an astute approach to temporal affairs. No news of the event was permitted to escape, not a whisper, even, in the parochial halls. The dean had everything under his own hand. He would raise his hand only when he was ready.

The incident, so miraculously unexpected, was a breath of new life to him. Not for many years had he known such inner satisfaction: both spiritual and material. He was a strange mixture of piety and ambition. His exceptional attributes of mind and body had seemed to destine him, automatically, for advancement in the church. And he longed passionately for that advancement as much, perhaps, as he longed for the advancement of Holy Church herself. A keen student of contemporary history, he likened himself often in his own mind to Newman. He merited equal eminence. Yet he remained, becalmed, at St. Dominic's. The only preferment they had given him, the reward of twenty distinguished years, was this petty elevation to the rank of dean, an infrequent title in the Catholic Church and one that often embarrassed him on his journeying beyond the city, causing him to be mistaken for an Anglican clergyman, an inference he most cordially resented.

Perhaps he realized that while he was admired he was not liked. With the passage of each day he was growing more and more a disappointed man. He strove for resignation. Yet when he bent his head and said "O Lord, thy will be done!" deep down beneath his humility was the burning thought: *By this time they should have given me my mozzetta.*

Now everything was changed. Let them keep him at St. Dominic's. He would make St. Dominic's a shrine of light. Lourdes was his exemplar and, nearer in time and space, the recent striking instance of Digby in the Midlands, where the foundation of a miraculous grotto, with many authenticated cures, had transformed the dreary hamlet into a thriving town, and elevated, at the same time, an unknown but resourceful parish priest to the status of a national figure.

The dean sank into a splendid vision of a new city, a great basilica, a solemn triduum, himself enthroned in stiff vestments . . . then sharply took himself in hand and scrutinized the draft contracts. His first action had been to place immediately a Dominican nun, Sister Teresa, trustworthy and discreet, in Charlotte Neily's home. Reassured by her impeccable reports he had taken to the law.

It was fortunate that Marywell and all the land adjacent formed the estate of the old and wealthy Hollis family. Though not a Catholic, Captain Hollis had married one, Sir George Renshaw's sister. He was friendly and well disposed. He and his solicitor, Malcom Glennie, were closeted with the dean upon successive days, holding long conferences over sherry and biscuits. A fair and amicable arrangement was at length worked out. The dean had no personal interest in money. He regarded it contemptuously as so much dross. But the things that money could purchase were important, and he must ensure the future of his shining project. No one but a fool could fail to realize that the value of the land would rocket to the sky.

On the last day of the negotiations Francis ran into Glennie in the upper corridor. Frankly, he was surprised to find Malcom dealing with the Hollis affairs. But the solicitor, when articled, had shrewdly bought himself into an old established firm with his wife's money, and quietly succeeded to some first-rate practice.

"Well, Malcom!" Francis held out his hand. "Glad to see you again."

Glennie shook hands with damp effusiveness.

"But I'm amazed," Francis smiled, "to find you in the house of the scarlet woman!"

The solicitor's answering smile was thin. He mumbled: "I'm a liberal man, Francis . . . besides being obliged to chase the pennies."

There was a silence. Francis had often thought to restore his relationship with the Glennies. But news of the death of Daniel had dissuaded him—and a chance encounter with Mrs. Glennie in Tynecastle when, as he crossed the street to greet her, she had sighted him from the corner of her eye and shied away, as though she spied the devil.

He said: "It made me very sad to hear of your father's death."

"Ay, ay! We miss him of course. But the old man was such a failure."

"It's no great failure to get into heaven," Francis joked.

"Well, yes, I suppose he's there." Glennie vaguely twisted the emblem on his watch chain. He was already tending toward an early middle age, his figure slack, shoulders and stomach pendulous, his thin hair plastered in streaks over his bare scalp. But his eye, though palely evasive, was gimlet sharp. As he moved toward the stairs he threw off a tepid invitation.

"Look us up when you have time. I'm married, as you know—two of a family—but Mother still lives with us."

Malcom Glennie had his own peculiar interest in the beatific vision of Charlotte Neily. Since his early youth he had been patiently seeking an opportunity to acquire wealth. He inherited from his mother a burning avarice and something of her long-nosed cunning. He smelled money in this ridiculous

Romish scheme. Its very uniqueness convinced him of its possibilities. His opportunity was here, dangling like a ripe fruit. It would never occur again, never in a lifetime.

Working disingenuously for his client, Malcom remembered what everyone else had forgotten. Secretly, and at considerable expense, he had a geological survey carried out. Then he was sure of what he had already suspected. The flow of water to the property came exclusively through an upper tract of heathland, above and remote from the estate.

Malcom was not rich. Not yet. But by taking all his savings, by mortgaging his house and business, he had just enough to execute a three months' option on this land. He knew what an artesian bore would do. That bore would never be driven. But a bargain would be driven, later, on the threat of that bore, which would make Malcom Glennie a landed gentleman.

Meanwhile the water still gushed clear and sweet. Charlotte Neily still maintained her rapture and her stigmata, still existed without sustenance. And Francis still prayed, broodingly, for the gift of faith.

If only he could believe like Anselm who, without a struggle, blandly, smilingly, accepted everything from Adam's rib to the less probable details of Jonah's sojourn in the whale! He did believe, he did, he did . . . but not in the shallows, only in the depths . . . only by an effort of love, by keeping his nose to the grindstone in the slums, when shaking the fleas from his clothing into the empty bath . . . never, never easily . . . except when he sat with the sick, the crippled, those of stricken, ashen countenance. The cruelty of this present test, its unfairness, was wrecking his nerves, withering in him the joy of prayer.

It was the girl herself who disturbed him. Doubtless he was prejudiced: he could not overlook the fact that Charlotte's mother was Thaddeus Gilfoyle's sister. And her father was a vague and windy character, pious yet lazy, who stole away from his small chandler's premises every day to light candles before the side altar for success in his neglected business. Charlotte had all her father's fondness for the church. But Francis had a worried suspicion that the incidentals drew her, the smell of incense and of candle grease, that the darkness of the confessional struck overtures upon her nerves. He did not deny her unblemished goodness, the regularity with which she carried out her duties. As against that, she washed sketchily, and her breath was rancid.

On the following Saturday as Francis walked down Glanville Street, feeling absurdly depressed, he observed Dr. Tulloch come out of Number 143, the house of Owen Warren. He called; the doctor turned, stopped, then fell into step beside his friend.

Willie had broadened with the years, but had otherwise changed little. Slow, tenacious, and canny, loyal to his friends, hostile to his enemies, he had, in manhood, all his father's honesty, but little of his charm and nothing of his looks. His blunt-nosed face was red and stolid, topped by a shock of unmanageable hair. He had an air of plodding decency. His medical career had not been brilliant, but he was sound and enjoyed his work. He was quite contemptuous of all orthodox ambitions.

Though he spoke occasionally of "seeing the world," of pursuing adventure in far-off romantic lands, he remained in his poor-law appointment—which demanded no hateful bedside falsities and enabled him at most times to speak his mind—anchored by the humdrum, by his matter-of-fact capacity of living from day to day. Besides, he never could save money. His salary was not large; and much of it was spent on whiskey.

Always careless of his appearance, this morning he had not shaved. And his deep-set eyes were somber, his expression unusually put out: as though today he had a grudge against the world. He indicated briefly that the Warren boy was worse. He had been in to take a shred of tissue for pathological examination.

They continued along the street, linked by one of their peculiar silences. Suddenly, on an unaccountable impulse, Francis divulged the story of Charlotte Neily.

Tulloch's face did not change; he trudged along, fists in his deep coat pockets, collar up, head down.

"Yes," he said at last. "A little bird told me."

"What do you think of it?"

"Why ask me?"

"At least you're honest."

Tulloch looked oddly at Francis. For one so modest, so conscious of his mental limitations, the doctor's rejection of the myth of God was strangely positive. "Religion isn't my province; I inherited a most satisfying atheism . . . which the anatomy room confirmed. But if you want it straight—in my old dad's words, I have my doubts. See here, though! Why don't we take a look at her? We're not far from the house. We'll go in together."

"Won't that get you into trouble with Dr. Brine?"

"No. I can square it with Salty tomorrow. In dealing with my colleagues I find it pays to act first and apologize afterward." He threw Francis a singular smile. "Unless you're afraid of the hierarchy?"

Francis flushed but controlled his answer. He said a minute later: "Yes, I'm afraid, but we'll go in."

It proved surprisingly easy to effect an entrance. Mrs. Neily, worn-out by a night of watching, was asleep. Neily, for once, was at his business. Sister Teresa, short, quiet, and amiable, opened the door. Since she came from a distant section of Tynecastle she had no knowledge of Tulloch, but she knew and recognized Francis, at once. She admitted them to the polished, immaculately tidy room where Charlotte lay on spotless pillows, washed and clothed in a high white nightgown, the brasses of the bedstead shining. Sister Teresa bent over the girl, not a little proud of her stainless handiwork.

"Charlotte, dear. Father Chisholm has come to see you. And brought a doctor who is a great friend of Dr. Brine."

Charlotte Neily smiled. The smile was conscious, vaguely languid, yet charged with curious rapture. It lit up the pale, already luminous face, motionless upon the pillow. It was deeply impressive. Francis felt a stir of genuine compunction. There was no doubt that something existed, here, in this still white room, outside the bonds of natural experience.

"You don't mind if I examine you, Charlotte?" Tulloch spoke kindly.

At his tone, her smile lingered. She did not move. She had the cushioned repose of one who is watched, who knows that she is watched, yet is undisturbed, rather exalted, by such watching: a consciousness of inner power, a mollification, a dreamy and elevated awareness of the deference and reverence evoked among the watchers. Her pale eyelids fluttered. Her voice was untroubled, remote.

"Why should I mind, doctor? I'm only too glad. I'm not worthy to be chosen as God's vessel . . . but since I am chosen I can only joyfully submit."

She allowed the respectful Tulloch to examine her.

"You don't eat anything, Charlotte?"

"No, doctor."

"You've no appetite?"

"I never think of food. I just seem sustained by an inner grace."

Sister Teresa said quietly: "I can assure you she hasn't put a bite in her mouth since I came into this house."

A silence fell in the hushed white room. Dr. Tulloch straightened himself, pushing back his unruly hair. He said simply:

"Thank you, Charlotte. Thank you, Sister Teresa. I'm much indebted to you for your kindness." He went toward the bedroom door.

As Francis made to follow the doctor a shadow fluttered over Charlotte's face.

"Don't you want to see too, Father? Look . . . my hands! My feet are just the same."

She extended both her arms, gently, sacrificially. Upon both her pale palms, unmistakably, were the blood-stained marks of nails.

Outside, Dr. Tulloch maintained his attitude of reserve. He kept his lips shut until they reached the end of the street. Then, at the point where their ways diverged, he spoke rapidly. "You want my opinion I suppose. Here it is. A borderline case, or just over: manic-depressive in the exalted stage. Certainly a hysteric bleeder. If she steers clear of the asylum, she'll probably be canonized!" His composure, his perfect manner left him. His red plain face became congested. His words choked him. "Damn it to hell! When I think of her trigged up there in her simpering holiness, like an anemic angel in a flour bag—and little Owney Warren, stuck in a dirty garret, with worse pain than your hellfire in his gangrenous leg, and the threat of malignant sarcoma over him, I could just about explode. Bite on that when you say your prayers. You're probably going back to say them now. Well, I'm going home to have a drink." He walked rapidly away before Francis could reply.

That same evening when Francis returned from Tenebrae an urgent summons awaited him, written on the slate that hung in the presbytery vestibule. With a premonition of misfortune, he went upstairs to the study. The dean was wearing out his temper and his carpet with short exasperated paces.

"Father Chisholm! I am both amazed and indignant. Really, I expected better of you than this. To think that you should bring in—from the streets—an atheistic doctor; I resent it violently!"

"I'm sorry." Francis answered heavily. "It's just—oh, well, he happens to be my friend."

"That in itself is highly reprehensible. I find it wildly improper that one of my curates should associate with a character like Dr. Tulloch."

"We . . . we were boys together."

"That is no excuse. I'm hurt and disappointed. I'm thoroughly and justifiably incensed. From the very beginning your attitude toward this great event has been cold and unsympathetic. I daresay you are jealous that the honor of the discovery should have fallen to the senior curate. Or is there some deeper motive behind your manifest antagonism?"

A sense of wretchedness flowed over Francis. He felt that the dean was right. He mumbled:

"I'm terribly sorry. I'm not disloyal. That's the last in the world I'd want to be. But I admit I've been lukewarm. It's because I've been troubled. That's why I took Tulloch in today. I have such doubts—"

"Doubts! Do you deny the miracles of Lourdes?"

"No, no. They're unimpeachable. Authenticated by doctors of all creeds."

"Then why deny us the opportunity to create another monument of faith—here—in our very midst?" The dean's brow darkened. "If you disregard the spiritual implications, at least respect the physical." He sneered. "Do you fondly imagine that a young girl can go nine days without food or drink—and remain well and perfectly nourished—unless she is receiving other sustenance?"

"What sustenance?"

"Spiritual sustenance." The dean fumed. "Didn't St. Catherine of Siena receive a spiritual mystic drink, which supplanted all earthly food? Such insufferable doubting! Can you wonder that I lose my temper?"

Francis hung his head. "St. Thomas doubted. In the presence of all the disciples. Even to putting his fingers in our Lord's side. But no one lost their temper."

There was a sudden shocked pause. The dean paled, then recovered himself. He bent over his desk, fumbling at some papers, not looking at Francis. He said in a restrained tone:

"This is not the first time you have proved obstructive. You are getting yourself into very bad odor in the diocese. You may go."

Francis left the room with a dreadful sense of his own deficiencies. He had a sudden overwhelming impulse to take his troubles to Bishop MacNabb. But he suppressed it. Rusty Mac seemed no longer approachable. He would be too fully occupied by his new high office to concern himself with the worries of a wretched curate.

Next day, Sunday, at the eleven o'clock High Mass, Dean Fitzgerald broke the news in the finest sermon he had ever preached.

The sensation was immediate and tremendous. The entire congregation stood outside the church talking in hushed voices, unwilling to go home. A spontaneous procession formed up and departed, under the leadership of Father Mealey, for Marywell. In the afternoon crowds collected outside the Neily home. A band of young women of the confraternity, to which Charlotte belonged, kneeled in the street reciting the rosary.

In the evening the dean consented to be interviewed by a highly curious press. He conducted himself with dignity and restraint. Already esteemed in the city, rated as a public-spirited clergyman, he produced a most favorable impression. Next morning the newspapers gave him generously of their space. He was on the front page of the *Tribune,* had a eulogistic double spread inside the *Globe.* "Another Digby," proclaimed the *Northumberland Herald.* Said the *Yorkshire Echo,* "Miraculous Grotto Brings Hope to Thousands." The *Weekly High Anglican* hedged, rather cattily, "We await further evidence." But the London *Times* was superb with a scholarly article from its theological correspondent tracing the history of the well back to Aidan and St. Ethelwulf. The dean flushed with gratification. Father Mealey could eat no breakfast, and Malcom Glennie was beside himself with joy.

Eight days later Francis paid an evening visit to Polly's little flat in Clermont, at the north end of the city. He was tired, after a long day's visiting in the dingy tenements of his district, and most desperately depressed. That afternoon a note had come round from Dr. Tulloch which curtly signed young Warren's death warrant. The condition had been revealed as malignant sarcoma of the leg. There was no hope whatsoever for the boy: he was dying and might not last the month.

At Clermont, Polly was her indomitable self, Ned, perhaps, a trifle more trying than usual. Hunched in his wheeled chair, a blanket wrapped about his knees, he talked much and rather foolishly. Some sort of final settlement had at last been squeezed out of Gilfoyle on account of the remnants of Ned's interest in the Union Tavern. A pitiful sum. But Ned had boasted as though it were a fortune. As the result of his complaint his tongue seemed too large for his mouth; he was distressingly inarticulate.

Judy was already asleep when Francis arrived, and although Polly said nothing there was a hint in her manner that the child had misbehaved and been sent off early. The thought saddened him further.

Eleven o'clock was striking when he left the flat. The last tram to Tynecastle had gone. Tramping home, his shoulders drooping slightly under this final discomfiture, he entered Glanville Street. As he drew opposite the Neily home he observed that the double window on the ground floor, which marked Charlotte's room, was still illuminated. He made out the movements of figures, vague shadows on the yellow blind.

A rush of contrition overcame him. Oppressed by the realization of his obduracy, he had a sudden desire to see the Neilys and make amends. The instinct of reparation was strong within him as he crossed the street and went up the three front steps. He raised his hand toward the knocker, altered his mind, and turned the old-fashioned handle of the door. He had acquired that facility, common to priests and physicians, of making his sick visits unannounced.

The bedroom, opening off the small lobby, projected a wide slant of gaslight. He tapped gently on the lintel and entered the room. Then he stood, suddenly transformed to stone.

Charlotte, propped up in bed, with an oval tray before her laden with breast of chicken and a custard, was stuffing herself with food. Mrs. Neily, wrapped in a faded blue dressing gown, bent with solicitude, was noiselessly decanting stout.

It was the mother who saw Francis first. Arrested, she gave a neighing cry of terror. Her hand flew to her throat, dropping the glass, spilling the stout upon the bed.

Charlotte raised her gaze from the tray. Her pale eyes dilated. She gazed at her mother; her mouth opened; she began to whimper. She slid down on the bed, shielding her face. The tray crashed onto the floor. No one had spoken. Mrs. Neily's throat worked convulsively. She made a stupid, feeble effort to secrete the bottle in her dressing gown. At last she gasped: "I've got to keep her strength up somehow . . . all she's been through . . . it's invalid's stout!"

Her look of frightened guilt revealed everything. It sickened him. He felt debased and humiliated. He had difficulty in finding words.

"I suppose you've given her food every night . . . when Sister left her, thinking she was asleep?"

"No, Father! As God is my witness!" She made a last desperate attempt at denial, then broke down, lost her head completely. "What if I did? I couldn't see my poor child starve, not for nobody. But dear St. Joseph . . . I'd never have let her do it if I'd known it would mean so much . . . with the crowds . . . and the papers . . . I'm glad to be through with it. . . . Don't . . . don't be hard on us, Father."

He said in a low voice: "I'm not going to judge you, Mrs. Neily."

She wept.

He waited patiently until her sobs subsided, seated on a chair at the door, gazing at his hat, between his hands. The folly of what she had done, the folly, at that moment, of all human life, appalled him. When the two were quieter he said: "Tell me about it."

The story came, gulped out, mostly by Charlotte.

She had read such a nice book, from the church library, about Blessed Bernardette. One day when she was passing Marywell—it was her favorite walk—she noticed the water running. *That's funny,* she thought. Then the coincidence struck her, among the water, Bernadette, and herself. It was a shock. She had almost, in a sort of way, fancied she saw the Blessed Virgin. When she got home, the more she thought of it the surer she became. It gave her quite a turn. She was all white and trembling; she had to take to her bed and send for Father Mealey. And before she knew where she was, she was telling him the whole story.

All that night she'd lain in a kind of ecstasy; her body seemed to go rigid, stiff as a board. Next morning, when she woke up, the marks were there. She'd always bruised terrible, but these were different.

Well, that convinced her. All that day, when food came, she refused it, just waved it away. She was too happy, too excited to eat. Besides, lots of saints had lived without food. That idea fixed itself on her, too. When Father Mealey and the dean heard she was living on grace—and perhaps she was too—it was a glorious feeling. The attention she had, it was like she was a bride. But of course, after a bit, she got dreadfully hungry. She couldn't disappoint Father Mealey and the dean: the way she was looked up to by Father Mealey especially. She just told her mother. And things had gone so far her mother had to help her. She had a big meal, sometimes two, every night.

But then, oh, dear, things had gone even further. "At first, as I told you, Father, it was wonderful. The best of all was the confraternity girls praying to me outside the window!" But when the newspapers started and all that, she got really frightened. She wished to God she had never done it. Sister Teresa was harder to pull the wool over. The marks on her hands were getting faint, instead of being all lifted up and excited she was turning low, depressed . . .

A fresh burst of sobbing terminated the pitiful revelation—tawdry as an illiterate scrawl upon a wall. Yet tragic, somehow, with the idiocy of all humanity.

The mother interposed.

"You won't tell Dean Fitzgerald on us, will you, Father?"

Francis was no longer angry, only sad and strangely merciful. If only the wretched business had not gone so far. He sighed.

"I won't tell him, Mrs. Neily, I won't say a word. But—" He paused. "I'm afraid you must."

Terror leaped again in her eyes. "No, no . . . for pity's sake no, Father."

He began, quietly, to explain why they must confess, how the scheme that the dean contemplated could not be built upon a lie, especially one that must soon be palpable. He comforted them with the thought that the nine days' wonder would soon subside and be forgotten.

He left them an hour later, somewhat appeased, and with their faithful promise that they would follow out his advice. But as he directed his echoing footsteps homeward through the empty streets his heart ached for Dean Gerald Fitzgerald.

The next day passed. He was out visiting most of the time, and did not see the dean. But a curious hollowness, a kind of suspended animation, seemed to float within the presbytery. He was sensitive to atmosphere. He felt this strongly.

At eleven o'clock on the following forenoon, Malcom Glennie broke into his room.

"Francis! You've got to help me. He's not going on with it. For God's sake, come in and talk to him."

Glennie was painfully distressed. He was pale; his lips worked; there was a wildness in his eye. He stuttered:

"I don't know what's taken him. He must be out of his mind. It's such a beautiful scheme. It'll do so much good—"

"I have no influence with him."

"But you have—he thinks the world of you. And you're a priest. You owe it to your flock. It'll be good for the Catholics—"

"That hardly interests you, Malcom."

"But it does," Glennie babbled. "I'm a liberal man. I admire the Catholics. It's a beautiful religion. I often wish—oh, for God's sake, Francis, come in, quick, before it's too late."

"I'm sorry, Malcom. It's disappointing for all of us." He turned away toward the window.

At that Glennie lost all control of himself. He caught hold of Francis's arm. He sniveled abjectly.

"Don't turn me down, Francis. You owe everything to us. I've bought a little bit of land, put all my savings in it; it's worthless if the scheme falls through. Don't see my poor family ruined. My poor old mother! Think of how she brought you up, Francis. Please, please persuade him. I'd do anything in the world. I'll even turn a Catholic for you!"

Francis kept staring out of the window, his hand gripping the curtain, his eyes fixed on the church gable, pointed with a gray stone cross. A dull thought crossed his mind. What would mankind do for money? Everything. Even to selling its immortal soul.

Glennie exhausted himself at last. Convinced, finally, that nothing could be gained from Francis, he struggled for the remnants of his dignity. His manner altered.

"So you won't help me. Well, I'll remember you for this." He moved toward the door. "I'll get even with you all. If it's the last thing I do."

He paused on his way out, his pallid face contorted with malice. "I should have known you'd bite the hand that fed you. What else could you expect from a lot of dirty papists!"

He slammed the door behind him.

The hollowness continued within the presbytery: that kind of vacuum in which people lose their clear outlines, become unsubstantial, transitory. The servants moved on tiptoe, as though it were a house of death. The Lithuanian father wore a look of sheer bewilderment. Father Mealey went about with his eyes cast down. He had received a grave hurt. But he kept silence, which in one so naturally effusive was a singular grace. When he spoke it was of other matters. He distracted himself, passionately, with his work at the foreign missions office.

For more than a week after Glennie's outburst Francis had no encounter with Fitzgerald. Then, one morning, as he entered the sacristy, he found the dean unvesting. The altar boys had gone; the two were alone.

Whatever his personal humiliation, the dean's control of the disaster had been consummate. Indeed, in his hands it ceased to be disaster. Captain Hollis had willingly torn up the contracts. An occupation had been found for Neily in a distant town: the first step toward discreet withdrawal of the family. The clangor in the journals was tactfully stilled. Then, on Sunday, the dean climbed again into the pulpit. Facing the hushed congregation, he gave the text: "O Ye of Little Faith!"

Quietly, with still intensity, he developed his thesis: what need had the church of additional miracles? Had she not fully justified herself, miraculously, already? Her foundations were planted deep, foursquare, upon the miracles of Christ. It was pleasant, no doubt exciting, to meet a manifestation like that of Marywell. They had all, himself included, been carried away with it. But on sober reflection, why all this outcry about a single blossom, when the very flower of heaven bloomed here in the church, before their eyes? Were they so weak, so pusillanimous in their faith they needed further material evidence? Had they forgotten the solemn words: "Blessed are they that have not seen, and have believed"? It was a superb feat of oratory. It surpassed his triumph of the previous Sunday. Gerald Fitzgerald, still a dean, alone knew what it cost him.

At first, in the sacristy, the dean seemed about to maintain his inflexible reserve. But, when ready to leave, with his black coat cast about his shoulders, he suddenly swung round. In the clear light of the sacristy Francis was shocked to see the deep lines on the handsome face, the weariness in the full gray eyes.

"Not one lie, Father, but a tissue of lies. Well! God's will be done!" He paused. "You're a good fellow, Chisholm. It's a pity you and I are incompatible." He went out of the sacristy, erect.

By the end of Easter the event had almost been forgotten. The neat white railing that had been erected round the well in the dean's first ardor still stood; but the little entrance gate remained unlocked, swinging, rather pathetically, in the light spring air. A few good souls went occasionally to pray and bless themselves with the sparkling, ever-gushing water.

Francis, caught by a spurt of parish work, rejoiced in his own forgetfulness. The smear of the experience was gradually wearing off. What remained was only a faint ugliness at the back of his mind, which he quickly suppressed and would soon bury completely. His idea of a new playing field for the boys and young men of the parish had taken tangible form. He had been offered the use of a strip of the public park by the local council. Dean Fitzgerald had given his consent. He was now immersed in a pile of catalogs.

On the eve of Ascension Day he received an urgent call to visit Owen Warren. His face clouded. He rose immediately, the cricket folder falling from his knee. Though he had expected this summons for many weeks, he dreaded it. He went quickly to the church and, with the viaticum upon his person, hurried through the crowded town to Glanville Street.

His expression was fixed and sad as he saw Dr. Tulloch pacing restlessly outside the Warren home. Tulloch was attached to Owen too. He looked deeply upset as Francis approached.

"Has it come at last?" Francis said.

"Yes, it's come!" As an afterthought: "Yesterday the main artery thrombosed. It wasn't any use—even to amputate."

"Am I too late?"

"No." Tulloch's manner held a subdued violence. He shouldered roughly past Francis. "But I've been in three times at the boy while you've been strolling along. Come in, damn it . . . if you're coming in at all."

Francis followed the other up the steps. Mrs. Warren opened the door. She was a spare woman of fifty, worn out by the weeks of anxiety, plainly dressed in gray. He saw that her face was wet with tears. He pressed her hand in sympathy.

"I'm so sorry, Mrs. Warren."

She laughed—weakly, chokingly.

"Go into the room, Father!"

He was shocked. He thought that grief had momentarily turned her mind. He went into the room.

Owen was lying on the counterpane of his bed. His lower limbs were unbandaged, bare. They were rather thin, showing the wasting of disease. Both were sound, unblemished.

Dazed, Francis watched Dr. Tulloch lift up the right leg and run his hand firmly down the sound straight shin, which yesterday had been a festering malignant mass. Finding no answer in the doctor's challenging eyes, he turned giddily to Mrs. Warren, saw that her tears were tears of joy. She nodded blindly, through these tears.

"I bundled him up warm in the old gocar' this morning before anybody was about. We wouldn't give up, Owney and me. He had always believed . . . if he could only get up there to the well. . . . We prayed and dipped his leg in the water. . . . When we got back . . . Owney . . . took the bandage off himself!"

The stillness in the room was absolute. It was Owen who finally broke it.

"Don't forget to put me down for your new cricket team, Father."

In the street, outside, Willie Tulloch stared doggedly at his friend.

"There's bound to be a scientific explanation beyond the scope of our present knowledge. An intense desire for recovery—psychological regeneration of the cells." He stopped short, his big hand trembling on Francis's arm. "Oh, God!—if there is a God!—let's all keep our bloody mouths shut about it!"

That night Francis could not rest. He stared with sleepless eyes into the blackness above his head. The miracle of faith. Yes, faith itself was the miracle. The waters of Jordan, Lourdes, or Marywell—they mattered not a jot. Any muddy pool would answer, if it were the mirror of God's face.

Momentarily, the seismograph of his mind faintly registered the shock: a glimmering of the knowledge of the incomprehensibility of God. He prayed fervently. O dear God, we don't even know the beginning. We are like tiny ants in a bottomless abyss, covered with a million layers of cotton wool, striving . . . striving to see the sky. O God . . . dear God, give me humility . . . and give me faith!

3

It was three months later when the bishop's summons arrived. Francis had expected it for some time now, yet its actual arrival somewhat dismayed him. Heavy rain began as he walked up the hill toward the palace; only by racing the intervening distance did he avoid a thorough drenching. Out of breath, wet, and splashed with mud, he felt his arrival somewhat lacking in dignity. Insensibly his anxiety increased as he sat, slightly shivering, in the formal parlor, gazing at his mired boots, so incongruous upon the red pile carpet.

At last the bishop's secretary appeared, ushered him up a shallow flight of marble stairs, and silently indicated a dark mahogany door. Francis knocked and went in.

His Lordship was at his desk, not bent at work but resting, his cheek against his hand, elbow on the arm of his leather chair. The fading light, striking sideways through the velvet pelmets of the tall window, enriched the violet of his biretta but found his face in shadow.

Francis paused uncertainly, disconcerted by the impassive figure, asking himself if this were really his old friend of Holywell and San Morales. There was no sound but the faint ticking of the Buhl clock on the mantelpiece. Then a severe voice said:

"Well, Father, any miracles to report tonight? And by the by, before I forget, how is the dance-hall business doing now?"

Francis felt a thickness in his throat; he could have cried for sheer relief. His Lordship continued his scrutiny of the figure marooned on the wide rug. "I must confess it affords some relief to my old eyes to see a priest so manifestly unprosperous as you. Usually they come in here looking like successful undertakers. That's an abominable suit you're wearing—and dreadful boots!" He rose slowly, and advanced toward Francis. "My dear boy, I am delighted to see you. But you're horribly thin." He placed his hand on the other's shoulder. "And good gracious, horribly wet, too!"

"I got caught in the rain, Your Grace."

"What! No umbrella! Come over to the fire. We must get you something warm." Leaving Francis, he went to a small escritoire and produced a decanter and two liqueur glasses. "I am not yet properly acclimatized to my new dignity. I ought to ring and command some of these fine vintages used by all the bishops one reads about. This is only Glenlivet, but it's fit tipple for two Scots." He handed Francis a tiny glassful of the neat spirit, watched him drink it, then drank his own. He sat down on the other side of the fireplace. "Speaking of dignity, do not look so scared of me. I'm bedizened now—I admit. But underneath is the same clumsy anatomy you saw wading through the Stinchar!"

Francis reddened. "Yes, Your Grace."

There was a pause, then His Lordship said, directly and quietly: "You've had a pretty thin time, I imagine, since you left San Morales."

Francis answered in a low voice. "I've been a pretty good failure."

"Indeed?"

"Yes, I felt this coming . . . this disciplinary interview. I knew I wasn't pleasing Dean Fitzgerald lately."

"Just pleasing Almighty God, eh?"

"No, no. I'm really ashamed, dissatisfied with myself. It's my incorrigibly rebellious nature." A pause.

"Your culminating iniquity seems to be that you failed to attend a banquet in honor of Alderman Shand . . . who has just made a magnificent donation of five hundred pounds to the new high altar fund. Can it be that you disapprove of the good alderman—who, I am told, is slightly less pious in his dealings with the tenants of his slum property in Shand Street?"

"Well . . ." Francis halted in confusion. "I don't know. I was wrong not to go. Dean Fitzgerald specially advised us we must attend . . . he attached great importance to it. But something else cropped up . . ."

"Oh?" The bishop waited.

"I was called to see someone that afternoon." Francis spoke with great reluctance. "You may remember . . . Edward Bannon . . . though he's unrecognizable now, in his illness, paralyzed, drooling, a caricature of God-made man. When it was time for me to go he clutched my hand, implored me not to leave him. I couldn't help myself . . . or restrain a terrible sick pity for this . . . grotesque, dying outcast. He fell asleep mumbling, 'John the Father, John the Son, John the Holy Ghost,' saliva running down his gray unshaven chin, holding my hand. . . . I remained with him till morning."

A longer pause. "No wonder the dean was annoyed that you preferred the sinner to the saint."

Francis hung his head. "I am annoyed with myself. I keep trying to do better. It's strange—when I was a boy I had the conviction that priests were all quite infallibly good . . ."

"And now you are discovering how terribly human we are. Yes, it's unholy that your 'rebellious nature' should fill me with joy, but I find it a wonderful antidote to the monotonous piety I am subjected to. You are the stray cat, Francis, who comes stalking up the aisle when everyone is yawning their head off at a dull sermon. That's not a bad metaphor—for you *are* in the church even if you don't match up with those who find it all by the well-known rule. I am not flattering myself, when I say that I am probably the only cleric in this diocese who really understands you. It's fortunate I am now your bishop."

"I know that, Your Grace."

"To me," His Lordship meditated, "you are not a failure, but a howling success. You can do with a little cheering up—so I'll risk giving you a swelled head. You've got inquisitiveness and tenderness. You're sensible of the distinction between thinking and doubting. You're not one of our ecclesiastical milliners who must have everything stitched up in neat little packets—

convenient for handing out. And quite the nicest thing about you, my dear boy, is this—you haven't got that bumptious security that springs from dogma rather than from faith."

There was a silence. Francis felt his heart melt toward the old man. He kept his eyes cast down. The quiet voice went on.

"Of course, unless we do something about it you're going to get hurt. If we go on with cudgels there'll be too many bloody heads—including your own! Oh, yes, I know—you're not afraid. But I am. You're too valuable to be fed to the lions. That's why I have something to put before you."

Francis raised his head quickly, met His Lordship's wise and affectionate gaze. The bishop smiled.

"You don't imagine I'd be treating you as a boon companion if I didn't want you to do something for me!"

"Anything . . ." Francis stumbled on the words.

There was a long pause. The bishop's face was gravely chiseled. "It's a big thing to ask . . . a great change to suggest . . . if it is too much . . . you must tell me. But I think it is the very life for you." Again a pause. "Our foreign missions society has at last been promised a vicariate in China. When all the formalities are completed, and you've had some preparation, will you go there as our first unprincipled adventurer?"

Francis remained completely still, numb with surprise. The walls seemed to crumble about him. The request was so unexpected, so tremendous, it took his breath away. To leave home, his friends, and move into a great unknown void . . . He could not think. But slowly, mysteriously, a strange animation filled his being. He answered haltingly: "Yes . . . I will go."

Rusty Mac leaned over and took Francis's hand in his. His eyes were moist and had a poignant fixity. "I thought you would, dear boy. And I know you'll do me credit. But you'll get no salmon fishing there, I warn you."

PART IV

The China Incident

1

Early in the year 1902 a lopsided junk making dilatory passage up the endless yellow reaches of the Ta-Hwang River in the province of Chek-kow, not less than one thousand miles inland from Tientsin, bore a somewhat unusual figurehead in the shape of a medium-sized Catholic priest wearing list slippers and an already wilted topee. With his legs astride the stubby bowsprit and his breviary balanced on one knee, Francis ceased momentarily his vocal combat with the Chinese tongue, in which every syllable seemed to his exhausted larynx to have as many inflections as a chromatic scale, and let his gaze rest on the drifting brown and ocher landscape. Fatigued after his tenth night in the three-foot den between decks that was his cabin, he had, in the hope of a breath of air, forced himself forward into the bows through the packed welter of his fellow passengers: farm laborers, basket and leather workers from Sen-siang, bandits and fishermen, soldiers and merchants on their way to Pai-tan, squatting elbow to elbow, smoking, talking, and tending their cooking pots among the crates of ducks, the pigpens, and the heaving net that held the solitary but fractious goat.

Although Francis had vowed not to be fastidious the sounds, sights, and smells of this final yet interminable stage of his journey had tried him severely. He thanked God and St. Andrew that tonight, short of further delay, he would at last reach Pai-tan.

Even yet he could not believe himself a part of this new fantastic world, so remote and alien, so incredibly divorced from all that he had known, or hoped to know. He felt as if his life had suddenly been bent, grotesquely, away from its natural form. He checked his sigh. Others lived to a smooth and normal pattern. He was the oddity, the misfit, the little crooked man.

It had been hard to say good-bye to those at home. Ned, mercifully, had passed away three months ago, a blessed ending to that grotesque and pitiful epilogue of life. But Polly . . . he hoped, he prayed he might see Polly in the future. There was consolation in the fact that Judy had been accepted as a shorthand typist in the Tynecastle council offices—a post that offered security and good chances of promotion.

As if to steel himself anew he pulled from his inside pocket the final letter relating to his appointment. It was from Father Mealey, now relieved of his parish duties at St. Dominic's to devote himself exclusively to the FMS administration.

Addressed to him at Liverpool University, where for the past twelve months he had hammered out his language course, the letter ran:

My dear Francis,

I am overjoyed to be the bearer of glad tidings! We have just received news that Pai-tan, in the vicariate of Chek-kow, which, as you well know, was presented to us by the AFMS in December, has now been ratified by the Congregation of Propaganda. It was decided at our meeting held at the FMS in Tynecastle tonight that nothing need delay your departure. At last, at last, I am able to speed you on your glorious mission to the Orient.

So far as I can ascertain Pai-tan is a delightful spot, some miles inland, but on a pleasant river, a thriving city specializing in the manufacture of baskets, with an abundance of cereal, meat, poultry, and tropical fruits. But the supremely important, the blessed fact is that the mission itself, while somewhat remote and for the past twelve months unfortunately without a priest, is in a highly flourishing condition. I'm sorry we have no photographs but I can assure you the layout is most satisfactory: comprising chapel, priest's house, and compound. (What an exciting sound that word *compound* has! Don't you remember as boys when we played Indians? Forgive my enthusiasms.)

But *la crème de la crème* lies in our proved statistics. Enclosed you will find the annual report of the late incumbent, Father Lawler, who, a year ago, returned to San Francisco. I don't propose to analyze this for you since you will indubitably con it over, nay, digest it in the wee small hours. Nevertheless I may stress these figures: that although established only three years ago the Pai-tan mission can boast of four hundred communicants and over one thousand baptisms, only a third of which were *in articulo mortis.* Is it not gratifying, Francis? An example of how the dear old grace of God leavens even heathen hearts amid pagan temple bells.

My dear fellow, I rejoice that this prize is to be yours. And I have no doubt that by your labors in the field you will materially increase the vineyard's crop. I look forward to your first report. I feel that you have at last found your métier and that the little eccentricities of tongue and temper that have been your trouble in the past will no longer be part and parcel of your daily life. Humility, Francis, is the lifeblood of God's saints. I pray for you every night.

I will be writing you later. Meanwhile don't neglect your outfit. Get good strong durable soutanes. Short drawers are the best, and I advise a body belt. Go to Hanson & Son; they are sound people; and cousins of the organist at the cathedral.

It is just possible I may be seeing you sooner than you imagine. My new post may make me quite a globe-trotter. Wouldn't it be grand if we met in the shady compound of Pai-tan?

Again my congratulations and with every good wish,

I remain, your devoted brother in J. C.

Anselm Mealey

Secretary to the Foreign Missions Society,

Diocese of Tynecastle.

Toward sundown a heightening of the commotion in the junk indicated the imminence of their arrival. As the vessel yawed round a bend into a great bight of dirty water, mobbed by a pack of sampans, Francis eagerly scanned the low tiered reaches of the town. It seemed like a great low hive, humming with sound and yellow light, fronted by the reedy mudflats with their flotsam of rafts and boats, backed distantly by mountains, pink and of a pearly translucency.

He had hoped the mission might send a boat for him, but the only private wherry was for Mr. Chia, merchant and wealthy resident of Pai-tan, who now emerged for the first time, silent and satin clad, from the recesses of the junk.

This personage was about thirty-five, but of such composure he looked older, with a supple golden skin and hair so black it seemed moist. He stood with leisurely indifference while the *kapong* fussed around him. Though his lashes did not once flicker in the direction of the priest, Francis had the odd conviction he was being taken in minutely.

Owing to the preoccupation of the purser, some time elapsed before the new missioner secured passage for himself and his japanned tin trunk. As he stepped down to the sampan he clutched his large silk umbrella, a glorious thing covered in Chisholm tartan, which Bishop MacNabb had pressed upon him as a parting gift.

His excitement rose when, nearing the bank, he saw a great press of people on the landing steps. Was it a welcome from his congregation? What a splendid thought for the end of his long, long journey! His heart began to beat almost painfully, with happy expectation. But alas, when he landed he saw he was mistaken. No one greeted him. He had to push his way through the staring yet incurious throng.

At the end of the steps, however, he stopped short. Before him, smiling happily, dressed in neat blue and bearing, as a symbol of their credentials, a brightly colored picture of the Holy

Family, were a Chinese man and woman. As he stood, the two small figures approached him, their smiles deepening, overjoyed to see him, bowing and zealously blessing themselves.

Introductions began—less difficult than he had supposed. He asked warmly:

"Who are you?"

"We are Hosannah and Philomena Wang—your beloved catechists, Father."

"From the mission?"

"Yes, yes; Father Lawler made a most excellent mission, Father."

"You will conduct me to the mission?"

"By all means, let us go. But perhaps Father will honor us and come first to our humble abode."

"Thank you. But I am eager to reach the mission."

"Of course. We will go to the mission. We have bearers and a chair for Father."

"You are very kind, but I would prefer to walk."

Still smiling, though less perceptibly, Hosannah turned and in a rapid unintelligible exchange, which had some semblance of an argument, dismissed the sedan chair and the string of porters that he had in tow. Two coolies remained: one shouldered the trunk, the other the umbrella, and the party set off on foot.

Even in the tortuous and dirty streets it was agreeable for Francis to stretch his legs, cramped from confinement in the junk. A quick fervor stirred his blood. Amid the strangeness he could feel the pulse of humanity. Here were hearts to be won, souls to be saved!

He became aware of one of the Wangs, pausing, to address him.

"There is an agreeable dwelling in the Street of the Net Makers . . . only five taels by the month . . . where Father might wish to spend the night."

Francis looked down in amused surprise. "No, no, Hosannah. Onward to the mission!"

There was a pause. Philomena coughed. Francis realized that they were standing still. Hosannah politely smiled.

"Here, Father, is the mission."

At first he did not fully understand.

Before them on the riverbank was an acre of deserted earth, sun scorched, gullied by the rains, encircled by a tramped-down piece of kaolin. At one end stood the remnants of a mud-brick chapel, the roof blown off, one wall collapsed, the others crumbling. Alongside lay a mass of caved-in rubble, which might once have been a house. Tall feathery weeds were sprouting there. A single meager shell remained amid the ruins, leaning yet still straw-roofed—the stable.

For three minutes Francis stood in a kind of stupor, then he slowly turned to the Wangs, who were close together, watching him, neat, unfathomable, similar as Siamese twins.

"Why has this taken place?"

"It was a beautiful mission, Father. It cost much—and we made many financial arrangements for its building. But alas, the good Father Lawler placed it near the river. And the devil sent much wicked rain."

"Then where are the people of the congregation?"

"They are wicked people without belief in the Lord of Heaven." The two spoke more rapidly now, helping each other, gesticulating. "Father must understand how much depends upon his catechists. Alas! Since the good Father Lawler has gone away we have not been paid our lawful stipend of fifteen taels each month. It has been impossible to keep these wicked people properly instructed."

Crushed and devastated, Father Chisholm removed his gaze. This was his mission, these two his sole parishioners. The recollection of the letter within his pocket sent a sudden upsurge of passion over him. He clenched his hands, stood thinking, rigidly.

The Wangs were still talking fluently, trying to persuade him to return to the town. With an effort he rid himself of their importunities, their unctuous presence. It was, at least, a relief to be alone.

Determinedly, he carried his box into the stable. At one time a stable had been good enough for Christ. Gazing round he saw that some straw still littered the earthen floor. Though he had neither food nor water, at least he had a bed. He unpacked his blankets, began to make the place as habitable as he could. Suddenly a gong sounded. He ran out of the stable. Across the decapitated fence, outside the nearest of the temples that stippled the adjacent hill, stood an aged bonze wearing thick stockings and a quilted yellow robe, beating his metal plaque into the short unheeding twilight with measured boredom. The two priests—of Buddha and of Christ—inspected each other in silence; then the old man turned, expressionless, mounted the steps, and vanished.

Night fell with the swiftness of a blow. Francis knelt down in the darkness of the devastated compound and lifted his eyes to the dawning constellations. He prayed with fierce, with terrible intensity. Dear God, you wish me to begin from nothing. This is the answer to my vanity, my stubborn human arrogance. It's better so! I'll work, I'll fight for you. I'll never give up . . . never . . . never!

Back in the stable, trying to rest, while the shrill ping of mosquitoes and the crack of flying beetles split the sweltering air, he forced himself to smile. He did not feel heroic, but a dreadful fool. St. Teresa had likened life to a night in a hotel. This one they had sent him to was not the Ritz!

Morning came at last. He rose. Taking his chalice from its cedar box, he made an altar of his trunk and offered up his Mass, kneeling on the stable floor. He felt refreshed, happy, and strong. The arrival of Hosannah Wang failed to discompose him.

"Father should have let me serve his Mass. That is always included in our pay. And now—shall we find a room in the Street of the Net Makers?"

Francis reflected. Though he had stubbornly made up his mind to live here till the situation cleared, it was true that he must find a more fitting center for his ministrations. He said: "Let us go there now."

The streets were already thronged. Dogs raced between their legs; pigs were rooting for garbage in the gutter. Children followed them, jeering and shouting. Beggars wailed with importunate palms. An old man setting out his wares, in the Street of the Lantern Makers, spat sullenly across the foreign devil's feet.

Outside the yamen of justice, a peripatetic barber stood twanging his long tongs. There were many poor, many crippled, and some, blinded by smallpox, who tapped their way forward with a long bamboo and a queer high whistle.

It was an upper room Wang brought him to, clumsily partitioned with paper and bamboo, but sufficient for any service he would conduct. From his small store of money he paid a month's rent to the shopkeeper, named Hung, and began to set out his crucifix and solitary altar cloth. His lack of vestments, of altar furnishings, fretted him. Led to expect a full equipment at the "flourishing" mission, he had brought little. But his standard, at least, was planted.

Wang had preceded him to the shop below and as he turned to descend he observed Hung take two of the silver taels which he had given him and pass them, with a bow, to Wang. Though he had early guessed the worth of Father Lawler's legacy Francis was conscious of a sudden mounting of his blood. Outside, in the street, he turned quietly to Wang.

"I regret, Hosannah, I cannot pay your stipend of fifteen taels a month."

"Father Lawler could pay. Why cannot the father pay?"

"I am poor, Hosannah, just as poor as was my master."

"How much will the father pay?"

"Nothing, Hosannah! Even as I am paid nothing. It is the good Lord of Heaven who will reward us!"

Wang's smile did not falter. "Perhaps Hosannah and Philomena must go where they are appreciated. At Sen-siang the Methodys pay sixteen taels for highly respected catechists. But doubtless the good father will change his mind. There is much animosity in Pai-tan. The people consider the feng shui of the city—the laws of wind and order—destroyed by the intrusion of the missionary."

He waited for the priest's reply. But Francis did not speak. There was a strained pause. Then Wang bowed politely and departed.

A coldness settled upon Francis as he watched the other disappear. Had he done right in alienating the friendly Wangs? The answer was that the Wangs were not his friends, but lickspittle opportunists who believed in the Christian God because of Christian money. And yet . . . his one contact with the community was severed. He had a sudden, frightening sense of being alone.

As the days passed this horrible loneliness increased, coupled with a paralyzing impotence. Lawler, his predecessor, had built upon sand. Incompetent, credulous, and supplied with ample funds, he had rushed about, giving money and taking names, baptizing promiscuously, acquiring a string of "rice Christians," filling long reports, unconsciously the victim of a hundred subtle squeezes, sanguine, bombastic, gloriously triumphant. He had not even scratched the surface. Of his work nothing remained except perhaps—in the city's official circles—a lingering contempt for such lamentable foreign folly.

Beyond a small sum set for his living expenses, and a five-pound note pressed into his hand by Polly on his departure, Francis had no money whatsoever. He had been warned, too, on the futility of requesting grants from the new society at home. Sickened by Lawler's example, he rejoiced in his poverty. He swore, with a feverish intensity, that he would not hire his congregation. What must be done would be done with God's help and his own two hands.

Yet so far he had done nothing. He hung a sign outside his makeshift chapel; it made no difference: none appeared to hear his mass. The Wangs had spread a wide report that he was destitute, with nothing to distribute but bitter words.

He attempted an open-air meeting outside the courts of justice. He was laughed at, then ignored. His failure humiliated him. A Chinese laundryman preaching Confucianism in pidgin English in the streets of Liverpool would have met with more success. Wildly he fought that insidious demon, the inner whisper of his own incompetence.

He prayed, he prayed most desperately. He ardently believed in the efficacy of prayer. "Oh God, you've helped me in the past. Help me now, for God's sake, please."

He had hours of raging fury. Why had they sent him, with plausible assurances, to this outlandish hole? The task was beyond any man, beyond God himself! Cut from all communications, buried in the hinterland, with the nearest missioner, Father Thibodeau, at Sen-siang, four hundred miles away, the place was quite untenable.

Fostered by the Wangs, the popular hostility toward him increased. He was used to the jeers of the children. Now, on his passage through the town, a crowd of young coolies followed, throwing out insults. When he stopped a member of the gang would advance and perform his natural functions in the vicinity.

One night, as he returned to the stable, a stone sailed out of the darkness and struck him on the brow.

All Francis's combativeness rose hotly in response. As he bandaged his broken head, his own wound gave him a wild idea, making him pause, rigid and intent. Yes . . . he must . . . he must get closer to the people . . . and this . . . no matter how primitive . . . this new endeavor might help him to that end.

Next morning, for two extra taels a month, he rented the lower back room of the shop from Hung and opened a public dispensary. He was no expert—God knew. But he had his St. John's certificate, and his long acquaintance with Dr. Tulloch had grounded him soundly in hygiene.

At first no one ventured near him, and he sweated with despair. But gradually, drawn by curiosity, one or two came in. There was always sickness in the city, and the methods of the native doctors were barbaric. He had some success. He exacted nothing in money or devotion. Slowly his clientele grew. He wrote urgently to Dr. Tulloch, enclosing Polly's five pounds, clamoring for an additional supply of dressings, bandages, and simple drugs. While the chapel remained empty the dispensary was often full.

At night, he brooded frantically amongst the ruins of the mission. He could never rebuild on that eroded site. And he gazed across the way in fierce desire at the pleasant Hill of Brilliant Green Jade where, above the scattered temples, a lovely slope extended, sheltered by a grove of cedars. What a noble situation for a monument to God!

The owner of this property, a civil judge named Pao, member of that inner intermarried community of merchants and magistrates who controlled the city's affairs, was rarely to be seen. But on most afternoons, his cousin, a tall dignified mandarin of forty, who managed the estate for Mr. Pao, came to inspect and to pay the laborers who worked the clay pits in the cedar grove.

Worn by weeks of solitude, desolate, and persecuted, Francis was undoubtedly a little mad. He had nothing; he was nothing. Yet one day, on an impulse, he stopped the tall mandarin as he crossed the road toward his chair. He did not understand the impropriety of this direct approach. In fact he knew little of what he did: he had not been eating properly, and was lightheaded from a touch of fever.

"I have often admired this beautiful property which you so wisely administer."

Taken wholly by surprise, Mr. Pao's cousin formally viewed the short alien figure with its burning eyes, and the soiled bandage on its forehead. In frigid politeness he bore with the priest's continued assaults upon the syntax, briefly deprecated himself, his family, his miserable possessions, remarked on the weather, the crops, and the difficulty the city had experienced last year in buying off the Wai-Chu bandits; then pointedly opened the door of his chair. When Francis, with swimming head, strove to return the conversation to the Green Jade land, he smiled coldly.

"The Green Jade property is a pearl without price, in extent more than sixty *mous* . . . shade, water, pasture . . . in addition a rich and extraordinary clay pit for the purpose of tiles, pottery, and bricks. Mr. Pao has no desire to sell. Already, for the estate, he has refused . . . fifteen thousand silver dollars."

At the price, ten times greater than his most fearful estimate, Francis's legs shook. The fever left him; he suddenly felt weak and giddy, ashamed at the absurdity into which his dreams had led him. With splitting head, he thanked Mr. Pao's cousin, muttered a confused apology.

Observing the priest's disappointed sadness, the lean, middle-aged, cultured Chinese allowed a flicker of disdain to escape his watchful secrecy.

"Why does the Shang-Foo come here? Are there no wicked men to regenerate in his own land? For we are not wicked people. We have our own religion. Our own gods are older than his. The other Shang-Foo made many Christians by pouring water from a little bottle upon dying men and singing 'Ya . . . ya!' Also, by giving food and clothing, to many more who would sing any tune to have their skins covered and their bellies full. Does the Shang-Foo wish to do this also?"

Francis gazed at the other in silence. His thin face had a worn pallor; there were deep shadows beneath his eyes. He said quietly: "Do you think that is my wish?"

There was a strange pause. All at once, Mr. Pao's cousin dropped his eyes.

"Forgive me," he said, in a low tone. "I did not understand. You are a good man." A vague friendliness tinctured his compunction. "I regret that my cousin's land is not available. Perhaps in some other manner I may assist you?"

Mr. Pao's cousin waited with a new courtesy, as if anxious to make amends. Francis thought for a moment, then asked heavily: "Tell me, since we are being honest. . . . Are there no true Christians here?"

Mr. Pao's cousin answered slowly: "Perhaps. But I should not seek them in Pai-tan." He paused. "I have heard, however, of a village in the Kwang Mountains." He made a vague gesture toward the distant peaks. "A village Christian for many years . . . but it is far away, many many *li* from here."

A gleam of light shot into the haggard gloom of Francis's mind.

"That interests me deeply. Can you give me further information?"

The other shook his head regretfully. "It is a small place on the uplands—almost unknown. My cousin only learned of it from his trade in sheepskins."

Francis's eagerness sustained him. "Could you ask him? Could you procure directions for me . . . perhaps a map?"

Mr. Pao's cousin reflected, then nodded gravely. "It should be possible. I shall ask Mr. Pao. Moreover I shall be careful to inform him that you have spoken with me in a most honorable fashion."

He bowed and went away.

Overwhelmed with this wholly unexpected hope, Francis returned to the ruined compound where, with some blankets, a water skin, and the few utensils purchased in the town, he had made his primitive encampment. As he prepared himself a simple meal of rice, his hands trembled, as from shock. A

Christian village! He must find it—at all costs. It was his first sense of guidance, of divine inspiration, in all these weary, fruitless months.

As he sat tensely thinking in the dusk he was disturbed by a hoarse barking of crows, fighting and tearing at some carrion by the water's edge. He went over at length, to drive them off. And there, as the great ugly birds flapped and squawked at him, he saw their prey to be the body of a newly born female child.

Shuddering, he took up the infant's torn body from the river, saw it to be asphyxiated, thrown in and drowned. He wrapped the little thing in linen, buried it in a corner of the compound. And as he prayed he thought: yes, despite my doubts, there is need for me, in this strange land, after all.

2

Two weeks later, when the early summer burgeoned, he was ready. Placing a painted notice of temporary closure on his premises in Net Maker Street, he strapped a pack of blankets and food upon his back, took up his umbrella, and set off briskly on foot.

The map given him by Mr. Pao's cousin was beautifully executed, with wind-belching dragons in the corners and a wealth of topographic detail as far as the mountains. Beyond it was sketchy, with little drawings of animals instead of place-names. But from their conversations and his own sense of direction Francis had in his head a fair notion of his route. He set his face toward the Kwang Gap.

For two days his journey lay through easy country, the green wet rice fields giving place to woods of spruce, where the fallen needles made a soft resilient carpet for his feet. Immediately below the Kwangs he traversed a sheltered valley aflame with wild rhododendrons, and later, that same dreamy afternoon, a glade of flowering apricots whose perfume pricked the nostrils like the fume of sparkling wine. Then he began the steep ascent of the ravine.

It grew colder with every step up the narrow stony track. At night he folded himself under the shelter of a rock, hearing the whistle of the wind, the thunder of snow water in the gorge. In the daytime, the cold blazing whiteness of the higher peaks burned his eyes. The thin iced air was painful to his lungs.

On the fifth day he crossed the summit of the ridge, a frozen wilderness of glacier and rock, and thankfully descended the other side. The pass led him to a wide plateau, beneath the snow line, green with verdure, melting into softly rounded hills. These were the grasslands of which Mr. Pao's cousin had spoken.

Thus far the sheer mountains had defined his twisted course. Now he must rely on providence, a compass, and his good Scot's sense. He struck out directly toward the west. The country was like the uplands of his home. He came on great herds of stoic grazing goats and mountain sheep that streamed off wildly at his approach. He caught the fleeting image of a gazelle. From the bunchgrass of a vast dun marsh thousands of nesting ducks rose screaming, darkening the sky. Since his food was running low, he filled his satchel gratefully with the warm eggs.

It was trackless, treeless plain: he began to despair of stumbling on the village. But early on the ninth day when he felt he must soon turn back, he sighted a shepherd's hut, the first sign of habitation since he'd left the southern slopes. He hastened eagerly toward it. The door was sealed with mud; there was no one inside. But as he swung round, his eyes sharp with disappointment, he saw a boy approaching over the hill behind his flock.

The young shepherd was about seventeen, small and wiry, like his sheep, with a cheerful and intelligent face now caught between wonderment and laughter. He wore short sheepskin trousers and a woolen cape. Round his neck was a small bronze yuan cross, wafer thin with age, and roughly scratched with the symbol of a dove. Father Chisholm gazed from the boy's open face to the antique cross in silence. At last he found his voice and greeted him, asking if he were from the Liu village.

The lad smiled. "I am from the Christian village. I am Liu-Ta. My father is the village priest." He added, not to be thought boasting, "One of the village priests!"

Again, there was a silence. Father Chisholm thought better of questioning the boy further. He said: "I have come a long distance, and I too am a priest. I should be grateful if you would take me to your home."

The village lay in an undulating valley five *li* farther to the westward, a cluster of some thirty houses, tucked away in this fold of the uplands, surrounded by little stone-walled fields of grain. Prominent, upon a central hillock, behind a queer conical mound of stones shaded by a ginkgo tree, was a small stone church.

As he entered the village the entire community immediately surrounded him—men, women, children, and dogs—all crowding round in curiosity and excited welcome, pulling at his sleeves, touching his boots, examining his umbrella with cries of admiration, while Ta threw off a rapid explanation in a dialect he could not understand. There were perhaps sixty persons in the throng, primitive and healthy, with naive, friendly eyes and features that bore the imprint of their common family. Presently, with a proprietary smile, Ta brought forward his father Liu-Chi, a short and sturdy man of fifty with a small gray beard, simple and dignified in his manner.

Speaking slowly, to make himself understood, Liu-Chi said: "We welcome you with joy, Father. Come to my house and rest a little before prayer."

He led the way to the largest house, built on a stone foundation next the church, and showed Father Chisholm, with courteous urbanity, into a low cool room. At the end of the room stood a mahogany spinet and a Portuguese wheel clock. Bewildered, lost in wonder, Francis stared at the clock. The brass dial was engraved: "Lisbon 1632."

He had no time for closer inspection; Liu-Chi was addressing him again. "Is it your wish to offer Mass, Father? Or shall I?"

As in a dream Father Chisholm nodded his head toward the other. Something within him answered: "You . . . please!" He was groping in a great confusion. He knew he could not rudely break this mystery with speech. He must penetrate it graciously, in patience, with his eyes.

Half an hour later they were all within the church. Though small it had been built with taste in a style that showed the Moorish influence on the Renaissance. There were three simple arcades, beautifully fluted. The doorway and the windows were supported by flat pilasters. On the walls, partly incomplete, free mosaics had been traced.

He sat in the front row of an attentive congregation. Every one had ceremonially washed his hands before entering. Most of the men and a few of the women wore praying caps upon their heads. Suddenly a tongueless bell was struck, and Liu-Chi approached the altar, wearing a faded yellow alb and supported by two young men. Turning, he bowed ceremoniously to Father Chisholm and the congregation. Then the service began.

Father Chisholm watched, kneeling erect, spellbound, like a man beholding the slow enactment of a dream. He saw now that the ceremony was a strange survival, a touching relic of the Mass. Liu-Chi must know no Latin, for he prayed in Chinese. First came the confiteor, then the creed. When he ascended the altar and opened the parchment missal on its wooden rest, Francis clearly heard a portion of the gospel solemnly intoned in the native tongue. An original translation. . . . He drew a quick breath of awe.

The whole congregation advanced to take communion. Even children at the breast were carried to the altar steps. Liu-Chi descended, bearing a chalice of rice wine. Moistening his forefinger he placed a drop upon the lips of each.

Before leaving the church, the congregation gathered at the statue of the Savior, placing lighted joss sticks on the heavy candelabrum before the feet. Then each person made three prostrations and reverently withdrew.

Father Chisholm remained behind, his eyes moist, his heart wrung by the simple childish piety—the same piety, the same simplicity he had so often witnessed in peasant Spain. Of course this ceremony was not valid—he smiled faintly, visualizing Father Tarrant's horror at the spectacle—but he had no doubt it was pleasing to God Almighty nonetheless.

Liu-Chi was waiting outside to conduct him to the house. There a meal awaited them. Famished, Father Chisholm did full justice to the stew of mountain mutton—little savory balls floating in cabbage soup—and the strange dish of rice and wild honey that followed. He had never tasted such a delicious sweet in all his life.

When they had both finished, he began tactfully to question Liu-Chi. He would have bitten out his tongue rather than give offense. The gentle old man answered trustingly. His beliefs were Christian, quite childlike and curiously mingled with the traditions of *Tâo-tê.* Perhaps, thought Father Chisholm, with an inward smile, a touch of Nestorianism thrown in for value. . . .

Chi explained that the faith had been handed down from father to son through many generations. The village was not dramatically isolated from the world. But it was sufficiently remote; and so small, so integrated in its family life, that strangers rarely troubled it. They were one great family. Existence was purely pastoral and self-supporting. They had grain and mutton in plenty even through the hardest times; cheese, which they sealed in the stomach of a sheep, and two kinds of butter, red and black, both made from beans and named *chiang.* For clothing they had home-carded wool, sheepskins for extra warmth. They beat a special parchment from the skins that was much prized in Pekin. There were many wild ponies on the uplands. Rarely, a member of the family went out with a pony-load of vellum.

In the little tribe there were three fathers, each chosen for this honored position while still in infancy. For certain religious offices a fee of rice was paid. They had a special devotion to the Three Precious Ones—the Trinity. Within living memory they had never seen an ordained priest.

Father Chisholm had listened with rapt attention and now he put the question uppermost in his mind.

"You have not told me how it first began!"

Liu-Chi looked at his visitor with final appraisal. Then with a faint reassured smile he got up and went into the adjoining room. When he returned he bore under his arm a sheepskin-covered bundle. He handed it over silently, watched Father Chisholm open it, then, as the priest's absorption became apparent, silently withdrew.

It was the journal of Father Ribiero, written in Portuguese, brown, stained, and tattered, but mostly legible. From his knowledge of Spanish, Francis was able slowly to decipher it. The fascinating interest of the document made the labor as nothing. It held him riveted. He remained motionless, except for the slow movement of his hand turning, at intervals, a heavy page. Time flew back three hundred years: the old stopped clock took up its measured tick.

Manoel Ribiero was a missioner of Lisbon who came to Pekin in 1625. Francis saw the Portuguese vividly before him: a young man of twenty-nine, spare, olive skinned, a little fiery, his swart eyes ardent yet humble. In Pekin the young missionary had been fortunate in his friendship with Father Adam Schall, the great German Jesuit, missionary, courtier, astronomer, trusted friend, and canon founder extraordinary to the Emperor Tchoun-Tchin. For several years Father Ribiero shared a little of the glory of this astounding man who moved untouched through the seething intrigues of the courts of heaven, advancing the Christian faith, even in the celestial harem, confounding virulent hatreds with his accurate predictions of comets and eclipses, compiling a new calendar, winning friendship and illustrious titles for himself and all his ancestors.

Then the Portuguese had pressed to be sent on a distant mission to the royal court of Tartary. Adam Schall had granted his request. A caravan was sumptuously equipped and formidably armed. It started from Pekin on the Feast of the Assumption, 1629.

But the caravan had failed to reach the Tartar royal courts. Ambushed by a horde of barbarians on the northern slopes of the Kwang Mountains the formidable defenders dropped their arms and fled. The valuable caravan was plundered. Father Ribiero escaped, desperately wounded by flint arrows, with only his personal belongings and the least of his ecclesiastical equipment. Benighted in the snow, he thought his last hour had come and offered himself, bleeding, to God. But the cold froze his wounds. He dragged himself next morning to a shepherd's hut, where he lay for six months neither dead nor alive. Meanwhile an authentic report reached Pekin that Father Ribiero was massacred. No expedition was sent out to search for him.

When the Portuguese decided he might live, he made plans to return to Adam Schall. But time went on, and he still remained. In these wide grasslands, he gained a new sense of values, a new habit of contemplation. Besides, he was three thousand *li* from Pekin, a forbidding distance, even to his intrepid spirit. Quietly he took his decision. He collected the handful of shepherds into one small settlement. He built a church. He became friend and pastor—not to the king of Tartary but to this humble little flock.

⊕

With a strange sigh Francis put down the journal. In the failing light he sat thinking, thinking, and seeing many things. Then he rose and went out to the great mound of stones beside the church. Kneeling, he prayed at Father Ribiero's tomb.

He remained at the Liu village for a week. Persuasively, in a manner to hurt no one, he suggested a ratification of all baptisms and marriages. He said Mass. Gently he dropped a hint, now here, now there, suggesting an emendation of certain practices. It would take a long time to regularize the village to hidebound orthodoxy: months—no, years. What did that matter? He was content to go slowly. The little community was as clean and sound as a good apple.

He spoke to them of many things. In the evenings a fire would be lit outside Liu-Chi's house, and when they had all seated themselves about it, he would rest himself on the doorstep and talk to the silent, flame-lit circle. Best of all they liked to hear of the presence of their own religion in the great outside world. He drew no captious differences. It enthralled them when he spoke of the churches of Europe, the great cathedrals, the thousands of worshipers flocking to St. Peter's, great kings and princes, statesmen and nobles, all prostrating themselves before the Lord of Heaven, that same Lord of Heaven whom they worshiped here, their master too, their friend. This sense of unity, hitherto but dimly surmised, gave them a joyful pride.

As the intent faces, flickering with light and shadow, gazed up at him in happy wonderment, he felt Father Ribiero at his elbow smiling a little, darkly, not displeased with him. At such moments he had a terrible impulse to throw up Pai-tan and devote himself entirely to these simple people. How happy he could be here! How lovingly he would tend and polish this jewel he had found so unexpectedly in the wilderness! But no, the village was too small, and too remote. He could never make it a center for true missionary work. Resolutely, he put the temptation away from him.

The boy Ta had become his constant follower. Now he no longer called him Ta but Joseph, for that was the name the youngster had demanded at his conditional baptism. Fortified by the new name, he had begged permission to serve Father Chisholm's Mass; and though he naturally knew not a shred of Latin, the priest had smilingly consented. On the eve of his departure Father Chisholm was seated at the doorway of the house when Joseph appeared, his usually cheerful features set and woebegone, the first arrival for the final lecture. Studying the boy, the priest had an intuition of his regret, followed by a sudden happy thought.

"Joseph! Would it please you to come with me—if your father would permit it? There are many things you might do to help me."

The boy jumped up with a cry of joy, fell before the priest, and kissed his hand.

"Master, I have waited for you to ask me. My father is willing. I will serve you with all my heart."

"There may be many rough roads, Joseph."

"We shall travel them together, Master."

Father Chisholm raised the young man to his feet. He was moved and pleased. He knew he had done a wise thing.

Next morning the preparations for departure were completed.

Scrubbed and smiling, Joseph stood with the bundles, beside the two shaggy mountain ponies he had rounded up at dawn. A small group of younger boys surrounded him; already he was awing his companions with the wonders of the world. In the church Father Chisholm was finishing his thanksgiving. As he rose, Liu-Chi beckoned him to the cryptlike sanctuary. From a cedar chest he drew an embroidered cope, an exquisite thing, stiff with gold. In parts the satin had rubbed paper-thin but the vestment was intact, usable, and priceless. The old man smiled at the expression on Francis's face.

"This poor thing pleases you?"

"It is beautiful."

"Take it. It is yours!"

No protestations could prevent Liu-Chi from making the superb gift. It was folded, wrapped in clean flax cloth, and placed in Joseph's pack.

At last Francis had to bid them all farewell. He blessed them, gave repeated assurances that he would return within six months. It would be easier next time, mounted, and with Joseph as his guide. Then the two departed, together, their ponies nodding neck-to-neck, climbing to the uplands. The eyes of the little village followed them with affection.

With Joseph beside him, Father Chisholm set a good round pace. He felt his faith restored, gloriously fortified. His breast throbbed with fresh hope.

3

The summer that followed their return to Pai-tan had passed. And now the cold season fell upon the land. With Joseph's help he made the stable snug, patching the cracks with fresh mud and kaolin. Two wooden bunks now buttressed the weakest wall and a flat iron brazier made a hearth upon the beaten-earth floor. Joseph, whose appetite was healthy, had already acquired an interesting collection of cooking pots. The boy, now less angelic, improved upon acquaintance: he was a great prattler, loved to be praised, and could be willful at times, with a naive facility for abstracting ripe muskmelons from the market garden down the way.

Francis was still determined not to quit their lowly shelter until he saw his course ahead. Gradually a few timid souls were creeping to his chapel room in Net Maker Street, the first an old woman, ragged and ashamed, furtively pulling her beads from the sacking that served her for a coat, looking as though a single word would send her scurrying. Firmly, he restrained himself, pretended not to notice her. Next morning she returned with her daughter.

The pitiful sparsity of his followers did not discourage him. His resolve neither to cajole nor to buy his converts was tempered, like fine steel.

His dispensary was going with a swing. Apparently his absence from the little clinic had been regretted. On his return he found a nondescript assembly awaiting him outside Hung's premises. With practice, his judgment, and indeed his skill, increased. All sorts of conditions came his way: skin diseases, colics and coughs, enteritis, dreadful suppurations of the eyes and ears; and most were the result of dirt and overcrowding. It was amazing what cleanliness and a simple bitter tonic did for them. A grain of potassium permanganate was worth its weight in gold.

When his meager supplies threatened to run out, an answer came to his supplication to Dr. Tulloch—a big nailed-up box of lint, wool and gauze, iodine and antiseptics, castor oil and Chlorodyne, with a scrawled torn-off prescription sheet crumpled at the foot.

"Your Holiness: I thought I was the one to go doctoring in the tropics! And where is your degree? Never mind—cure what you can and kill what you can't. Here is a little bag of tricks to help you."

It was a neatly packed first-aid case of lancet, scissors, and forceps. A postscript added: "For your information, I am reporting you to the BMA, the pope, and Chung-lung-soo."

Francis smiled at the irrepressible facetiousness. But his throat was tight with gratitude. With this stimulation of his own endeavor and the comfort of Joseph's companionship, he felt a new and thrilling exaltation. He had never worked harder, nor slept sounder, in his life.

But one night in November his sleep was light and troubled, and after midnight he suddenly awoke. It was piercing cold.

In the still darkness he could hear Joseph's deep and peaceful breathing. He lay for a moment, trying to reason away his vague distress. But he could not. He got up, cautiously, so that he might not wake the sleeping boy, and slipped out of the stable into the compound. The frozen night stabbed him: the air was razor-edged with cold, each breath a cutting pain. There were no stars, but from the frosted snow came a strange and luminous whiteness. The silence seemed to reach a hundred miles. It was terrifying.

Suddenly, through that stillness, he fancied he heard a faint and uncertain cry. He knew he was mistaken, listened, and heard no more. But as he turned to reenter the stable the sound was repeated, like the feeble squawking of a dying bird. He stood indecisively, then slowly crunched his way across the crusted snow, toward the sound.

Outside the compound, fifty paces down the path, he stumbled on a stiff dark shadow: the prostrate form of a woman, her face sunk into the snow, starkly frozen. She was quite dead, but under her, in the garments about her bosom, he saw the feeble writhings of a child.

He stooped and lifted up the tiny thing, cold as a fish, but soft. His heart was beating like a drum. He ran back, slipping, almost falling, to the stable, calling in a loud voice to Joseph.

When the brazier was blazing with fresh wood, throwing out light and heat, the priest and his servant bent over the child. It was not more than twelve months old. Its eyes were dark and wild, unbelieving toward the warmth of the fire. From time to time it whimpered.

"It is hungry," Joseph said in a wise tone.

They warmed some milk and poured it into an altar vial. Father Chisholm then tore a strip of clean linen and coaxed it, like a wick, into the flask's narrow neck. The child sucked greedily. In five minutes the milk was finished and the child asleep. The priest wrapped it in a blanket from his own bed.

He was deeply moved. The strangeness of his premonition, the simplicity of the coming of the little thing, into the stable, out of the cold nothingness, was like a sign from God. There was nothing upon the mother's body to tell who she might be, but her features, worn by hardship and poverty, had a thin, fine Tartar cast. A band of nomads had passed through the day before: perhaps she had been overcome by cold, had fallen behind to die. He sought in his mind for a name for the child. It was the feast day of St. Anna. Yes, he would name her Anna.

"Tomorrow, Joseph, we shall find a woman to take care of this gift from heaven."

Joseph shrugged. "Master, you cannot give away a female child."

"I shall not give the child away," Father Chisholm said sternly.

His purpose was already clear and fixed. This babe, sent to him by God, would be his first foundling—yes, the foundation of his children's home . . . that dream he had cherished since his arrival in Pai-tan. He would need help of course, the sisters must one day come—it was all a long way off. But, seated on the earth floor, by the dark red embers, gazing upon the sleeping infant, he felt it was a pledge from heaven that he would, in the end, succeed.

It was Joseph, the prize gossip, who first told Father Chisholm that Mr. Chia's son was sick. The cold season was late in breaking, the Kwang Mountains were still deep in snow; and the cheerful Joseph blew upon his nipped fingers as he chattered away after Mass, assisting the priest to put away his vestments. "Tch! My hand is as useless as that of the little Chia-Yu."

Chia-Yu had scratched his thumb upon no one knew what; but in consequence, his five elements had been disturbed, and the lower humors had gained ascendancy, flowing entirely into one arm, distending it, leaving the boy's body burning and wasted. The three highest physicians of the city were in attendance, and the most costly remedies had been applied. Now a messenger had been dispatched to Sen-siang for the *elixir vitae:* a priceless extract of frog's eyes, obtained only in the circle of the dragon's moon.

"He will recover," Joseph concluded, showing his white teeth in a sanguine smile. "This *hao kao* never fails . . . which is important for Mr. Chia, since Yu is his only son."

Four days later, at the same hour, two closed chairs, one of which was empty, drew up outside the chapel shop in the Street of the Net Makers, and a moment later the tall figure of Mr. Pao's cousin, wrapped in a cotton-padded tunic, gravely confronted Father Chisholm. He apologized for his unseemly intrusion. He asked the priest to accompany him to Mr. Chia's house.

Stunned by the implication of the invitation, Francis hesitated. Close relationship, through business and marriage ties, existed between the Paos and the Chias; both were highly influential families. Since his return from the Liu village he had not infrequently encountered the lean, aloof, and pleasantly cynical cousin of Mr. Pao, who was, indeed, also first cousin to Mr. Chia. He had some evidence of the tall mandarin's regard. But this abrupt call, this sponsorship, was different. As he turned silently to get his hat and coat, he felt a sudden hollow fear.

The Chia house was very quiet, the trellised verandas empty, the fishpond brittle with a film of ice. Their steps rang softly, but with a momentous air, upon the paved, deserted courtyards. Two flanking jasmine trees, swathed in sacking, lolled like sleeping giants, against the tented, red-gold gateway. From the women's quarters across the terraces came the strangled sound of weeping.

It was darkish in the sick chamber, where Chia-Yu lay upon a heated *kang,* watched by the three bearded physicians in long full robes seated upon fresh rush matting. From time to time one of the physicians bent forward and placed a charcoal lump beneath the boxlike *kang.* In the corner of the room, a Taoist priest in a slate-colored robe was mumbling, exorcising, to the accompaniment of flutes behind the bamboo partition.

Yu had been a pretty child of six, with soft cream coloring and sloe black eyes, reared in the strictest traditions of parental respect, idolized, yet unspoiled. Now, consumed by remorseless fever and the terrible novelty of pain, he was stretched upon his back, his bones sticking through his skin, his dry lips twisting, his gaze upon the ceiling, motionless. His right arm, livid, swollen out of recognition, was encased in a horrible plaster of dirt mixed with little printed paper scraps.

When Mr. Pao's cousin entered with Father Chisholm there was a tiny stillness; then the Taoist mumbling was resumed, while the three physicians, more strictly immobilized, maintained their vigil by the *kang.*

Bent over the unconscious child, his hand upon the burning brow, Father Chisholm knew the full import of that limpid and passionless restraint. His present troubles would be as nothing to the persecution that must follow a futile intervention. But the desperate sickness of the boy and this noxious pretense of treatment whipped his blood. He began, quickly yet gently, to remove from the infected arm the *hao kao,* that filthy dressing he had so often met with in his little dispensary.

At last the arm was free, washed in warm water. It floated almost, a bladder of corruption, with a shiny greenish skin. Though now his heart was thudding in his side, Francis went on steadfastly, drew from his pocket the little leather case that Tulloch had given him, took from that case the single lancet. He knew his inexperience. He knew also that if he did not incise the arm the child, already moribund, would die. He felt every unwatching eye upon him, sensed the terrible anxiety, the growing doubt gripping Mr. Pao's cousin as he stood motionless behind him. He made an ejaculation to St. Andrew. He steeled himself to cut, to cut deep, deep and long.

A great gush of putrid matter came heaving through the wound, flowing and bubbling into the earthenware bowl beneath. The stench was dreadful, evil. In all his life Francis had never savored anything so gratefully. As he pressed, with both his hands, on either side of the wound, encouraging the exudation, seeing the limb collapse to half its size, a great relief surged through him, leaving him weak.

When, at last, he straightened up, having packed the wound with clean wet linen, he heard himself murmur, foolishly, in English: "I think he'll do now, with a little luck!" It was old Dr. Tulloch's famous phrase: it demonstrated the tension of his nerves. Yet on his way out he strove to maintain an attitude of cheerful unconcern, declaring to the completely silent cousin of Mr. Pao, who accompanied him to his chair: "Give him nourishing soup if he wakes up. And no more *hao kao.* I will come tomorrow."

On the next day little Yu was greatly better. His fever was almost gone; he had slept naturally and drunk several cups of chicken broth. Without the miracle of the shining lancet he would almost certainly have been dead.

"Continue to nourish him." Father Chisholm genuinely smiled as he took his departure. "I shall call again tomorrow!"

"Thank you." Mr. Pao's cousin cleared his throat. "It is not necessary." There was an awkward pause. "We are deeply grateful. Mr. Chia has been prostrate with grief. Now that his son is recovering he also is recovering. Soon he may be able to present himself in public!" The mandarin bowed, hands discreetly in his sleeves, and was gone.

Father Chisholm strode down the street—he had angrily refused the chair—fighting a dark and bitter indignation. This was gratitude. To be thrown out, without a word, when he had saved the child's life, at the risk, perhaps, of his own . . . From first to last he had not even seen the wretched Mr. Chia, who, even on the junk, that day of his arrival, had not deigned to glance at him. He clenched his fists, fighting his familiar demon: "O God, let me be calm! Don't let this cursed sin of anger master me again. Let me be meek and patient of heart. Give me humility, dear Lord. After all it was thy merciful goodness, thy divine providence, that saved the little boy. Do with me what thou wilt, dear Lord. You see, I am resigned. But, O God!"—with sudden heat: "You must admit it was such damned ingratitude after all!"

During the next few days Francis rigorously shunned the merchant's quarter of the city. More than his pride had been hurt. He listened in silence while Joseph gossiped of the remarkable progress of little Yu, of the largesse distributed by Mr. Chia to the wise physicians, the donation to the temple of Lao-tzu, for the exorcising of the demon that had troubled his beloved son. "Is it not truly remarkable, dear Father, how many sources have benefited by the mandarin's noble generosity?"

"Truly remarkable," said Father Chisholm dryly, but wincing.

A week later, when about to close his dispensary after a stale and profitless afternoon, he suddenly observed, across the flask of permanganate he had been mixing, the discreet apparition of Mr. Chia.

He started hotly, but said nothing. The merchant wore his finest clothes: a rich black satin robe with yellow jacket, embroidered velvet boots in one of which was thrust the ceremonial fan, a fine flat satin cap, and an expression both formal and dignified. His too-long fingernails were protected by gold metal cases. He had an air of culture and intelligence; his manners expressed perfect breeding. There was a gentle, enlightened melancholy on his brow.

"I have come," he said.

"Indeed!" Francis's tone was not encouraging. He went on stirring with his glass rod, mixing the mauve solution.

"There have been many matters to attend to, much business to settle. But now," a resigned bow, "I am here."

"Why?" Shortly, from Francis.

Mr. Chia's face indicated mild surprise. "Naturally . . . to become a Christian."

There was a moment of dead silence—a moment that, traditionally, should have marked the climax of these meager toiling months, the thrilling firstfruits of the missionary's achievement: here, the leading savage, bowing the head for baptism. But there was little exultation in Father Chisholm's face. He chewed his lip crossly, then he said slowly: "Do you believe?"

"No!" Sadly.

"Are you prepared to be instructed?"

"I have not time to be instructed." A subdued bow. "I am only eager to become a Christian."

"Eager? You mean you want to?"

Mr. Chia smiled wanly. "Is it not apparent—my wish to profess your faith?"

"No, it is not apparent. And you have not the slightest wish to profess my faith. Why are you doing this?" The priest's color was high.

"To repay you," Mr. Chia said simply. "You have done the greatest good to me. I must do the greatest good for you."

Father Chisholm moved irritably. Because the temptation was so alluring, because he wished to yield and could not, his temper flared. "It is not good. It is bad. You have neither inclination nor belief. My acceptance of you would be a forgery for God. You owe me nothing. Now please go!"

At first Mr. Chia did not believe his ears.

"You mean you reject me?"

"That is putting it politely," growled Father Chisholm.

The change in the merchant was seraphic. His eyes brightened, glistened; his melancholy dropped from him like a shroud. He had to struggle to contain himself; but although he had the semblance of desiring to leap into the air he did contain himself. Formally, he made the kowtow three times. He succeeded in mastering his voice.

"I regret that I am not acceptable. I am of course most unworthy. Nevertheless, perhaps in some slight manner . . ." He broke off, again he made the kowtow three times and, moving backward, went out.

That evening, as Father Chisholm sat by the brazier with a sternness of countenance that caused Joseph, who was cooking tasty river mussels in his rice, to gaze at him timidly, there came the sudden sound of firecrackers. Six of Mr. Chia's servants were exploding them, ceremoniously, in the road outside. Then Mr. Pao's cousin advanced, bowed, handed Father Chisholm a parchment wrapped in vermilion paper.

"Mr. Chia begs that you will honor him by accepting this most unworthy gift—the deeds of the Brilliant Green Jade property with all land and water rights and the rights to the crimson clay pit. The property is yours, without restraint, forever. Mr. Chia further begs that you accept the help of twenty of his workmen till any building you may wish to carry out is fully accomplished."

So completely taken aback was Francis he could not speak a word. He watched the retreating figure of the cousin of Mr. Pao, and of Mr. Chia, with a strange still tensity. Then he wildly scanned the title deeds and cried out joyfully, "Joseph! Joseph!"

Joseph came hurrying, fearing another misfortune had befallen them. His master's expression reassured him. They went together to the Hill of Brilliant Green Jade and there, standing under the moon amid the tall cedars, they sang aloud the Magnificat.

Francis remained bareheaded, seeing in a vision what he would create on this noble brow of land. He had prayed with faith, and his prayer had been answered.

Joseph, made hungry by the keen wind, waited uncomplainingly, finding his own vision in the priest's rapt face, glad he had shown the presence of mind to take his rice pot from the fire.

4

Eighteen months later, in the month of May, when all Chek-kow Province lay basking in that span of short perfection between the winter snows and the swelterings of summer, Father Chisholm crossed the paved courtyard of his new Mission of St. Andrew.

Never, perhaps, had such a sense of quiet contentment suffused him. The crystal air, where a cloud of white pigeons wheeled, was sweet and sparkling. As he reached the great banyan tree that, through his design, now shaded the forecourt of the mission, he threw a look across his shoulder, partly of pride, part in wry wonderment, as though still apprehensive of a mirage that might vanish overnight.

But it was there, shining and splendid: the slender church sentineled between the cedars, his house, vivid with scarlet lattices, adjoining the little schoolroom, the snug dispensary opening through the outer wall, and a further dwelling screened by the foliage of pawpaw and catalpa, which sheltered his freshly planted garden. He sighed, his lips smiling, blessing the miracle of the fruitful clay pit, which had yielded, through many blendings and experimental bakings, bricks of a lovely soft pale rose, making his mission a symphony in cinnabar.

He blessed, indeed, each subsequent wonder: the implacable kindness of Mr. Chia; the skillful patience of his workers; the incorruptibility—almost complete—of his sturdy foreman; even the weather, this recent brilliant spell, which had made his opening ceremony, held last week and politely attended by the Chia and Pao families, a notable success.

For the sole purpose of viewing the empty classroom he took the long way round: peering, like a schoolboy, through the window at the brand-new pictures upon the whitewashed wall, at the shining benches that, like the blackboard, he had carpentered himself. The knowledge that his handiwork was in that particular room lay warmly round his heart. But recollection of the task he had in mind drove him to the end of the garden where, near the lower gate, and beside his private workshop, was a small brick kiln.

Happily, he jettisoned his old soutane and, in stained denim trousers, shirtsleeves, and suspenders, he took a wooden spade and began to puddle up some clay.

Tomorrow the three sisters would arrive. Their house was ready—cool, curtained, already smelling of beeswax. But his final conceit, a secluded loggia in which they might rest and meditate, was not quite finished, demanding at least another batch of bricks from his own especial oven. As he shaped the marl he shaped the future in his mind.

Nothing was more vital than the advent of these nuns. He had seen this from the outset; he had worked and prayed for it, sending letter upon letter to Father Mealey and even to the bishop, while the mission slowly rose before his eyes. Conversion of the Chinese adult was, he felt, a labor for archangels. Race, illiteracy, the tug of an older faith—these were formidable barriers to break down honestly, and one knew that the Almighty hated being asked to do conjuring tricks with each individual case. True, now that he was sustained in "face" by his fine new church, increasing numbers of repentant souls were adventuring to Mass. He had some sixty persons in his congregation. As their pious cadences ascended at the Kyrie it sounded quite a multitude.

Nevertheless, his vision was focused, brightly, on the children. Here, quite literally, children went two a penny. Famine, grinding poverty, and the Confucianism of masculine perpetuation made female infants, at least, a drug upon the market. In no time at all he would have a schoolful of children, fed and cared for by the sisters, here in the mission, spinning their hoops, making the place gay with laughter, learning their letters and their catechism. The future belonged to the children: and the children . . . his children . . . would belong to God!

He smiled self-consciously at his thoughts as he shoved the molds into the oven. He could not call himself, precisely, a ladies' man. Yet he had hungered, these long months, amid this alien race, for the comfort of intercourse with his own kind. Mother Maria-Veronica, though Bavarian by birth, had spent the past five years with the Bon Secours in London. And the two whom she led, the French Sister Clotilde and Sister Martha, a Belgian, had equal experience in Liverpool. Coming direct from England they would bring him, at least, a friendly breath of home.

A trifle anxiously—for he had taken enormous trouble—he reviewed his preparations for their arrival on the following day: a few fireworks in the best Chinese style, but not enough to alarm the ladies, at the river landing stage, where the three best chairs in Pai-tan would await them. Tea served immediately they reached the mission. A short rest followed by benediction—he hoped they would like the flowers—and then, a special supper.

He almost chuckled as he conned, in his mind's eye, the menu of that supper. Well . . . they'd get down to hardtack soon enough, poor things! His own appetite was scandalously meager. During the building of the mission he had subsisted abstractedly, standing on scaffolds, or fingering a plan with Mr. Chia's foreman, upon rice and bean curd. But now he had sent Joseph scouring the city for mangos, chowchow, and, rarest delicacy of all, fresh bustard from Shon-see in the North.

Suddenly, across his meditation, came the sound of footsteps. He lifted his head. As he turned, the gate was thrown open. Signed forward by their guide, a ragged riverside coolie, three nuns appeared. They were travel stained, with a vague uneasiness in their uncertain glances. They hesitated, then advanced wearily up the garden path. The foremost, about forty years of age, had both dignity and beauty. There was high breeding in the fine bones of her face and in her wide heavy blue eyes. Pale with fatigue, impelled by a kind of inward fire, she forced herself on. Barely looking at Francis, she addressed him in fair Chinese.

"Please take us immediately to the mission, Father."

Dreadfully put out at their obvious distress, he answered in the same tongue.

"You were not expected till tomorrow."

"Are we to return to that dreadful ship?" She shivered with contained indignation. "Take us to your master at once."

He said slowly, in English: "I am Father Chisholm."

Her eyes, which had been searching the mission buildings, returned incredulously to his short shirtsleeved figure. She stared with growing dismay at his working clothes, dirty hands, and caked boots, the smear of mud across his cheek. He murmured awkwardly: "I'm sorry . . . most distressed you weren't met."

For a moment her resentment mastered her. "One might have supposed some welcome at the end of six thousand miles."

"But you see . . . the letter said quite definitely—"

She cut him short with a repressed gesture.

"Perhaps you will show us to our quarters. My companions," with a proud negation of her own exhaustion, "are completely worn-out."

He was about to make a final explanation, but the sight of the two other sisters, staring and very frightened, restrained him. He led the way in painful silence to their house. Here he stopped.

"I hope you will be comfortable. I will send for your baggage. Perhaps . . . perhaps you will dine with me tonight."

"Thank you. It is impossible." Her tone was cold. Once again her eyes, holding back haughty tears, touched his disreputable garments. "But if we could be spared some milk and fruit . . . tomorrow we shall be fit for work."

Subdued and mortified, he returned slowly to his house, bathed, and changed. From among his papers he found and carefully examined the letter from Tientsin. The date given was May 19, which, as he had said, was tomorrow. He tore the letter into little pieces. He thought of that fine, that foolish, bustard. He flushed. Downstairs he was confronted by Joseph, bubbling with spirits, his arms full of purchases.

"Joseph! Carry the fruit you have bought to the sisters' house. Take everything else and distribute it to the poor."

"But, Master . . ." Stupefied at the tone of the command, the expression on the priest's face, Joseph swallowed rapidly; then, his jubilation gone, he gulped: "Yes, Master."

Francis went toward the church, his lips compressed as though they sealed an unexpected hurt.

Next morning the three sisters heard his Mass. And he hurried, unconsciously, through his thanksgiving, hoping to find Mother Maria-Veronica awaiting him outside. She was not there. Nor did she come, for her instructions, to his house. An hour later he found her writing in the schoolroom. She rose quietly.

"Please sit down, Reverend Mother."

"Thank you." She spoke pleasantly. Yet she continued to stand, pen in hand, notepaper before her on the desk. "I have been waiting on my pupils."

"You shall have twenty by this afternoon. I've been picking them for many weeks." He strove to make his tone light and agreeable. "They seem intelligent little things."

She smiled gravely. "We shall do our utmost for them."

"Then there is the dispensary. I am hoping you will assist me there. I've very little knowledge—but it's amazing what even a little does here."

"If you will tell me the dispensary hours I shall be there."

A brief silence. Through her quiet civility, he felt her reserve deeply. His gaze, downcast, moving awkwardly, lit suddenly upon a small framed photograph that she had already established on the desk.

"What a beautiful scene!" He spoke at random, striving to break the impersonal barrier between them.

"Yes, it is beautiful." Her heavy eyes followed his to the picture of a fine old house, white and castellated against a dark wall of mountain pines, with a sweep of terraces and gardens running down toward the lake. "It is the Schloss Anheim."

"I have heard that name before. It is historic, surely. Is it near your home?"

She looked at him for the first time straight in the face. Her expression was completely colorless. "Quite near," she said.

Her tone absolutely closed the subject. She seemed to wait for him to speak, and when he did not she said, rather quickly:

"The sisters and I . . . we are most earnest in our desire to work for the success of the mission. You have only to mention your wishes and they will be carried out. At the same time—" Her voice chilled slightly, "I trust you will afford us a certain freedom of action."

He stared at her oddly. "What do you mean?"

"You know our rule is partly contemplative. We should like to enjoy as much privacy as possible." She gazed straight in front of her. "Take our meals alone . . . maintain our separate establishment."

He flushed. "I never dreamed of anything else. Your little house is your convent."

"Then you permit me to manage all our convent affairs."

Her meaning was quite plain to him. It settled like a weight upon his heart. He smiled, unexpectedly, rather sadly.

"By all means. Only be careful about money. We are very poor."

"My order has made itself responsible for our support."

He could not resist the question. "Does not your order enforce holy poverty?"

"Yes," she gave back swiftly, "but not meanness."

There was a pause. They remained standing side by side. She had broken off sharply, with a catch in her breath, her fingers tight upon the pen. His own face was burning; he had a strange reluctance to look at her.

"I will send Joseph with a note of the dispensary hours . . . and of church services. Good morning, Sister."

When he had gone she sat down, slowly, at the desk, her gaze still fixed ahead, her expression proudly unreadable. Then a single tear broke and rolled mysteriously down her cheek. Her worst forebodings were justified. Passionately, almost, she dipped her pen in the inkwell and resumed her letter.

". . . It has happened, already, as I feared, my dear, dear brother, and I have sinned again in my dreadful . . . my ineradicable Hohenlohe pride. Yet who could blame me? He has just been here, washed free of earth and approximately shaved—I could see the scrubby razor cuts upon his chin—and armed with such a dumb authority. I saw instantly, yesterday, what a little bourgeois it was. This morning he surpassed himself. Were you aware, dear count, that Anheim was historic? I almost laughed as his eyes fumbled at the photograph: you remember the one I took from the boathouse that day we went sailing with Mother on the lake—it's gone with me everywhere—my sole temporal treasure. He said, in effect, 'Which Cook's tour did you take to view it?' I felt like saying, 'I was born there!' My pride restrained me. Yet had I done so he would probably have kept on gazing at his boots, still creviced with mud, where he had failed to clean them—and muttered: 'Oh, indeed! Our blessed Lord was born in a stable.'

"You see, there is something about him that strikes at one. Do you recollect Herr Spinner, our first tutor . . . we were such brutes to him . . . and the way he had of looking up suddenly with such hurt, yet humble restraint? His eyes, here, are the same. Probably his father was a woodcutter like Herr Spinner's, and he too has struggled up, precariously, with dogged humility. But, dear Ernst, it is the future that I dread, shut up in this strange and isolated spot, which intensifies every aspect of the situation. The danger is a lowering of one's inborn standards, yielding to a kind of mental intimacy with a person one instinctively despises. That odious familiar cheerfulness! I must drop a hint to Martha and Clotilde—who has been such a poor sick calf all the way from Liverpool. I am resolved to be pleasant and to work myself to the bone. But only complete detachment, an absolute reserve, will . . ."

She broke off, gazing again, remote and troubled, through the window.

Father Chisholm soon perceived that the two under sisters went out of their way to avoid him.

Clotilde was not yet thirty, flat bosomed, and delicate, with bloodless lips and a nervous smile. She was very devout and when she prayed, with her head inclined to one side, tears would gush from her pale green eyes. Martha was a different person: past forty, stocky, and strong, a peasant type, dark complexioned and with a net of wrinkles round her eyes. Bustling and outspoken, a trifle coarse in manner, she looked as though she would be immediately at home in a kitchen or a farmyard.

When by chance he met them in the garden the Belgian sister would drop a quick curtsy while Clotilde's sallow face flushed nervously as she smiled and fluttered on. He knew himself to be the subject of their whisperings. He had the impulse, often, to stop them violently. *Don't be so scared of me. We've made a stupid beginning. But I'm a much better fellow than I look.*

He restrained himself. He had no grounds whatsoever for complaint. Their work was executed scrupulously, with minute perfection of purpose. New altar linen, exquisitely stitched, appeared in the sacristy, and an embroidered stole, which must have taken days of patient labor. Bandages and dressings, rolled, cut to all sizes, filled the store cupboard in the surgery.

The children had come and were comfortably housed in the big ground-floor dormitory of the sisters' house. And presently the schoolroom hummed with little voices, or with the chanted rhythm of a much-repeated lesson. He would stand outside, open breviary in hand, sheltered by the bushes, listening. It meant so much to him, this tiny school; he had so joyfully anticipated its opening. Now he rarely went in; and never without a sense of his intrusion. He withdrew into himself, accepting the situation with a somber logic. It was very simple. Mother Maria-Veronica was a good woman, fine, fastidious, devoted to her work. Yet from the first she had conceived a natural aversion to him. Such things cannot be overcome. After all, he was not a prepossessing character; he had been right when he judged himself no squire of dames. It was a sad disappointment, nevertheless.

The dispensary brought them together on three afternoons each week when, for four hours at a stretch, Maria-Veronica worked close beside him. He could see that she was interested, often so deeply as to forget her aversion. Though they spoke little he had on such occasions a strange sense of comradeship with her.

One day, a month after her arrival, as he finished dressing a severe whitlow, she exclaimed, involuntarily: "You would have made a surgeon."

He flushed. "I've always liked working with my hands."

"That is because you are clever with them."

He was ridiculously pleased. Her manner was friendlier than it had ever been. At the end of the clinic, as he put away his simple medicines, she gazed at him questioningly. "I've been meaning to ask you . . . Sister Clotilde has had too much to do lately, preparing the children's meals with Martha in the kitchen. She isn't strong, and I'm afraid it is too much for her. If you have no objection I would like to get some help."

"But of course." He agreed at once—even happier that she should have asked his permission. "Shall I find you a servant?"

"No thank you. I already have a good couple in mind!"

Next morning when crossing the compound, he observed on the convent balcony, airing and brushing the matting, the unmistakable figures of Hosannah and Philomena Wang. He stopped short, his face darkening, then he took immediate steps toward the sisters' house.

He found Maria-Veronica in the linen room checking over the sheets. He spoke hurriedly: "I'm sorry to disturb you. But—these new servants—I'm afraid you won't find them satisfactory."

She turned slowly from the cupboard, sudden displeasure in her face. "Surely I am the best judge of that?"

"I don't want you to think I'm interfering. But I'm bound to warn you that they are far from reliable characters."

Her lip curled. "Is that your Christian charity?"

He paled. She was placing him in a horrible position. But he went on determinedly. "I am obliged to be practical. I am thinking of the mission. And of you."

"Please do not trouble about me." Her smile was icy. "I am quite capable of looking after myself."

"I tell you these Wangs are a really bad lot."

She answered with peculiar emphasis: "I know they've had a really bad time. They told me."

His temper flared. "I advise you to get rid of them."

"I won't get rid of them!" Her voice was cold as steel. She had always suspected him, and now she knew. Because she had relaxed her vigilance yesterday, for a moment, in the dispensary, he had rushed to interfere, to show his authority, on this frivolous pretext. Never, never would she be weak with him again. "You already agreed that I am not responsible to you for the administration of my house. I must ask you to keep your word."

He was silent. There was nothing more that he could say. He had meant to help her. But he had made a bad mistake. As he turned away he knew that their relationship, which he had thought to be improving, was now worse than it had been before.

The situation began to affect him seriously. It was hard to keep his expression unruffled when the Wangs passed him, with an air of muted triumph, many times a day. One morning, toward the end of July, Joseph brought him his breakfast of fruit and tea with swollen knuckles and a sheepish air—part triumphant, part subdued.

"Master, I am sorry. I have had to give that rascal Wang a beating."

Father Chisholm sat up sharply, his eye stern: "Why so, Joseph?"

Joseph hung his head. "He says many unkind words about us. That Reverend Mother is a great lady and we are simply dust."

"We all are dust, Joseph." The priest's smile was faint.

"He says harder words than that."

"We can put up with hard words."

"It is more than words, Master. He has become puffed up beyond measure. And all the time he is making a bad squeeze on the sisters' housekeeping."

It was quite true. Because of his opposition, the reverend mother was indulgent toward the Wangs. Hosannah was now the majordomo of the sisters' house while Philomena departed, every day, with a basket on her arm, to do the shopping as if she owned the place. At the end of each month, when Martha paid the bills with the roll of notes that the reverend mother gave her, the precious pair would depart for the town, in their best clothes, to collect a staggering commission from the tradesmen. It was barefaced robbery, anathema to Francis's Scottish thrift.

Gazing at Joseph he said grimly: "I hope you did not hurt Wang much."

"Alas! I fear I hurt him greatly, Master."

"I am cross with you, Joseph. As a punishment you shall have a holiday tomorrow. And that new suit you have long been asking of me."

That afternoon, in the dispensary, Maria-Veronica broke her rule of silence. Before the patients were admitted she said to Francis:

"So you have chosen to victimize poor Wang again?"

He answered bluntly: "On the contrary. It is he who is victimizing you."

"I do not understand you."

"He is robbing you. The man is a born thief, and you are encouraging him."

She bit her lip fiercely. "I do not believe you. I am accustomed to trust my servants."

"Very well then, we shall see." He dismissed the matter quietly.

In the next few weeks his silent face showed deeper lines of strain. It was dreadful to live in close community with a person who detested, despised, him—and to be responsible for that person's spiritual welfare. Maria-Veronica's confessions, which contained nothing, were torture to him. And he judged they were equal torture for her. When he placed the sacred wafer between her lips while her long delicate fingers upheld the altar cloth in the still and pallid dawn of each new day, her upturned pale face, with eyelids veined and tremulous, seemed still to scorn him. He began to rest badly and to walk in the garden at night. So far, their disagreement had been limited to the sphere of her authority. Constrained, more silent than ever, he waited for the moment when he must enforce his will.

It was autumn when that necessity arose, quite simply, out of her inexperience. Yet he could not pass it by. He sighed as he walked over to the sisters' house.

"Reverend Mother . . ." To his annoyance he found himself trembling. He stood before her, his eyes upon those memorable boots. "You have been going into the city these last few afternoons with Sister Clotilde?"

She looked surprised. "Yes, that is true."

There was a pause.

On guard, she inquired with irony: "Are you curious to know what we are doing?"

"I already know." He spoke as mildly as he could. "You go to visit the sick poor of the city. As far away as the Manchu Bridge. It is commendable. But I'm afraid it must cease."

"May I ask why?" She tried to match his quietness but did not quite succeed.

"Really, I'd rather not tell you."

Her fine nostrils were tense. "If you are prohibiting my acts of charity . . . I have a right . . . I insist on knowing."

"Joseph tells me there are bandits in the city. Wai-Chu has begun fighting again. His soldiers are dangerous."

She laughed outright proudly, contemptuously.

"I am not afraid. The men in my family have always been soldiers."

"That is most interesting." He gazed at her steadily. "But you are not a man, nor is Sister Clotilde. And Wai-Chu's soldiers are not exactly the kid-gloved cavalry officers infallibly found in the best Bavarian families."

He had never used that tone with her before. She reddened, then paled. Her features, her whole figure seemed to contract. "Your outlook is common and cowardly. You forget that I have given myself to God. I came here prepared for anything—sickness, accident, disaster, if necessary death—but not to listen to a lot of cheap sensational rubbish."

His eyes remained fixed on her, so that they burned her, like points of light. He said unconditionally: "Then we will cease to be sensational. It would, as you infer, be a small matter if you were captured and carried off. But there is a stronger reason why you should restrain your charitable promenades. The position of women in China is very different from that to which you are accustomed. In China women have been rigidly excluded from society for centuries. You give grave offense by walking openly in the streets. From a religious standpoint it is highly damaging to the work of the mission. For that reason I forbid you, absolutely, to enter Pai-tan unescorted, without my permission."

She flushed, as though he had struck her in the face. There was a mortal stillness. She had nothing whatever to say.

He was about to leave her when there came a sudden scud of footsteps in the passage and Sister Martha bundled into the room. Her agitation was so great she did not observe Francis, half-hidden by the shadow of the door. Nor did she guess the tension of the moment. Her gaze, distraught beneath her rumpled wimple, was bent on Maria-Veronica. Wringing her hands, she lamented wildly:

"They've run away . . . taken everything . . . the ninety dollars you gave me yesterday to pay the bills . . . the silver . . . even Sister Clotilde's ivory crucifix . . . they've gone, gone . . ."

"Who has gone?" The words came, with a dreadful effort, from Maria-Veronica's stiff lips.

"The Wangs, of course . . . the low, dirty thieves. I always knew they were a pair of rogues and hypocrites."

Francis did not dare to look at the mother superior. She stood there, motionless. He felt a strange pity for her. He made his way clumsily from the room.

5

As Father Chisholm returned to his own house he became aware, through the strained preoccupation of his mind, of Mr. Chia and his son, standing by the fishpond, watching the carp, with a quiet air of waiting. Both figures were warmly padded against the chill—it was a "six-coat cold day"—the boy's hand was in his father's, and the slow dusk, stealing from the shadows of the banyan tree, seemed reluctant to envelop them, and to efface a charming picture.

The two were frequent visitors to the mission and perfectly at home there; they smiled, as Father Chisholm hurried over, greeted him with courteous formality. But Mr. Chia, for once, gently turned aside the priest's invitation to enter his house.

"We come instead to bid you to our house. Yes, tonight, we are leaving for our mountain retreat. It would afford me the greatest happiness if you would accompany us."

Francis stood amazed. "But we are entering upon winter!"

"It is true, my friend, that I and my unworthy family have hitherto ventured to our secluded villa in the Kwangs only during the inclement heat of summer." Mr. Chia paused blandly. "Now we make an innovation which may be even more agreeable. We have many cords of wood and much store of food. Do you not think, Father, it would be edifying to meditate, a little, among these snowy peaks?"

Searching the maze of circumlocution with a puzzled frown, Father Chisholm shot a swift glance of interrogation at the merchant.

"Is Wai-Chu about to loot the town?"

Mr. Chia's shoulders mildly deprecated the directness of the query but his expression did not falter. "On the contrary, I myself have paid Wai considerable tribute and billeted him comfortably. I trust he will remain in Pai-tan for many days."

A silence. Father Chisholm's brows were drawn in complete perplexity.

"However, my dear friend, there are other matters that occasionally make the wise man seek the solitudes. I beg of you to come."

The priest shook his head slowly. "I am sorry, Mr. Chia—I am too busy in the mission. . . . How could I leave this noble place that you have so generously given me?"

Mr. Chia smiled amiably. "It is most salubrious here at present. If you change your mind do not fail to inform me. Come, Yu . . . the wagons will be loaded now. Give your hand to the holy father in the English fashion."

Father Chisholm shook hands with the little wrapped-up boy. Then he blessed them both. The air of restrained regret in Mr. Chia's manner disturbed him. His heart was strangely heavy as he watched them go.

The next two days passed in a queer atmosphere of stress. He saw little of the sisters. The weather turned worse. Great flocks of birds were seen flying to the south. The sky darkened and lay like lead upon all living things. But except for a few flurries no snow came. Even the cheerful Joseph showed unusual signs of grievance, coming to the priest and expressing his desire to go home.

"It is a long time since I have seen my parents. It is fitting for me to visit them."

When questioned, he waved his hand around vaguely, grumbling that there were rumors in Pai-tan of evil things traveling from the north, the east, the west.

"Wait till the evil spirits come, Joseph, before you run away." Father Chisholm tried to rally his servant's spirits. And his own.

Next morning, after early Mass, he went down to the town, alone, in determined quest of news. The streets were teeming, life apparently pulsed undisturbed, but a hush hung about the larger dwellings, and many of the shops were closed. In the Street of the Net Makers, he found Hung boarding up his windows with unobtrusive urgency.

"There is no denying it, Shang-Foo!" The old shopkeeper paused to give the father a calamitous glance over his small pebble spectacles. "It is sickness . . . the great coughing sickness that they name the black death. Already six provinces are stricken. People are fleeing with the wind. The first came last night to Pai-tan. And one of the women fell dead inside the Manchu Gate. A wise man knows what that portends. Ay, ay, when there is famine we march and when there is pestilence we march again. Life is not easy when the gods show their wrath."

Father Chisholm climbed the hill to the mission with a shadow upon his face. He seemed already to smell the sickness in the air.

Suddenly he drew up. Outside the mission wall, and directly in his path, lay three dead rats. Judging by the priest's expression there was, in this stiff trinity, a dire foreboding. He shivered unexpectedly, thinking of his children. He went himself for kerosene, and poured it on the corpses of the rats, ignited the oil, and watched their slow cremation. Hurriedly, he took up the remains with tongs and buried them.

He stood thinking deeply. He was five hundred miles from the nearest telegraph terminal. To send a messenger to Sen-siang by sampan, even by the fastest pony, might take at least six days. And yet he must at all costs establish some contact with the outer world.

Suddenly his expression lifted. He found Joseph and led him quickly by the arm to his room. His face was set with gravity as he addressed the boy.

"Joseph! I am sending you on an errand of the first importance. You will take Mr. Chia's new launch. Tell the *kapong* you have Mr. Chia's permission and mine. I even command you to steal the launch if it is necessary. Do you understand?"

"Yes, Father." Joseph's eyes flashed. "It will not be a sin."

"When you have the boat, proceed with all speed to Sen-siang. There you will go to Father Thibodeau at the mission. If he is away go to the offices of the American oil company. Find someone in authority. Tell him the plague is upon us, that we need immediately medicine, supplies, and doctors. Then go to the telegraph company, send these two messages I have written for you. See . . . take the papers . . . the first to the vicariate at Pekin, the second to the Union General Hospital at Nankin.

Here is money. Do not fail me, Joseph. Now go . . . go. And the good God go with you!"

He felt better an hour later as the lad went padding down the hill, his blue bundle bobbing on his back, his intelligent features screwed to a staunch tenacity. The better to view the departure of the launch, the priest hastened to the belfry tower. But here, as he perched himself against the pediment, his eye darkened. On the vast plain before him he saw two thinly moving streams of beasts and straggling humans, reduced, alike, by distance to the size of little ants—two moving streams, the one approaching, the other departing from the city.

He could not wait; but, descending, crossed immediately to the school. In the wooden corridor Sister Martha was on her knees scrubbing the boards. He stopped.

"Where is Reverend Mother?"

She raised a damp hand to straighten her wimple. "In the classroom." She added, in a sibilant, confederate's whisper: "And lately much disarranged."

He went into the classroom, which, at his entry, fell immediately to silence. The rows of bright childish faces gave him, suddenly, a gripping pang. Quickly, quickly, he fought back that unbearable fear.

Maria-Veronica had turned toward him with a pale, unreadable brow. He approached and addressed her in an undertone.

"There are signs of an epidemic in the city. I am afraid it may be plague. If so, it is important for us to be prepared." He paused, under her silence, then went on. "At all costs we must try to keep the sickness from the children. That means isolating the school and the sisters' house. I shall arrange at once for some kind of barrier to be put up. The children and all three sisters should remain inside, with one sister always on duty at the entrance." He paused again, forcing himself to be calm. "Don't you think that wise?"

She faced him, cold and undismayed. "Profoundly wise."

"Are there any details we might discuss?"

She answered bitterly: "You have already familiarized us with the principle of segregation."

He took no notice. "You know how the contagion is spread?"

"Yes."

There was a silence. He turned toward the door, somber from her fixed refusal to make peace. "If God sends this great trouble upon us, we must work hard together. Let us try to forget our personal relations."

"They are best forgotten." She spoke in her most frigid tone, submissive upon the surface, yet charged, beneath, with high disdainful breeding.

He left the classroom. He could not but admire her courage. The news he had conveyed to her would have terrified most women. He reflected tensely that they might need all their spirit before the month was past.

Convinced of the need of haste, he recrossed the compound and dispatched the gardener for Mr. Chia's foreman and six of the men who had worked on the church. Immediately, when these arrived, he set them to build a thick fence of kaolin on the boundary he had marked off. The dried stalks of maize made an excellent barricade. While it rose under his anxious eyes, girding the school and convent house, he trenched a narrow ditch around the base. This could be flooded with disinfectant if the need arose.

The work went on all day and was not completed until late at night. Even after the men had gone he could not rest, a mounting tide of dread was in his blood. He took most of his stores into the enclosure, carrying sacks of potatoes and flour on his shoulders, butter, bacon, condensed milk, and all the tinned goods of the mission. His small stock of medicines he likewise transferred. Only then did he feel some degree of relief. He looked at his watch: three o'clock in the morning. It was not worthwhile to go to bed. He went into the church and spent the hours remaining until dawn in prayer.

When it was light, before the mission was astir he set out for the yamen of the chief magistrate. At the Manchu Gate fugitives from the stricken provinces were still crowding unhindered into the city. Scores had taken up their lodging beneath the stars, in the lee of the Great Wall. As he passed the silent figures, huddled under sacking, half-frozen by the bitter wind, he heard the racking sound of coughing. His heart flowed out toward these poor exhausted creatures, many already stricken, enduring humbly, suffering without hope; and a burning, impetuous desire to help them suffused his soul. One old man lay dead and naked, stripped of the garments he no longer needed. His wrinkled toothless face was upturned toward the sky.

Spurred by the pity in his breast, Francis reached the yamen of justice. But here a blow awaited him. Mr. Pao's cousin was gone. All the Paos had departed, the closed shutters of their house stared back at him like sightless eyes.

He took a swift and painful breath and turned, chafing, into the courts. The passages were deserted, the main chamber a vault of echoing emptiness. He could see no one, except a few clerks scurrying with a furtive air. From one of these he learned that the chief magistrate had been called away to the obsequies of a distant relative in Tchientin, eight hundred *li* due south. It was plain to the harassed priest that all but the lowest court officials had been "summoned" from Pai-tan. The civil administration of the city had ceased to exist.

The furrow between Francis's eyes was deeply cut, a haggard wound. Only one course lay open to him now. And he knew that it was futile. Nevertheless, he turned and made his way rapidly to the cantonment.

With the bandit Wai-Chu complete overlord of the province, ferociously exacting voluntary gifts, the position of the regular military forces was academic. They dissolved or seceded as a matter of routine on the bandit's periodic visits to the town. Now, as Francis reached the barracks, a bare dozen soldiers hung about, conspicuously without arms, in dirty gray-cotton tunics.

They stopped him at the gate. But nothing could withstand the fire that now consumed him. He forced his way to an inner chamber, where a young lieutenant in a clean and elegant uniform lounged by the paper-latticed window, reflectively polishing his white teeth with a willow twig.

Lieutenant Shon and the priest inspected one another, the young dandy with polite guardedness, his visitor with all the dark and hopeless ardor of his purpose.

"The city is threatened by a great sickness." Francis fought to inject his tone with deliberate restraint. "I am seeking for someone with courage and authority, to combat the grave danger."

Shon continued dispassionately to consider the priest. "General Wai-Chu has the monopoly of authority. And he is leaving for Tou-en-lai tomorrow."

"That will make it easier for those who remain. I beg of you to help me."

Shon shrugged his shoulders virtuously. "Nothing would afford me greater satisfaction than to work with the Shang-Foo entirely without prospect of reward, for the supreme benefit of suffering mankind. But I have no more than fifty soldiers. And no supplies."

"I have sent to Sen-siang for supplies." Francis spoke more rapidly. "They will arrive soon. But meanwhile we must do all in our command to quarantine the refugees and prevent the pestilence from starting in the city."

"It has already started." Shon answered coolly. "In the Street of the Basket Makers there are more than sixty cases. Many dead. The rest dying."

A terrible urgency tautened the priest's nerves, a surge of protest, a burning refusal to accept defeat. He took a quick step forward.

"I am going to aid these people. If you do not come I shall go alone. But I am perfectly assured that you are coming."

For the first time the lieutenant looked uncomfortable. He was a bold youngster, despite his foppish air, with ideas of his own advancement and a sense of personal integrity that had caused him to reject the price offered him by Wai-Chu, as dishonorably inadequate. Without the slightest interest in the fate of his fellow citizens, he had been, on the priest's arrival, idly debating the advisability of joining his few remaining men in the Street of the Stolen Hours. Now, he was disagreeably embarrassed and reluctantly impressed. Like a man moving against his own will, he rose, threw away his twig, and slowly buckled on his revolver.

"This does not shoot well. But as a symbol it encourages the unswerving obedience of my most trusted followers."

They went out together into the cold gray day.

From the Street of the Stolen Hours they routed some thirty soldiers and marched to the teeming warrens of the basket weavers' quarters by the river. Here the plague had already settled, with the instinct of a dunghill fly. The river dwellings, tiers of cardboard hovels, leaning one on top of another, against the high mud bank, were festering with dirt, vermin, and the disease. Francis saw that unless immediate measures were taken, the contagion would spread in this congestion like a raging conflagration.

He said to the lieutenant, as they emerged, bent double, from the end hovel of the row:

"We must find some place to house the sick."

Shon reflected. He was enjoying himself more than he had expected. This foreign priest had shown much "face" in stooping close to the stricken persons. He admired "face" greatly.

"We shall commandeer the yamen of the *yu shih*—the imperial recorder." For many months Shon had been at violent enmity with this official, who had defrauded him of his share of the salt tax. "I am confident that my absent friend's abode will make a pleasing hospital."

They went immediately to the recorder's yamen. It was large and richly furnished, situated in the best part of the city. Shon effected entry by the simple expedient of breaking down the door. While Francis remained with half a dozen men to make some preparations for receiving the sick, he departed with the remainder. Presently the first cases arrived in litters and were arranged in rows on quilted mats upon the floor.

That night, as Francis went up the hill toward the mission, tired from his long day's work, he heard above the faint incessant death music the shouts of wild carousing and sporadic rifle shots. Behind him, Wai-Chu's irregulars were looting the shuttered shops. But presently the city fell again to silence. In the still moonlight he could see the bandits, streaming from the eastern gate, spurring their stolen ponies across the plains. He was glad to see them go.

At the summit of the hill the moon suddenly was dimmed. It began at last to snow. When he drew near the gateway in the kaolin fence the air was alive and fluttering. Soft dry blinding flakes came whirling out of the darkness, settling on eyes and brow, entering his lips like tiny hosts, whirling so dense and thick that in a minute the ground was carpeted in white. He stood outside, in the white coldness, rent by anxiety, and called in a low voice. Immediately Mother Maria-Veronica came to the gate, holding up a lantern that cast a beam of spectral brightness on the snow.

He scarcely dared to put the question. "Are you all well?"

"Yes."

His heart stopped pounding in sheer relief. He waited, suddenly conscious of his fatigue and the fact that he had not eaten all that day. Then he said: "We have established a hospital in the town . . . not much . . . but the best we could do." Again he waited, as if for her to speak, deeply sensible of the difficulty of his position, and the greatness of the favor he must ask. "If one of the sisters could be spared . . . would volunteer to come . . . to help us with the nursing . . . I should be most grateful."

There was a pause. He could almost see her lips shape themselves to answer coldly: "You ordered us to remain in here. You forbade us to enter the town." Perhaps the sight of his face, worn, drawn, and heavy eyed, through the maze of snowflakes, restrained her. She said: "I will come."

His heart lifted. Despite her fixed antagonism toward him she was incomparably more efficient than Martha or Clotilde. "It means moving your quarters to the yamen. Wrap up warmly. And take all you need."

Ten minutes later he took her bag; they went down to the yamen together in silence. The dark lines of their footprints in the fresh snow were far apart.

Next morning sixteen of those admitted to the yamen were dead. But three times that number were coming in. It was pneumonic plague and its virulence surpassed the fiercest venom. People dropped with it as if bludgeoned and were dead before the next dawn. It seemed to congeal the blood, to rot the lungs, which threw up a thin white speckled sputum, swarming with lethal germs. Often one hour spaced the interval between a man's heedless laugh and the grin that was his death mask.

The three physicians of Pai-tan had failed to arrest the epidemic by the method of acupuncture. On the second day they ceased prickling the limbs of their patients with needles, and discreetly withdrew to a more salubrious practice.

By the end of that week the city was riddled from end to end. A wave of panic struck through the apathy of the people. The southern exits of the city were choked with carts, chairs, overburdened mules, and a struggling, hysterical populace.

The cold intensified. A great blight seemed to lie on the afflicted land, here and beyond. Dazed with overwork and lack of sleep, Francis nevertheless dimly sensed the calamity at Pai-tan to be but a portion of the major tragedy. He had no news. He did not grasp the immensity of the disaster: a hundred thousand miles of territory stricken, and half a million dead beneath the snow. Nor could he know that the eyes of the civilized world were bent in sympathy on China, that expeditions quickly organized in America and Britain had arrived to combat the disease.

His torturing suspense deepened daily. There was still no sign of Joseph's return. Would help never reach them from Sen-siang? A dozen times each day he plodded to the wharfside for the sight of the upcoming boat.

Then, at the beginning of the second week, Joseph suddenly appeared, weary and spent, but with a pale smile of achievement. He had encountered every obstacle. The countryside was in a ferment, Sen-siang a place of torment, the mission there ravaged by the disease. But he had persisted. He had sent his telegrams and bravely waited, hiding in his launch in a creek of the river. Now he had a letter. He produced it with a grimed and shaking hand. More: a doctor who knew the father, an old and respected friend of the father, would arrive on the supply boat!

With beating excitement, and a strange wild premonition, Father Chisholm took the letter from Joseph, opened it, and read:

Lord Leighton Relief Expedition
Chek-kow

Dear Francis,

I have been in China five weeks now with the Leighton expedition. This should not surprise you if you remember my youthful longings for the decks of oceangoing freighters and the exotic jungles that lay beyond. Quite truly, I thought I had forgotten all that nonsense myself. But at home, when they began asking for volunteers for the relief party, I suddenly surprised myself by joining up. It certainly was not the desire to become a national hero that prompted the absurd impulse. Probably a reaction, long deferred, against my humdrum life in Tynecastle. And perhaps, if I may say it, a very real hope of seeing you.

Anyhow, ever since we arrived, I've been working my way up-country, trying to push myself into your sacred presence. Your telegram to Nankin was turned over to our headquarters there and word of it reached me at Hai-chang next day.

I immediately asked Leighton, who is a very decent fellow, despite his title, if I might push off to give you a hand. He agreed and even let me have one of our few remaining power-boats. I've just reached Sen-siang and am collecting supplies. I will be along full steam ahead, probably arriving twenty-four hours behind your servant. Take care of yourself till then. All my news later.

In haste,
Yours,
Willie Tulloch

The priest smiled, slowly, for the first time in many days, and with a deep and secret warmth. He felt no great amazement; it was so typical of Tulloch to sponsor such a cause. He was braced, fortified by the unexpected fortune of his friend's arrival.

It was difficult to hold his eagerness in check. Next day when the relief boat was sighted he hastened to the wharf. Even before the launch drew alongside, Tulloch had stepped ashore, older, stouter, yet unchangeably the same dour quiet Scot, careless as ever in his dress, shy, strong and prejudiced as a Highland steer, as plain and honest as homespun tweed.

The priest's vision was absurdly blurred.

"Man, Francis, it's you!" Willie could say no more. He kept on shaking hands, confused by his emotion, debarred by his northern blood from more overt demonstration. At last he muttered, as if conscious of the need of speech: "When we walked down Darrow High Street we never dreamed we'd forgather in a place like this." He tried a half laugh, but with little success.

"Where's your coat and gum boots? You can't stroll through the pest in these shoes. It's high time I kept an eye on you."

"And on our hospital." Francis smiled.

"What!" The doctor's sandy eyebrows lifted. "You have a hospital of sorts? Let's see it."

"As soon as you are ready."

Instructing the crew of the launch to follow him with the supplies, Tulloch set off, at the priest's side, agile despite his increased girth, his eyes intent in his red hard-wearing face, his thinned hair showing a mass of freckles on his ruddy scalp as he punctuated his friend's brief report with comprehending nods.

At the end of it, as they reached the yamen, he remarked with a dry twinkle: "You might have done worse. Is this your center?" Across his shoulder he told his bearers to bring in the cases.

Inside the hospital he made a quick inspection, his eyes darting right, left, and with an odd curiosity toward Mother Maria-Veronica, who now accompanied them. He took a swift glance at Shon, when the young dandy came in, then firmly shook hands with him. Finally as they stood, all four, at the entrance to the long suite of rooms that formed the main ward, he addressed them quietly.

"I think you have done wonders. And I hope you don't expect melodramatic miracles from me. Forget all your preconceived ideas and face the truth—I'm not the dark handsome doctor with the portable laboratory. I'm here to work with you, like one of yourselves, which means . . . flatly . . . like a navvy. I haven't a drop of vaccine in my bag—in the first place because it isn't one damn bit of good outside the storybooks. And in the second because every flask we brought to China was used up in a week. Ye'll note," he inserted mildly, "it didn't check the epidemic. Remember! This is practically a fatal disease once it gets you. In such circumstances, as my old dad used to say," he smiled faintly, "an ounce of prevention is better than a ton of cure. That's why, if you don't mind, we'll turn our attention—not to the living—but to the dead."

There was a silence while they slowly grasped his meaning. Lieutenant Shon smiled.

"Cadavers are accumulating in the side streets at a disconcerting rate. It is discouraging to stumble in the darkness and fall into the arms of an unresponsive corpse."

Francis shot a quick glance at Maria-Veronica's expressionless face. Sometimes the young lieutenant was a little indiscreet.

The doctor had moved to the nearest crate and, with stolid competence, was prying off the lid.

"The first thing we do is fit you out properly. Oh! I know you two believe in God. And the lieutenant in Confucius." He bent and produced rubber boots from the case. "But I believe in prophylaxis."

He completed the unpacking of his supplies, fitting white overalls and goggles upon them, berating their negligence of their own safety. His remarks ran on, matter-of-fact, composed. "Don't you realize, you confounded innocents . . . one cough in your eye and you're done for . . . penetration of the cornea. They knew that even in the fourteenth century. . . . They wore visors of isinglass against this thing. . . . It was brought down from Siberia by a band of marmoset hunters. Well, now, I'll come back later, Sister, and have a real look at your patients. But first of all, Shon, the reverend and myself will take a peek round."

In his stress of mind, Francis had overlooked the grim necessity of swift interment before the germ-infested bodies were attacked by rats. Individual burial was impossible in that iron ground, and the supply of coffins had run out long ago. All the fuel in China would not have burned the bodies—for as Shon again remarked, nothing is less inflammable than frozen human flesh. One practical solution remained. They dug a great pit outside the walls, lined it with quicklime, and requisitioned carts. The loaded carts, driven by Shon's men, bumped through the streets and shot their cargo into this common grave.

Three days later, when the city was cleared and the stray carcasses half-devoured and dragged away by dogs, collected from the ice-encrusted fields, stricter measures were enforced. Afraid lest the spirits of their ancestors be defiled by an unholy tomb, people were hiding the bodies of their relatives, storing scores of infected corpses under the floorboards of their houses and in the kaolin roofs.

At the doctor's suggestion Lieutenant Shon promulgated an edict that all such hoarders would be shot. When the death carts rumbled through the city his soldiers shouted: "Bring out your dead. Or you yourselves will die."

Meanwhile, they were ruthlessly destroying certain properties that Tulloch had marked as breeding grounds of the disease. Experience and dire necessity made the doctor vengefully efficient. They entered, cleared the rooms, demolished the bamboo partitions with axes, spread kerosene, and made a pyre for the rats.

The Street of the Basket Makers was the first they razed. Returning, scorched and grimed, a hatchet still in his hand, Tulloch cast a queer glance at the priest, walking wearily beside him through the deserted streets. He said, in sudden compunction:

"This isn't your job, Francis. And you're worn so fine you're just about to drop. Why don't you get up the hill for a few days, back to those kids you're worrying yourself stiff over?"

"That would be a pretty sight. The man of God taking his ease while the city burns."

"Who is there to see you in this out-of-the-way hole?"

Francis smiled strangely. "We are not unseen."

Tulloch dropped the matter abruptly. Outside the yamen he swung round, gazing glumly at the redness still smoldering in the low dim sky. "The fire of London was a logical necessity." Suddenly his nerves rasped. "Damn it, Francis, kill yourself if you want to. But keep your motives to yourself."

The strain was telling on them. For ten days Francis had not been out of his clothes; they were stiff with frozen sweat. Occasionally he dragged his boots off, obeyed Tulloch's command to rub his feet with colza oil—even so his right great toe was inflamed with agonizing frostbite. He was dead with fatigue, but always there was more . . . more to be done.

They had no water, only melted snow; the wells were solid ice. Cooking was near impossible. Yet every day, Tulloch insisted that they all meet to have their midday meal together, to counteract the growing nightmare of their lives. At this hour, doggedly, he exerted himself to be cheerful, occasionally giving them Edison Bell selections on the phonograph he had brought out with him. He had a fund of North Country anecdotes, stories of the Tynecastle "Georgies," which he drew on freely. Sometimes he had the triumph of bringing a pale smile to Maria-Veronica's lips. Lieutenant Shon could never understand the jokes, though he listened politely while they were explained to him. Sometimes Shon was a little late in coming to the meal. Though they guessed that he was solacing some pretty lady who still, like themselves, survived, the empty chair took an unsuspected toll upon their nerves.

As the third week began Maria-Veronica showed signs of breaking down. Tulloch was bewailing the lack of floor space in the yamen, when she remarked: "If we took hammocks from the Street of the Net Makers we could house double our number of patients . . . more comfortably, too."

The doctor paused, gazed at her with grim approbation. "Why didn't I think of that before? It's a grand suggestion."

She colored deeply under his praise, cast down her eyes, and tried to go on with her dish of rice. But she could not. Her arm began to shake. It shook so violently the food dropped off her fork. She could not raise a grain of rice toward her lips. Her flush deepened, spread into her neck. Several times she repeated the attempt and failed. She sat with bent head, enduring the absurd humiliation. Then she rose without a word and left the table.

Later, Father Chisholm found her at work in the women's ward. He had never known such calm and pitiless self-sacrifice. She performed the most hateful duties for the sick, work that the lowest Chinese sweeper would have spurned. He dared not look at her, so unbearable had their relationship become. He had not addressed her directly for many days.

"Reverend Mother, Dr. Tulloch thinks . . . we all think you have been doing too much . . . that Sister Martha should come down to relieve you."

She had regained only a vestige of her cold aloofness. His suggestion disturbed her anew. She drew herself up. "You mean that I am not doing enough?"

"Far from it. Your work is magnificent."

"Then why attempt to keep me from it?" Her lips were trembling.

He said clumsily, "We are considering you."

His tone seemed to sting her to the quick. Holding back her tears, she answered passionately: "Do not consider me. The more work you give me . . . and the less sympathy . . . the better I shall like it."

He had to leave it at that. He raised his eyes to look at her, but her gaze was fixedly averted. He sadly turned away.

The snow, which had held off for a week, suddenly began again. It fell and fell unendingly. Francis had never seen such snow, the flakes so large and soft. Each added snowflake made an added silence. Houses were walled up in the silent whiteness. The streets were choked with drifts, hindering their work, increasing the sufferings of the sick. His heart was wrung again . . . again. In the endless days he lost all sense of time and place and fear. As he bent over the dying, succoring them with deep compassion in his eyes, stray thoughts swam through his dizzy brain. . . . Christ promised us suffering. . . . This life was given us only as a preparation for the next . . . when God will wipe all sorrow from our eyes, weeping and mourning shall be no more.

Now they were halting all nomads outside the walls, disinfecting and holding them in quarantine until assured of their freedom from the disease. As they came back from the isolation huts they had thrown up, Tulloch inquired of him, overtaxed, frayed to a raw anger:

"Is hell any worse than this?"

He answered, through the fog of his fatigue, blundering forward, unheroic, yet undismayed: "Hell is that state where one has ceased to hope."

None of them knew when the epidemic eased. There was no climax of achievement, no operatic crowning of their efforts. Visible evidence of death no longer lingered in the streets. The worst slums lay as dirty ashes on the snow. The mass flight from the northern provinces gradually ceased. It was as if a great dark cloud, immovably above them, were at last rolling slowly southward.

Tulloch expressed his feelings in a single dazed and jaded phrase.

"Your God alone knows if we've done anything, Francis . . . I think . . ." He broke off, haggard, limp, and for the first time seemed about to break. He swore. "The admissions are down again today. . . . Let's take time off, or I'll go mad."

That evening the two took a brief respite, for the first time, from the hospital and climbed to the mission to spend the night at the priest's house. It was after ten o'clock, and a few stars were faintly visible in the dark bowl of sky.

The doctor paused on the brow of the snow-embowered hill, which they had ascended with great effort, studying the soft outlines of the mission, lit by the whiteness of the earth. He spoke with unusual quietness: "It's a bonny place you've made, Francis. I don't wonder you've fought so hard to keep your little brats safe. Well, if I've helped at all, I'm mortal glad." His lips twitched. "It must be pleasant to spend your days here with a fine-looking woman like Maria-Veronica,"

The priest knew his friend too well to take offense. But he answered, with a strained and wounded smile:

"I'm afraid she does not find it agreeable."

"No?"

"You must have seen that she loathes me."

There was a pause. Tulloch gave the priest a queer glance.

"Your most endearing virtue, my holy man, has always been your painful lack of vanity." He moved on. "Let's go in and have some toddy. It's something to have worked through this scourge and to have the end of it in sight. It sort of lifts one up above the level of the brutes. But don't try to use that on me as an argument to prove the existence of the soul."

Seated in Francis's room they knew a moment of exhausted exaltation, talked of home late into the night. Briefly, Tulloch satirized his own career. He had done nothing, acquired nothing but a taste for whiskey. But now, in his sentimental middle age, aware of his limitations, having proved the fallacy of the world's wide-open spaces, he was hankering for his home in Darrow and the greater adventure of matrimony. He excused himself with a shamed smile.

"My dad wants me in the practice. Wants to see me raise a brood of young Ingersolls. Dear old boy, he never fails to mention you, Francis . . . his Roman Voltaire."

He spoke with rare affection of his sister Jean, now married and comfortably settled in Tynecastle. He said, oddly, not looking at Francis:

"It took her a long time to reconcile herself to the celibacy of the clergy."

His silence on the subject of Judy was strangely suspect. But he could not speak enough of Polly. He had met her six months ago in Tynecastle, still going strong. "What a woman!" He nodded across his glass. "Mark my words; she may astound you one day. Polly is, was, and always will be a holy trump." They slept in their chairs.

By the end of that week the epidemic showed further indications of abatement. Now the death carts seldom rattled through the streets, vultures ceased to swoop from the horizon, and snow no longer fell.

On the following Saturday Father Chisholm stood again on his balcony at the mission, inhaling the ice-cold air, with a deep and blessed thankfulness. From his vantage he could see the children playing in complete unconsciousness behind the tall kaolin fence. He felt like a man toward whom sweet daylight slowly filters after a long and dreadful dream.

Suddenly his gaze was caught by a figure of a soldier, dark against the snowbanks, moving rapidly up the road toward the mission. At first he took the man for one of the lieutenant's followers. Then, with some surprise, he saw that it was Shon himself.

This was the first time the young officer had visited him. A puzzled light hovered about Francis's eyes as he turned and went down the stairs to meet him.

On the doorstep, the sight of Shon's face stopped the welcome on his lips. It was lemon pale, tight drawn, and of a mortal gravity. A faint dew of perspiration on the brow bespoke his haste, as did the half-unbuttoned tunic, an unbelievable laxity in one so precise.

The lieutenant wasted no time. "Please come to the yamen at once. Your friend the doctor is taken ill."

Francis felt a great coldness, a cold shock, like the impact of a frigid blast. He shivered. He gazed back at Shon. After what seemed a long time he heard himself say: "He has been working too much. He has collapsed."

Shon's hard dark eyes winced imperceptibly. "Yes, he has collapsed."

There was another pause. Then Francis knew it was the worst. He turned pale. He set out, as he was, with the lieutenant.

They walked half the way in complete silence. Then Shon, with a military precision that suppressed all feeling, revealed briefly what had occurred. Dr. Tulloch had come in with a tired air and gone to take a drink. While he poured the drink he had coughed explosively, and steadied himself against the bamboo table, his face a dingy gray, except for the prune-juice froth upon his lips. As Maria-Veronica ran to help him, he gave her before he collapsed a weak, peculiar smile: "Now is the time to send for the priest."

When they reached the yamen a soft gray mist was drooping, like a tired cloud, across the snow-banked roofs. They entered quickly. Tulloch lay in the small end room, on his narrow camp bed, covered with a quilted mat of purple silk. The rich deep color of the quilt intensified his dreadful pallor, threw a livid shadow upon his face. It was agony for Francis to see how swiftly the fever had struck. Willie might have been a different man. He was shrunken, unbelievably, as though after weeks of wasting. His tongue and lips were swollen, his eyeballs glazed and shot with blood.

Beside the bed Maria-Veronica was kneeling, replenishing the pack of snow upon the sick man's forehead. She held herself erect—tensely, her expression rigid in its fixed control. She rose as Francis and the lieutenant entered. She did not speak.

Francis went over to the bedside. A great fear was in his heart. Death had walked with them these past few weeks, familiar and casual, a dreadful commonplace. But now that death's shadow lay upon his friend, the pain that struck at him was strange and terrible.

Tulloch was still conscious, the light of recognition remained in his congested gaze. "I came out for adventure." He tried to smile. "I seem to have got it." A moment later, he added, half-closing his eyes, as a kind of afterthought: "Man, I'm weak as a cat."

Francis sat down on the low stool at the head of the bed. Shon and Maria-Veronica were at the end of the room.

The stillness, the painful sense of waiting, was insupportable, growing, alike, with a frightful feeling of intrusion upon the privacy of things unknown.

"Are you quite comfortable?"

"I might be worse. Spare me a drop of that Japanese whiskey. It'll help me along. Man, it's an awful conventional thing to die like this . . . me that damned the storybooks."

When Francis had given him a sip of spirits he closed his eyes and seemed to rest. But soon he lapsed into a low delirium.

"Another drink, lad. Bless you, that's the stuff! I've drunk plenty in my time, round the slums of Tynecastle. And now I'm away home to dear old Darrow. On the banks of Allan Water, when the sweet springtime had fled. D'you mind that one, Francis . . . it's a bonny song. Sing it, Jean. Come on, louder, louder . . . I cannot hear you in the dark." Francis gritted his teeth, fighting the tumult in his breast. "That's right, Your Reverence. I'll keep quiet and save my strength. . . . It's a queer business . . . altogether . . . we've all got to toe the line sometime." Muttering, he sank into unconsciousness.

The priest knelt in prayer by the bedside. He prayed for help, for inspiration. But he was strangely dumb, gripped by a kind of stupor. The city outside was ghostly in its silence. Twilight came. Maria-Veronica rose to light the lamp, then returned to the far corner of the room outside the beam of lamplight, her lips unmoving, silent, but her fingers steadily enumerating the beads beneath her gown.

Tulloch was getting worse: his tongue black, his throat so swollen his bouts of vomiting were an agony to watch.

But suddenly he seemed to rally; he dimly opened his eyes.

"What o'clock is it?" His voice crouped huskily. "Near five . . . at home . . . that's when we had our tea. D'you mind, Francis, the crowd of us at the big round table . . . ?" A longer pause. ". . . Ye'll write the old man and tell him that his son died game. Funny . . . I still can't believe in God."

"Does that matter now?" What was he saying? Francis did not know. He was crying and, in the stupid humiliation of his weakness, the words came from him, in blind confusion. "He believes in you."

"Don't delude yourself . . . I'm not repentant."

"All human suffering is an act of repentance."

There was a silence. The priest said no more. Weakly, Tulloch reached out his hand and let it fall on Francis's arm.

"Man, I've never loved ye so much as I do now . . . for not trying to bully me to heaven. Ye see—" His lids dropped wearily. "I've such an awful headache."

His voice failed. He lay on his back, exhausted, his breathing quick and shallow, his gaze upturned as though fixed far beyond the ceiling. His throat was closed; he could not even cough.

The end was near. Maria-Veronica was kneeling now, at the window, her back toward them, her gaze directed fixedly into the darkness. Shon stood at the foot of the bed. His face was set immovably.

Suddenly Willie moved his eyes, in which a lingering spark still flickered. Francis saw that he was trying, vainly, to whisper.

He knelt, slipped his arm about the dying man's neck, brought his cheek close to the other's breath. At first he could hear nothing. Then weakly came the words: "Our fight . . . Francis . . . more than sixpence to get my sins forgiven."

The sockets of Tulloch's eyes filled up with shadow. He yielded to an unaccountable weariness. The priest felt rather than heard the last faint sigh. The room was suddenly more quiet. Still holding the body, as a mother might hold her child, he began blindly, in a low and strangled voice, the De Profundis.

"Out of the depths have I cried unto thee, O Lord. Lord, hear my voice . . . because with the Lord there is mercy: and with him plentiful redemption."

He rose at last, closed the eyes, composed the limp hands.

As he went out of the room he saw Sister Maria-Veronica still bowed at the window. As though still within a dream he gazed at the lieutenant. He saw, in a kind of dim surprise, that Shon's shoulders were shaking convulsively.

6

The plague had passed, but a great apathy gripped the snow-bound land. In the country the rice fields were frozen lakes. The few remaining peasants could not work a soil so mercilessly entombed. There was no sign of life. In the town, survivors emerged as from a painful hibernation, began dully to gather up their daily lives. The merchants and magistrates had not yet returned. It was said that many distant roads were quite impassable. None could remember such evil weather. All the passes were reported blocked and avalanches hurtled down the distant Kwangs like puffs of pure white smoke. The river, in its upper reaches, was frozen solid, a great gray wasteland over which the wind drove powder snow, in blinding desolation. Lower down there was a channel. Huge lumps of ice crashed and pounded in the current under the Manchu Bridge. Hardship was in every home, and famine lurked not far behind.

One boat had risked the jagged floes and steamed upriver from Sen-siang, bringing food and medical comforts from the Leighton expedition, and a long-delayed packet of letters. After a brief stay it had cast off, taking the remaining members of Dr. Tulloch's party back to Nankin.

In the mail that arrived, one communication surpassed the others in importance. As Father Chisholm came slowly up from the end of the mission garden where a small wooden cross marked Dr. Tulloch's grave, he bore this letter in his hand, and his thoughts were busy with the visit it announced. He hoped his work was satisfactory—the mission was surely worthy of his pride in it. If only the weather would break—thaw quickly—in the next two weeks!

When he reached the church Mother Maria-Veronica was coming down the steps. He must tell her—though he had come to dread these rare occasions when official business forced him to break the silence that lay between them.

"Reverend Mother . . . the provincial administrator of our foreign missions society, Canon Mealey, is making a tour of inspection of the Chinese missions. He sailed five weeks ago. He will arrive in about a month's time . . . to visit us." He paused. "I thought you'd like to have notice . . . in case there is anything you wish to put before him."

Muffled against the cold, she raised her gaze, impenetrable, behind the rimed vapor of her breath. Yet she started faintly. Now she so seldom saw him closely, the change that those last weeks had brought was strikingly manifest. He was thin, quite emaciated. The bones of his face had become prominent, the skin drawn tighter, cheeks slightly sunken, so that his eyes seemed larger and oddly luminous. A terrible impulse took possession of her.

"There is only one thing I wish to put before him." She spoke instinctively, the sudden news lifting from the recesses of her soul a deeply buried thought. "I shall ask to be transferred to another mission."

There was a long pause. Though not wholly taken by surprise, he felt chilled, defeated. He sighed. "You are unhappy here?"

"Happiness has nothing to do with it. As I told you, when I entered the religious life I prepared myself to endure everything."

"Even the enforced association of someone whom you despise?"

She colored with a proud defiance. That deep throbbing in her bosom drove her to continue. "You mistake me completely. It is obvious. It is something deeper . . . spiritual."

"Spiritual? Will you try to tell me?"

"I feel," she took a quick breath, "that you are upsetting me . . . in my inner life . . . my spiritual beliefs."

"That is a serious matter." He stared at the letter unseeingly, twisting it in his bony hands. "It hurts me . . . as much, I am sure, as it hurts you to say it. But perhaps you have misunderstood me. To what do you refer?"

"Do you think I have prepared a list?" Despite her control she felt her agitation rising. "It is your attitude. . . . For instance, some remarks you made when Dr. Tulloch was dying . . . and afterward, when he was dead."

"Please go on."

"He was an atheist, and yet you virtually promised he would have his eternal reward . . . he who didn't believe . . ."

He said quickly: "God judges us not only by what we believe . . . but by what we do."

"He was not a Catholic . . . not even a Christian!"

"How do you define a Christian? One who goes to church one day of the seven and lies, slanders, cheats his fellow men the other six?" He smiled faintly. "Dr. Tulloch didn't live like that. And he died—helping others . . . like Christ himself."

She repeated stubbornly: "He was a freethinker."

"My child, our Lord's contemporaries thought him a dreadful freethinker. . . . That's why they killed him."

She was pale now, quite distraught. "It is inexcusable to make such a comparison—outrageous!"

"I wonder! . . . Christ was a very tolerant man—and humble."

A rush of color again flooded her cheek. "He made certain rules. Your Dr. Tulloch did not obey them. You know that. Why, when he was unconscious, at the end, you did not even administer extreme unction."

"No, I didn't! And perhaps I should have." He stood, thinking worriedly, rather depressed. Then he seemed to cheer up. "But the good God may forgive him none the less." He paused, with simple frankness. "Didn't you love him too?"

She hesitated, lowered her eyes. "Yes. . . . Who could help that?"

"Then don't let us make his memory the occasion of a quarrel. There is one thing we most of us forget. Christ taught it. The church teaches it . . . though you wouldn't think so to hear a great many of us today. No one in good faith can ever be lost. No one. Buddhists, Mohammedans, Taoists . . . the blackest cannibals who ever devoured a missionary . . . if they are sincere, according to their own lights, they will be saved. That is the splendid mercy of God. So why shouldn't he enjoy confronting a decent agnostic at the judgment seat with a twinkle in his eye: 'I'm here you see, in spite of all they brought you up to believe. Enter the kingdom that you honestly denied.'" He made to smile, then, seeing her expression, sighed and shook his head. "I'm truly sorry you feel as you do. I know I'm hard to get on with, and perhaps a little odd in my beliefs. But you've worked so wonderfully here. . . . The children love you . . . and during the plague . . ." He broke off. "I know we haven't got on very well . . . but the mission would suffer terribly if you should go."

He gazed at her with a queer intentness, a sort of strained humility. He waited for her to speak. Then, as she did not, he slowly took his leave.

She continued on her way to the refectory where she superintended the serving of the children's dinner. Later, in her own bare room, she paced up and down in a strange continuance of her agitation. Suddenly, with a gesture of despair, she sat down and set herself to complete a further passage in another of those lengthy letters in which, from day to day, as the outlet for her emotions, a penance and a consolation, she compiled the record of her doings for her brother.

Pen in hand, she seemed calmer; the act of writing seemed to tranquilize her.

"I have just told him I must ask to be transferred. It came suddenly, a sort of climax to all I have suppressed, and something of a threat as well. I was amazed at myself, startled by the words issuing from my lips. Yet when the opportunity presented itself

I could not resist; I wanted instantly to startle, to hurt him. But, my dear, dear Ernst, I am no happier. . . . After that second of triumph when I saw dismay cloud his face I am even more restless and distressed. I look out at the vast desolation of these gray wastes—so different from our cozy winter landscape with its golden air, its sleigh bells and clustered chalet roofs—and I want to cry . . . as if my heart would break.

"It is his silence that defeats me—that stoic quality of enduring, and of fighting, all without speech. I've told you of his work during the plague, when he went about among foul sickness and sudden repulsive death as carelessly as if he were walking down the main street of his dreadful Scottish village. Well, it wasn't merely his courage, but the muteness of that courage, which was so unbelievably heroic. When his friend, the doctor, died, he held him in his arms, unmindful of the contagion, of that final cough that spattered his cheek with clotted blood. And the look upon his face . . . in its compassion and utter selflessness . . . it pierced my heart. Only my pride saved me the humiliation of weeping in his sight! Then I became angry. What irks me most of all is that I once wrote you that he was despicable. Ernst, I was wrong—what an admission from your stubborn sister!—I can no longer despise him. Instead I despise myself. But I detest him. And I won't, I won't let him beat me down to his level of harrowing simplicity.

"The two others here have both been conquered. They love him—that is another mortification I must sustain. Martha, the stolid peasant, with bunions but no brains, is prepared to adore anything in a cassock. But Clotilde, shy and timid, flushing on the slightest provocation, a gently sweet and sensitive creature, has become a perfect devotee. During her enforced quarantine she worked him a thick quilted bed mat, soft and warm, really beautiful. She took it to Joseph, his servant, with instructions to place it on the father's bed—she is much too modest even to whisper the word *bed* in his hearing. Joseph smiled: 'I am sorry, Sister; there is no bed!' It appears he sleeps upon the bare floor, with no covering but his overcoat, a greenish garment of uncertain age, which he is fond of, and of which, caressing the frayed and threadbare sleeves, he says proudly, 'Actually! I had it when I was a student at Holywell!'

"Martha and Clotilde have been making inquiries in his kitchen, nervous and perturbed, convinced that he does not look after himself. Their expressions, like shocked tabbies, almost made me laugh as they told me what I already knew, that he eats nothing but black bread, potatoes, and bean curd.

"'Joseph has instructions to boil a pot of potatoes and place them in a wicker basket,' Clotilde mewed. 'He eats one cold when he is hungry, dipping it in bean curd. Often they are quite musty before the basketful is finished.'

"'Isn't it dreadful?' I answered curtly. 'But then some stomachs have never known a good cuisine—it is not hardship for them to do without it.'

"'Yes, Reverend Mother,' murmured Clotilde, blushing, and retreating.

"She would do penance for a week to come and see him eat one nice hot meal. Oh, Ernst, you know how I abominate the sedulous and fawning nun who in the presence of a priest exposes the whites of her eyes and dissolves in obsequious rapture. Never, never, will I descend to such a level. I vowed it at Koblenz when I took the veil, and again at Liverpool . . . and will keep that vow . . . even in Pai-tan. But bean curd! *You* will not encounter it. A thin pinkish paste tasting of stagnant water and chewed wood!" She raised her head at an unexpected sound. "Ernst . . . it is unbelievable. . . . It is raining. . . ." She stopped writing, as if unable to continue, and slowly laid down her pen. With dark and self-distrustful eyes she sat watching the novelty of the rain, which trickled down the pane like heavy tears.

A fortnight later it was still raining. The skies, dull as tallow, were open sluices from which a steady deluge fell. The drops were large, pitting the upper crust of yellowish snow. It seemed everlasting . . . the snow. Great frozen slabs of it still came sliding from the church roof, with unpremeditated acceleration, landing soddenly upon the slushy snow beneath. Rivulets of rain went rushing across the dun-colored sludge, channeling, undercutting the banks, which toppled with a slow splash into the stream beneath. The mission was a quagmire of slush.

Then the first patch of brown earth appeared, momentous as the tip of Ararat. Further patches sprouted and coalesced, forming a landscape of bleached grass and scabby desert all fissured and cratered with the flood. And still the rain continued. The mission roofs broke down at last and leaked incessantly. Water came in cataracts from the eaves. The children sat, green and miserable, in the classroom, while Sister Martha placed pails for the larger drips. Sister Clotilde had a dreadful cold and took lessons at her desk beneath Reverend Mother's umbrella.

The light soil of the mission garden could not withstand the scouring fusion of rain and thaw. It swept down the hill in a yellow turbulence on which floated up-torn *sareta* plants and oleander shrubs. Carp from the fishpond darted frightened, through the flood. The trees were slowly undermined. For a painful day the lychees and catalpas stood upright on their naked roots, which groped like pallid tentacles, then slowly toppled. The young white mulberries followed next, then the lovely row of flowering plum, these on the day that the lower wall was washed away. Only the toughened cedars stood, with the giant banyan, amid the muddied desolation.

On the afternoon before Canon Mealey's arrival Father Chisholm heavily surveyed the dreary havoc on his way to children's benediction. He turned to Fu, the gardener, who stood beside him.

"I wished for a thaw. The good God has punished me by sending one."

Fu, like most gardeners, was not a cheerful man. "The great Shang-Foo who arrives from across the seas will think much ill of us. Ah! If only he had seen my bloom of lilies last spring!"

"Let us be of good heart, Fu. The damage is not irreparable."

"My plantings are lost." Fu gloomed. "We shall have to begin all over again."

"That is life . . . to begin again when everything is lost!"

Despite his exhortation, Francis was deeply depressed as he went into the church. Kneeling before the lighted altar, while the rain still drummed upon the roof, he seemed to hear, above the childish treble of the *Tantum Ergo,* a liquid murmuring beneath him. But the sound of flowing water had long been echoing in his ears. His mind was burdened by the wretched appearance that the mission must present to his visitor upon the following day. He put the thing away as an obsession.

When the service was over and Joseph had snuffed the candles and left the sacristy he came slowly down the aisle. A dank vapor hung about the whitewashed nave. Sister Martha had taken the children across the compound for their supper. But still in prayer upon the damp boards were Reverend Mother and Sister Clotilde. He passed them in silence; then suddenly stopped short. Clotilde's running head catarrh made her a spectacle of woe and Maria-Veronica's lips were drawn with cold. He had an extraordinary inner conviction that they should neither of them be allowed to remain.

He stepped back to them and said: "I am sorry, I'm going to close the church now."

There was a pause. This interference was unlike him. They seemed surprised. But they rose obediently, in silence, and preceded him to the porch. He locked the front doors and followed them through the streaming dusk.

A moment later the sound broke upon them. A low rumble, swelling to a roll of subterranean thunder. As Sister Clotilde screamed, Francis swung round to see the slender structure of his church in motion. Glistening, wetly luminous, it swayed gracefully in the fading light; then, like a reluctant woman, yielded. His heart stood still in horror. With a rending crash, the undermined foundations broke. One side caved in, the roof's spire snapped; the rest was a blinding vision of torn timbers and shattered glass. Then his church, his lovely church, lay dissolved into nothing at his feet.

He stood rooted, for an instant, in a daze of pain, then ran toward the wreckage. But the altar lay smashed to rubble, the tabernacle crushed to splinters beneath a beam. He could not even save the sacred species. And his vestments, the precious Ribiero relic, these were in shreds. Standing there, bareheaded in the teeming rain, he was conscious, amid the frightened babble that now surrounded him, of Sister Martha's lamentation.

"Why . . . why . . . why has this come on us?" She was moaning, wringing her hands. "Dear God! What worse could you have done to us?"

He muttered, not moving, desperately sustaining his own faith rather than hers:

"Ten minutes sooner . . . we should every one of us have been killed."

There was nothing to be done. They left the fallen wreckage to the darkness and the rain.

Next day, at three o'clock punctually, Canon Mealey arrived. Because of the turbulence of the flooded river, his junk had dropped anchor in a backwater five *li* below Pai-tan. There were no chairs available: only some wheelbarrows, long-shafted like ploughs, with solid wooden wheels that, since the plague, were used by the few remaining runners to transport their passengers. The situation was difficult for a man of dignity. But there was no alternative. The canon, mud-spattered and with dangling legs, reached the mission in a wheelbarrow.

The modest reception rehearsed by Sister Clotilde—a song of welcome, with waving of little flags, by the children—had been abandoned. Watching from his balcony, Father Chisholm hurried to the gate to meet his visitor.

"My dear Father!" cried Mealey, stiffly straightening himself and warmly grasping both Francis's hands. "This is the happiest day in many months—to see you again. I told you I should one day run the gamut of the Orient. With the interest of the world centered upon suffering China it was inevitable my resolve should crystallize to action!" He broke off, his eye bulging across the other's shoulder at the scene of desolation. "Why . . . I don't understand. Where is the church?"

"You see all that is left of it."

"But this mess . . . you reported a splendid establishment."

"We have had some reverses." Francis spoke quietly.

"Why, really, it's incomprehensible . . . most disturbing."

Francis intervened with a hospitable smile. "When you have had a hot bath and a change I will tell you."

An hour later, pink from his tub, in a new tussah suit, Anselm sat stirring his hot soup, with an aggrieved expression.

"I must confess this is the greatest disappointment of my life . . . to come here, to the very outposts . . ." He took a mouthful of soup, meeting the spoon with plump, pursed lips. He had filled out in these last years. He was big now, full shouldered and stately, still smooth skinned and clear-eyed, with big palps of hands, hearty or pontifical at will. "I had set my heart on celebrating High Mass in your church, Francis. These foundations must have been badly laid."

"It is a wonder they were laid at all."

"Nonsense! You've had lots of time to establish yourself. What in heaven's name am I to tell them at home?" He laughed shortly, dolefully. "I even promised a lecture at London headquarters of the FMS—'St. Andrew's: or God in Darkest China.' I'd brought my quarter plate Zeiss to get lantern slides. It places me . . . all of us . . . in a most awkward position."

There was a silence.

"Of course I know you've had your difficulties," Mealey continued between annoyance and compunction. "But who hasn't? I assure you we've had ours. Especially lately since we merged the two divisions . . . after Bishop MacNabb's death!"

Father Chisholm stiffened, as in pain.

"He's dead?"

"Yes, yes, the old man went at last. Pneumonia—this March. He was past his best, very muddled and queer, quite a relief to all of us when he went, very peacefully. The coadjutor, Bishop Tarrant, succeeded him. A great success."

Again a silence fell. Father Chisholm raised his hand to shield his eyes. Rusty Mac gone. . . . A rush of unbearable recollection swept him: that day by the Stinchar, the glorious salmon, those kind wise peering eyes and the warmth of them when he was worried at Holywell; the quiet voice in the study at Tynecastle before he sailed, "Keep fighting, Francis, for God and good old Scotland."

Anselm was reflecting, with friendly generosity: "Well, well! We must face things, I suppose. Now that I'm here I'll do my best to get things straight for you. I've a great deal of organizing experience. It may interest you, some day, to hear how I have put the society on its feet. In my personal appeals, delivered in London, Liverpool, and Tynecastle, I raised thirty thousand pounds—and that is only the beginning." He showed his sound teeth in a competent smile. "Don't be so depressed, my dear fellow. I'm not unduly censorious. . . . The first thing we'll do is have Reverend Mother over to lunch—she seems an able woman—and have a real roundtable parochial conference!"

With an effort Francis pulled himself back from the dear forgotten days. "Reverend Mother doesn't care to take her meals outside the sisters' house."

"You haven't asked her properly." Mealey gazed at the other's spare figure with a hearty, pitying kindliness. "Poor Francis! I'd hardly expect you to understand women. She'll come all right . . . just leave it to me!"

On the following day, Maria-Veronica did, in fact, present herself for lunch. Anselm was in high spirits after an excellent night's rest and an energetic morning of inspection. Still benevolent from his visit to the schoolroom, he greeted the reverend mother, though he had parted from her only five minutes before, with effusive dignity.

"This, Reverend Mother, is indeed an honor. A glass of sherry? No? I assure you it is fine—pale amontillado. A little traveled perhaps," he beamed, "since it came with me from home. Coddlesome, maybe . . . but a palate, acquired in Spain, is hard to deny."

They sat down at table.

"Now, Francis, what are you giving us? No Chinese mysteries, I trust, no bird's nest soup or puree of chopsticks. Ha! Ha!" Mealey laughed heartily as he helped himself to boiled chicken. "Though I must confess I am somewhat enamored of the Oriental cuisine. Coming over on the boat—a stormy passage, incidentally; for four days no one appeared at the skipper's table but your humble servant—we were served with a quite delicious Chinese dish, chow mein."

Mother Maria-Veronica raised her eyes from the tablecloth. "Is chow mein a Chinese dish? Or an American edition of the Chinese custom of collecting scraps?"

He stared at her, mouth slightly agape. "My dear Reverend Mother! Chow mein! Why . . ." He glanced at Francis for support, found none, and laughed again. "At any rate, I assure you, I chewed mine! Ha! Ha!"

Swinging round, for better access to the dish of salad that Joseph was presenting, he ran on: "Food apart, the lure of the Orient is immensely fascinating! We Occidentals are too apt to condemn the Chinese as a greatly inferior race. Now I for one will shake hands with any Chinaman, provided he believes in God and . . ." he bubbled . . . "carbolic soap!"

Father Chisholm shot a quick glance at Joseph's face, which, though expressionless, showed a faint tightening of the nostrils.

"And now," Mealey paused suddenly, his manner dropping to pontifical solemnity. "We have important business on our agenda. As a boy, Reverend Mother, our good mission father was always leading me into scrapes. Now it's my task to get him out of this one!"

Nothing definite emerged from the conference. Except, perhaps, a modest summary of Anselm's achievements at home.

Free of the limitations of a parish, he had set himself wholeheartedly to work for the missions, mindful that the Holy Father was especially devoted to the propagation of the faith and eager to encourage the workers who so selflessly espoused his favorite cause.

It had not been long before he won recognition. He began to move about the country, to preach sermons of impassioned eloquence in the great English cities. Through his genius for collecting friends, no contact of any consequence was ever thrown away. On his return from Manchester, or Birmingham, he would sit down and write a score of charming letters, thanking this person for a delightful lunch, the next for a generous donation to the foreign mission fund. Soon his correspondence was voluminous, and employed a full-time secretary.

Presently, London acknowledged him as a distinguished visitor. His debut, in the pulpit of Westminster, was spectacular. Women had always idolized him. Now he was adopted by the wealthy coterie of cathedral spinsters who collected cats and clergymen in their rich mansions south of the park. His manners had always been engaging. That same year he became a country member of the athenaeum. And the sudden engorgement of the FM moneybags evoked a most gracious token of appreciation, direct from Rome.

When he became the youngest canon in the northern diocese, few grudged him the success. Even the cynics who traced his exuberant rise to an overactive thyroid gland admitted his business acumen. For all his gush he was no fool. He had a level head for figures and could manage money. In five years he had founded two fresh missions in Japan and a native seminary in Nankin. The new FMS offices in Tynecastle were imposing, efficient, and completely free of debt.

In brief, Anselm had made a fine thing of his life. With Bishop Tarrant at his elbow there was every chance that his most admirable work would continue to expand.

Two days after his official meeting with Francis and Reverend Mother, the rain ceased and a watery sun sent pale feelers toward the forgotten earth. Mealey's spirits bounded. He joked to Francis.

"I've brought fine weather with me. Some people follow the sun around. But the sun follows me."

He unlimbered his camera and began to take countless photographs. His energy was tremendous. He bounded out of bed in the morning shouting "Boy! Boy!" for Joseph to get his bath. He said Mass in the schoolroom. After a hearty breakfast he departed in his solar topee, a stout stick in hand, the camera swinging on his hip.

He made many excursions, even poking discreetly for souvenirs amongst the ashes of Pai-tan's plague spots. At each scene of blackened desolation he murmured reverently: "The hand of God!" He would stop suddenly, at a city gate, arresting his companion with a dramatic gesture. "Wait! I must get this one. The light is perfect."

On Sunday, he came in to lunch greatly elated. "It's just struck me; I can still give that lecture. Treat it from the angle of dangers and difficulties in the mission field. Work in the plague and the flood. This morning I got a glorious view of the ruins of the church. What a slide it will make, titled 'God Chastiseth His Own'! Isn't that magnificent?"

But on the eve of his departure Anselm's manner altered, and his tone, as he sat with the mission priest on the balcony after supper, was grave.

"I have to thank you for extending hospitality to a wanderer, Francis. But I am not happy about you. I can't see how you are going to rebuild the church. The society cannot let you have the money."

"I haven't asked for it." The strain of the past two weeks was beginning to tell on Francis, his stern self-discipline was wearing thin.

Mealey threw his companion a sharp glance. "If only you had been more successful with some of the better-class Chinese, the rich merchants. If only your friend Mr. Chia had seen the light."

"He hasn't." Father Chisholm spoke with unusual shortness. "And he has given munificently. I shall not ask him for another tael."

Anselm shrugged his shoulders, annoyed. "Of course that's your affair. But I must tell you, frankly, I'm sadly disappointed in your conduct of this mission. Take your convert rate. It doesn't compare with our other statistics. We run them as a graph at headquarters, and you're the lowest in the whole chart."

Father Chisholm gazed straight ahead, his lips firmly compressed. He answered with unusual irony: "I suppose missionaries differ in their individual capabilities."

"And in their enthusiasm." Anselm, sensitive to satire, was now justly incensed. "Why do you persist in refusing to employ catechists? It's the universal custom. If you had even three active men, at forty taels a month, why, one thousand baptisms would only cost you fifteen hundred Chinese dollars!"

Francis did not answer. He was praying desperately that he might control his temper, suffer this humiliation as something he deserved.

"You're not getting behind your work here," Mealey went on. "You live, personally, in such poor style. You ought to impress the natives, keep a chair, servants; make more of a show."

"You are mistaken." Francis spoke steadily. "The Chinese hate ostentation. They call it *ti-mien*. And priests who practice it are regarded as dishonorable."

Anselm flushed angrily. "You're referring to their own low heathen priests, I presume."

"Does it matter?" Father Chisholm smiled palely. "Many of these priests are good and noble men."

There was a strained silence. Anselm drew his coat about him with a shocked finality.

"After that, of course, there is nothing to be said. I must confess your attitude pains me deeply. Even Reverend Mother is embarrassed by it. Ever since I arrived it has been plain how much she is at variance with you." He got up and went into his own room.

Francis remained a long time in the gathering mist. That last remark had cut him worst of all: the stab of a premonition confirmed. Now he had no doubt that Maria-Veronica had submitted her request to be transferred.

Next morning Canon Mealey took his departure. He was returning to Nankin to spend a week at the vicariate and would go from there to Nagasaki to inspect six missions in Japan. His bags were packed; a chair waited to bear him to the junk; he had taken his farewells of the sisters and the children. Now, dressed for the journey, wearing sunglasses, his topee draped with green gauze, he stood in final conversation with Father Chisholm in the hall.

"Well, Francis!" Mealey extended his hand in grudging forgiveness. "We must part friends. The gift of tongues is not given to all of us. I suppose you are a well-meaning fellow at heart." He threw out his chest. "Strange! I'm itching to be off. I have travel in my blood. Good-bye. Au revoir. Auf Wiedersehen. And last but not least—God bless you!"

Dropping the mosquito veil he stepped into his chair. The runners groaningly bent their shoulders, supported him, and shuffled off. At the sagging mission gates he leaned through the window of the chair, fluttered his white handkerchief in farewell.

At sundown, when he took his evening walk, his beloved hour of stealing twilight and far-off echoing stillness, Father Chisholm found himself meditating, among the debris of the church. He seated himself upon a lump of rubble, thinking of his old headmaster—somehow he always saw Rusty Mac with schoolboy's eyes—and of his exhortation to courage. There was little courage in him now. These last two weeks, the perpetual effort to sustain his visitor's patronizing tone, had left him void. Yet perhaps Anselm was justified. Was he not a failure, in God's sight and in man's? He had done so little. And that little, so labored and inadequate, was almost undone. How was he to proceed? A weary hopelessness of spirit took hold of him.

Resting there, with bent head, he did not hear a footstep behind him. Mother Maria-Veronica was compelled to make her presence known to him.

"Am I disturbing you?"

He glanced up, quite startled. "No . . . no. As you observe," he could not suppress a wincing smile, "I am doing nothing."

There was a pause. In the indistinctness her face had a swimming pallor. He could not see the nerve twitching in her cheek, yet he sensed in her figure a strange rigidity.

Her voice was colorless. "I have something to say to you. I—"

"Yes?"

"This is no doubt humiliating for you. But I am obliged to tell you. I—I am sorry." The words, torn from her, gained momentum, then came in a tumbled flood. "I am most bitterly and grievously sorry for my conduct toward you. From our first meeting I have behaved shamefully, sinfully. The devil of pride was in me. It's always been in me, ever since I was a little child and flung things at my nurse's head. I have known now for weeks that I wanted to come to you . . . to tell you . . . but my pride, my stubborn malice restrained me. These past ten days, in my heart, I have wept for you . . . the slights and humiliations you have endured from that gross and worldly priest, who is unworthy to untie your shoe. Father, I hate myself—forgive me, forgive me . . ." Her voice was lost; she crouched, sobbing into her hands, before him.

The sky was strained of all color, except the greenish afterglow behind the peaks. This faded swiftly, and the kind dusk enfolded her. An interval of time, in which a single tear fell upon her check. . . .

"So now you will not leave the mission?"

"No, no . . ." Her heart was breaking. "If you will let me stay. I have never known anyone whom I wished so much to serve. . . . Yours is the best . . . the finest spirit I have ever known."

"Hush, my child. I am a poor and insignificant creature . . . you were right . . . a common man . . ."

"Father, pity me." Her sobs went choking into the earth.

"And you are a great lady. But in God's sight we are both of us children. If we may work together . . . help each other . . ."

"I will help with all my power. One thing at least I can do. It is so easy to write to my brother. He will rebuild the church . . . restore the mission. He has great possessions; he will do it gladly. If only you will help me . . . help me to defeat my pride."

There was a long silence. She sobbed more softly. A great warmth filled his heart. He took her arm to raise her but she would not rise. So he knelt beside her and gazed, without praying, into the pure and peaceful night where, across the ages, among the shadows of a garden, another poor and common man also knelt and watched them both.

7

One sunny forenoon in the year 1912 Father Chisholm was separating beeswax from his season's yield of honey. His workshop, built in Bavarian style, at the end of the kitchen garden—trim, practical, with a pedal lathe and tools neatly racked, as much a source of delight to him as on the day Mother Maria-Veronica had handed him the key—was sweet with the fume of melted sugar. A great bowl of cool yellow honey stood among fresh shavings upon the floor. On the bench, setting, was the flat copper pan of tawny wax from which, tomorrow, he would make his candles. And such candles—smooth burning and sweet scented; even in St. Peter's one would not find the like!

With a sigh of contentment, he wiped his brow; his short fingernails blobbed with the rich wax. Then, shouldering the big honey jar, he pulled the door behind him and set off through the mission grounds. He was happy. Waking in the morning with the starlings chattering in the eaves, and the coolness of the dawn still dewed upon the grass, his second thought was that there could be no greater happiness than to work—much with his hands, a little with his head, but mostly with his heart—and to live, simply, like this, close to the earth which, to him, never seemed far from heaven.

The province was prospering, and the people, forgetting flood, pestilence, and famine, were at peace. In the five years that had elapsed since its reconstruction, through the generosity of Count Ernst von Hohenlohe, the mission had flourished in a quiet fashion. The church was bigger, stouter than the first. He had built it solidly, with grim compunction, using neither plaster nor stucco, after the monastic model that Queen Margaret had introduced to Scotland centuries before. Classic and severe, with a simple bell tower, and aisles supported by groined arches, its plainness grew on him until he preferred it to the other. And it was safe.

The school had been enlarged, a new children's home added to the building. And the purchase of the two adjoining irrigated fields provided a model home farm with pigpen, byre, and a chicken run down which Martha stalked, thin shanked, in wooden shoes and kilted habit, casting corn and clucking joyously in Flemish.

Now his congregation comprised two hundred faithful souls, not one of whom knelt under duress before his altar. The orphanage had trebled in size and was beginning to bear the first fruits of his patient foresight. The older girls helped the sisters with the little ones; some were already novices; others would soon be going into the world. Why, last Christmas he had married the eldest, at nineteen, to a young farmer from the Liu village. He smiled ruefully at the implications of his cunning. At his recent pastoral visit to Liu—a happy and successful expedition from which he had returned only last week—the young wife had hung her head and told him he must return presently to perform another baptism.

As he shifted the heavy honey to his other shoulder, a bent little man of forty-three, growing bald, with rheumatism already nibbling at his joints, a bough of jasmine flailed him on the cheek. The garden had seldom been so lovely: that, also, he owed to Maria-Veronica. Admitting some adroitness with his hands, he could not remotely claim to have green fingers. But Reverend Mother had revealed an unsuspected skill in growing things. Seeds had arrived from her home in Germany, bundles of shoots wrapped tenderly in sacking. Her letters, begging for this cutting and for that, had sped to famous gardens in Canton and Pekin—like his own swift white doves, importunate and homing. This beauty that now surrounded him, this sun-shot sanctuary, alive with twittering hum, was her work.

Their comradeship was not unlike this precious garden. Here, indeed, when he took his evening walk, he would find her, intent, coarsely gloved, cutting the full white peonies that grew so freely, training a stray clematis, watering the golden azaleas. There they would briefly discuss the business of the day. Sometimes they did not speak. When the fireflies flitted in the garden they had gone their separate ways.

As he approached the upper gate he saw the children march in twos across the compound. Dinner. He smiled and hastened. They were seated at the long low table in the new annex to the dormitory, two-score little blue-black polls and shining yellow faces, with Maria-Veronica at one end, Clotilde at the other. Martha, aided by the Chinese novices, was ladling steaming rice broth into a battery of blue bowls. Anna, his foundling of the snow, now a handsome girl, handed round the bowls with her usual air of dark and frowning reserve.

The clamor stilled upon his entry. He shot a shamed boyish look at the reverend mother, craving indulgence, and placed the honey jar triumphantly on the table.

"Fresh honey today, children! It is a great pity. I am sure no one wishes it!"

Shrill, immediate denial rose like the chatter of little monkeys. Suppressing his smile, he shook his head dolefully at the youngest, a solemn mandarin of three who sat swallowing his spoon, swaying dreamily, his soft small buttocks unstable on the bench.

"I cannot believe a good child could enjoy such monstrous depravity! Tell me, Symphorien—" It was dreadful the way in which new converts chose the most resounding saint names for their children—"Tell me, Symphorien . . . would you not rather learn nice catechism than eat honey?"

"Honey!" answered Symphorien dreamily. He stared at the lined brown face above him. Then, surprised by his own temerity, he burst into tears and fell off the bench.

Laughing, Father Chisholm picked up the child. "There, there! You are a good boy, Symphorien. God loves you. And for speaking the truth you shall have double honey."

He felt Maria-Veronica's reproving gaze upon him. She would presently follow him to the door and murmur: "Father . . . we must consider discipline!" But today—it seemed so long since he stood outside the buzzing classroom, troubled and unhappy, afraid to penetrate the chill unfriendly air—nothing could restrain his manner with the children. His fondness toward them had always been absurd; it was what he named his patriarchal privilege.

As he expected, Maria-Veronica accompanied him from the room but, though her brow seemed unusually clouded, she did not even mildly rebuke him. Instead, after some hesitation, she remarked: "Joseph had a strange story this morning."

"Yes. The rascal wants to get married . . . naturally. But he is deafening me with the beauties and convenience of a lodge . . . to be built at the mission gate . . . not, of course, for Joseph or for Joseph's wife . . . but solely for the benefit of the mission."

"No, it isn't the lodge." Unsmiling, she bit her lip. "The building is taking place elsewhere, in the Street of the Lanterns—you know that splendid central site—and on a grander scale, much grander than anything we have accomplished here." Her tone was strangely bitter. "Scores of workmen have arrived, barges of white stone from Sen-siang. Everything. I assure you money is being spent as only American millionaires can spend it. Soon we shall have the finest establishment in Pai-tan, with schools, for both boys and girls, a playground, public rice kitchen, free dispensary, and a hospital with resident doctor!" She broke off, gazing at him with tears in her troubled eyes.

"What establishment?" He spoke automatically, stunned by a presage of her answer.

"Another mission. Protestant. The American Methodists."

There was a long pause. Secure in the remoteness of his situation, he had never contemplated even the possibility of such intrusion. Reverend Mother, recalled to the refectory by Clotilde, left him in painful silence.

He walked slowly toward his house, all the brightness of the morning dimmed. Where was his medieval fortress now? In a quick throwback to his childhood, he had the same sensation of injustice as when, out berry picking, another boy had encroached upon a secret bush of his own discovery and rudely begun to strip it of its fruit. He knew the hatreds that developed between rival missions, the ugly jealousies, above all, the bickerings on points of doctrine, the charge and countercharge, the raucous denunciation that made the Christian faith appear, to the tolerant Chinese mind, an infernal Tower of Babel where all shouted at lung pitch: "Behold, it is here! Here! Here!" But where? Alas! When one looked, there was nothing but rage and sound and execration.

At his house he found Joseph, duster in hand, idling about the hall, in pretense of work, waiting to bemoan the news.

"Has the father heard of the hateful coming of these Americans who worship the false God?"

"Be silent, Joseph!" The priest answered harshly. "They do not worship the false God, but the same true God as we. If you speak such words again you will never get your gatehouse!"

Joseph edged away, grumbling beneath his breath.

In the afternoon Father Chisholm went down to Pai-tan and, in the Street of the Lanterns, received the fateful confirmation of his eyes. Yes, the new mission was begun—was rising rapidly under the hands of many squads of masons, carpenters, and coolies. He watched a string of laborers, swaying along a strip of planking, bearing baskets of the finest Soochin glaze. He saw that the scale of operations was princely.

As he lingered there, with his thoughts for company, he suddenly discovered Mr. Chia at his elbow. He greeted his old friend quietly.

As they talked of the fineness of the weather and the general excellence of trade, Francis sensed more than usual kindness in the merchant's manner.

Suddenly, having appeased the proprieties, Mr. Chia guilelessly remarked: "It is pleasant to observe the excess growth of goodness, though many would consider it a superfluity. For myself I much enjoy walking in other mission gardens. Moreover, when the father came here many years ago he received much ill usage." A gentle and suggestive pause. "It seems highly probable, even to such an uninfluential and lowly placed citizen as I, that the new missioners could receive such execrable treatment on their arrival that they might be most regretfully forced to depart."

A shiver passed over Father Chisholm as an unbelievable temptation assailed him. The ambiguity, the forced understatement, of the merchant's remark was more significant than the direst threat. Mr. Chia, in many subtle and subterranean ways, wielded the greatest power in the district. Francis knew that he need only answer, gazing into space: "It would certainly be a great misfortune if disaster befell the coming missioners. . . . But then, who can prevent the will of heaven?" to foredoom the threatened invasion of his pastorate. But he recoiled, abhorring himself for the thought. Conscious of a cold perspiration on his brow, he replied as calmly as he could:

"There are many gates to heaven. We enter by one, these new preachers by another. How can we deny them the right to practice virtue in their own way? If they desire it, then they must come."

He did not observe that spark of singular regard that for once irradiated Mr. Chia's placid eye. Still deeply disturbed, he parted from his friend and walked homeward up the hill. He entered the church and seated himself, for he was tired, before the crucifix on the side altar. Gazing at the face, haloed with thorns, he prayed, in his mind, for endurance, wisdom, and forbearance.

By the end of June the Methodist mission was near completion. For all his fortitude, Father Chisholm had not brought himself to view the successive stages of construction; he had somberly avoided the Street of the Lanterns. But when Joseph, who had not failed as a baleful informant, brought news that the two foreign devils had arrived, the little priest sighed, put on his one good suit, took his tartan umbrella, and steeled himself to call.

When he rang the doorbell the sound echoed emptily into the new smell of paint and plaster. But after waiting indeterminately for a minute under the green-glass portico, he heard hastening steps within, and the door was opened by a small faded middle-aged woman in a gray alpaca skirt and high-necked blouse.

"Good afternoon. I am Father Chisholm. I took the liberty of calling to welcome you to Pai-tan."

She started nervously and a look of quick apprehension flooded her pale blue eyes.

"Oh, yes. Please come in. I am Mrs. Fiske. Wilbur . . . my husband . . . Dr. Fiske . . . he's upstairs. I'm afraid we are all alone, and not quite settled yet!" Hurriedly, she silenced his regretful protest. "No, no . . . you must step in."

He followed her upstairs to a cool, lofty room, where a man of forty, clean shaven, with a short-cropped moustache, and of her own diminutive size, was perched on a stepladder methodically arranging books upon the shelves. He wore strong glasses over his intelligent, apologetic, shortsighted eyes. His baggy cotton knickers gave his thin little calves an indescribable pathos. Descending the ladder, he stumbled, almost fell.

"Do be careful, Wilbur!" Her hands fluttered protectively. She introduced the two men. "Now let's sit down . . . if we can." She unsuccessfully attempted a smile. "It's too bad not having our furniture . . . but then one gets used to anything in China."

They sat down. Father Chisholm said pleasantly:

"You have a magnificent building here."

"Yes." Dr. Fiske deprecated. "We're very lucky. Mr. Chandler, the oil magnate, is most generous with us."

A strained silence. They so little fulfilled the priest's uneasy expectations, he felt taken unawares. He could not claim gigantic stature, yet the Fiskes, by the very sparseness of their physical economy, silenced the merest whisper of aggression. The little doctor was mild, with a bookish, even timid air, and a smile, deprecating, about his lips, as though afraid to settle. His wife, more clearly distinguishable in this good light, was a gentle, steadfast creature, her blue eyes easily receptive of tears, her hands alternating between her thin gold locket chain and a frizzy pad of rich, net-enclosed brown hair which, with a slight shock, Francis perceived to be a wig.

Suddenly Dr. Fiske cleared his throat. He said, simply: "How you must hate our coming here!"

"Oh, no . . . not at all." It was the priest's turn to look awkward.

"We had the same experience once. We were up-country in the Lan-hi Province, a lovely place. I wish you'd seen our peach trees. We had it all to ourselves for nine years. Then another missionary came. Not," he inserted swiftly, "a Catholic priest. But, well . . . we did resent it, didn't we, Agnes?"

"We did, dear." She nodded tremulously. "Still . . . we got over it. We are old campaigners, Father."

"Have you been long in China?"

"Over twenty years! We came as an insanely young couple the day we were married. We have given our lives to it." The moisture in her eyes receded before a bright and eager smile. "Wilbur! I must show Father Chisholm John's photograph." She rose, proudly took a silver-framed portrait from the bare mantelpiece. "This is our boy, taken when he was at Harvard, before he went as Rhodes Scholar to Oxford. Yes, he's still in England . . . working in our dockland settlement in Tynecastle."

The name shattered his strained politeness. "Tynecastle!" He smiled. "That is very near my home."

She gazed at him, enchanted, smiling back, holding the photograph to her bosom with tender hands.

"Isn't that amazing? The world is such a small place after all." Briskly she replaced the photograph on the mantel. "Now

I'm going to bring in coffee and some of my very own doughnuts . . . a family receipt." Again she silenced his protests. "It's no trouble. I always make Wilbur take a little refreshment at this hour. He has had some bother with his duodenum. If I didn't look after him who would?"

He had meant to stay for five minutes; he remained for more than an hour.

They were New England people, natives of the town of Biddeford, in Maine, born, reared, and married in the tenets of their own strict faith. As they spoke of their youth he had a swift and strangely sympathetic vision of a cold crisp countryside, of great salty rivers flowing between wands of silver birches to the misty sea, past white wooden houses amid the wine of maples, and sumac, velvet red in winter, a thin white steeple above the village, with bells and dark silent figures in the frosted street, following their quiet destiny.

But the Fiskes had chosen another and harder path. They had suffered. Both had almost died of cholera. During the Boxer Rebellion, when many of their fellow missioners were massacred, they had spent six months in a filthy prison under daily threat of execution. Their devotion to each other, and to their son, was touching. She had, for all her tremulousness, an indomitable maternal solicitude toward her two men.

Despite her antecedents, Agnes Fiske was a pure romantic whose life was written in the host of tender souvenirs she so carefully preserved. Soon she was showing Francis a letter of her dear mother's, a quarter of a century old, with the formula for these doughnuts, and a curl from John's head worn within her locket. Upstairs in her drawer were many more such tokens: bundles of yellowing correspondence, her withered bridal bouquet, a front tooth her son had shed, the ribbon she had worn at her first Biddeford church social. . . .

Her health was frail and presently, once this new venture was established, she was leaving for a six months' vacation, which she would spend in England with her son. Already, with an earnestness that presaged her goodwill, she pressed Father Chisholm to entrust her with any commissions he might wish executed at home.

When, at last, he took his leave, she escorted him beyond the portico, where Dr. Fiske stood, to the outer gate. Her eyes filled up with tears. "I can't tell you how relieved, how glad I am at your kindness, your friendliness in calling . . . especially for Wilbur's sake. At our last station he had such a painful experience . . . hatreds stirred up, frightful bigotry. It got so bad, latterly, when he went out to see a sick man he was struck and knocked senseless by a young brute of a . . . a missionary who accused him of stealing the man's immortal soul." She suppressed her emotion. "Let us help one another. Wilbur is such a clever doctor. Call on him any time you wish." She pressed his hand quickly and turned away.

Father Chisholm went home in a curious state of mind. For the next few days he had no news of the Fiskes. But on Saturday a batch of home-baked cookies arrived at St. Andrew's. As he took them, still warm and wrapped in the white napkin, to the children's refectory, Sister Martha scowled.

"Does she think we cannot bake here—this new woman?"

"She is trying to be kind, Martha. And we also must try."

For several months Sister Clotilde had suffered from a painful irritation of her skin. All sorts of lotions had been used, from calamine to carbolic, but without success. So distressing was the affliction, she made a special novena for a cure. The following week Father Chisholm saw her rubbing her red excoriated hands in a torment of itching. He frowned and, fighting his own reluctance, sent a note to Dr. Fiske.

The doctor arrived within half an hour, quietly examined the patient in Reverend Mother's presence, used no resounding words, praised the treatment that had been given and, having mixed a special physic to be taken internally every three hours, unobtrusively departed. In ten days the ugly rash had vanished, and Sister Clotilde was a new woman. But after the first radiance she brought a troubling scruple to her confession.

"Father . . . I prayed to God so earnestly . . . and . . ."

"It was the Protestant missionary who cured you?"

"Yes, Father."

"My child . . . don't let your faith be troubled. God did answer your prayer. We are his instruments . . . every one of us." He smiled suddenly. "Don't forget what old Lao-tzu said—'Religions are many; reason is one; we are all brothers.'"

That same evening as he walked in the garden Maria-Veronica said to him, almost unwillingly:

"This American . . . he is a good doctor."

He nodded. "And a good man."

The work of the two missions marched forward without conflict. There was room for both in Pai-tan, and each was careful not to give offense. The wisdom of Father Chisholm's determination to have no rice Christians in his flock was now apparent. Only one of his congregation betook himself to Lantern Street, and he was returned with a brief note: "Dear Chisholm, The bearer is a bad Catholic but would be a worse Methodist. Ever, Your friend in the Universal God, Wilbur Fiske, MD. *PS.* If any of your people need hospitalization send them along. They'll receive no dark hints on the fallibility of the Borgias!"

The priest's heart glowed. Dear Lord, he thought, kindness and toleration—with these two virtues how wonderful thy earth would be!

Fiske's accomplishments were not worn on his sleeve: he was revealed gradually as an archeologist and Chinese scholar of the first order. He contributed abstruse articles to the archives of obscure societies at home. His hobby was Chien-lung porcelain, and his collection of eighteenth-century *famille noire,* picked up with unobtrusive guile, was genuinely fine. Like most small men ruled by their wives, he loved an argument, and it was not long before Francis and he were friends enough to debate, warily, with cunning on both sides, and sometimes, alas, with rising heat, certain points that separated their respective creeds. Occasionally, carried away by the fervor of their opposite views, they parted with a certain tightness of the lips—for the pedantic little doctor could be querulous when roused. But it soon passed.

Once, after such a disagreement, Fiske met the mission priest. He stopped abruptly. "My dear Chisholm, I have been reflecting on a sermon that I once heard from the lips of Dr. Elder Cummings, our eminent divine, in which he declared:

'The greatest evil of today is the growth of the Romish Church through the nefarious and diabolical intrigues of its priests.' I should like you to know that since I have had the honor of your acquaintance I believe the Reverend Cummings to have been talking through his hat."

Francis, smiling grimly, consulted his theological books and ten days later formally bowed.

"My dear Fiske, in Cardinal Cuesta's catechism I find, plainly printed, this illuminating phrase: 'Protestantism is an immoral practice, which blasphemes God, degrades man, and endangers society.' I should like you to know, my dear Fiske, that even before I had the honor of your acquaintance I considered the cardinal unpardonable!" Raising his hat he solemnly marched off.

Neighboring Chinese thought the "doubled-up-with-laughter small-foreign-devil Methody" had completely lost his reason.

One gusty day toward the end of October Father Chisholm met the doctor's good lady on the Manchu Bridge. Mrs. Fiske was returning from marketing, one hand holding a net bag, the other clasping her hat securely to her head.

"Goodness!" she exclaimed cheerfully. "Isn't this a gale? It does blow the dust into my hair. I shall have to shampoo it again tonight!"

Familiar now with this one eccentricity, this single blot upon a blameless soul, Francis did not smile. Upon every possible occasion she guilelessly assumed her dreadful toupee to be a perfect mane of hair. His heart went out to her for the gentle little lie.

"I hope you are all well."

She smiled, head inclined, being very careful of her hat. "I am in rude health. But Wilbur is sulking—because I am off tomorrow. He will be so lonely, poor fellow. But then you are always lonely—what a solitary life you have!" She paused. "Do tell me, now that I am going to England, if there is anything I can do for you. I am bringing Wilbur back some new winter underwear—there's no place like Britain for woolens. Shall I do the same for you?"

He shook his head, smiling; then an odd thought struck him. "If you have nothing better to do one day . . . look up a dear old aunt of mine in Tynecastle. Miss Polly Bannon is the name. Wait, I'll write down her address."

He scribbled the address with a stub of pencil on a scrap of paper torn from a package in her shopping bag. She tucked it into her glove.

"Shall I give her any message?"

"Tell her how well and happy I am . . . and what a grand place this is. Tell her I'm—next to your husband—the most important man in China."

Her eyes were bright and warm toward him. "Perhaps I shall tell her more than you think. Women have a way of talking when they get together. Good-bye. See that you look in on Wilbur occasionally. And do take care of yourself."

She shook hands and went off, a poor weak woman with a will of iron.

He promised himself he would call on Dr. Fiske. But as the weeks slipped past he seemed never to have an hour of leisure.

There was the matter of Joseph's house to be arranged, and, when the little lodge was nicely built, the marriage ceremony itself, a full nuptial Mass with six of the youngest children as trainbearers. Once Joseph and his bride were suitably installed, he returned to the Liu village with Joseph's father and brothers. He had long cherished the dream of an outpost, a small secondary mission at Liu. There was talk of a great trade route being constructed through the Kwangs. At some future date he might well have a younger priest to help him, one who might operate from this new center in the hills. He had a strange impulse to set his plans in motion by increasing the area of the village grain fields, arranging with his friends in Liu to clear, plow, and sow an additional sixty *mu* of arable upland.

These affairs offered a genuine excuse, yet he experienced a sharp twinge of self-reproach as, some five months later, he unexpectedly encountered Fiske. The doctor, however, was in good spirits, lit by a guarded, oddly jocose animation, which permitted only one deduction.

"Yes." He chuckled, then corrected himself to a fitting gravity. "You're quite right. Mrs. Fiske rejoins me at the beginning of next month."

"I'm glad. It has been a long journey for her to take alone."

"She was fortunate in finding a most congenial fellow passenger."

"Your wife is a very friendly person."

"And with a great talent," Dr. Fiske seemed to suppress a preposterous tendency to giggle, "for not minding her own business. You must come and dine with us when she arrives."

Father Chisholm rarely went out; his mode of life did not permit it, but now compunction drove him to accept. "Thank you, I will."

Three weeks later he was reminded of his commitment, not altogether willingly, by a copperplate note from the Street of the Lanterns: "Tonight, without fail, seven-thirty."

It was inconvenient, when he had arranged for Vespers at seven o'clock. But he advanced the service by half an hour, sent Joseph to procure a chair, and that evening set out in formal style.

The Methodist mission was brightly illuminated, exuding an unusual air of festivity. As he stepped out into the courtyard he hoped it would not be a large or lengthy affair. He was not anti-social, but his life had grown increasingly interior in these last years, and that strain of Scots reserve, inherited from his father, had deepened into an odd guardedness toward strangers.

He was relieved, on entering the upper room, now gay with flowers and festoons of colored paper, to find only his host and hostess, standing together on the hearth rug, rather flushed from the warm room, like children before a party. While the doctor's thick lenses scintillated rays of welcome, Mrs. Fiske came quickly forward and took his hand.

"I am so glad to see you again, my poor neglected and misguided creature."

There was no mistaking the warmth of her greeting. She seemed quite taken out of herself. "You're happy to be back anyway. But I'm sure you've had a wonderful trip."

"Yes, yes, a wonderful trip. Our dear son is doing splendidly. How I wish he were with us tonight." She rattled on, ingenuous as a girl, her eyes bright with excitement. "Such things I have to tell you. But you'll hear . . . indeed, you'll hear . . . when our other guest comes in."

He could not prevent a questioning elevation of his brows.

"Yes, we are four tonight. A lady . . . in spite of our different viewpoints . . . now a most particular friend of mine. She is here on a visit." She stumbled, aware of his amazement, then faltered nervously. "My dear good Father, you are not to be cross with me." She faced the door and clapped her hands, in prearranged signal.

The door opened, and Aunt Polly came into the room.

8

In the convent kitchen on that September day of 1914 neither Polly nor Sister Martha gave the slightest heed to the faint familiar sound of rifle fire in the hills. While Martha cooked the dinner, using her spotless battery of copper pans, Polly stood by the window ironing a pile of linen wimples. In three months the two had become as inseparable as two brown hens in a strange farmyard. They respected each other's qualities. Martha had acclaimed Polly's crochet as the finest she had ever seen, while Polly, after fingering Martha's cross-stitch, admitted her own inferior for the first time in her life. And they had, of course, a topic that never failed them.

Now, as Polly damped the linen and raised the iron expertly to her cheek to test its heat, she complained: "He is looking very poorly again." With one hand Martha put some more wood into the stove while she stirred the soup reflectively with the other. "What would one expect? He eats nothing."

"When he was a young man he had a good appetite."

The Belgian sister shrugged her shoulders in exasperation. "He is the worst feeder of all the priests I have known. Ah! I have known some great feeders. There was our abbé at Métiers—six courses of fish in Lent. Of course I have a theory. When one eats little the stomach contracts. Thereafter it becomes impossible."

Polly shook her head in mild disagreement. "Yesterday when I took him some new baked scones he looked at them and said, 'How can one eat when thousands are hungry, within sight of this room?' "

"Bah! They are always hungry. In this country it is customary to eat grass."

"But now he says it will be worse because of all this fighting that is going on."

Sister Martha tasted the soup, her famous pot-au-feu, and her face registered critical approval. But as she turned to Polly she made a grimace. "There is always fighting. Just as there is always starving. We have bandits with our coffee in Pai-tan. They pop a few guns—like you hear now. Then the city buys them off, and they go home. Tell me, did he eat my scones?"

"He ate one. Yes, and said it was excellent. Then he told me to give the set to Reverend Mother for our poor."

"That good father will drive me to distraction." Though Sister Martha was, outside her kitchen, as mild as mother's milk, she scowled as if she were a creature of splendid rages. "Give, give, give! Until one's skin cracks with the strain. Shall I tell you what occurred last winter? One day in the town when it was snowing he took his coat off, his fine new coat that we sisters had made for him of best imported wool cloth, and gave it to some already half-frozen good-for-nothing. I would have let him have a tonguing, I assure you. But Mother Superior chose to correct him. He looked at her with those surprised eyes, which hurt you deep inside. 'But why not? What's the use of preaching Christianity if we don't live as Christians? The great Christ would have given that beggar his coat. Why shouldn't I?' When Reverend Mother answered very crossly that the coat was a gift from us he smiled, standing there, shivering with cold. 'Then you are the good Christians—not I.' Was not that incredible? You wouldn't believe it if, like me, you were brought up in a country where thrift is inculcated. Enough! Let us sit and drink our soup. If we wait until these greedy children have done we may faint for weakness."

Walking past the uncurtained window on his way back from the town Father Chisholm caught a glimpse of the two seated at their early lunch. The deep shadow of anxiety lifted momentarily from his face; his lips faintly smiled.

Despite his first premonitions, the accident of Polly's visit was an immense success; she fitted miraculously into the frame of the mission, and was enjoying herself with the same placidity that she would have displayed during a short weekend at Blackpool. Undismayed by clime or season, she would stalk silently to her seat in the kitchen garden and knit for hours among the cabbages with shoulders squared, elbows angled, and needles flashing, her mouth slightly pursed, her eyes remotely complacent, the yellow mission cat purring like mad, crouched half beneath her skirts. She was the closest crony of old Fu and became a hub round which the gloomy gardener revolved, exhibiting prodigious vegetables for her approval and prognosticating the weather with signs and baleful portents.

In her contact with the sisters she never interfered, never assumed a privilege. Her tact was instinctive and beautiful, springing from her gift of silence, from the prosaic simplicity of her life. She had never been happier. She was realizing her cherished longing to see Francis at his missionary work, a priest of God, helped, perhaps, to the worthy end—though she would never have dreamed of voicing such a thought—by her own humble effort. The length of her stay, set primarily at two months, had been extended until January.

Her one regret, naively expressed, was that she had been unable to take this trip earlier in her life. Though she had served Ned hand and foot so long, his death had not freed her from responsibility. Judy remained, a constant anxiety, with her whims and giddiness, her capricious inconstancy of purpose. From her first employment with the Tynecastle council she had passed through half a dozen secretarial positions, each acclaimed as perfect in the beginning, then presently thrown up in disgust. From a business career she had turned to pupil teaching, but her course at the Normal College soon bored her, and she vaguely entertained the idea of entering a convent. At this stage, when twenty-seven years of age, she had suddenly discovered that her true vocation was to become a nurse and had joined the staff of the Northumberland General Hospital as a probationer. This was the circumstance that had provided Polly with her present opportunity—a freedom that, alas, seemed only momentary. Already, after four short months, the hardships of the probationer's life were discouraging Judy, and letters kept coming, full of petulance and grievance, hinting that Aunt Polly must return soon to look after her poor neglected niece.

As Francis pieced together the pattern of Polly's life at home—gradually, for she was never garrulous—he came to see her as a saint. Yet her fixity was not that of a plaster image. She had her foibles, and her genius for the malapropos still remained. For instance, with remarkable initiative, and a loyal desire to aid Francis in his work, she had practically reconverted two errant souls who, on one of her staid excursions through Pai-tan, obsequiously attached themselves to her person and her purse. It had cost Francis some trouble to rid her of Hosannah and Philomena Wang.

If only for the consolation of their daily conversations, he had reason to value this amazing woman. Now, in the trials that had suddenly confronted him, he clung to her common sense.

As he reached his house, there, awaiting him on the porch veranda, stood Sister Clotilde and Anna. He sighed. Was he never to have peace to consider the disquieting news he had received?

Clotilde's sallow face wore a nervous flush. She stood close to the girl, almost like a jailer, restraining her with a freshly bandaged hand. Anna's eyes were dark with defiance. She also smelled of perfume.

Under his interrogating gaze Clotilde took a quick breath. "I had to ask Reverend Mother to let me bring Anna over. After all, in the basket workroom, she's under my special charge."

"Yes, Sister?" Father Chisholm forced himself to speak patiently. Sister Clotilde was quivering with hysterical indignation.

"I've put up with so much from her. Insolence and disobedience and laziness. Watching her upset the other girls. Yes, and steal! Why, even now she's reeking of Miss Bannon's eau de cologne. But this last—"

"Yes, Sister?"

Sister Clotilde reddened more deeply. It was a greater ordeal for her than for the graceless Anna.

"She's taken to going out at night. You know the place is infested with soldiers just now. She was out all last night with one of Wai-Chu's men, her bed not even slept in. And when I reasoned with her this morning, she struggled with me and bit me."

Father Chisholm turned his eyes on Anna. It seemed incredible that the little child he had held in his arms that winter night, who had come to him like a gift from heaven, should now confront him as a sulky and unruly young woman. In her teens, she was quite mature, with a full bosom, heavy eyes, and a plummy ripeness on her lips. She had always been different from the other children: uncaring, bold, never submissive. He thought: for once the copybooks are wrong—Anna has turned out no angel.

The heavy burden upon his mind made his voice mild. "Have you anything to say, Anna?"

"No."

"No, Father," Sister Clotilde hissed. Anna gave her a sullen glance of hatred.

"It seems a pity, after all we've tried to do for you, Anna, that you should repay us like this. Aren't you happy here?"

"No, I am not."

"Why?"

"I didn't ask to come to the convent. You didn't even buy me. I came for nothing. And I am tired of praying."

"But you don't pray all the time. You've got your work."

"I don't want to make baskets."

"Then we'll find something else for you to do."

"What else? Sewing? Am I to go on sewing all my life?"

Father Chisholm forced a smile. "Of course not. When you've learned all those useful things, one of our young men will want to marry you."

She gave him a sullen sneer, which said plainly: "I want something more exciting than your nice young men."

He was silent; then he said, somewhat bitterly, for her lack of gratitude hurt him: "No one wishes to keep you against your will. But until the district is more settled you must remain. Great trouble may be coming to the town. Indeed, great trouble may be coming to the world. While you are here you are safe. But you must keep the rule. Now go with Sister and obey her. If I find that you do not I shall be very angry."

He dismissed them both, then as Clotilde turned he said: "Ask Reverend Mother to come and see me, Sister." He watched them cross the compound, then went slowly to his room. As if he had not enough to weigh him down!

Five minutes later when Maria-Veronica entered he stood at the window viewing the city below. He let her join him there, keeping silent. At last he said: "My dear friend, I have two bad pieces of news for you, and the first is that we are likely to have a war here—before the year is out."

She gazed at him calmly, waiting. He swung round and faced her.

"I have just come from Mr. Chia. It is inevitable. For years the province has been dominated by Wai-Chu. As you know, he has bled the peasants to death with taxation and forced levies. If they didn't pay, their villages were destroyed—whole families slaughtered. But—brute though he is—the merchants of Pai-tan have always managed to buy him off." He paused. "Now another warlord is moving into the district—General Naian, from the lower Yangtze. He's reported to be not so bad as Wai—in fact our old friend Shon has gone over to him. But he wants Wai's province, that is, the privilege of squeezing the people there. He will march into Pai-tan. It is impossible to buy off both leaders. Only the victor can be bought off. So this time they must fight it out."

She smiled slightly. "I knew most of this before. Why are you so ominous today?"

"Perhaps because war is in the air." He gave her a queer strained glance. "Besides, it will be a bitter battle."

Her smile deepened. "Neither you nor I are afraid of a battle."

There was a silence. He glanced away. "Of course, I am thinking of ourselves, exposed here outside the city walls—if Wai attacks Pai-tan we shall be in the middle of it. But I am thinking more of the people—so poor, so helpless, and so hungry. I have come to love them here with all my heart. They only beg to be left in peace, to get a simple living from the soil, to live in their homes quietly with their families. For years they've been oppressed by one tyrant. Now, because another appears on the scene, guns are being thrust into their hands; yes, into the hands of the men of our congregation, flags are being waved, the usual cries are already raised—freedom and liberty. Hatreds are being worked up. Then, because two dictators wish it, these poor creatures will fall upon one another. And to what purpose? After the slaughter, when the smoke and the shooting have cleared away, there will be more taxation, more oppression, a heavier yoke than before." He sighed, "Can one help feeling sad for poor mankind?"

She moved somewhat restively. "You have not a great opinion of war. Surely some wars can be just and glorious? History proves it. My family has fought in many such."

He did not answer for a long time. When at last he turned to her the lines about his eyes had deepened. He spoke slowly, heavily. "It is strange you should say that at this moment." He paused, averting his eyes. "Our little trouble here is only the echo of a greater disorder." He found it difficult, most difficult, to continue. But he forced himself on. "Mr. Chia has had word by special courier from his business associates in Sen-siang. Germany has invaded Belgium and is at war with France and Britain."

There was a short pause. Her face altered; she did not speak, but stood silent, her head immobile, unnaturally arrested.

At length he said: "The others will soon know. But we must not let it make any difference to us at the mission."

"No, we must not." She answered mechanically, as though her gaze were fixed thousands of miles away.

The first sign came some days later: a small Belgian flag, sewn hurriedly with colored threads upon a square of silk, and placed prominently in Sister Martha's bedroom window. That same day, indeed, Martha scurried in early to the sisters' house from the dispensary, with her new eagerness, then gave a cluck of nervous satisfaction. They had come—what she looked forward to with all her soul: the newspapers. It was the *Intelligence,* an American daily published in Shanghai, and it arrived, in batches, erratically, about once a month. Hurriedly, her fingers trembling between expectation and apprehension, she undid the wrappers at the window.

For a minute she turned the pages, hastily. Then she gave an outraged cry.

"What monsters! Oh my God, it is insupportable!" She beckoned urgently, not lifting her head, to Clotilde, who had come quickly into the room, drawn by the same magnetic force. "Look, Sister! They are in Louvain—the cathedral is in ruins—shelled to pieces. And Metrieux—ten kilometers from my home—destroyed to the ground. Oh, dear God! Such a fine and prosperous town!"

Linked by common calamity, the two sisters bent over the sheets, punctuating their reading with exclamations of horror.

"The very altar blown to pieces!" Martha wrung her hands. "Metrieux! I drove there with my father in the high cart when I was a little thing of seven. Such a market! We bought twelve gray geese that day . . . so fat and beautiful . . . and now . . ."

Clotilde, with dilated eyes, was reading of the battle of the Marne. "They are slaughtering our brave people. Such butchery, such vileness!"

Though Reverend Mother had entered and seated herself quietly at the table, Clotilde remained unconscious of her presence. But Martha saw her, from the corner of her eye, and Martha was beside herself.

Suffused with indignation, her voice shaking, she pointed her finger to a paragraph. "Consider this, Sister Clotilde. 'It is reliably reported that the convent of Louvain was violated by the German invaders. Unimpeachable sources confirm the fact that many innocent children have been mercilessly butchered.' "

Clotilde was pale as ivory. "In the Franco-Prussian War it was the same. They are inhuman. No wonder, in this good American journal, they already call them Huns." She hissed the word.

"I cannot allow you to speak in such terms of my people."

Clotilde spun round, supporting herself on the window frame, taken aback. But Martha was prepared.

"Your people, Reverend Mother? I would not be so proud to own them if I were you. Brutal barbarians. Murderers of women and little children."

"The German Army is comprised of gentlemen. I do not believe that vulgar sheet. It is not true."

Martha spread her hands on her hips; her harsh peasant voice grated with resentment. "Is it true when the vulgar sheet reports the ruthless invasion of a little peaceful country by your gentlemanly army?"

Reverend Mother was paler now than Clotilde.

"Germany must have her place in the sun."

"So she kills and plunders, blows up cathedrals, and the marketplace I went to as a girl, because she wants the sun and the moon, the greedy swine—"

"Sister!" Dignified even in her agitation, Reverend Mother rose up. "There is such a thing as justice in this world. Germany and Austria have never had justice. And do not forget that my brother is fighting even now to forge the new Teutonic destiny. Therefore I forbid you both, as your superior, to speak any such slanders as have just defiled your lips."

There was an intolerable pause, then she turned to leave the room. As she reached the door Martha cried: "Your famous destiny isn't forged yet. The Allies will win the war."

Maria-Veronica gave her a cold and pitying smile. She went out.

The feud intensified, fanned by the stray news that filtered to the far-off mission itself under threat of war. Though the French sister and the Belgian had never greatly liked each other, now they were linked in bosom friendship. Martha was protective toward the weaker Clotilde, solicitous for her health, dosing her troublesome cough, giving her choice pieces from every dish. Together, openly, they knitted mittens and socks to be sent to the brave *blessés*. They would talk of their beloved countries, over Reverend Mother's head, with many sighs and innuendoes—careful, oh so careful, to give no offence. Then Martha with a strange significance would remark: "Let us go over a moment to pray for our intention."

Maria-Veronica endured it all with a proud silence. She, too, prayed for victory. Father Chisholm could see the three faces in a row, beatifically upturned, praying for opposing victories while he, careworn and harassed, watching Wai's forces march and countermarch among the hills, hearing of Naian's final mobilization, prayed for peace . . . safety for his people . . . and enough food for the children.

Presently Sister Clotilde began to teach her class the *Marseillaise.* She did it secretly, when Reverend Mother was engaged in the basket room at the other end of the mission. The class, being imitative, picked it up quickly. Then, one forenoon as Maria-Veronica came slowly across the compound, her air fatigued and noticeably constrained, there burst, through the open windows of Clotilde's classroom, to the accompaniment of a thumped piano, the full-throated blast of the French national anthem: "Allons, enfants de la patrie . . ."

For an instant Maria-Veronica's step faltered; then her figure, which showed signs of softening, became steeled. All her fortitude was summoned to sustain her. She walked on with her head high.

One afternoon toward the end of the month, Clotilde was again in her schoolroom. The class, having given its daily rendering of the *Marseillaise,* had now concluded its catechism lesson. And Sister Clotilde, following her recently instituted custom, remarked:

"Kneel down, dear children, and we will say a little prayer for the brave French soldiers."

The children knelt down obediently and repeated the three Hail Marys after her.

Clotilde was about to signal them to rise when, with a slight shock, she became aware of Reverend Mother standing behind her. Maria-Veronica was calm and pleasant. Gazing across Sister Clotilde's shoulder she addressed the class.

"And now, children, it is only right that you should say the same prayer for the brave German soldiers."

Clotilde turned a dirty green. Her breath seemed to choke her.

"This is my classroom, Reverend Mother."

Maria-Veronica ignored her. "Come now, dear children, for the brave Germans, 'Hail Mary full of grace . . .' "

Clotilde's breast heaved; her pale lips retracted from her narrow teeth. Convulsively, she drew back her hand and slapped her superior on the face.

There was a terrified hush. Then Clotilde burst into tears and ran sobbing from the room.

Maria-Veronica moved not a muscle. With that same agreeable smile she said to the children:

"Sister Clotilde is unwell. You see how she knocked against me. I will finish the class. But first, children, three Hail Marys for the good German soldiers."

When the prayer concluded she seated herself, unruffled, at the high desk and opened the book.

That evening, entering the dispensary unexpectedly, Father Chisholm surprised Sister Clotilde measuring herself a liberal dose of Chlorodyne. She whipped round at his step and almost dropped the full minim glass, her cheek flooded by a painful flush. The episode in the classroom had strung her to breaking pitch.

She stammered: "I take a little for my stomach. We have so much to worry us these days." He knew, from the measure and her manner, that she was using the drug as a sedative.

"I wouldn't take it too often, Sister. It contains a good deal of morphine."

When she had gone he locked the bottle in the poison cupboard. As he stood in the empty dispensary, torn by the anxiety of their danger here, weighed down by the sheer futility of that far-off, awful war, he felt a slow surge of anger at the senseless rancor of these women. He had hoped it would settle. But it had not settled. He compressed his lips in sudden resolution.

After school that day he sent for the three sisters. He made them stand before his desk, his face unusually stern, choosing his words, almost with bitterness.

"Your behavior at a time like this is greatly distressing me. It must cease. You have no justification for it whatsoever."

There was a short pause. Clotilde was shaking with contention. "But we have justification." She fumbled in the pocket of her robe and agitatedly thrust into his hand a much-creased, cut-out section of newsprint. "Read this, I beg of you. From a prince of the church."

He scanned the cutting, slowly read it aloud. It was the report of a pronouncement by Cardinal Amette, from the pulpit of the Cathedral of Notre Dame in Paris. "'Beloved Brethren, Comrades in Arms of France and her Glorious Allies, Almighty God is upon our side. God has helped us to our greatness in the past. He will help us once again in our hour of need. God stands beside our brave soldiers in the battlefield, strengthening their arms, girding them against the enemy. God protects his own. God will give us victory . . .'"

He broke off; he would go no further.

A rigid silence followed. Clotilde's head trembled with nervous triumph, and Martha's face was dogged with vindication. But Maria-Veronica remained undefeated. Stiffly, from the black cloth bag she wore upon her girdle, she unfolded a neat square clipping.

"I know nothing of the prejudiced opinion of any French cardinal. But here is the joint statement to the German people of the archbishops of Cologne, Munich, and Essen." In a cold and haughty voice she read: "'Beloved People of the Fatherland, God is with us in this most righteous struggle which has been forced upon us. Therefore we command you in God's name to fight to the last drop of your blood for the honor and glory of our country. God knows in his wisdom and justice that we are in the right and God will give us . . .'"

"That is enough."

Francis stopped her, struggling for self-control, his soul suffused by wave upon wave of anger and despair. Here, before him, was the essence of man's malice and hypocrisy. The senselessness of life seemed suddenly to overwhelm him. Its hopelessness crushed him.

He remained with his head resting upon his hand, then in a low voice he said: "God knows God must get sick of all this crying out to God!"

Mastered by his emotion he rose abruptly and began to pace the room. "I can't refute the contradictions of cardinals and archbishops with still more contradictions. I wouldn't presume to. I'm nobody—an insignificant Scottish priest stuck in the wilds of China on the edge of a bandit's war. But don't you see the folly and the baseness of the whole transaction? We, the Holy Catholic Church—yes, all the great churches of Christendom—condone this world war. We go further—we sanctify it. We send millions of our faithful sons to be maimed and slaughtered, to be mangled in their bodies and their souls, to kill and destroy one another, with a hypocritical smile, an apostolic blessing. Die for your country and all will be forgiven you. Patriotism! King and emperor! From ten thousand smug pulpits: 'Render to Caesar the things that are Caesar's . . .'" He broke off, hands clenched, eyes remotely burning. "There is no Caesar nowadays—only financiers and statesmen who want diamond mines in Africa and rubber in the slave-driven Congo. Christ preached everlasting love. He preached the brotherhood of man. He did not climb the mountain and shout, 'Kill! Kill! Go forth in hatred and plunge a bayonet into thy brother's belly!' It isn't his voice that resounds in the churches and high cathedrals of Christendom today—but the voice of timeservers and cowards." His lips quivered. "How in the name of the God we serve can we come to these foreign lands, the lands we call pagan, presuming to convert the people to a doctrine we give the lie to by our every deed? Small wonder they jeer at us. Christianity—the religion of lies! Of class and money and national hatreds! Of wicked wars!" He stopped short, perspiration beading his brow, his eyes dark with anguish. "Why doesn't the church seize her opportunity? What a chance to justify herself as the living bride of Christ! Instead of preaching hatred and incitement, to cry, in every land, with the tongues of her pontiff and all her priests: 'Throw down your weapons. Thou shalt not kill. We command you *not* to fight.' Yes, there would be persecutions and many executions. But these would be martyrdoms—not murders. The dead would decorate, not desecrate, our altars." His voice dropped, his attitude was calmer, strangely prophetic. "The church will suffer for its cowardice. A viper nourished in one's bosom will one day strike that bosom. To sanction the might of arms is to invite destruction. The day may come when great military forces will break loose and turn upon the church, corrupting millions of her children, sending her down again—a timid shadow—into the catacombs."

There was a strained stillness when he concluded. Martha and Clotilde hung their heads, as though touched, against their will. But Maria-Veronica, with something of the arrogance that marked those early days of strife, faced him with a cold clear gaze, hardened by a glint of mockery.

"That was most impressive, Father . . . worthy of these cathedrals you decry. . . . But aren't your words rather empty if you don't live up to them . . . here in Pai-tan?"

The blood rushed to his brow, then quickly ebbed. He answered without anger.

"I have solemnly forbidden every man in my congregation to fight in this wicked conflict that threatens us. I have made them swear to come with their families inside the mission gates, when trouble breaks. Whatever the consequences I shall be responsible."

All three sisters looked at him. A faint tremor passed over Maria-Veronica's cold still face. Yet, as they filed from the room, he could see they were not reconciled. He suddenly felt a shiver of unnameable fear. He had the strange sensation that time swung suspended, balanced in fateful expectation of what might come to pass.

9

On a Sunday morning, he was awakened by a sound that he had dreaded for many days—the dull concussion of artillery in action. He jumped up and hurried to the window. On the western hills, a few miles distant, six light field pieces had begun to shell the city. He dressed rapidly and went downstairs. At the same moment Joseph came running from the porch.

"It has begun, Master. Last night General Naian marched into Pai-tan and the Wai forces are attacking him. Already our people are arriving at the gates."

He glanced swiftly over Joseph's shoulder. "Admit them at once."

While his servant went back to unlock the gates he hastened over to the home. The children were collected at breakfast and amazingly undisturbed. One or two of the smaller girls whimpered at the sudden distant banging. He went round the long tables, forcing himself to smile. "It is only firecrackers, children. For a few days we are going to have big ones."

The three sisters stood apart at the head of the refectory. Maria-Veronica was calm as marble, but he saw at once that Clotilde was upset. She seemed to hold herself in, and her hands were clenched in her long sleeves. Every time the guns went off she paled. Nodding toward the children, he joked expressly for her. "If only we could keep them eating all the time!"

Sister Martha cackled too quickly: "Yes, yes, then it would be easy." As Clotilde's stiff face made the effort to smile the far-off guns rolled again.

After a moment he left the refectory and pressed on to the lodge where Joseph and Fu stood at the wide-open gates. His people were pouring in with their belongings, young and old, poor humble illiterate creatures, frightened, eager for safety, the very substance of suffering mortality. His heart swelled as he thought of the sanctuary he was giving them. The good brick walls would afford them sound protection. He blessed the vanity that had made him build them high. With a queer tenderness, he watched one aged ragged dame, whose withered face bespoke a patient resignation to a long life of privation, stumble in with her bundle, establish herself quietly in a corner of the crowded compound, and painstakingly begin to cook a handful of beans in an old condensed-milk can.

At his side, Fu was imperturbable but Joseph, the valiant, showed a slight variation of his normal color. Marriage had altered him; he was no longer a careless youth, but a husband and a father, with all the responsibilities of a man of property.

"They should hurry," he muttered restively. "We must lock and barricade the gates."

Father Chisholm put his hand on his servant's shoulder. "Only when they are all inside, Joseph."

"We are going to have trouble," Joseph answered with a shrug. "Some of our men who have come in were conscripted by Wai. He will not be pleased when he finds they prefer to be here rather than to fight."

"Nevertheless they will not fight." The priest answered firmly. "Come, now, don't be despondent. Run up our flag, while I watch at the gate."

Joseph departed, grumbling, and in a few minutes the mission flag, of pale blue silk with a deeper blue St. Andrew's cross, broke and fluttered on the flagstaff. Father Chisholm's heart gave an added bound of pride; his breast was filled with a quick elation. That flag stood for peace and goodwill to all men, a neutral flag, the flag of universal love.

When the last straggler had entered they locked the gates provisionally. At that moment Fu drew the priest's attention to the cedar grove, some three hundred yards to the left, on their own jade hillside. In this clump of trees a long gun had unexpectedly appeared. Indistinctly, between the branches, he could see the quick movements of soldiers, in Wai green tunics, trenching and fortifying the position. Though he knew little of such matters the gun seemed a far more powerful weapon than the ordinary field pieces now in action. And even as he gazed there came a swift flash, followed instantly by a terrifying concussion and the wild scream of the shell overhead.

The change was devastating. As the new heavy gun deafeningly pounded the city, it was answered by a Naian battery of ineffectual range. Small shells, falling short of the cedar grove, rained about the mission. One plunged into the kitchen garden, erupting a shower of earth. Immediately a cry of terror rose in the crowded compound, and Francis ran to shepherd his congregation from the open into the greater safety of the church.

The noise and confusion increased. In the classroom the children were in a milling stampede. It was Reverend Mother who stemmed the panic. Calm and smiling, but shouting above the bursting shells, she drew the children round her, made them close their ears with their fingers and sing at the pitch of their lungs. When they became calmer they were herded quickly across the courtyard into the cellars of the convent. Joseph's wife and the two children were already there. It was strange to see all these small yellow faces, in the half-light, among stores of oil and candles and sweet potatoes, below the long shelves on which stood Sister Martha's preserves. The screaming of the shells was less down below. But from time to time there was a heavy shock; the building shook to its foundations.

While Polly remained below with the children, Martha and Clotilde scurried to fetch them lunch. Clotilde, always highly strung, was now almost out of her wits. As she crossed the compound a spent piece of metal struck her lightly on her cheek.

"Oh, God!" she cried, sinking down. "I'm killed!" Pale as death she began to make an act of contrition.

"Don't be a fool." Martha shook her fiercely by the shoulder. "Come and get these wretched brats some porridge."

Father Chisholm had been called by Joseph to the dispensary. One of the women had been slightly wounded in the hand.

When the bleeding was controlled and the wound bandaged, the priest sent both Joseph and the patient over to the church, then hurried to the window, anxiously gauging the effects of the bursts, damaging puffs of debris, as the shells from the Wai gun exploded in Pai-tan. Sworn to neutrality, he could not repress a terrible desire, surging and devastating, that Wai, the unspeakable, might be defeated.

Suddenly, as he stood there, he saw a detachment of Naian soldiers strike out from the Manchu Gate. They flowed out like a stream of gray ants, perhaps two hundred of them, and began in a ragged line to mount the hill.

He watched them with a dreadful fascination. They came quickly, at first, in little sudden rushes. He could see them vividly against the untroubled green of the hillside. Bent double, each man bolted forward, carrying his rifle, for a dozen yards, then flung himself, desperately, upon the earth.

The Wai gun continued firing into the city. The gray figures drew nearer. They were crawling now, flat on their stomachs, completing their toiling ascent in that blazing sun. At a distance of a hundred paces from the cypress grove they paused, hugging the slope, for a full three minutes. Then their leader gave a sign. With a shout they jumped erect and rushed on the emplacement.

They covered half the distance rapidly. A few seconds and they would have reached their objective. Then the harsh vibration of machine guns resounded in the brilliant air.

There were three, manned and waiting, in the cypress grove. At their jarring impact the rushing gray figures seemed to stop, to fall in sheer bewilderment. Some fell forward, others on their backs, some for a moment upon their knees, as though in prayer. They fell all ways, comically, then lay still, in the sunshine. At that, the rattling of the maxims ceased. All was stillness, warm and quiet, until the heavy concussion of the big gun boomed again, reawakening everything to life—all but those quiet little figures on the green hillside.

Father Chisholm stood rigid, consumed by the torment of his mind. This was war. This toylike pantomime of destruction, magnified a million times, was what was happening now on the fertile plains of France. He shuddered, and prayed passionately: "O Lord, let me live and die for peace."

Suddenly his haggard eye picked up a sign of movement on the hill. One of the Naian soldiers was not dead. Slowly and painfully, he was dragging himself down the slope in the direction of the mission. It was possible to observe the ebbing of his strength in the gradual slowing of his progress. Finally he came to rest, utterly spent, lying on his side, some sixty yards from the upper gate.

Francis thought, *He is dead . . . this is no time for mock-heroics. If I go out there I will get a bullet in my head. . . . I must not do it.* But he found himself leaving the dispensary and moving toward the upper gate. He had a shamed consciousness as he opened the gate: fortunately no one was watching from the mission. He walked out into the bright sunshine upon the hillside.

His short black figure and long black shadow were shockingly obvious. If the mission windows were blank he felt many eyes upon him from the cypress grove. He dared not hurry.

The wounded soldier was breathing in sobbing gasps. Both hands were pressed weakly against his lacerated belly. His human eyes gazed back at Francis with an anguished interrogation.

Francis lifted him on his back and carried him into the mission. He propped him up while he relocked the gate. Then he pulled him gently into shelter. When he had given him a drink of water he found Maria-Veronica and told her she must prepare a cot in the dispensary.

That afternoon another unsuccessful raid was made on the gun position. And when night fell Father Chisholm and Joseph brought in five more wounded men. The dispensary assumed the appearance of a hospital.

Next morning the shelling continued without interruption. The noise was interminable. The city took severe punishment, and it looked as if a breach were being driven in the western wall. Suddenly, at the angle of the western gate, about a mile away, Francis saw the main body of the Wai forces bearing in upon the broken parapet. He thought with a sinking heart, *They are in the city.* But he could not judge.

The remainder of the day passed in a state of sick uncertainty. In the late afternoon he liberated the children from the cellar and his congregation from the church to let them have a breath of air. At least they were unharmed. As he went among them, heartening them, he buoyed himself with this simple fact.

Then, as he finished his round, he found Joseph at his side, wearing for the first time a look of unmistakable fear.

"Master, a messenger has come over from the Wai gun in the cedar grove."

At the main gate three Wai soldiers were peering between the bars while an officer, whom Father Chisholm took to be the captain of the gun crew, stood by. Without hesitation Francis unlocked the gate and went outside.

"What do you wish of me?"

The officer was short, thickset, and middle-aged, with a heavy face and thick mulish lips. He breathed through his mouth, which hung open, showing his stained upper teeth. He wore the usual peaked cap and green uniform with a leather belt, bearing a green tassel. His puttees ended in a pair of broken canvas plimsolls.

"General Wai favors you with several requests. In the first place you are to cease sheltering the enemy wounded."

Francis flushed sharply, nervously. "The wounded are doing no harm. They are beyond fighting."

The other took no notice of this protest. "Secondly, General Wai affords you the privilege of contributing to his commissariat. Your first donation will be eight hundred pounds of rice and all American canned goods in your storerooms."

"We are already short of food." Despite his resolution, Francis felt his temper rise; he spoke heatedly. "You cannot rob us in this fashion."

As before, the gun captain let the argument pass unheeded. He had a way of standing sideways, with his feet apart, delivering each word across his shoulder, like an insult.

"Thirdly, it is essential that you clear your compound of all whom you are protecting there. General Wai believes you are harboring deserters from his forces. If this is so they will be shot. All other able-bodied men must enlist immediately in the Wai army."

This time Father Chisholm made no protest. He stood tense and pale, his hands clenched, his eyes blazing with indignation. The air before him vibrated on a red haze. "Suppose I refuse to comply with these most moderate solicitations?"

The obstinate face before him almost smiled. "That, I assure you, would be a mistake. I should then most reluctantly turn our gun upon you and in five minutes reduce your mission, and all within, to an inconsiderable powder."

There was a silence. The three soldiers were grimacing, making signs to some of the younger women in the compound. Francis saw the situation as cold and clear-cut as a picture etched on steel. He must yield, under threat of annihilation, to these inhuman demands. And that yielding would be but the prelude to greater and still greater demands. A dreadful sweep of anger conquered him. His mouth went dry; he kept his burning eyes on the ground.

"General Wai must realize that it will take some hours to make ready these stores for him . . . and to prepare my people . . . for their departure. How much time does he afford me?"

"Until tomorrow." The officer answered promptly. "Provided you deliver to me before midnight at my gun position a personal offering of tinned goods together with sufficient valuables to constitute a suitable present."

Again there was a silence. Francis felt a dark choking swelling of his heart. He lied in a suppressed voice: "I agree. I have no alternative. I will bring you your gift tonight."

"I commend your wisdom. I shall expect you. And I advise you not to fail."

The captain's tone held a heavy irony. He bowed to the priest, shouted a command to his men, and marched off squatly toward the cedar grove.

Francis reentered the mission in a trembling fury. The clang of the heavy iron gate behind him set a chain of febrile echoes ringing through his brain. What a fool he had been, in his fatuous elation, to imagine he could escape this trial. He . . . the dovelike pacifist. He gritted his teeth as wave after wave of pitiless self-anger assailed him. Abruptly, he rid himself of Joseph and of the silent gathering who timidly searched his face for the answer to their fears.

Usually he took his troubles to the church, but now he could not bow his head and tamely murmur: "Lord, I will suffer and submit." He went to his room and flung himself violently into the wicker chair. His thoughts for once ran riot, without the rein of meekness or forbearance. He groaned as he thought of his pretty gospel of peace. What was to happen to his fine words now? What was to happen to them all?

Another barb struck him—the needlessness, the crass inanity of Polly's presence in the mission at such a time. Under his breath he cursed Mrs. Fiske for the interfering officiousness that had subjected his poor old aunt to this fantastic tribulation. God! He seemed to have the cares of all the world upon his bent incompetent shoulders. He jumped up. He could not, he would not, yield, weakly, to the maddening menace of Wai's threat and the deadlier menace of that gun, which grew in his feverish imagination, swelled to such gigantic size it became the symbol of all wars, and of every brutal weapon built by man for the slaughter of mankind.

As he paced his room, tense and sweating, there came a mild knock at his door. Polly entered the room.

"I don't like to disturb you, Francis . . . but if you have a minute to spare. . . ." She smiled remotely, using the privilege of her affection to disturb his privacy.

"What is it, Aunt Polly?" He composed his features with a great effort. Perhaps she had further news, another message from Wai.

"I'd be glad if you'd try on this comforter, Francis. I don't want to get it too large. It should keep you nice and warm in the winter." Under his bloodshot gaze she produced a woolen balaclava helmet she was knitting him.

He scarcely knew whether to weep or laugh. It was so like Polly. When the crack of doom resounded she would no doubt pause to offer him a cup of tea. There was nothing for it but to comply. He stood and let her fit the half-finished capote upon his head.

"It looks all right," she murmured critically. "Maybe a trifle wide about the neck." With her head on one side and her long wrinkled upper lip pursed, she counted the stitches with her bone knitting needle. "Sixty-eight. I'll take it in four. Thank you, Francis. I hope I haven't troubled you."

Tears started to his eyes. He had an almost irresistible desire to put his head on her hard shoulder and cry brokenly, outrageously: "Aunt Polly! I'm in such a mess. What in God's name am I to do?"

As it was, he gazed at her a long time. He muttered: "Don't you worry, Polly, about the danger we're all in here?"

She smiled faintly. "Worry killed the cat. Besides . . . aren't you looking after us?"

Her ineradicable belief in him was like a breath of pure cold air. He watched her wrap up her work, skewer it with needles, and, giving her competent nod, silently withdraw. Somehow, beneath her casualness, her air of commonplace, there lay a hint of deeper knowledge. He had no doubts now as to what he must do. He took his hat and coat, made his way secretly toward the lower gate.

Outside the mission the deep darkness blindfolded him. But he went down the Brilliant Green Jade road toward the city, rapidly, heedless of any obstacle.

At the Manchu Gate he was sharply halted and a lantern thrust close against his face, while the sentries scrutinized him. He had counted on being recognized—he was, after all, a familiar figure in the city—yet his luck went further still. One of the three soldiers was a follower of Shon who had worked all through the plague epidemic. The man vouched for him immediately and after a short exchange with his companions agreed to take him at once to the lieutenant.

The streets were deserted, choked in parts with rubble and ominously silent. From the distant eastern section there came occasional bursts of firing. As the priest followed the quick padding footsteps of his guide he had a strange exhilarating sense of guilt.

Shon was in his old quarters at the cantonment, snatching a short rest, fully dressed, on that same camp bed that had been Dr. Tulloch's. He was unshaven, his puttees white with mud, and there were dark shadows of fatigue beneath his eyes. He propped himself upon his elbow as Francis entered.

"Well!" he said slowly. "I have been dreaming about you, my friend, and your excellent establishment on the hill."

He slid from the bed, turned up the lamp and sat down at the table. "You do not want some tea? No more do I. But I am glad to see you. I regret I cannot present you to General Naiain. He is leading an attack on the east section . . . or perhaps executing some spies. He is a most enlightened man."

Francis sat down at the table, still in silence. He knew Shon well enough to let him talk himself out. And tonight the other had less to say than usual. He glanced guardedly at the priest. "Why don't you ask it, my friend? You are here for help which I cannot give. We should have been in your mission two days ago except that then we should merely have been blown to pieces together by that infamous Sorana."

"You mean the gun?"

"Yes, the gun," Shon answered with polite irony. "I have known it too well for a period of years. . . . It came originally from a French gunboat. General Hsiah had it first. Twice I took it from him with great trouble, but each time he bought it back from my commandant. Then Wai had a concubine from Pekin who cost him twenty thousand silver dollars. She was an Armenian lady, very beautiful, named Sorana. When he ceased to regard her with affection he exchanged her to Hsiah for the gun. You saw us try to capture it yesterday. It is not possible. . . . Fortified . . . across that open country . . . with only our piff-paff battery to protect us. Perhaps it is going to lose us our war . . . just when I am making a great personal advancement with General Naian."

There was a pause. The priest said stiffly: "Suppose it were possible to capture the gun?"

"No. Do not entice me." Shon shook his head with concealed bitterness. "But if ever I get near that dishonorable weapon I shall finish it for good."

"We can get very near the gun."

Shon raised his head deliberately, sounding Francis with his eyes. A glint of excitement enlivened him. He waited.

Father Chisholm leaned forward, his lips making a tight line, "This evening under threat of shelling the mission, the Wai officer who commands the gun crew ordered me to bring food and money to him before midnight . . ."

He went on, gazing at Shon, then abruptly broke off, conscious that he need say no more. For a full minute nothing was said. Shon was thinking, behind his careless brow. At last he smiled—at least the muscles of his face went through the act of smiling, but there was nothing of humor in his eyes.

"My friend, I must continue to regard you as a gift from heaven."

A cloud passed over the priest's set face. "I have forgotten about heaven tonight."

Shon nodded, not thinking of that remark. "Now listen and I will tell you what we shall do."

An hour later Francis and Shon left the cantonment and made their way through the Manchu Gate toward the mission. Shon had changed his uniform for a worn blue blouse and a pair of coolie's slacks, rolled to the knee. A flat pleated hat covered his head. On his back he carried a large sack, tightly sewn with twine. Following silently, at a distance of some three hundred paces, were twenty of his men.

Halfway up the Brilliant Green Jade road Francis touched his companion on the arm. "Now it is my turn."

"It is not heavy." Shon shifted the bundle tenderly to his other shoulder. "And I am perhaps more used to it than you."

They reached the shelter of the mission walls. No lights were showing, the outline that compassed everything he loved lay shadowy and unprotected. The silence was absolute. Suddenly, from within the lodge, he heard the melodious strike of the American chiming clock he had given Joseph for a wedding present. He counted automatically. Eleven o'clock.

Shon had given the men a final word of instruction. One of them, squatting against the wall, suppressed a cough that seemed to echo out across the hill. Shon cursed him in a violent whisper. The men were not important. It was what Shon and he must do together that mattered. He felt his friend peering at him through the silent darkness.

"You know exactly what is going to occur?"

"Yes."

"When I fire into the can of gasoline it will ignite instantly and explode the cordite. But before that, even before I raise my revolver, you must begin to move away. You must be well away.

The concussion will be extreme." He paused. "Let us go if you are ready. And for the love of your Lord of Heaven keep the torch away from the sack."

Nerving himself, Francis took matches from his pocket and let the split reed flare. Then, holding it up, he stepped from the cover of the mission wall and walked openly toward the cypress grove. Shon came behind him, like a servant, bearing the sack on his back, as if groaning beneath its weight, taking care to make a noise.

The distance was not great. At the edge of the grove he halted, called out into the watchful stillness of the invisible trees:

"I have come as requested. Take me to your leader."

There was an interval of silence; then, close behind them, a sudden movement. Francis swung round and saw two of Wai's men standing in the pool of smoky glare.

"You are expected, bewitcher. Proceed without undue fear."

They were escorted through a formidable maze of shallow trenches and sharp-ended bamboo stakes to the center of the grove. Here the priest's heart sharply missed a beat. Behind a breastwork of earth and cedar branches, the crew dispersed in attitudes of care beside it, stood the long-muzzled gun.

"Have you brought all that was demanded of you?"

Francis recognized the voice of his visitor earlier that evening. He lied more readily this time.

"I have brought a great load of tinned goods . . . which will certainly please you."

Shon exhibited the sack, moving nearer, a trifle nearer, to the gun.

"It is not so great a load." The captain of the gun crew stepped into the light. "Have you brought money also?"

"Yes."

"Where is it?" The captain felt the neck of the sack.

"Not there." Francis spoke hurriedly, with a start. "I have the money in my purse."

The captain gazed at him, diverted from his examination of the sack, his expression lit by a sudden cupidity. A group of soldiers had collected, their staring faces all bent upon the priest.

"Listen, all of you." Francis held their attention, with a desperate intensity. He could see Shon edging imperceptibly into the fringe of shadow, closer, still closer to the gun. "I ask you—I beg you—to leave us unmolested in the mission."

Contempt showed in the captain's face. He smiled derisively. "You shall be unmolested . . . until tomorrow." Someone laughed in the background. "Then we shall protect your women."

Francis hardened his heart. Shon, as though exhausted, had unloaded the sack under the breech of the gun. Pretending to wipe the perspiration from his brow he came back a little toward the priest. The crowd of soldiers had increased and were growing impatient. Francis strove to gain one minute of extra time for Shon.

"I do not doubt your word, but I should value some assurance from General Wai."

"General Wai is in the city. You will see him later."

The captain spoke curtly and stepped out to get the money. From the corner of his eye, Francis saw Shon's hand go beneath his blouse. *It is coming now,* he thought. In the same moment, he heard the loud report of the revolver shot and the impact of the bullet as it struck the oil tin inside the sack. Braced for the convulsion, he could not understand. There was no explosion. Shon in swift succession fired three further shots into the tin. Francis saw the gasoline flood all over the sacking. He thought, with a kind of sick disillusionment yet quicker than the thudding shots: *Shon was mistaken, the bullets won't ignite the gasoline, or perhaps it is only kerosene they put inside the tin.* He saw Shon shooting into the crowd now, struggling to free his gun, shouting hopelessly to his own men to rush in. He saw the captain and a dozen soldiers closing on him. It all happened as swiftly as his thought. He felt a final, devastating wave of anger and despair. Deliberately, as though casting with a salmon rod, he drew back his arm and threw his torch.

His accuracy was beautiful. The blazing flare arched like a comet through the night and hit the oil-soaked sacking squarely in the center. Instantly a great sheet of sound and light struck at him. He no more than sensed the brilliant flash when the earth erupted and amid a frightful detonation a blast of scorching air blew him backward into crashing darkness. He had never lost consciousness before. He seemed falling, falling, into space and blackness, clutching for support and finding none, falling to annihilation, to oblivion.

When his senses returned he found himself stretched in the open, limp but unhurt, with Shon pulling his earlobes to bring him round. Dimly he saw the red sky above him. The whole cypress grove was ablaze, crackling and roaring like a pyre.

"Is the gun finished?"

Shon stopped the ear tweaking and sat up, relieved.

"Yes, it is finished. And some thirty of Wai's soldiers blown to pieces with it." His teeth showed white in his scorched face. "My friend, I congratulate you. I have never seen such a lovely killing in my life. Another such and you may have me for a Christian."

The next few days brought a terrible confusion of mind and spirit to Father Chisholm. The physical reaction to his adventure almost prostrated him. He was no virile hero of romantic fiction but a stubby, short-winded little man well over forty. He felt shaken and dizzy. His head ached so persistently he had to drag himself to his room several times a day to plunge his splitting brow in the tepid water of his ewer. And through this bodily suffering ran the greater anguish of his soul, a chaotic mixture of triumph and remorse, a heavy and relentless wonder that he, a priest of God, should have raised his hand to slay his fellow men. He could barely find self-vindication in the safety of his people. His strangest torment lay in the stabbing recollection of his own unconsciousness under the shock of the explosion. Was death like that? A total oblivion . . .

No one but Polly suspected that he had left the mission grounds that night. He could feel her tranquil gaze traveling from his own silent and diminished form to the charred cedar stumps that marked the remnants of the gun emplacement. There was infinite understanding in the banal phrase she spoke to him:

"Somebody has done us a good turn by getting that nuisance out of the way."

Fighting continued in the outskirts of the city and in the hills to the eastward. By the fourth day, reports reaching the mission indicated that the struggle was turning against Wai.

The end of that week came gray and overcast, with heavy gathering clouds. On Saturday the firing in Pai-tan dwindled to a few spasmodic rattles. Watching from his balcony Father Chisholm saw strings of figures in the Wai green retreating from the western gate. Many of these had thrown away their arms in the fear of being captured and shot as rebels. This Francis knew to be an indication of Wai's reverses and of his inability to effect a compromise with General Naian.

Outside the mission, behind the upper wall where some bamboo canes screened them from observation from the city, a number of these scattered soldiers had collected. Their voices, indeterminate and plainly frightened, could be heard inside the mission.

Toward three o'clock in the afternoon Sister Clotilde came with renewed agitation to Father Chisholm as he paced the courtyard, too disturbed to rest.

"Anna is throwing food over the upper wall." She wailed out the complaint. "I am sure her soldier is there . . . they were talking together."

His own nerves were near to breaking point. "There is no harm in giving food to those who need it."

"But he is one of those dreadful cutthroats. Oh, dear, we shall all be murdered in our beds!"

"Don't think so much about your own throat." He flushed with annoyance. "Martyrdom is an easy way to heaven."

As twilight fell, masses of the beaten Wai forces poured from all the city gates. They came by the Manchu Bridge, swarming up the Brilliant Green Jade road past the mission, in great confusion. The dirty faces of the men were stamped with the urgency of flight.

The night that followed was one of darkness and disorder, filled with shouting and shots, with galloping horses and the flare of torches on the far-off plain below. The priest watched with a strange melancholy from the lower mission gate. Suddenly, as he stood there, he heard a cautious step behind him. He turned. As he had half-expected, it was Anna, her mission coat buttoned closely to her chin, a cloth-wrapped bundle in her hand.

"Where are you going, Anna?"

She drew back with a stifled cry, but immediately regained her sullen boldness.

"It is my own affair."

"You will not tell me?"

"No."

His mood had fallen to quieter key, his attitude was changed. What was the use of more compulsion here?

"You have made up your mind to leave us, Anna. That is evident. And nothing that I can say or do will change it."

She said bitterly: "You have caught me now. But the next time you will not do so."

"There need be no next time, Anna." He took the key from his pocket and unlocked the gate. "You are free to go."

He could feel her start in sheer amazement, feel the impact of those full sultry eyes. Then without a word of gratitude or farewell she gripped her bundle and darted through the opening. Her running form was lost in the crowded roadway.

He stood, bareheaded, while the rabble swept past him. Now the exodus had turned to a rout. Suddenly there was a louder shouting, and he saw in the bobbing glare of upheld torches a group of men on horses. They approached rapidly, beating their way through the slow unmounted stream that hindered them. As they reached the gate one of the riders wrenched his lathered pony to a stop. In the torchlight the priest had a vision of incredible evil, a death's-head face, with narrowed slits of eyes, and a low receding brow. The horseman shouted at him, an insult charged with hatred, then raised his hand with immediate deadly menace. Francis did not move. His perfect immobility, uncaring and resigned, seemed to disconcert the other. While he hesitated for an instant a pressing cry was raised from behind. "On, on, Wai . . . to Tou-en-lai . . . they are coming!"

Wai dropped his hand, holding the weapon, with a queer fatalism. As he spurred his beast forward he bent in the saddle and spat venomously in the priest's face. The night enclosed him.

Next morning, which dawned bright and sunny, the mission bells were ringing gaily. Fu, of his own accord, had clambered to the tower. He swung on the long rope, his thin beard wagging with delight. Most of the refugees were ready to go home, their faces jubilant, waiting only to have the mission father's word before departing. All the children were in the compound, laughing and skipping, watched by Martha and Maria-Veronica, who had patched up their differences sufficiently to stand no more than six feet apart.

Even Clotilde was playing, the gayest of all, bouncing a ball, running with the little ones, giggling. Polly, upright in her favorite place in the vegetable garden, sat winding a new skein of wool as though life were nothing but a round of calm normality.

When Father Chisholm came slowly down the steps of his house Joseph met him joyfully, carrying his chubby infant on his arm. "It is over, Master. Victory for the Naians. The new general is truly great. No more war in Pai-tan. He promises it. Peace for all of us in our time." He bounced the baby tenderly, triumphantly. "No fighting for you my little Joshua, no more tears and blood. Peace! Peace!"

Inexplicably, a shaft of utter sadness pierced the priest's heart. He took the babe's tiny cheek, soft and golden, between his thumb and finger, caressingly. He stifled his sigh and smiled. They were all running toward him, his children, his people whom he loved—whom, at the cost of his dearest principle, he had saved.

10

The end of January brought the first glorious fruits of victory to Pai-tan. And Francis felt relief that Aunt Polly was spared the sight of them. She had departed for England the week before, and although the parting had been difficult he knew in his heart that it was wiser for her to go.

This morning as he crossed to the dispensary he speculated on the length of the rice line. Yesterday it had stretched the whole length of the mission wall. Wai, in the fury of defeat, had burned every stalk of grain for miles around. The sweet-potato crop was poor. The rice fields, tended only by the women, with men and water oxen commandeered by the army, had produced less than half the usual yield. Everything was scarce and costly. In the city, the value of tinned goods had multiplied five times. Prices were soaring daily.

He hastened into the crowded building. All three sisters were there, each with a wooden measure and a black japanned bin of rice, engaged in the interminable task of scooping three ounces of the grain, running it into the proffered bowls.

He stood watching. His people were patient, quite silent. But the motion of the dry kernels made a constant hissing in the room. He said in a low voice to Maria-Veronica: "We can't keep this up. Tomorrow we must cut the allowance in half."

"Very well." She made a gesture of acquiescence. The strain of the past weeks had taken toll of her; he thought her unusually pale. She kept her eyes on the bin.

He went to the outer door, once or twice, counting the numbers. At last, to his relief, the line began to thin. He recrossed the compound and descended to the store cellars, recasting the inventory of their supplies. Fortunately he had placed an order with Mr. Chia two months ago, and it had been faithfully delivered. But the stock of rice and sweet potatoes, which they used in great quantity, was dangerously low.

He stood thinking. Though prices were exorbitant, food could still be purchased in Pai-tan. He took a sudden resolution and decided, for the first time in the mission's history, to cable the society for an emergency grant.

A week later he received the answering cable:

> Quite impossible allocate any monies. Kindly remember we are at war. You are not and therefore extremely lucky. Am immersed Red Cross work. Best regards Anselm Mealey.

Francis crumpled the green slip with an expressionless face. That afternoon he mustered all the available financial resources of the mission and went to the town. But now it was too late—he could buy nothing. The grain market was closed. The principal shops showed only a minimum of perishable produce: some melons, radishes, and small river fish.

Disturbed, he stopped at the Lantern Street mission, where he had a long conversation with Dr. Fiske. Then, on his way back, he visited Mr. Chia's house.

Mr. Chia made Francis welcome. They drank tea together in the latticed little office smelling of spice and musk and cedar.

"Yes," Mr. Chia agreed gravely, when they had fully discussed the shortage. "It is a matter of some small concern. Mr. Pao has gone to Chek-kow to endeavor to procure certain assurances from the new government."

"With some chance of success?"

"With every chance." The mandarin added, with the nearest approach to cynicism Father Chisholm had heard from him: "But assurances are not supplies."

"It was reported that the granary held many tons of reserve grain."

"General Naian took every bushel for himself. He has gutted the city of food."

"But surely," the mission father spoke frowningly, "he cannot see the people starve. He promised them great benefit if they fought for him."

"Now he has mildly expressed the belief that some slight depopulation might benefit the community."

There was a silence. Father Chisholm reflected. "At least it is a blessing that Dr. Fiske will have large supplies. He is promised three full junkloads from his headquarters in Pekin."

"Ah!"

Again the silence.

"You are dubious?"

Mr. Chia responded with his gentle smile. "It is two thousand *li* from Pekin to Pai-tan. And there are many hungry people on the way. In my unworthy opinion, my most esteemed friend, we must prepare for six months of greatest hardship. These things come to China. But what matter? We may go. China remains."

Next morning Father Chisholm was obliged to turn back the rice line. It cut him to the heart to do so, yet he had to close the doors. He instructed Joseph to paint a notice that cases of utter destitution might leave their names at the lodge. He would investigate them personally.

Back in his house he set himself to work out a plan for rationing the mission. And the following week he introduced it. As the scheme began to operate, the children wondered, then passed through fretfulness into a kind of puzzled dullness. They were lethargic, and they asked for more at every meal. The insufficiency of sugar and starchy stuffs seemed to cause them most discomfort. They were losing weight.

From the Methodist mission came no word of the relief stores. The junks were now nearly three weeks overdue, and Dr. Fiske's anxiety was too significant to be mistaken. His public rice kitchen had been closed for more than a month. In Pai-tan the people had a sluggish air, a heavy apathy. There was no light upon their faces, no briskness in their movements.

Then it began and gradually gathered strength: the timeless transmigration, old as China itself, the silent departure of men and women with their children from the city toward the south.

When Father Chisholm saw this symptom his heart chilled. A horrible vision attacked him of his little community, emaciated, relaxed in the final debility of starvation. He drew the lesson, swiftly, from the slow procession now beginning before his eyes.

As in the days of plague, he summoned Joseph to him, spoke to him, and sped him upon an urgent errand.

On the morning following Joseph's departure he came over to the refectory and ordered an extra portion of rice to be given to the children. One last box of figs remained in the larder. He went down the long table giving each child a sweet sticky mouthful.

This sign of better feeding made the community more cheerful. But Martha, with one eye on the almost empty store cellar and the other upon Father Chisholm, muttered her perplexity.

"What is in the wind, Father? There's something . . . I'm sure."

"You shall know on Saturday, Martha. Meanwhile, please tell Reverend Mother we shall continue on the extra rice for the remainder of this week."

Martha went off to do his bidding but could not find Reverend Mother anywhere. It was strange.

All that afternoon Maria-Veronica did not appear. She failed to take her weaving class, which was always held on Wednesdays, in the basket room. At three o'clock she could not be found. Perhaps it was an oversight. Shortly after five, she came in for refectory duty as usual, pale and composed, offering no explanation of her absence. But that night in the convent both Clotilde and Martha were awakened by a startling sound which came, unmistakably, from Maria-Veronica's room.

Appalled, they talked of it next morning in whispers, in the corner of the laundry, watching Reverend Mother through the window as she crossed the courtyard, dignified and upright, yet much slower than before.

"She has broken at last." Martha's words seemed constricted in her throat. "Blessed Virgin, did you hear her weep last night?"

Clotilde stood twisting an end of linen in her hands. "Perhaps she has news of a great German defeat we have not heard of yet."

"Yes, yes . . . it is something terrible." Martha's face suddenly puckered up. "Truly, if she were not an accursed Boche I would feel almost sorry for her."

"I have never known her to weep before." Clotilde meditated, her fingers twisting indecisively. "She is a proud woman. That must make it doubly hard."

"Pride goeth before a fall. Would she have had sympathy for us if we had yielded first? Nevertheless I must admit—Bah! Let us continue with our ironing."

Early on Sunday morning a small cavalcade approached the mission, winding downward from the mountains. Advised by Joseph of its arrival, Father Chisholm hastened to the lodge to welcome Liu-Chi and his three companions from the Liu village. He clasped the old shepherd's hands as though he would never let them go.

"This is true kindness. The good God will bless you for it."

Liu-Chi smiled, naively pleased by the warmth of his reception. "We would have come sooner. But we took much time to collect the ponies."

There were perhaps thirty of the short shaggy uplands ponies, bridled but unsaddled, with big double panniers strapped upon their backs. They were contentedly munching the swathes of dried grass strewn for them. The priest's heart lifted. He pressed the four men to the refreshments that Joseph's wife had already prepared in the lodge, told them they must rest when they had eaten.

He found Reverend Mother in the linen room silently passing out fresh white bundles of the week's requirements: table covers, sheets, and towels, to Martha, Clotilde, and one of the senior students. He no longer attempted to conceal his satisfaction.

"I must prepare you for a change. Because of the threat of famine we are moving to the Liu village. You'll find plenty there, I assure you." He smiled. "Sister Martha, you'll find many ways of cooking mountain mutton before you return. I know you will enjoy the experience. And for the children . . . it will be a fine holiday."

There was a moment's sheer surprise. Then Martha and Clotilde both smiled, conscious of a coming break in the monotony of life, already stirring to the excitement of the adventure.

"Doubtless you will expect us to be organized in five minutes," Martha grumbled amiably, casting her eye instructively, for the first time in many weeks, upon Reverend Mother, as if for her approval.

It was the first faint gesture of atonement. But Maria-Veronica, standing by, with a colorless face, gave no answering sign.

"Yes, you must look sharp." Father Chisholm spoke almost gaily. "The little ones will be packed into the panniers. The others must take turns of walking and riding. The nights are warm and fine. Liu-Chi will look after you. If you leave today you should reach the village in a week."

Clotilde giggled. "We shall be like one of the tribes of Egypt."

The priest nodded. "I am giving Joseph a basket of my fantails. Every evening he must release one to bring me a message of your progress.

"What!" Martha and Clotilde exclaimed together. "You are not coming with us?"

"I may follow at a later date." Francis felt happy that they should want him. "You see, someone must remain at the mission. Reverend Mother and you two will be the pioneers."

Maria-Veronica said slowly: "I cannot go."

There was a silence.

At first he thought it a continuation of her pique, a disinclination to accompany the other two, but one glance at her face told him otherwise.

He said persuasively: "It will be a pleasant trip. The change would do you good."

She shook her head slowly. "I shall be obliged to take a longer trip . . . quite soon."

There was a longer pause. Then standing very still, she spoke with a toneless lack of emotion. "I must return to Germany . . . to see about the disposal . . . to our order . . . of my estate." She gazed into the distance. "My brother has been killed in action."

The previous silence had been deep, but now there was a mortal stillness. It was Clotilde who burst into violent tears. Then Martha, as though trapped, like an animal, hung her head unwillingly, in sympathy. Father Chisholm glanced from one to the other in deep distress, then walked silently away.

A fortnight after the party had arrived at Liu, the day of Maria-Veronica's departure was, incredibly, upon him. The latest information from the village, received by pigeon post, indicated that the children were primitively yet comfortably billeted, and wild with health in the keen high air. Father Chisholm had good reason to congratulate himself upon his own resourcefulness. Yet as he walked beside Maria-Veronica to the landing steps, preceded by two bearers with long poles, supporting her baggage upon their shoulders, he felt a desperate forlornness.

They stood on the jetty while the men placed the bundles in the sampan. Behind them the city lay, murmuring in still dejection. Before them, in midriver, lay the outgoing junk. The dun water that lapped its hull reached out to a gray horizon.

He could find no words to express himself. She had meant so much to him, this gracious and distinguished woman, with her help, encouragement, and comradeship. The future had stretched before them, indefinitely, a future filled with their work together. Now she was going, unexpectedly, almost furtively, it seemed, in a haze of darkness and confusion.

He sighed, at last, giving her his troubled smile. "Even if my country remains at war with yours . . . remember I am not your enemy."

The understatement was so like him, and all that she admired in him, it shook her determination to be strong. As she gazed at his spare figure, gaunt face, and thinning hair, tears clouded her beautiful eyes.

"My dear . . . dear friend . . . I will never forget you."

She gave him her warm firm clasp and stepped quickly into the little craft that would take her to the junk.

He stood there, leaning on his old tartan umbrella, his eyes screwed against the water's glitter, until the vessel was a speck, floating, vanishing beyond the rim of the sky.

Unknown to her, he had placed among her baggage the little antique figure of the Spanish Virgin that Father Tarrant had given him. It was his sole possession of any value. She had often admired it.

He turned and slowly plodded home. In the garden, which she had made and loved so much, he paused, grateful for the silence and the peace there. The scent of lilies was in the air. Old Fu, the gardener, his sole companion in the deserted mission, was pruning the azalea bushes with gentle, inquiring hands. He felt worn-out by all that he had lately undergone. A chapter in his life was ended; for the first time, he dimly sensed that he was growing old. He seated himself on the bench beneath the banyan tree, rested his elbows on the pinewood table she had placed there. Old Fu, pruning the azaleas, pretended not to see him as, after a moment, he laid his head upon his arms.

11

The broad leaves of the banyan tree still shaded him as he sat at the garden table turning the pages of his journal with hands which, as by some strange illusion, were veined and vaguely tremulous. Of course, old Fu no longer watched him, unless through a chink of heaven. Instead, two young gardeners bent by the azalea bed while Father Chou, his Chinese priest, small, gentle, and demure, pacing with his breviary at a respectful distance, kept a warm brown filial eye upon him.

In the August sunshine the mission compound was aquiver with dry light, like the sparkle of a golden wine. From the playground the happy shouts of the children at their playtime told him the forenoon hour: eleven o'clock. His children, or rather, he corrected himself wryly, his children's children . . . How unfairly time had flashed across him, tumbling the years into his lap, one upon another, too fast for him to marshal them.

A jolly red face, plump and smiling, swam into his abstracted vision, above a tumblerful of milk. He forced a frown as Mother Mercy Mary drew near, annoyed to be reminded of his age by another of her coddling tricks. He was only sixty-seven . . . well, sixty-eight next month . . . a mere nothing and . . . fitter than any youngster.

"Haven't I told you not to bring me that stuff?"

She smiled soothingly—vigorous, bustling, and matronly. "You need it today, Father, if you will insist on taking that long unnecessary trip." She paused. "I don't see why Father Chou and Dr. Fiske couldn't go themselves?"

"Don't you?"

"No, indeed."

"Dear Sister, that's too bad. Your mind must be breaking up." She laughed indulgently and tried to coax him.

"Shall I tell Joshua you've decided not to go?"

"Tell him to have the ponies saddled in an hour."

He saw her depart, shaking her head reproachfully. He smiled again, with the dry triumph of a man who has had his way. Then, sipping his milk, without, now that she was gone, the necessity of a grimace, he resumed his leisured perusal of the diary before him. It was a habit into which he had lately fallen, a kind of willful retrospection, evoked by turning the frayed and dog-eared pages at random.

This morning it opened, strangely, first at the date *October 1917*.

"Despite the improving conditions in Pai-tan, the good rice crop, and the safe homecoming of my little ones from Liu, I have been downcast lately; yet today a simple incident gave me preposterous happiness.

"I had been away for four days at the annual conference that the prefect apostolic has thought fit to institute at Sen-siang. As the farthest outpost of the vicariate I had fancied myself immune from such junkets. Indeed, we missioners are so widely scattered and so few—only Father Surette, poor Thibodeau's successor, the three Chek-kow Chinese priests and Father Van Dwyn the Dutchman from Rakai—that the occasion seemed scarcely worth the long river journey. But there we were 'exchanging viewpoints.' And naturally I talked indiscreetly against 'aggressive Christianizing methods,' got hot under the collar, and quoted Mr. Pao's cousin: 'You missionaries walk in with your gospel and walk off with our land.' I fell into disgrace with Father Surette, a bustling father who rejoices in his muscles, which he has used to destroy all the pleasant little Buddhist wayside shrines within twenty *li* of Sen-siang, and who in addition claims the amazing record of fifty thousand pious ejaculations in one day.

"On my return trip I was overcome with remorse. How often have I had to write in this journal: 'Failed again. Dear Lord, help me restrain my tongue!' And they thought me such a queer fish at Sen-siang!

"To mortify myself I had dispensed with a cabin on the boat. Next to me on deck was a man with a cage of prime rats, which he dined on, progressively, under my jaundiced eye. In addition it rained hard, blew down streams, and I was, as I deserved to be, extremely sick.

"Then, as I stepped off the vessel at Pai-tan, more dead than alive, I found an old woman waiting for me on the drenched, deserted jetty. As she approached I saw her to be my friend, old mother Hsu, she who cooked beans in the milk can in the compound. She is the poorest, the lowest person in my parish.

"To my amazement her face was illuminated at the sight of me. Quickly she told me she had missed me so much she had stood there in the rain these past three afternoons, waiting my arrival. She produced six little ceremonial cakes of rice flour and sugar, not for eating—the kind they place before the images of Buddha—the same images that Father Surette knocks down. A comic gesture . . . but the joy of knowing that to one person at least one is dear . . . and indispensable . . ."

"*May 1918.* This lovely morning my first batch of young settlers departed for Liu, twenty-four in all—I might discreetly add, twelve of each kind—amid great enthusiasm and many knowing nods and practical admonitions from our good Reverend Mother Mercy Mary. Though I resented her coming intensely—weighing her sulkily against the memory of Maria-Veronica—she is a fine, capable, cheerful person, and for a holy nun she has an amazing insight into the exigencies of the marriage bed.

"Old Meg Paxton, the Cannelgate fishwife, used to reassure me that I wasn't such a fool as I looked; and I'm quite proud of my inspiration to colonize Liu—with the finest produce of this mission of St. Andrew's. There simply aren't enough jobs here for my growing-up young people. It would seem the worst kind of stupidity, having pulled them out of the gutter, to throw them back again, benevolently, now they are educated. And Liu itself will profit by an infusion of fresh blood. There is ample land, a stirring climate. Once the numbers are adequate I shall establish a young priest there. Anselm must send me one; until he does so, I shall deafen him with my importunities. . . .

"I am tired tonight from the excitement and the ceremonies—these mass marriages are no joke, and Chinese ceremonial oratory leaves the vocal cords in ruins. Perhaps my depression is reactionary, perhaps physical. I do need a holiday quite badly; I am a little stale. The Fiskes have gone off for their routine six months' rest, to visit their son, now established in Virginia. I miss them. Their relief, the Reverend Ezra Salkins, makes me realize how fortunate I am to have such sweet and gentle neighbors. Shang-Foo Ezra is neither—a big man with a fixed beam, a Rotarian handshake, and a smile like melting lard. He boomed at me as he cracked my finger bones: 'Anything I can do to help you, brother, anything at all.'

"The Fiskes would be my honored guests at Liu. But to Ezra I am dumb. In just sixty seconds he would have Father Ribiero's tomb plastered with bill heads: 'Brother are you saved?' Oh, blow! I am crabbed and sour; it's that plum pie Mercy Mary made me eat at the wedding breakfast. . . .

"I have been made truly happy by a long letter dated June 10th, 1922, from Mother Maria-Veronica. After many vicissitudes, the trials of the war, and the humiliations of the armistice, she has at last been rewarded by her appointment as superior of the Sistine Convent in Rome. This is the mother house of her order, a fine old foundation on the high slopes between the Corso and the Quirinal overlooking the Saporelli and the lovely church of Santi Apostoli. It is an office of the first importance but no more than she deserves. She seems contented . . . at peace. Her letter brings me such a fragrance of the Holy City—that might be one of Anselm's phrases!—always the object of my tender longings, I have dared to make a plan. When my sick leave, already twice postponed, does arrive, what is to prevent my visiting Rome, wearing my boots out on the mosaics of St. Peter's, and seeing Mother Maria-Veronica in the bargain? When I wrote in April congratulating Anselm on his appointment as rector of the Tynecastle Cathedral Church he assured me, in his reply, that I should have an assistant priest within six months and my 'much-needed vacation' before the year was out.

"An absurd thrill pervades my sun-bleached bones when I think that such happiness may be in store for me. Enough! I must start to save to buy myself a suit of clothes. What would the good abbess of Santi Apostoli think if the little bricklayer who claimed her acquaintance turned out to have a patch on the backside of his pants. . . ."

"*September 17th, 1923.* Breathless excitement! Today, my new priest arrived; at last I have a colleague, and it seems almost too good to be true.

"Although, at first, Anselm's voluminous hieratics gave me hope of a stout young Scot, preferably with freckles and sandy hair, later advices had prepared me for a native father from the college at Pekin. It was like my perverted humor to tell the sisters nothing of the coming denouement. For weeks they had been gathering themselves to coddle the young missioner from home—Clotilde and Martha wanted something Gallic with a beard, but poor Mother Mercy Mary had made a very special novena for an Irish one. The look on her honest Hibernian face as she burst into my room, purple with tragedy! 'The new father is a Chinese!'

"But Father Chou seems a splendid little fellow, not only quiet and amiable, but conveying a deep sense of that extraordinary interior life that is such an admirable characteristic of the Chinese. I have met several native priests on my infrequent pilgrimages to Sen-siang, and I have always been impressed. If I wished to be pompous I should say that the good ones appear to combine the wisdom of Confucius with the virtue of Christ.

"And now I am off to Rome, next month . . . my first holiday in nineteen years. I am like a Holywell schoolboy, at the end of term, banging his desk and chanting:

> 'Two more weeks and I shall be,
> Outside the gates of mis-er-ee.'

"I wonder if Mother Maria-Veronica has lost her taste for fine-stem ginger. I shall take her a jar and risk being told she has turned to macaroni. Heigh-ho! This life is most jolly. Through my window I see the young cedars swaying in the wind with a wild joy. I must write now to Shanghai for my tickets. Hurrah!"

"*October 1923.* Yesterday the cable came canceling my trip to Rome, and I have just returned from my evening walk by the riverbank where I stood a long time in a soft mist watching the cormorant fishers. It is a sad way of catching fish, or perhaps I had a sad way of looking at it. The great birds are ringed by the neck to prevent their swallowing the fish. They crouch indolently on the gunwale of the boat as though dreadfully bored with the whole proceeding. Suddenly there is a dip and a splutter and up comes the great bill, pouched with fish, a tail wriggling at the tip. An embarrassing undulation of the neck follows next. When relieved of their catch the birds shake their heads, disconsolate, yet as though experience had taught them nothing. Then they squat again, brooding blackly, recuperating for a fresh defeat.

"My own mood was dark and defeated enough, God knows. As I stood by the slate water, from which the night wind threw waves upon the weed coiled like hair upon the shore, my thoughts, strangely, were not of Rome but of the streams of Tweedside, with myself, barefoot in the rippling crystal, casting a withy rod for trout.

"More and more of late I find myself living in the memory of my childhood, recollected so vividly it might be yesterday—a sure symptom of approaching age! . . . I even dream, tenderly, wistfully—isn't this unbelievable?—of my boyish love: my own dear Nora.

"You see, I have reached the sentimental stage of disappointment, which is next to getting over it, but when the telegram arrived, in old Meg's words, 'it was hard to thole.'

"Now I am almost resigned to the utter finality of my exile. The principle is probably correct that a return to Europe unsettles the missionary priest. After all, we give ourselves entirely; there is no retreat. I am here for life. And I'll lay myself, at last, in that little piece of Scotland where Willie Tulloch rests.

"Moreover, it is certainly logical and just that Anselm's trip to Rome is more necessary than mine. The funds of the society cannot sustain two such excursions. And he can better tell the Holy Father of the advances of 'his troops'—as he calls us. Where my tongue would be stiff and clumsy his will captivate—garner funds and support for all the FS missions. He has promised to write me fully of his doings. I must enjoy Rome vicariously, have my audience in imagination, meet Maria-Veronica in spirit. I could not bring myself to accept Anselm's suggestion of a short vacation in Manila. Its gaiety would have troubled me; I should have laughed at the solitary little man, poking round the harbor, fancying himself on the Pontine Hill. . . ."

"*A month later.* . . . Father Chou is nicely established in the Liu village and our pigeons pass one another at celestial speed. What a joy that my scheme is working so beautifully. I wonder if Anselm will mention it, perhaps, when he sees the Holy Father, just a word of that tiny jewel, set in the great wilderness, once forgotten . . . by all but God. . . ."

"*November 22nd, 1928.* How can one compass a sublime experience in mere words—in one bald and arid phrase? Last night Sister Clotilde died. Death is a topic I have not often dwelled upon in this sketchy record of my own imperfect life.

"Thus, twelve months ago when Aunt Polly passed away in her sleep at Tynecastle, uneventfully and of pure goodness and old age, and the news reached me in Judy's tear-smudged letter, I made no comment here beyond the simple entry: 'Polly died, October 17th, 1927.' There is an inevitability in the death of those whom we know to be good. But there are others . . . sometimes we tough old priests are staggered, as by a revelation.

"Clotilde had been ailing, slightly it seemed, for several days. . . . When they called me just after midnight I was shocked to see the change in her. I sent at once to tell Joshua, Joseph's eldest boy—to run for Dr. Fiske. But Clotilde, with a strange expression, restrained me. She indicated, with a peculiar smile, that Joshua might spare himself the journey. She said very little; but enough.

"When I recollected how, years ago, I tartly reproached her for that inexplicable recourse to Chlorodyne, I could have wept for my stupidity. I had never thought enough of Clotilde: the tension of her manner, which she could not help, her morbid dread of flushing, of people, of her own overcharged nerves, made her superficially unattractive, even ridiculous. One should have reflected on the struggles of such a nature to overcome itself; one should have thought of the invisible victories. Instead, one thought only of the visible defeats.

"For eighteen months she had been suffering from a growth of the stomach arising out of a chronic ulcer. When she learned from Dr. Fiske that nothing could be done she pledged him to secrecy and set herself to fight an unsung battle. Before I was called the first bad hemorrhage had prostrated her. At six next morning she had the second and succumbed quite quietly. Between, we talked . . . but I dare not make a record of that conversation. Broken and disjointed, it would seem meaningless . . . a prey for easy sneers . . . and alas, the world cannot be reformed by a sneer . . .

"We are all much upset, Martha especially. She is like me, strong as a mule, and will go on forever. Poor Clotilde! I think of her as a gentle creature so strung to sacrifice that sometimes she vibrated harshly. To see a face become at peace, a quiet acceptance of death, without fear . . . it ennobles the heart of man."

"*November 30th, 1929.* Today Joseph's fifth child was born. How life flies on! Who would have dreamed that my shy, brave, garrulous, touchy youngster had in him the makings of a patriarch? Perhaps his early fondness for sugar should have warned me! Really, he is quite a personage now—officious, uxorious, a little pompous, very curt to callers he thinks I should not see—I am rather scared of him myself. . . ."

"*A week later.* More local news . . . Mr. Chia's dress boots have been hung up at the Manchu Gate. This is a tremendous honor here . . . and I rejoice for my old friend, whose ascetic, contemplative, generous nature has always been devoted to the reasonable and the beautiful, to that which is eternal.

"Yesterday the mail came in. Even without the presage of his immense success in Rome, I had long realized that Anselm must achieve high honor in the church. And at last his work for the foreign missions has earned him a fitting reward from the Vatican. He is the new bishop of Tynecastle. Perhaps the greatest strain is thrown upon our moral vision by the spectacle of another's success. The dazzle hurts us. But now, in my approaching old age, I'm shortsighted. I don't mind Anselm's luster; I'm rather glad, because I know that he will be supremely glad himself. Jealousy is so hateful a quality. One should remember that the defeated still have everything if they still have God.

"I wish I might take credit for my magnanimity. But this is not magnanimity, merely an awareness of the difference between Anselm and myself . . . of the ridiculous presumption of myself aspiring to the crozier. Though we started from the same mark, Anselm has far outstripped me. He has developed his talents to the full, is now, I observe from the *Tynecastle Chronicle,* 'an accomplished linguist, a notable musician, a patron of arts and science in the diocese, with a vast circle of influential friends.' How lucky! I have had no more than six friends in my uneventful life, and all except one were humble folk. I must write to Anselm to congratulate him, making it clear, however, that I do not presume upon our friendship and have no intention of asking for preferment. *Viva Anselmo!* I am sad when I think how much you have made of your life and how little I have made of mine. I have bumped my head so often . . . and so hard, in my strivings after God."

"*December 30th, 1929.* I have not written in this journal for almost a month . . . not since the news of Judy arrived. I still find it difficult to set down even the barest outline of what has taken place at home . . . and here, within myself.

"I flattered myself I had achieved a beatific resignation toward the finality of my exile. Two weeks ago today, I was remarkably complacent. Having made a survey of my recent additions to the mission, the four rice fields by the river, which I bought last year, the enlarged stockyard beyond the white mulberry grove, and the new pony farm, I came into the church to help the children make the Christmas crib. This is a job I particularly enjoy, partly from that lamentable obsession that has stuck to me all my life; I suppose the ribald would call it a suppressed paternal instinct: a love of children—from the dear Christ child down to the meanest little yellow waif who ever crawled into this mission of St. Andrew's.

"We had made a splendid manger with a snowy roof of real cotton wool and were arranging the ox and ass in their stall behind. I had all sorts of things up my sleeve too, colored lights, and a fine crystal star to hang on the spruce-branched sky. As I saw the shining faces about me and listened to the excited chatter—this is one of the occasions when distractions are permissible in church—I had a wonderful sense of lightness, a vision of all the Christmas cribs in all the Christian churches of the world, dignifying this sweet festival of the Nativity, which, even to those who cannot believe, must at least be beautiful as the feast of all motherhood.

"At that moment one of the bigger boys, sent by Mother Mercy Mary, hurried in with the cablegram. Surely ill tidings come fast enough without flashing them round the earth. As I read, my expression must have changed. One of the smallest girls began to cry. The brightness in my breast was quenched.

"Perhaps I might be judged absurd for taking this so much to heart. I lost Judy when in her teens, on my departure for Pai-tan. But I have lived her life with her in thought. The infrequency of her letters made them stand out like beads upon a chain.

"The hand of heredity propelled Judy forward without mercy. She never quite knew what she wanted or where she was going. But so long as Polly stood beside her she could not become the victim of her own caprice. All through the war she prospered, like many other young women, working for high wages in a munitions factory. She bought a fur coat and a piano—how well I recollect the letter in which the joyful information reached me—and was keyed to sustain her effort by the sense of emergency in the air. This was her heyday. When the war ended, she was over thirty; opportunities were scarce; she gradually abandoned all thought of a career and lapsed into a quiet life with Polly, sharing the small flat in Tynecastle and gaining, one hoped, with maturity, an added balance.

"Judy seemed always to have a queer suspicion toward the other sex and had never been attracted by the thought of marriage. She was forty when Polly died, and one never dreamed that she would change her single state. Nevertheless, within eight months of the funeral, Judy was married . . . and later deserted.

"One does not disguise the brutal fact that women do strange things before the climacteric. But this was not the explanation of the pitiful comedy. Polly's legacy to Judy was some two thousand pounds, enough to provide a modest annual competence. Not until Judy's letter arrived did I guess how she had been persuaded to realize her capital, to transfer it to her sober, upright, and gentlemanly husband whom she had first met, apparently, in a boardinghouse at Scarborough.

"No doubt whole volumes might be written on this basic mundane theme . . . dramatic . . . analytical . . . in the grand Victorian manner . . . perhaps with that sly smirk that sees a rich deep humor in the gullibility of our human nature. But the epilogue was briefly written in ten words on the telegraph form that I held in my hands before the Christmas crib. A child had been born to Judy of this belated, transitory union. And she had died in bearing it.

"Now I reflect there had always been a dark thread running through the flimsy fabric of Judy's inconsequential life. She was the visible evidence, not of sin—how I detest and distrust that word!—but of man's weakness and stupidity. She was the reason, the explanation of our presence here on earth, the tragic evidence of our common mortality. And now, differently, yet with the same essential sadness, that mortal tragedy is again perpetuated.

"I cannot bring myself to contemplate the fate of this unlucky infant, with no one to look after it but the woman who attended Judy—she who has now sent me the news. It is easy to fit her to the pattern of events: one of those handy wives who take in expectant mothers, in straitened, slightly dubious circumstances. I must reply to her at once . . . send some money, what little I have. When we bind ourselves to holy poverty we are strangely selfish, forgetful of the awful obligations that life may place upon us. Poor Nora . . . poor Judy . . . poor unnamed little child . . ."

⊕

"*June 19th, 1930.* A grand day of early summer sunshine, and my heart is lighter for the letter received this afternoon. The child is baptized Andrew, after this same infamous mission, and the news makes me chuckle with senile vanity, as though I, myself, were the little wretch's grandfather. Perhaps, whether I wish it or not, this relationship will devolve on me. The father has vanished, and we shall make no attempt to trace him. But if I send a certain sum each month, this woman, Mrs. Stevens, who seems a worthy creature, will care for Andrew. Again I can't help smiling . . . my priestly career has been a hodgepodge of peculiarities . . . to rear an infant at a distance of eight thousand miles will be its crowning oddity!

"Wait a moment! I've flicked myself on the raw with that phrase: 'my priestly career.' The other day, during one of our friendly tiffs, on purgatory I think it was, Fiske declared—heatedly, for I was getting the better of him: 'You argue like a mixed convention of holy rollers and high Anglicans!'

"That brought me up short. I daresay my upbringing, and that early bit of the uncalculable influence of dear old Daniel Glennie, shaped me toward undue liberality. I love my religion, into which I was born, which I have taught, as best I could, for over thirty years, and which has led me unfailingly to the source of all joy, of everlasting sweetness. Yet in my isolation here my outlook has simplified, clarified with my advancing years. I've tied up, and neatly tucked away, all the complex, pettifogging little quirks of doctrine. Frankly, I can't believe that any of God's creatures will grill for all eternity because of eating a mutton chop on Friday. If we have the fundamentals—love for God and our neighbor—surely we're all right? And isn't it time for the churches of the world to cease hating one another . . . and unite? The world is one living, breathing body, dependent for its health on the billions of cells that comprise it . . . and each tiny cell is the heart of man . . ."

"*December 15th, 1932.* Today the new patron saint of this mission was three years old. I hope he had a pleasant birthday and didn't eat too much of the toffee I wrote Burley's, in Tweedside, to send him."

"*September 1st, 1935.* Oh Lord, don't let me be a silly old man . . . this journal is becoming more and more the fatuous record of a child I have not seen and shall never see. I cannot return, and he cannot come here. Even my obstinacy balks at that absurdity . . . though I did in fact inquire of Dr. Fiske, who told me that the climate would be deadly for an English child of such tender years.

"Yet I must confess I'm troubled. Reading between her letters it would seem as though Mrs. Stevens had lately come down a little in her luck. She has moved to Kirkbridge, which, as I remember it, is a cotton town, not prepossessing, near Manchester. Her tone has altered, too, and I am beginning to wonder if she is more interested in the money she receives than in Andrew. Yet her parish priest gave her an excellent character. And hitherto she has been admirable.

"Of course, it's all my own fault. I could have secured Andrew's future, after a fashion, by turning him over to one of our excellent Catholic institutions. But somehow . . . he's my one 'blood relation,' a living memento of my dear lost Nora. . . . I can't and I won't be so impersonal. . . . It's my inveterate crankiness, I suppose, that makes me fight against officialdom. Well . . . if that is so . . . I . . . and Andrew . . . must take the consequences . . . we are in God's hands and he will . . ."

Here, as Father Chisholm turned another page, his concentration was disturbed by the sound of ponies stamping in the compound. He hesitated, listening, half unwilling to relinquish his mood of precious reverie. But the sound increased, mingled with brisk voices. His lips drew together in acceptance. He turned to the last entry in the journal and, taking his pen, added a paragraph.

"*April 30th, 1936.* I am on the point of leaving for the Liu settlement with Father Chou and the Fiskes. Yesterday Father Chou came in, anxious for my advice about a young herdsman he had isolated at the settlement, fearing he might have the smallpox. I decided to go back with him myself—with our good ponies and the new trail, it is only a two days' journey. Then I amplified the idea. Since I have repeatedly promised to show Dr. and Mrs. Fiske our model village, I decided we might all four take the trip. It will be my last opportunity to fulfill my long-outstanding pledge to the doctor and his wife. They are returning home to America at the end of this month. I hear them calling now. They are looking forward to the excursion . . . I'll tackle Fiske en route on his confounded impudence . . . holy roller, indeed! . . ."

12

The sun was already dropping toward the bare rim of the hills that enclosed the narrow valley. Riding ahead of the returning party, occupied by thoughts of Liu, where they had left Father Chou with medicine for the sick herdsman, Father Chisholm had resigned himself to another night encampment before reaching the mission when, at a bend of the road, he met three men in dirty cotton uniforms slouching head down with rifles on their hips.

It was a familiar sight: the province was swarming with irregulars, disbanded soldiers with smuggled weapons who had formed themselves into roving gangs. He passed them with a muttered, "Peace be with you," and slowed down till the others of the party made up to him. But as he turned he was surprised to see terror on the faces of the two porters from the Methodist mission and a sudden anxiety in his own servant's eyes.

"These look like followers of Wai." Joshua made a gesture toward the road ahead. "And there are others."

The priest swung round stiffly. About twenty of the gray-green figures were approaching down the path, kicking up a cloud of slow white dust. On the shadowed hill, straggling in a winding line, were at least another score. He exchanged a glance with Fiske.

"Let's push on."

The two parties met a moment later. Father Chisholm, smiling, with his usual greeting, kept his beast moving steadily down the middle of the path. The soldiers, gaping stupidly, gave way automatically. The only mounted man, a youngster with a broken peaked cap and some air of authority, enhanced by a corporal's stripe misplaced upon his cuff, halted his shaggy pony indecisively.

"Who are you? And whither are you going?"

"We are missionaries, returning to Pai-tan." Father Chisholm gave the answer calmly across his shoulder, still leading the others forward. They were now almost through the dirty, puzzled, staring mob: Mrs. Fiske and the doctor behind him, followed by Joshua and the two bearers.

The corporal was uncertain but partly satisfied. The encounter was robbed of danger, reduced to commonplace, when suddenly the elder of the two porters lost his head. Prodded by a rifle butt in his passage between the men, he dropped his bundle with a screech of panic and bolted for the cover of the brushwood on the hill.

Father Chisholm suppressed a bitter exclamation. In the gathering twilight, there was a second's dubious immobility. Then a shot rang out, another, and another. The echoes went volleying down the hills. As the blue figure of the bearer, bent double, vanished into the bushes, a loud defrauded outcry broke amongst the soldiers. No longer dumbly wondering, they crowded around the missionaries, in furious, chattering resentment.

"You must come with us." As Father Chisholm had foreseen, the corporal's reaction was immediate.

"We are only missionaries," Dr. Fiske protested heatedly. "We have no possessions. We are honest people."

"Honest people do not run away. You must come to our leader, Wai."

"I assure you—"

"Wilbur!" Mrs. Fiske interposed quietly. "You'll only make it worse. Save your breath."

Bundled about, surrounded by the soldiers, they were roughly pushed along the path that they had recently traversed. About five *li* back, the young officer turned west into a dry watercourse that took a tortuous and stony course into the hills. At the head of the gully the company halted.

Here perhaps a hundred ill-conditioned soldiers were scattered about in postures of ease—smoking, chewing betel nut, scraping lice from their armpits and caked mud from between their bare toes. On a flat stone, cross-legged, eating his evening meal before a small dung fire, with his back against the wall of the ravine, was Wai-Chu.

Wai was now about fifty-five, gross but full-bellied, with a greater and more evil immobility. His ghee-oiled hair, worn long and parted in the middle, fell over a forehead so drawn down by a perpetual frown as to narrow the oblique eyes to slits. Three years before, a bullet had sheared away his front teeth and upper lip. The scar was horrible. Despite it, Francis plainly recognized the horseman who had spat into his face at the mission gate that night of the retreat. Hitherto he had sustained their detention with composure. But now, under that hidden, subhuman gaze, charged beneath its blankness with an answering recognition, the priest was conscious of a sharp constriction of his heart.

While the corporal volubly related the circumstances of the capture, Wai continued unfathomably to eat, the twin sticks sending a stream of liquid rice and pork lumps into his gullet from the bowl pressed beneath his chin. Suddenly two soldiers broke up the ravine at the double, dragging the fugitive bearer between them. With a final heave they threw him into the circle of fire glow. The unhappy man fell on his knees close to Wai, his arms skewered behind him, panting and gibbering, in an ecstasy of fear.

Wai continued to eat. Then, casually, he pulled his revolver from his belt and fired it. Caught in the act of supplication, the porter fell forward, his body still jerking against the ground. A creamy pinkish pulp oozed from his blasted skull. Before the stunning reverberations of the report had died Wai had resumed his meal.

Mrs. Fiske had screamed faintly. But beyond a momentary lifting of their heads, the resting soldiers took no notice of the incident. The two who had brought in the bearer now pulled his corpse away and systematically dispossessed it of boots, clothing, and a string of copper cash. Numb and sick, the priest muttered to Dr. Fiske, who stood, very pale, beside him.

"Keep calm . . . show nothing . . . or it is hopeless for all of us."

They waited. The cold and senseless murder had charged the air with horror. At a sign from Wai the second bearer was driven forward and flung upon his knees. The priest felt his stomach turn with a dreadful premonition. But Wai merely said, addressing them all, impersonally:

"This man, your servant, will leave immediately for Pai-tan and inform your friends that you are temporarily in my care. For such hospitality a voluntary gift is customary. At noon on the day following tomorrow two of my men will await him, half a *li* outside the Manchu Gate. He will advance, quite alone." Wai paused blankly. "It is to be hoped he will bring the voluntary gift."

"There is little profit in making us your guests." Dr. Fiske spoke with a throb of indignation. "I have already indicated that we are without worldly goods."

"For each person five thousand dollars is requested. No more."

Fiske breathed more easily. The sum, though large, was not impossible to a mission as wealthy as his own.

"Then permit my wife to return with the messenger. She will ensure that the money is paid."

Wai gave no sign of having heard. For one apprehensive moment the priest thought his overwrought companion was about to make a scene. But Fiske stumbled back to his wife's side. The messenger was dispatched, sent bounding down the ravine with a last forceful injunction from the corporal. Wai then rose and, while his men made preparations for departure, walked forward to his tethered pony, so casually that the dead man's bare upturned feet, protruding from an arbutus bush, struck the eye like a hallucination.

The missionaries' ponies were now brought up, the four prisoners forced to mount, then roped together by long hemp cords. The cavalcade moved off into the gathering night.

Conversation was impossible at this bumping gallop. Father Chisholm was left to the mercy of his thoughts, which centered on the man now holding them for ransom.

Lately Wai's waning power had driven him to many excesses. From a traditional warlord, dominating the Chek-kow district of the province with his army of three thousand men, bought off by the various townships, levying taxes and imposts, living in feudal luxury in his walled fortress at Tou-en-lai, he had slowly fallen to ruinous days. At the height of his notoriety he had paid fifty thousand taels for a concubine from Pekin. Now he lived from hand-to-mouth by petty forays. Beaten decisively in two pitched battles with neighboring mercenaries, he had thrown in his lot first with the Min-tuan, then, in a fit of malice, with the opposing faction, the Yu-chi-tui. The truth was that neither desired his doubtful aid. Degenerate, vicious, he fought solely for his own hand. His men were steadily deserting. As the scale of his operations dwindled, his ferocity intensified. When he reached the humiliation of a bare two hundred followers, his round of pillage and burnings stood as a dreadful theme of terror. A fallen Lucifer, his hatreds fed on the glories he had lost; he was at enmity with mankind.

The night was interminable. They crossed a low range of hills, forded two rivulets, spattered for an hour through low-lying swamplands. Beyond that, and his conjecture from the polestar that they were traveling due west, Father Chisholm had no knowledge of the terrain they traversed. At his age, used to the quiet amble of his beast, the rapid jolting shook his bones until they rattled. But he reflected, with commiseration, that the Fiskes, too, were enduring the bone shaking, for the good God's sake. And Joshua, poor lad, though supple enough, was so young he must be sadly frightened. The priest told himself that on the return to the mission he would assuredly give the boy the roan pony he had coveted, silently, these past six months. Closing his eyes, he said a short prayer for the safety of their little party.

Dawn found them in a wilderness of rock and windblown sand, quite uninhabited, with no vegetation but scattered clumps of yellowish tuft grass. But within an hour, the sound of rushing water reached them, and there, behind an escarpment, was the ruined citadel of Tou-en-lai, a huddle of ancient mud-brick houses on the cliff slope, surrounded by a crenellated wall, scarred and scorched by many sieges, the old glazed pillars of a Buddhist temple standing roofless, by the riverside.

Within the walls, the party dismounted, and Wai, without a word, entered his house, the only habitable dwelling. The morning air was raw. As the missionaries stood shivering on the hard mud courtyard, still roped together, a number of women and older men came crowding from the little caves that honeycombed the cliff and joined the soldiers in a chattering inspection of the captives.

"We should be grateful for food and rest." Father Chisholm addressed the company at large.

"Food and rest." The words were repeated, passed from mouth to mouth, among the onlookers, as an amusing curiosity.

The priest proceeded patiently. "You observe how weary is the missionary woman." Mrs. Fiske was, indeed, half-fainting, on her feet. "Perhaps some well-disposed person would offer her hot tea."

"Tea . . . hot tea," echoed the mob, crowding closer.

They were now within touching distance of the missionaries and suddenly, with a simian acquisitiveness, an old man in the front rank snatched at the doctor's watch chain. It was the signal for a general spoliation—money, breviary, Bible, wedding ring, the priest's old silver pencil—in three minutes the little group stood divested of everything except their boots and clothing.

As the scramble ended, a woman's eye was caught by the dull sparkle of a jet buckle on the band of Mrs. Fiske's hat. Immediately, she clutched at it. Aware, desperately, of her awful hazard, Mrs. Fiske struggled, with a shrill defensive cry. But in vain. Buckle, hat, and wig came off together in her assailant's tenacious grasp. In a flash her bald head gleamed, like a bladder of lard, with grotesque and terrible nakedness, in the remorseless air.

There was a hush. Then a babble of derision broke, a paroxysm of shrieking mockery. Mrs. Fiske covered her face with her hands and burst into scalding tears. The doctor, attempting tremulously to cover his wife's scalp with his handkerchief, saw the colored silk snatched away. *Poor woman,* Father Chisholm thought, compassionately averting his eyes.

The sudden arrival of the corporal ended the hilarity as quickly as it had begun. The crowd scattered as the missionaries were led into one of the caves, which possessed the distinction of a hatch. This heavy-ribbed door was slammed and fastened. They were left alone.

"Well," said Father Chisholm—after a pause, "at least we have this to ourselves."

There was a longer silence. The little doctor, seated on the earth door with his arm about his weeping wife, said dully: "It was scarlet fever. She caught it the first year we were in China. She was so sensitive about it. We took such pains never to let a soul know."

"And no one will know," the priest lied swiftly. "Joshua and I are silent as the grave. When we return to Pai-tan the—the damage can be repaired."

"You hear that, Agnes, dear? Pray stop crying, my dearest love."

A slackening, then cessation of the muffled sobs. Mrs. Fiske slowly raised her tear-stained eyes, red-rimmed in that ostrich orb.

"You are very kind," she choked.

"Meanwhile, they seem to have left me with this. If it can be of any service." Father Chisholm produced a large maroon bandana from his inner pocket.

She took it humbly, gratefully; tied it, like a mobcap, with a butterfly knot behind her ear.

"There now, my dear." Fiske patted her on the back. "Why, you look quite captivating again."

"Do I, dear?" She smiled wanly, coquettishly. Her spirits lifted. "Now let's see what we can do to put this wretched *yao-fang* in order."

There was little they could do: the cave, no more than nine feet deep, held nothing but some broken crockery and its own dank gloom. The only light and air came from chinks in the barricaded entry. It was cheerless as a tomb. But they were worn-out. They stretched themselves on the floor. They slept.

It was afternoon when they were wakened by the creak of the opening hatch. A shaft of fantastic sunshine penetrated the *yao-fang;* then a middle-aged woman entered with a pitcher of hot water and two loaves of black bread. She stood watching as Father Chisholm handed one loaf to Dr. Fiske, then silently broke the other between Joshua and himself. Something in her attitude, in her dark and rather sullen face, caused the priest to gaze at her attentively.

"Why!" He gave a start of recognition. "You are Anna!" She did not answer. After sustaining his gaze, boldly, she turned and went out.

"Do you know that woman?" Fiske asked quickly.

"I am not sure. But yes, I am sure. She was a girl at the mission who . . . who ran away."

"Not a great tribute to your teaching." For the first time Fiske spoke acidly.

"We shall see."

That night they all slept badly. The discomforts of their confinement grew hourly. They took turns lying next to the hatch, for the privilege of breathing in the damp moist air. The little doctor kept groaning: "That awful bread! Dear heaven, it's tied my duodenum in a knot."

At noon, the next day, Anna came again with more hot water and a bowl of millet. Father Chisholm knew better than to address her by name.

"How long are we to be kept here?"

At first it seemed as though she would make no reply; then she said, indifferently: "The two men have departed for Pai-tan. When they return you will be free."

Dr. Fiske interposed restively: "Cannot you procure better food for us and blankets? We will pay."

She shook her head, scared off. But when she had retreated and let down the hatch she said, through the bars: "Pay me if you wish. It is not long to wait. It is nothing."

"Nothing." Fiske groaned again when she had gone. "I wish she had my insides."

"Don't give way, Wilbur." From the darkness beyond, Mrs. Fiske exhorted him. "Remember, we've been through this before."

"We were young, then. Not old crocks on the verge of going home. And this Wai . . . he's got his knife in us missionaries especially . . . for changing his good old order when crime paid."

She persisted: "We must all keep cheerful. Look, we've got to distract ourselves. Not talk—or you two will start quarrelling about religion. A game. The silliest we can think of! We'll play animal, vegetable, or mineral. Joshua, are you awake? Good. Now listen, and I'll explain how it goes."

They played the guessing game with heroic vigor. Joshua showed surprising aptitude. Then Mrs. Fiske's bright laugh cracked suddenly. They all fell very quiet. A dragging apathy succeeded; snatches of fitful sleep; uneasy, restless movements.

"Dear God, they must surely be back by now." All next day that phrase fell incessantly from Fiske's lips. His face and hands were hot to the touch. Lack of sleep and air had made him feverish. But it was evening before a loud shouting and the barking of dogs gave indication of a late arrival. The silence that followed was oppressive.

At last, footsteps approached, and the hatch was flung open. On being commanded, they scrambled out on their hands and knees. The freshness of the night air, the sense of space and freedom, induced a delirium, almost, of relief.

"Thank heaven!" Fiske cried. "We're all right now."

An escort of soldiers took them to Wai-Chu.

He was seated, in his dwelling, on a coir mat, a lamp and a long pipe beside him, the lofty dilapidated room impregnated with the faintly bitter reek of poppy. Beside him was a soldier with a soiled blood-stained rag tied round his forearm. Five others of his troop, including the corporal, stood by the walls with rattans in their hands.

A penetrating silence followed the introduction of the prisoners. Wai studied them with deep and meditative cruelty. It was a hidden cruelty, sensed rather than seen, behind the mask of his face.

"The voluntary gift has not been paid." His voice was flat, unemotional. "When my men advanced to the city to receive it one was killed and the other wounded."

A shiver passed over Father Chisholm. What he had dreaded had come to pass. He said:

"Probably the message was never delivered. The bearer was afraid and ran away to his home in Shansee without going to Pai-tan."

"You are too talkative. Ten strokes on the legs."

The priest had expected this. The punishment was severe; the edge of the long square rod, wielded by one of the soldiers, lacerating his shins and thighs.

"The messenger was our servant." Mrs. Fiske spoke with suppressed indignation, a high spot of color burning on her pale cheek. "It is not the Shang-Foo's fault if he ran away."

"You are also too talkative. Twenty slaps on the face."

She was beaten hard with the open palm on both cheeks while the doctor trembled and struggled beside her.

"Tell me, since you are so wise. If your servant ran away why should my emissaries be waited upon and ambushed?"

Father Chisholm wished to say that, in these times, the Pai-tan garrison was perpetually on the alert and would shoot any of Wai's men on sight. He knew this to be the explanation. He judged it wiser to hold his tongue.

"Now you are not so talkative. Ten strokes on the shoulders for keeping unnatural silence."

He was beaten again.

"Let us return to our missions." Fiske threw out his hands, gesticulating, like an agitated woman. "I assure you on my solemn oath that you will be paid without the slightest hesitation."

"I am not a fool!"

"Then send another of your soldiers to Lantern Street with a message that I will write. Send him now, immediately."

"And have him slaughtered also? Fifteen blows for assuming that I am a fool."

Under the blows the doctor burst into tears. "You are to be pitied," he blubbered. "I forgive you but I pity, I pity you."

There was a pause. It was almost possible to observe the dull flicker of gratification in Wai's contracted pupils. He turned to Joshua. The lad was healthy and strong. He desperately needed recruits.

"Tell me. Are you prepared to make atonement by enlisting under my banner?"

"I am sensible of the honor." Joshua spoke steadily. "But it is impossible."

"Renounce your foreign devil god and you will be spared."

Father Chisholm endured an instant of cruel suspense, preparing himself for the pain and humiliation of the boy's surrender.

"I will die gladly for the true Lord of Heaven."

"Thirty blows for being a contumacious wretch."

Joshua did not utter a cry. He took the punishment with eyes cast down. Not a moan escaped him. But every blow made Father Chisholm wince.

"Now will you advise your servant to repent?"

"Never." The priest answered firmly, his soul illuminated by the boy's courage.

"Twenty blows on the legs for reprehensible obduracy."

At the twelfth blow, delivered on the front of his shins, there was a sharp brittle crack. An agonizing pain shot through the broken limb. Oh Lord, thought Francis, that's the worst of old bones.

Wai considered them with an air of finality. "I cannot continue to shield you. If the money does not arrive tomorrow I have a foreboding that some evil may befall you."

He dismissed them blankly. Father Chisholm could barely limp across the courtyard. Back in the *yao-fang* Mrs. Fiske made him sit down and, kneeling beside him, stripped off his boot and sock. The doctor, somewhat recovered, then set the broken limb.

"I've no splint . . . nothing but these rags." His voice had a high and tremulous ring. "It's a nasty fracture. If you don't rest it'll turn compound. Feel how my hands are shaking. Help us, dear Lord! We're going home next month. We're not so—"

"Please, Wilbur." She soothed him with a quiet touch. He completed dressing the injury in silence. Then she added: "We must try to keep our spirits up. If we give in now, what's going to happen to us tomorrow?"

Perhaps it was well that she prepared them.

In the morning the four were led out into the courtyard, which was lined with the population of Tou-en-lai and humming with the promise of a spectacle. Their hands were tied behind their backs and a bamboo pole passed between their arms. Two soldiers then seized the ends of each spit and, raising the prisoners, marched them in procession round the arena six times, in narrowing circles, bringing up before the bullet-pocked facade of the house where Wai was seated.

Sick with the pain of his broken leg, Father Chisholm felt, through the stupid ignominy, a terrible dejection, amounting to despair, that the creatures of God's hand should make a careless festival out of the blood and tears of others. He had to still the dreadful whisper that God could never fashion men like this . . . that God did not exist.

He saw that several of the soldiers had their rifles; he hoped that a merciful end was near. But after a pause, at a sign from Wai, they were turned about and frog-marched down the steep path, past some beached sampans on a narrow spit of shingle, to the river. Here, before the reassembled crowd, they were dragged through the shallows and each secured with cord to a mooring stake in five feet of running water.

The switch from the threat of sudden execution was so unexpected, the contrast to the filthy squalor of the cave so profound, it was impossible to escape a sensation of relief. The shock of the water restored them. It was cold from mountain springs, and clear as crystal. The priest's leg ceased to pain him. Mrs. Fiske smiled feebly. Her courage was heartrending.

Her lips shaped the words: "At least we shall get clean."

But after half an hour a change set in. Father Chisholm dared not look at his companions. The river, at first so refreshing, gradually grew colder, colder, losing its gentle numbness, compressing their bodies and lower limbs in an algid vice. Each heartbeat, straining to force the blood through frozen arteries, was a throb of pulsing agony. The head, engorged, floated disembodied, in a reddish haze. With his swimming senses the priest still strove to find the reason of this torture, which now he dimly recollected as "the water ordeal," an intermittent sadism, hallowed by tradition, first conceived by the tyrant Tchang. It was a punishment well suited to Wai's purpose, since it probably expressed his lingering hope that the ransom might still be paid. Francis suppressed a groan. If this were true, their sufferings were not yet over.

"It's remarkable." With chattering teeth the doctor tried to talk. "This pain . . . perfect demonstration of angina pectoris . . . intermittent blood supply through constricted vascular system. O blessed Jesus!" He began to whimper. "O Lord God of Hosts—why hast thou forsaken us? My poor wife . . . thank God she has fainted. Where am I? . . . Agnes . . . Agnes . . ." He was unconscious.

The priest painfully turned his eyes toward Joshua. The boy's head, barely visible to his congested gaze, seemed decapitated, the head of a young St. John the Baptist on a streaming charger. Poor Joshua—and poor Joseph! How he would miss his eldest born. Francis said gently:

"My son, your courage and your faith—they are very pleasing to me."

"It is nothing, Master."

A pause. The priest, deeply moved, made a great effort to stem the torpor stealing over him.

"I meant to tell you, Joshua. You shall have the roan pony when we return to the mission."

"Does the master think we shall ever return to the mission?"

"If not, Joshua, the good God will give you a finer pony to ride in heaven."

Another pause. Joshua said faintly:

"I think, Father, I should prefer the little pony at the mission."

A great surging flowed into Francis's ears, ending their conversation with waves of darkness. When the priest came to himself again they were all back in the cave, flung together in a sodden heap. As he lay a moment, gathering his senses, he heard Fiske talking to his wife, in that querulous plaint to which his speech had fallen.

"At least we are out of it . . . that dreadful river."

"Yes, Wilbur dear, we are out of it. But unless I mistake that ruffian, tomorrow we shall be into it again." Her tone was quite practical as though she were discussing the menu for his dinner. "Don't let's delude ourselves, dearest. If he keeps us alive it's only because he means to kill us as horribly as possible."

"Aren't you . . . afraid, Agnes?"

"Not in the least, and you mustn't be either. You must show these poor pagans . . . and the father . . . how good New England Christians die."

"Agnes dear . . . you're a brave woman."

The priest could feel the pressure of her arm about her husband. He was greatly stirred, reshaken by a passionate concern for his companions, these three people, so different, yet each so dear to him. Was there no way of escape? He thought deeply, with gritted teeth, his brow pressed against the earth.

An hour later when the woman entered with a dish of rice he placed himself between her and the door.

"Anna! Do not deny that you are Anna! Have you no gratitude for all that was done for you at the mission? No—" She tried to push past him. "I shall not let you go until you listen. You are still a child of God. You cannot see us slowly murdered. I command you in his name to help us."

"I can do nothing." In the darkness of the cave it was impossible to see her face. But her voice, though sullen, was subdued.

"You can do much. Leave the hatch unfastened. No one will think to blame you."

"To what purpose? All the ponies are guarded."

"We need no ponies, Anna."

A spark of inquiry flashed in her lowering gaze. "If you leave Tou-en-lai on foot you will be retaken next day."

"We shall leave by sampan . . . and float downriver."

"Impossible." She shook her head with vehemence. "The rapids are too strong."

"Better to drown in the rapids than here."

"It is not my business where you drown." She answered with sudden passion: "Nor to help you in any manner whatsoever."

Unexpectedly, Dr. Fiske reached out in the darkness and gripped her hand. "Look, Anna, take my fingers and give heed. You must make it your business. Do you understand? Leave the door free tonight."

There was a pause.

"No." She hesitated, slowly withdrew her hand. "I cannot tonight."

"You must."

"I will do it tomorrow . . . tomorrow . . . tomorrow." With an odd change of manner, a sudden wildness, she bent her head and darted from the cave. The hatch closed behind her with a heavy slam.

And a heavier silence settled upon the cave. No one believed that the woman would keep her word. Even if she meant it, her promise was a feeble thing to weigh against the prospects of the coming day.

"I'm a sick man," Fiske muttered peevishly, laying his head against his wife's shoulder. In the darkness they could hear him percussing his own chest. "My clothes are still sopping. D'you hear that . . . it's quite dull . . . lobar consolidation. Oh, God, I thought the tortures of the Inquisition were matchless."

Somehow the night passed. The morning was cold and gray. As the light filtered through and sounds were heard in the courtyard, Mrs. Fiske straightened herself with a look of sublime resolution on her peaked and pallid face, still girded by the shrunken headdress. "Father Chisholm, you are the senior clergyman here. I ask you to say a prayer before we go out to what may be our martyrdom."

He knelt down beside her. They all joined hands. He prayed, as best he could, better than he had prayed in all his life. Then the soldiers came for them.

Weakened as they were, the river seemed colder than before. Fiske shouted hysterically as they drove him in. To Father Chisholm it now became a hazy vision.

Immersion, his thoughts ran mazily, purification by water, one drop and you were saved. How many drops were here? Millions and millions . . . four hundred million Chinese all waiting to be saved, each with a drop of water. . . .

"Father! Dear good Father Chisholm!" Mrs. Fiske was calling him, her eyes glassy with a sudden feverish gaiety. "They are all watching us from the bank. Let us show them. An example. Let us sing. What hymn have we in common? 'The Christmas Hymn,' of course. A sweet refrain. Come, Joshua . . . Wilbur . . . all of us."

She struck up, in a high quavering pipe:

"Oh, come, all ye faithful,
Joyful and triumphant . . ."

He joined with the others:

"Oh, come ye, oh, come ye, to Bethlehem."

Late afternoon. They were back in the cave again. The doctor lay on his side. His breath came raspingly. He spoke with an air of triumph.

"Lobar pneumonia. I knew it yesterday. Apical dullness and crepitations. I'm sorry, Agnes, but . . . I'm rather glad."

No one said anything. She began to stroke his hot forehead with her bleached sodden fingers. She was still stroking when Anna came to the cave. This time, however, the woman brought no food with her.

She did no more than stand in the entrance staring at them with a kind of grudging sullenness. At last she said:

"I have given the men your supper. They think it is a great joke. Go quickly before they discover their mistake."

There was an absolute silence. Father Chisholm felt his heart bound in his racked, exhausted body. It seemed impossible that they might leave the cave of their own free will. He said: "God will bless you, Anna. You have not forgotten him, and he has not forgotten you."

She gave no answer. She stared at him with her darkly inscrutable eyes, which he had never read, even on that first night amid the snow. Yet it gave him a burning satisfaction that she should justify his teaching, openly, before Dr. Fiske. She stood for a moment, then glided silently away.

Outside the cave it was dark. He could hear laughter and low voices from the neighboring *yao-fang.* Across the courtyard there was a light in Wai's house. The adjacent stables and soldiers' quarters showed a feeble illumination. The sudden barking of a dog sent a shock through his tortured nerves. This slender hope was like a new pain, suffocating in its intensity.

Cautiously, he tried to stand upon his feet. But it was impossible, he fell heavily, beads of perspiration breaking on his brow. His leg, swollen to three times its natural size, was quite unusable.

In a whisper he told Joshua to take the half-unconscious doctor on his back and carry him very quietly to the sampans. He saw them go off, accompanied by Mrs. Fiske, Joshua bent under his sacklike burden, keeping cleverly to the dense shadows of the rocks. The faint clatter of a loose stone came back to him, so loud it seemed to wake the dead. He breathed again; no one had heard it but himself. In five minutes Joshua returned. Leaning on the boy's shoulder, he dragged slowly and painfully down the path.

Fiske was already stretched out on the bottom of the sampan with his wife crouched beside him. The priest seated himself in the stern. Lifting his useless leg with both hands he arranged it out of the way, like a piece of timber, then propped himself against the gunwale with his elbow. As Joshua climbed into the bow and began to untie the mooring rope he seized the single stern oar in readiness to push off.

Suddenly a shout rang out from the top of the cliff, followed by another and the sound of running. A loud commotion broke; dogs set up a violent barking. Then two torches flared in the upper darkness and came rapidly, amid shrill voices and excited, clattering footsteps, down the river path.

The priest's lips moved in the anguished immobility of his body. But he remained silent. Joshua, fumbling and tearing at the matted rope, knew the danger, without the added confusion of a command.

At last, with a wild gasp, the boy pulled the rope loose, falling backward against the thwarts. Instantly, Father Chisholm felt the sampan float free, and with all his remaining strength he fended it into the current. Out of the slack water, they spun aimlessly, then began to slide downstream. Across and behind them, the flares now showed a group of running figures on the bank. A rifle shot cracked, followed by an irregular volley. The lead skipped the water with a twanging hum. They were sliding faster now, much faster; they were almost out of range. Father Chisholm was staring into the dark wall ahead with almost feverish relief when suddenly, amid the scattered shooting, a great weight struck at him out of the night. His head rocked under the impact of what seemed a heavy flying stone. Beyond the crashing blow he had no pain. He raised his hand to his wet face. The bullet had smashed through his upper jaw, torn out by his right check. He kept silent. The firing ceased. No one else was hit.

The river now moved them forward at intimidating speed. He was quite sure in his own mind that it must ultimately join the Hwang—no other outlet was possible. He leaned forward toward Fiske and, seeing him conscious, made an effort to cheer him.

"How do you feel?"

"Pretty comfortable, considering I'm dying." He repressed a short cough. "I'm sorry I've been such an old woman, Agnes."

"Please don't talk, dear."

The priest straightened himself, sadly. Fiske's life was ebbing away. His own resistance was almost gone. He had to fight an almost irresistible impulse to weep.

Presently an increase in the volume of the river's sound heralded their approach to broken water. The noise seemed to blot out what vision was left him. He could see nothing. With his single oar he pulled the sampan straight with the current. As they shot down, he commended their souls to God.

He was beyond caring, beyond realizing how the craft lived in that unseen thunder. The roar dulled him into stupor. He clung to the useless oar as they lurched and plunged, invisibly. At times they seemed to drop through empty space, as if the bottom had fallen from the boat. When a splintering crash arrested their momentum, he thought numbly that they must founder. But they plunged off again, the boiling water surging in on them as they whirled, down, down. Whenever he felt they must be free, a new roaring reared itself ahead, reached out, engulfed them. At a narrow bend they hit the rocky bank with stunning force, ripping low branches from overhanging trees, then bounced, spun, crashed on again. His brain was caught in the swirl, battered and jarred, down, down, down.

The peace of the quiet water, far below, brought him feebly to his senses. A faint streak of dawn lay ahead of them, limning a broad expanse of gentle pastoral waters. He could not guess what distance they had come, though dimly he surmised it must be many *li*. All he knew was this: they had reached the Hwang and were floating calmly on its bosom toward Pai-tan.

He tried to move, but could not, his weakness held him fettered. His damaged limb felt heavier than lead, the pain of his smashed face was like a raging toothache. But with incredible effort he turned and pulled himself slowly down the boat with his hands. The light increased. Joshua was huddled in the bow, his body limp, but breathing. He was asleep. In the bottom of the sampan Fiske and his wife lay together, her arm supporting his head, her body shielding him from the water they had shipped. She was awake and calmly reasonable. The priest was conscious of a great wonder as he gazed at her. She had shown the highest endurance of them all. Her eyes answered his unspoken inquiry with a wan negation. He could see that her husband was almost gone.

Fiske was breathing in little staccato spasms, with intervals when he did not breathe at all. He muttered constantly, but his eyes, though fixed, were open. And, suddenly, there appeared in them a vague, uncertain light of recognition. The shadow of a movement crossed his lips—nothing, yet in that nothingness hovered the suggestion of a smile. His muttering took on coherent form.

"Don't pride yourself . . . dear fellow . . . on Anna." A little gasp of breathing. "Not so much your teaching as—" Another spasm. "I bribed her." Weakly, the flutter of a laugh. "With the fifty-dollar bill I always carried in my shoe." A feeble triumphant pause. "But God bless you, dear fellow, all the same."

He seemed happier now he had scored his final point. He closed his eyes. As the sun rose in a flood of sudden light they saw that he was gone.

Back in the stern Father Chisholm watched Mrs. Fiske compose the dead man's hands. He looked dizzily at his own hands. The backs of both his wrists were covered peculiarly with raised red spots. When he touched them they rolled like buckshot beneath his skin. He thought, *Some insect has bitten me while I slept.*

Later, through the rising morning vapors, he saw downriver, in the distance, the flat boats of cormorant fishers. He closed his throbbing eyes. The sampan was drifting . . . drifting in the golden haze, toward them.

13

One afternoon six months later the two new missionary priests, Father Stephen Munsey, MB, and Father Jerome Craig, were earnestly discussing the arrangements over coffee and cigarettes.

"Everything has got to be perfect. Thank God the weather looks good."

"And settled." Father Jerome nodded. "It's a blessing we have the band."

They were young, healthy, full of vitality, with an immense belief in themselves and God. Father Munsey, the American priest, with a medical degree from Baltimore, was slightly the taller of the two, a fine six-footer, but Father Craig's shoulders had gained him a place in the Holywell boxing team. Though Craig was British he had a pleasant touch of American keenness, for he had taken a two years' missionary preparatory course at the College of St. Michael's in San Francisco. Here, indeed, he had met Father Munsey. The two had felt, instinctively, a mutual attraction, had soon become, affectionately, "Steve" and "Jerry" to each other—except on those occasions when a burst of self-conscious dignity induced a more formal tone. "Say, Jerry, old boy, are you playing basketball this afternoon?—And oh, er, by the way, Father, what time is your Mass tomorrow?" To be sent to Pai-tan together had set the seal upon their friendship.

"I asked Mother Mercy Mary to look in." Father Steve poured himself fresh coffee. He was clean-cut and virile, two years senior to Craig, admittedly the leader of the partnership. "Just to discuss the final touches. She's so cheery and obliging. She's going to be a great help to us."

"Yes, she's a grand person. Honestly, Jerry, we'll make things hum here when we have it to ourselves."

"Hist! Don't talk so loud," Father Steve warned. "The old boy's not so deaf as you'd think."

"He's a case." Father Jerry's blunt features melted to a reminiscent smile. "Of course I know you pulled him through. But at his age to shake off a broken leg, a smashed jaw, and the smallpox on top of it—well!—it says something for his pluck."

"He's terribly feeble though." Munsey spoke seriously. "It's quite finished him. I'm hoping the long voyage home'll do him good."

"He's a funny old devil—sorry, Father, I mean fogy. D'you remember, when he was so sick and Mrs. Fiske sent up the four-poster bed before she left for home? The awful trouble we had to get him into it? Remember how he kept saying 'How can I rest if I'm comfortable?'" Jerry laughed.

"And that other time he threw the beef tea at Mother Mercy Mary's head—" Father Steve stifled his grin. "No, no, Father, we mustn't let our tongues get the better of us. After all he's not so bad if you take him the right way. Anybody would get a bit queer in the topknot after being over thirty years out here alone. Thank God we're a pair. Come in."

Mother Mercy Mary entered, smiling, red cheeked, her eyes friendly and merry. She was very happy with her new priests, whom she thought of, instinctively, as two nice boys. She would mother them. It was good for the mission to have this infusion of young blood. It would be more human for her to have a proper priest's laundry to oversee, decent thick underwear to darn.

"Afternoon, Reverend Mother. Can we tempt you to the cup that cheers but doesn't inebriate? Good. Two lumps? We'll have to watch that sweet tooth of yours in Lent. Well now, about tomorrow's farewell ceremonies for Father Chisholm."

They talked together, amicably and earnestly, for half an hour. Then Mother Mercy Mary seemed to prick up her ears. Her expression of maternal protectiveness deepened. Listening acutely, she sounded a note of concern with her tongue.

"Do you hear him about? I don't. God bless my soul, I'm sure he's away out without telling us." She rose. "Excuse me, fathers. I'll have to find out what he's up to. If he goes and gets his feet wet it'll ruin everything."

Leaning on his old rolled umbrella, Father Chisholm had made a last pilgrimage of his mission of St. Andrew's. The slight exertion fatigued him absurdly; he realized, with an inward sigh, how sadly useless his long illness had left him. He was an old man. The thought was quite staggering—he felt so little different, within his heart, so unchanged. And tomorrow he must leave Pai-tan. Incredible! When he had made up his mind to lay his bones at the foot of the mission garden alongside Willie Tulloch. Phrases in the bishop's letter recurred to him: ". . . not up to it, solicitous your health, deeply appreciative, end your labors in the foreign mission field." Well, God's will be done!

He was standing, now, in the little churchyard, swept by a flood of tender, ghostly memories, noting the wooden crosses—Willie's, Sister Clotilde's, the gardener Fu's, a dozen more, each an end and a beginning, the milestones of their common pilgrimage.

He shook his head like an old horse amid a hum of insects in a sunny field: really he must not yield to reverie. He fixed his gaze across the low wall in the new pasture field. Joshua was putting the roan pony through its paces while four of his younger brothers watched admiringly. Joseph himself was not far off. Fat, complacent, and forty-five, shepherding the remainder of his nine children back from their afternoon stroll, he slowly pushed a wicker perambulator toward the lodge. What richer instance, thought the priest with a faint slow smile, of the subjugation of the noble male?

He had made the grand tour, as unobtrusively as possible, for he guessed what lay in store for him tomorrow. School, dormitory, refectory, the lace- and mat-making workrooms, the little annex he had opened last year to teach basket weaving to the blind children. Well . . . why continue the meager tally? In the past he had judged it some small achievement. In his present mood of gentle melancholy he measured it as nothing. He swung round stiffly. From the new hall came the ominous stertor of wind on brass. Again he suppressed a crooked smile, or was it perhaps a frown? These young curates with their explosive ideas! Only last night, when he was trying—vainly, of course—to instruct them in the topography of the parish, the doctor one had whispered: *airplane.* What were things coming to! Two hours by air to the Liu village. And his first trip had taken him two weeks on foot!

He ought not to go farther, for the afternoon was turning chill. But, though he knew his disobedience would earn a merited scolding, he pressed harder on his umbrella and went slowly down the Hill of Brilliant Green Jade toward the deserted site of the first forgotten mission. Though the compound was now rank with bamboo, the lower edge eroded to a muddy swamp, the mud-brick stable still remained.

He bowed his head and passed under the sagging roof, assailed, immediately, by another host of recollections, seeing a young priest, dark, eager, and intent, crouched before a brazier, his sole companion a Chinese boy. That first Mass he had celebrated here, on his japanned tin trunk without bell or server, no one but himself—how sharply it struck the taut chords of his memory. Clumsily, a stiff ungainly figure, he knelt down, and begged God to judge him less by his deeds than by his intention.

Back at the mission he let himself in by the side porch and went softly upstairs. He was fortunate; no one saw him come in. He did not wish "the grand slam," as he had come to call it, a flurry of feet and doors, with hot-water bottles and solicitous profferings of soup. But, as he opened the door of his room, he was surprised to find Mr. Chia inside. His disfigured face, now gray with cold, lit up to a sudden warmth. Heedless of formality, he took his old friend's hand and pressed it.

"I hoped you would come."

"How could I refrain from coming?" Mr. Chia spoke in a sad and strangely troubled voice. "My dear Father, I need not tell you how deeply I regret your departure. Our long friendship has meant much to me."

The priest answered quietly: "I, too, shall miss you much. Your kindness and benefactions have overwhelmed me."

"It is less than nothing," Mr. Chia waved the gratitude away, "beside your inestimable service to me. And have I not always enjoyed the peace and beauty of your mission garden? Without you, the garden will hold a great sadness." His tone lifted to a fitful gleam. "But then . . . perhaps, on your recovery . . . you may return to Pai-tan?"

"Never." The priest paused, with the suspicion of a smile. "We must look forward to our meeting in the celestial hereafter."

An odd silence fell. Mr. Chia broke it with constraint. "Since our time together is limited it might not be unfitting if we talked a moment regarding the hereafter."

"All my time is dedicated to such talk."

Mr. Chia hesitated, beset by unusual awkwardness. "I have never pondered deeply on what state lies beyond this life. But if such a state exists it would be very agreeable for me to enjoy your friendship there."

Despite his long experience, Father Chisholm did not grasp the import of the remark. He smiled but did not answer. And Mr. Chia was forced in great embarrassment to be direct.

"My friend, I have often said: there are many religions, and each has its gate to heaven." A faint color crept beneath his dark skin. "Now it would appear that I have the extraordinary desire to enter by your gate."

Dead silence. Father Chisholm's bent figure was immobilized, rigid.

"I cannot believe that you are serious."

"Once, many years ago, when you cured my son, I was not serious. But then I was unaware of the nature of your life . . . of its patience, quietness, and courage. The goodness of a religion is best judged by the goodness of its adherents. My friend . . . you have conquered me by example."

Father Chisholm raised his hand to his forehead, that familiar sign of hidden emotion. His conscience had often reproached him for his initial refusal to accept Mr. Chia, even without a true intention. He spoke slowly. "All day long my mouth has been bitter with the ashes of failure. Your words have rekindled the fires in my heart. Because of this one moment I feel that my work has not been worthless. In spite of that I say to you . . . don't do this for friendship—only if you have belief."

Mr. Chia answered firmly. "My mind is made up. I do it for friendship and belief. We are as brothers, you and I. Your Lord must also be mine. Then, even though you must depart tomorrow, I shall be content, knowing that in our Master's garden our spirits will one day meet."

At first the priest was unable to speak. He fought to conceal the depth of his feeling. He reached out his hand to Mr. Chia. In a low uncertain tone he said:

"Let us go down to the church. . . ."

Next morning broke warm and clear. Father Chisholm, awakened by the sound of singing, escaped from the sheets of Mrs. Fiske's bed and stumbled to the open window. Beneath his balcony twenty little girls from the junior school, none more than nine years of age, dressed in white and blue sashes, were serenading him: "Hail, smiling morn . . ." He grimaced at them. At the end of the tenth verse he called down:

"That's enough. Go and get your breakfast."

They stopped, smiled up at him, holding their music sheets. "Do you like it, Father?"

"No . . . Yes. But it's time for breakfast."

They started off again from the beginning and sang it all through with extra verses while he was shaving. At the words "on thy fresh cheek" he cut himself. Peering into the minute mirror at his own reflection, pocked and cicatrized, and now gory, he thought mildly, *Dear me, what a dreadful-looking ruffian I've become; I really must behave myself today.*

The breakfast gong sounded. Father Munsey and Father Craig were both waiting on him, alert, deferential, smiling—the one rushing to pull out his chair, the other to lift the cover from the kedgeree. They were so anxious to please they could scarcely sit still. He scowled.

"Will you young idiots kindly stop treating me like your great-grandmother on her hundredth birthday?"

Must humor the old boy, thought Father Jerry. He smiled tenderly. "Why, Father, we're just treating you like one of ourselves. Of course you can't escape the honor due to a pioneer who blazed the first trails. You don't want to, either. It's your natural reward, and don't you have any doubt about it."

"I have a great many doubts."

Father Steve said heartily: "Don't you worry, Father. I know how you feel, but we won't let you down. Why, Jerry—I mean Father Craig and I have schemes in hand for doubling the size and efficiency of St. Andrew's. We're going to have twenty catechists—pay them good wages too—start a rice kitchen in Lantern Street, right opposite your Methodist pals there. We'll poke them in the eye all right." He laughed good-naturedly, reassuringly. "It's going to be downright, honest, foursquare Catholicism. Wait till we get our plane! Wait till we start sending you our conversion graphs. Wait till—"

"The cows come home," said Father Chisholm dreamily.

The two young priests exchanged a sympathetic glance. Father Steve said kindly:

"You won't forget to take your medicine in the trip home, Father? One tablespoonful *ex aqua,* three times a day. There's a big bottle in your bag."

"No, there isn't. I threw it out before I came down." Suddenly Father Chisholm began to laugh. He laughed until he shook. "My dear boys, don't mind me. I'm a cantankerous scoundrel. You'll do grandly here if you're not too cocksure . . . if you're kind and tolerant, and especially if you don't try to teach every old Chinaman how to suck eggs."

"Why . . . yes . . . yes, of course, Father."

"Look! I have no airplanes to spare, but I'd like to leave you a useful little souvenir. It was given me by an old priest. It's been with me on most of my travels." He left the table, handed them from the corner of the room the tartan umbrella Rusty Mac had given him. "It has a certain status among the state umbrellas of Pai-tan. It may bring you luck."

Father Jerry took it gingerly as though it were a sort of a relic.

"Thank you, thank you, Father. What pretty colors. Are they Chinese?"

"Much worse, I'm afraid." The old priest smiled and shook his head. He would say no more.

Father Munsey put down his napkin with a surreptitious signal to his colleague. There was an organizing glitter in his eye. He rose.

"Well, Father, if you'll excuse Father Craig and myself. Time is getting on, and we're expecting Father Chou any moment now . . ."

They departed briskly.

He was due to leave at eleven o'clock. He returned to his room. When he had completed his modest packing he had still an hour in which to wander round. He descended, drawn instinctively toward the church. There, outside his house, he drew up, genuinely touched. His entire congregation, nearly five hundred, stood awaiting him, orderly and silent, in the courtyard. The contingent from the Liu village, under Father Chou, stood on one flank, the older girls and handicraft workers upon the other, with his beloved children, shepherded by Mother Mercy Mary, Martha, and the four Chinese sisters, in front. There was something in the mass attention of their eyes, all bent affectionately upon his insignificant form, which gripped him with a sudden pang.

A deeper hush. From his nervousness it was clear that Joseph had been entrusted with the honor of the address. Two chairs were produced like a conjuring trick. When the old father was seated in one, Joseph mounted unsteadily upon the other, almost overbalancing, and unrolled the vermilion scroll.

"Most reverend and worthy disciple of the Lord of Heaven, it is with the utmost anguish that we, thy children, witness thy departure across the broad oceans . . ."

The address was no different from a hundred other eulogies suffered in the past except that it was lachrymose. Despite a score of secret rehearsals before his wife, Joseph's delivery was vanquished by the open courtyard. He began to sweat, and his paunch quivered like a jelly. *Poor dear Joseph,* thought the priest, staring at his boots and thinking of a slim young boy running, unfaltering, at his bridle rein thirty years ago.

When it was over the entire congregation sang the *Gloria laus* quite beautifully. Still looking at his boots, as the clear voices ascended, the priest felt a melting of his old bones. "Dear God," he prayed, "don't let me make a fool of myself."

For the presentation, they had chosen the youngest girl in the basket-weaving center for the blind. She came forward, in her black skirt and white blouse, uncertain yet sure, guided by her instinct and Mother Mercy Mary's whispered instructions. As she knelt before him, holding out the ornate gilt chalice of execrable design, bought by mail order from Nankin, his eyes were sightless as her own. "Bless you, bless you, my child," he muttered. He could say no more.

Mr. Chia's number-one chair now swam into the orbit of his hazy vision. Disembodied hands helped him into it. The procession formed and set off amid the popping of firecrackers and a sudden burst of Sousa from the new school band.

As he swayed slowly down the hill, borne pontifically on the shoulders of the men, he tried to rivet his consciousness upon the gimcrack comedy of the band: twenty schoolboys in sky-blue uniforms, blowing their cheeks out, receded by a Chinese majorette aged eight in fleecy shako and high white boots, strutting, twirling a cane, kicking up her knees. But somehow, his sense of the ridiculous had ceased to function. In the town the doorways were crowded with friendly faces. More firecrackers welcomed him at every street crossing. As he neared the landing stage flowers were cast before him.

Mr. Chia's launch lay waiting at the steps, the engines quietly running. The chair was lowered, he stepped out. It had come at last. They were surrounding him, bidding him farewell: the two young priests, Father Chou, Reverend Mother, Martha, Mr. Chia, Joseph, Joshua . . . all of them, some of the women of the congregation weeping, kneeling to kiss his hand. He had meant to say something. He could not mumble one incoherent word. His breast was overflowing.

Blindly, he boarded the launch. As he turned again to face them there fell a bar of silence. At a prearranged signal, the children's choir began his favorite hymn: the *Veni Creator.* They had saved it till the last.

"Come, Holy Spirit, Creator, come,
From thy bright heav'nly throne."

He had always loved these noble words, written by the great Charlemagne in the ninth century, the loveliest hymn of the church. Everyone on the landing was singing now.

"Take possession of our souls,
And make them all thy own."

Oh, dear, he thought, yielding at last, that's kind, that's sweet of them . . . but oh, how wickedly unfair! A convulsive movement passed over his face.

As the launch moved away from the stage and he raised his hand to bless them, tears were streaming down his battered face.

PART V

The Return

1

His Grace Bishop Mealey was extremely late. Twice a nice young priest of the household had peeped round the parlor door to explain that His Lordship and His Lordship's secretary were detained, unavoidably, at a convocation. Father Chisholm blinked formidably over his copy of the *Tablet*.

"Punctuality is the politeness of prelates!"

"His Lordship is a very busy man." With an uncertain smile, the young priest withdrew, not quite sure of this old boy from China, half-wondering if he could be trusted with the silver. The appointment had been for eleven. Now the clock showed half past twelve.

It was the same room in which he had awaited his interview with Rusty Mac. How long ago? Good heavens . . . thirty-six years! He shook his head dolefully. It had amused him to intimidate the pretty stripling, but his mood was far from combative. He felt rather shaky this morning, and desperately nervous. He wanted something from the bishop. He hated asking favors, yet he must ask this one, and his heart had jumped when the summons to the interview arrived at the modest hotel where he had been staying since the ship unloaded him at Liverpool.

Valiantly, he straightened his wrinkled vest, spruced up his tired collar. He was not really old. There was plenty of go in him yet. Now that it was well past noon, Anselm would undoubtedly ask him to remain to luncheon. He would be spry, curb his outrageous tongue, listen to Anselm's stories, laugh at his jokes, not be above a little, or perhaps a lot of, flattery. He hoped to God the nerve wouldn't start twitching in his damaged cheek. That made him look a perfect lunatic!

It was ten minutes to one. At last there came a commotion of importance in the corridor outside and, decisively, Bishop Mealey entered the room. Perhaps he had been hurrying; his manner was brisk, his eye beaming toward Francis, not unconscious of the clock.

"My dear Francis. It's splendid to see you again. You must pardon this little delay. No, don't get up, I beg of you. We'll talk here. It's . . . it's more intimate than in my room."

Briskly, he pulled out a chair and seated himself with an easy grace beside Father Chisholm at the table. As he rested his fleshy, well-tended hand affectionately upon the other's sleeve, he thought: *Good heavens, how old and feeble he has become!*

"And how is dear Pai-tan? Not unflourishing, Monsignor Sleeth tells me. I vividly remember when I stood in that stricken city, amid deadly plague and desolation. Truly the hand of God lay upon it. Ah, those were my pioneering days, Francis. I pine for them sometimes. Now," he smiled, "I'm only a bishop. Do you see much change in me since we parted on that Orient strand?"

Francis studied his old friend with an odd admiration. There was no doubt of it—the years had improved Anselm Mealey.

Maturity had come late to him. His office had given him dignity, toned his early effusiveness to suavity. He had a fine presence and held his head high. The soft full ecclesiastic face was lit by the same velvety eye. He was well preserved, still had his own teeth, and a supple vigorous skin.

Francis said simply, "I've never seen you look better."

The bishop inclined his head, pleased. "O tempora! O mores! We're neither of us so young as we were. But I don't wear too badly. Frankly, I find perfect health essential to efficiency. If you knew what I have to cope with! They've put me on a balanced diet. And I have a masseur, a husky Swede, who literally pummels the fear of God into me. . . . I'm afraid," with a sudden genuine solicitude, "you've been very careless of yourself."

"I feel like an old ragman beside you, Anselm, and that is God's truth. . . . But I keep young in heart . . . or try to. And there's still some service left in me. I . . . I hope you're not altogether dissatisfied with my work in Pai-tan."

"My dear father, your efforts were heroic. Naturally we're a little disappointed in the figures. Monsignor Sleeth was showing me only yesterday . . ." The voice was quite benevolent. ". . . In all your thirty-six years you made less conversions than Father Lawler made in five. Please don't think I'm reproaching you—that would be too unkind. Someday when you have leisure we'll discuss it thoroughly. Meanwhile—" His eye was hovering round the clock. "Is there anything we can do for you?"

There was a pause; then, in a low tone, Francis answered: "Yes . . . there is, Your Grace. . . . I want a parish."

The bishop almost started out of his benign, affectionate composure. He slowly raised his brows as Father Chisholm continued, with that quiet intensity: "Give me Tweedside, Anselm. There's a vacancy at Renton . . . a bigger, better parish. Promote the Tweedside priest to Renton. And let me . . . let me go home."

The bishop's smile had become fixed, rather less easy, upon his handsome face. "My dear Francis, you seem to wish to administer my diocese."

"I have a special reason for asking you. I would be so very grateful . . ." To his horror Father Chisholm found his voice out of control. He broke off, then added huskily: "Bishop MacNabb promised I should have a parish if ever I came home." He began to fumble in his inside pocket. "I have his letter . . ."

Anselm raised his hand. "I can't be expected to honor the posthumous letters of my predecessor." A silence; then, with kindly urbanity, His Lordship continued: "Naturally, I will bear your request in mind. But I cannot promise. Tweedside has always been very dear to me. When the weight of the pro-cathedral is off my shoulders I had thought of building myself a retreat there—a little Castle Gondolfo." He paused—his ear, still keen, picking up the sound of an arriving car, followed by voices in the hall outside. Diplomatically his eye sought the clock. His pleasant manner quickened. "Well . . . it is all in God's hands. We shall see; we shall see."

"If you would let me explain—" Francis protested humbly. "I'm . . . rather anxious to make a home . . . for someone."

"You must tell me some other time." Another car outside and more voices. The bishop gathered up his violet cassock, his tone honeyed with regret. "It is quite a calamity, Francis, that I must slip away, just as I was looking forward to our long and interesting talk. I have an official luncheon at one. The lord mayor and city council are my guests. More politics, alas . . . school board, water board, finance . . . a quid pro quo . . . I have to be a stockbroker these days. . . . But I like it, Francis; I like it!"

"I wouldn't take more than a minute . . ." Francis stopped short, dropped his gaze to the floor.

The bishop had risen blandly. With his arm lightly on Father Chisholm's shoulder he aided him affectionately to the door. "I can't express what a great joy it has been for me to welcome you home. We will keep in touch with you, never fear. And now, I must leave you. Good-bye, Francis . . . and bless you."

Outside, a stream of large dark limousines flowed up the drive toward the high portico of the palace. The old priest had a vision of a purple face beneath a beaver hat, of more faces, hard and bloated, of miniver, gold chains of office. A wet wind was blowing, and it cut his old bones, used to sunshine and covered only by his thin tropic suit. As he moved away a car wheel churned near the curb, and a spurt of mud flew up and bit him in the eye. He wiped it off with his hand, gazing down the arches of the years, reflecting, with a faint grim smile: Anselm's mud bath is avenged.

His breast was cold, yet through his disappointment, his sinking weakness, a white flame burned, unquenchably. He must find a church at once. Across the street the great domed bulk of the new cathedral loomed, a million pounds in sterling, transmuted to massive stone and marble. He limped urgently toward it.

He reached the broad entrance steps, mounted them, then suddenly drew up. Before him, on the wet stone of the topmost step, a ragged cripple crouched in the wind, with a card pinned upon his chest: "Old Soldier, Please Help."

Francis contemplated the broken figure. He pulled out the solitary shilling from his pocket, placed it in the tin cup. The two unwanted soldiers gazed at each other in silence, then each gazed away.

He entered the procathedral, an echoing vastness of beauty and silence, pillared in marble, rich in oak and bronze, a temple of towering and intricate design, in which his mission chapel would have stood unnoticed, forgotten, in a corner of the transept. Undaunted, he marched toward the high altar. There he knelt and fiercely, with unshaken valor, prayed.

"Oh, Lord, for once—not thy will, but mine, be done."

2

Five weeks later Father Chisholm made his expedition, long deferred, to Kirkbridge. As he left the railway station the cotton-thread mills of that large industrial center were disgorging their workers for the dinner hour. Hundreds of women with shawls wrapped about their heads went hurrying through the drenching rain, yielding only to an occasional tram clanging over the greasy cobbles.

At the end of the main street he inquired his way, then took to the right, past an enormous statue erected to a local thread magnate, and entered a poorer locality: a squalid square imprisoned by high tenements. He crossed the square and plunged into a narrow alley, fetid with smells, so dark that, on the brightest day, no gleam of sun could penetrate. Despite his joy, his high excitement, the priest's heart sank. He had expected poverty but not this. . . . He thought: *What have I done in my stupidity and neglect!* Here, it was like being at the bottom of a well.

He inspected the numbers on the tenement entrances, singled out the right one, and began to climb the stairs, which were without light or air, the windows foul, the gas brackets plugged. A cracked soil pipe had drenched one landing.

Three flights up he stumbled and almost fell. A child was seated upon the stairs, a boy. The priest stared through the foggy gloom at the small rachitic figure, supporting his heavy head with one hand, bracing his sharp elbow against his bony knee. His skin was the color of candle tallow. He was almost transparent. He looked like a tired old man. He might have been seven years of age.

Suddenly the boy lifted his head so that a shaft from the broken skylight fell upon him. For the first time Francis saw the child's face. He gave a stifled exclamation, and a heavy wave of terrible emotion broke over him; he felt it as a ship might feel the buffet of a heavy wave. That pallid upturned face was unmistakable in its likeness to Nora's face. The eyes, especially, enormous in the pinched skin, could never be denied.

"What is your name?"

A pause. The boy answered: "Andrew."

Behind the landing door there was a single room where, cross-legged on a dirty mattress stretched on the bare boards, a woman stitched rapidly, her needle flying with deadly, automatic speed. Beside her, on an upturned egg box, was a bottle. There was no furniture, only a kettle, some sacking, and a cracked jug. Across the egg box lay a pile of half-finished coarse serge trousers.

Torn by his distress, Francis could barely speak. "You are Mrs. Stevens?" She nodded. "I came . . . about the boy."

She let her work fall nervously into her lap: a poor creature, not old, nor vicious, yet worn-out by adversity, sodden through and through. "Yes, I had your letter." She began to whimper out an explanation of her circumstances, to exonerate herself, to produce irrelevant evidence proving how misfortune had lowered her to this.

He stopped her quietly; the story was written in her face. He said: "I'll take him back with me today."

At this quietness, she dropped her eyes to her swollen hands, the fingers blue stippled by countless needle pricks. Though she made an effort to conceal it, his attitude agitated her more than any rebuke. She began to weep.

"Don't think I'm not fond of him. He helps me in a heap of ways. I've treated him well enough. But it's been a sore struggle." She looked up with sudden defiance, silent.

Ten minutes later he left the house. Beside him, clutching a paper bundle to his pigeon chest, was Andrew. The priest's feelings were deep and complex. He sensed the child's dumb alarm at the unprecedented excursion, yet felt he could best reassure him by silence. He thought, with a slow deep joy: God gave me my life, brought me from China . . . for this!

They walked to the railway station without a word between them. In the train, Andrew sat staring out of the window, hardly moving, his legs dangling over the edge of the seat. He was very dirty; grime was ingrained into his thin pallid neck. Once or twice he glanced sideways at Francis, then immediately he glanced away again. It was impossible to guess his thoughts, but in the depths of his eyes there lurked a dark glimmer of fear and suspicion.

"Don't be afraid."

"I'm not afraid." The boy's underlip quivered.

Once the train had quitted the smoke of Kirkbridge it sped across the country and down the riverside. A look of wonder dawned slowly on the boy's face. He had never dreamed that colors could be so bright, so different from the leaden squalor of the slums. The open fields and farmlands gave place to a wilder scene, where woods sprang up about them, rich with green bracken and the part's-tongue fern, where the glint of rushing water showed in little glens.

"Is this where we are going?"

"Yes, we're nearly there."

They ran into Tweedside toward three in the afternoon. The old town, clustered on the riverbank, so unchanged he might have left it only yesterday, lay basking in brilliant sunshine. As the familiar landmarks swam into his gaze Francis's throat constricted with a painful joy. They left the little station and walked to St. Columba's presbytery together.

PART VI

End of the Beginning

1

From the window of his room Monsignor Sleeth frowned down toward the garden where Miss Moffat, basket in hand, stood with Andrew and Father Chisholm, watching Dougal fork up the dinner vegetables. The tacit air of companionship surrounding the little group heightened his fretful feeling of exclusion, hardened his resolution. On the table behind him, typed on his portable machine, lay his finished report—a terse and lucid document, crammed with hanging evidence. He was leaving for Tynecastle in an hour. It would be in the bishop's hands this evening.

Despite the keen, incisive satisfaction of accomplishment it was undeniable that the past week at St. Columba's had been trying. He had found much to annoy, even to confuse him. Except for a group centered round the pious yet obese Mrs. Glendenning, the people of the parish had some regard, he might even say affection, for their eccentric pastor. Yesterday, he had been obliged to deal severely with the delegation that waited on him to protest their loyalty to the parish priest. As if he didn't know that every native son must have his claque! The height of his exasperation was touched that same evening when the local Presbyterian minister dropped in and, after hemming and hawing, ventured to hope that Father Chisholm was not "leaving them"—the "feeling" in the town had lately been so admirable. . . . Admirable—indeed!

While he meditated, the group beneath his eye broke up, and Andrew ran to the summerhouse to get his kite. The old man had a mania for making kites, great paper things with waving tails, which flew—Sleeth grudgingly admitted—like monster birds. On Tuesday, coming upon the two breezily attached to the clouds by humming twine, he had ventured to remonstrate.

"Really, Father. Do you think this pastime dignified?"

The old man had smiled—confound it, he was never rebellious: always that quiet, maddeningly gentle smile.

"The Chinese do. And they're a dignified people."

"It's one of their pagan customs, I presume."

"Ah, well! Surely a very innocent one!"

He remained aloof, his nose turning blue in the sharp wind, watching them. It appeared that the old priest was merging pleasure with instruction. From time to time, while he held the string, the boy would sit in the summerhouse taking down dictation on strips of paper. Completed, these labored scrawls were threaded on the string, sent soaring to the sky, amid joint jubilation.

An impulse of curiosity had mastered him. He took the latest missive from the boy's excited hands. It was clearly written and not ill spelled. He read: "I faithfully promise to oppose bravely all that is stupid and bigoted and cruel. Signed, ANDREW. *PS.* Toleration is the highest virtue. Humility comes next."

He looked at it bleakly, for a long time, before surrendering it. He even waited with a chilled face until the next was prepared. "Our bones may molder and become the earth of the fields, but the spirit issues forth and lives on high in a condition of glorious brightness. God is the common father of all mankind."

Mollified, Sleeth looked at Father Chisholm. "Excellent. Didn't St. Paul say that?"

"No." The old man shook his head apologetically. "It was Confucius."

Sleeth was staggered. He walked away without a word.

That night he misguidedly began an argument, which the old man evaded with disconcerting ease. At the end he burst out, provoked:

"Your notion of God is a strange one."

"Which of us has any notion of God?" Father Chisholm smiled. "Our word *God* is a human word . . . expressing reverence for our Creator. If we have that reverence, we shall see God . . . never fear."

To his annoyance, Sleeth had found himself flushing. "You seem to have a very slight regard for Holy Church."

"On the contrary . . . all my life I have rejoiced to feel her arms about me. The church is our great mother, leading us forward . . . a band of pilgrims, through the night. But perhaps there are other mothers. And perhaps even some poor solitary pilgrims who stumble home alone."

The scene, of which this was a fragment, seriously disconcerted Sleeth and gave him, when he returned that night, a shockingly distorted nightmare. He dreamed that while the house slept, his guardian angel and Father Chisholm's knocked off for an hour and went down to the living room for a drink. Chisholm's angel was a slight cherubic creature, but his own was an elderly angel with discontented eyes and a ruffled angry plumage. As they sipped their drink, wings at rest on the elbows of their chairs, they discussed their present charges. Chisholm, although indicted as a sentimentalist, escaped lightly. But he . . . he was torn to shreds. He sweated in his sleep as he heard his angel dismiss him with a final malediction. "One of the worst I ever had . . . prejudiced, pedantic, overambitious, and worst of all, a bore."

Sleeth wakened with a start in the darkness of his room. What a hateful, disgusting dream. He shivered. His head ached. He knew better than to give credence to such nightmares, no more than odious distortions of one's waking thoughts, altogether different from the good, authentic scriptural dreams, that of Pharaoh's wife, for instance. He dismissed his dream violently, like an impure thought. But it nagged him now, as he stood at the window: *prejudiced, pedantic, overambitious, and worst of all, a bore.*

Apparently he had misjudged Andrew, for the child emerged from the summerhouse bearing, not his kite, but a large wicker trug into which, with Dougal's aid, he began to place some fresh-picked plums and pears. When the task was accomplished the boy moved toward the house, carrying the long basket on his arm.

Sleeth had an inexplicable impulse to retreat. He sensed that the gift was for him. He resented it, was vaguely, absurdly disconcerted. The knock on his door made him pull his scattered wits together.

"Come in."

Andrew entered the room and put the fruits upon the chest of drawers. With the shamed consciousness of one who knows himself suspected, he delivered his message, memorized all the way upstairs. "Father Chisholm hopes you will take these with you—the plums are very sweet—and the pears are the very last we'll get."

Monsignor Sleeth looked sharply at the boy, wondering if a double meaning were intended in that final simple phrase.

"Where is Father Chisholm?"

"Downstairs. Waiting on you."

"And my car?"

"Dougal has just brought it round for you to the front door."

There was a pause. Andrew began, hesitantly, to move away.

"Wait!" Sleeth drew up. "Don't you think it would be more convenient . . . altogether politer . . . if you carried down the fruit and put it in my car?"

The boy colored nervously and turned to obey. As he lifted the basket from the chest one of the plums fell off and rolled below the bed. Darkly red, he stooped and clumsily retrieved it, its smooth skin burst, a trickle of juice upon his fingers. Sleeth watched him with a cold smile.

"That one won't be much good . . . will it?"

No answer.

"I said, will it?"

"No, sir."

Sleeth's strange pale smile deepened. "You are a remarkably stubborn child. I've been watching you all the week. Stubborn and ill bred. Why don't you look at me?"

With a tremendous effort the boy wrenched his eyes from the floor. He was trembling, like a nervous foal, as he met Sleeth's gaze.

"It is the sign of a guilty conscience not to look straight at a person. Besides being bad manners. They'll have to teach you better at Ralstone."

Another silence. The boy's face was white. Monsignor Sleeth still smiled. He moistened his lips.

"Why don't you answer? Is it because you do not wish to go to the home?"

The boy faltered: "I don't want to go."

"Ah! But you want to do what is right, don't you?"

"Yes, sir."

"Then you will go. In fact, I may tell you that you are going very soon. Now you may put the fruit in the car. If you can do so without dropping all of it."

When the boy had gone, Monsignor Sleeth remained motionless, the contour of his lips fixed into a stiff, straight mold. His arms stretched down at his sides. His hands were clenched.

With that same stiff look upon his face he moved to the table. He could not have believed himself capable of such sadism. But that very cruelty had purged the darkness from his soul. Without hesitation, inevitably, he took up his compiled report, and tore it into shreds. His fingers ripped the sheets with methodical violence. He threw the torn and twisted fragments from him, scattered them irrevocably on the floor. Then he groaned and sank upon his knees.

"Oh, Lord." His voice was simple and pleading. "Let me learn something from this old man. And dear Lord . . . don't let me be a bore."

That same afternoon, when Monsignor Sleeth had gone, Father Chisholm and Andrew came guardedly through the back door of the house. Though the boy's eyes were still swollen, their brightness was that of expectation, his face, at last, was reassured.

"Be careful of the nasturtiums, laddie." Francis urged the boy forward with a conspirator's whisper. "Heaven knows we've had enough trouble in one day without Dougal starting on us."

While Andrew dug the worms in the flower bed the old man went to the toolshed, brought out their trout rods, and stood waiting at the gate. When the child arrived, breathless, with a wriggling tinful, he chuckled.

"Aren't you the lucky boy to be going trouting with the best fisher in all Tweedside? The good God made the little fishes, Andrew . . . and sent us here to catch them."

Their two figures, hand in hand, dwindled and disappeared, down the pathway, to the river.

The End

Questions for Reflection and Discussion

Use the following questions as guides to deeper individual understanding of the novel or for group discussion.

1. What is your general impression of Father Francis Chisholm's personality and character?

2. Father Chisholm believes himself to be prideful. At one point he scolds himself for "my incorrigibly rebellious nature" (p. 194). Do you see these faults in him? Does he have other faults?

3. Father Chisholm endures great frustration in his work. Few of his superiors and coworkers are sympathetic. He suffers great hardship and personal danger. What equips him to persevere?

4. What kind of spiritual life does Father Chisholm have?

5. Father Chisholm makes no effort to lead the dying agnostic Dr. Tulloch to Christian faith, and Dr. Tulloch thanks him "for not trying to bully me to heaven" (p. 285). What is your reaction to this scene? Should Father Chisholm have acted differently?

6. A dramatic peak in the novel comes when Mother Maria-Veronica accuses Father Chisholm of error in suggesting that Dr. Tulloch might have been saved despite his unbelief. Father Chisholm replies by saying "God judges us not only by what we believe . . . but by what we do" (p. 289). Does one of them "win" this theological argument, or does each of them have a point?

7. Father Chisholm professes pacifist beliefs, yet he intervenes on one side of the battle between warlords, and his actions cause the death of dozens of men. Did he act rightly? Does Father Chisholm himself think he acted rightly?

8. What do you think of Cronin's portrayal of the Chinese characters in the novel? Are they convincingly portrayed? Are they as convincing as the European characters?

9. *The Keys of the Kingdom* critiques a harsh, legalistic approach to the Catholic faith. This approach is embodied in the callous attitude of Father Kezer: "'Do this or be damned' was imprinted on his heart" (p. 139). Why do Father Kezer and the religious people like him act this way? Is their understanding of the Christian faith deficient, or are they people with serious character defects?

10. The title of the book is a reference to the Gospel passage where Jesus confers authority on Peter and is often interpreted as scriptural basis for the authority of the hierarchy of the Catholic Church. However, the book is highly critical of the hierarchy. What, then, does the title mean?

About the Author

Archibald Joseph Cronin was born in 1896 in Cardross, Scotland, the only child of a Catholic father and a Protestant mother. His childhood was shadowed by the death of his father and poverty; his mother tried to struggle forward alone but eventually was forced to return to her parents' home. Cronin would later often write of poor young people from mixed religious backgrounds. He was a precocious student who won writing competitions and was awarded a scholarship to study medicine at the University of Glasgow.

After serving as a surgeon in the Royal Navy during World War I, Cronin set up a medical practice in an impoverished region of Wales, where he was also appointed the medical inspector of mines. His exposure to the terrible conditions in the mines and their effect on workers' health shaped his social conscience. He drew on these experiences for his fiction, most notably *The Citadel,* set in Wales, and *The Stars Look Down,* set in northeastern England. After several years in Wales, Cronin moved to London and established a successful practice on Harley Street.

While recuperating from an illness in the Scottish Highlands, Cronin wrote his first novel, *Hatter's Castle.* He said that at one point in the writing he gave up on the novel and threw away the manuscript. He was encouraged to finish by an old farmer, who was digging a ditch that his father had started and left uncompleted. *Hatter's Castle* was a huge popular success, and it permitted Cronin to give up medicine and take up writing full-time.

Cronin wrote thirty novels and story collections, many of them best sellers. His fiction is marked by strong plots, acutely observed settings, and graphic description. Several of his novels, including *The Citadel* and *The Keys of the Kingdom,* were made into popular movies. Gregory Peck received an Oscar nomination for his portrayal of Father Francis Chisholm, the hero of *The Keys of the Kingdom.* Pointed social criticism is a theme in much of Cronin's fiction. Some credit *The Citadel,* which vividly portrayed wretched medical care for the poor, with hastening the establishment of the National Health Service in the United Kingdom.

Religious faith is another important theme in Cronin's writing. As a youth he was mocked for his Catholic faith and he fell away from religion until the 1930s, when his faith reawakened. He detested religious bigotry and dreamed of brotherhood and ecumenical conciliation among the different churches.

Cronin moved to the United States in the 1930s with his wife and three sons. He later settled in Switzerland. He died in Montreaux, Switzerland, in 1981.

Readers,

We'd like to hear from you! What other classic Catholic novels would you like to see in the Loyola Classics series? Please e-mail your suggestions and comments to **loyolaclassics@loyolapress.com** or mail them to:

Loyola Classics
Loyola Press
3441 N. Ashland Avenue
Chicago, IL 60657

LOYOLA CLASSICS

Catholics	Brian Moore	978-0-8294-2333-4	$12.95
Cosmas or the Love of God	Pierre de Calan	978-0-8294-2395-2	$12.95
Dear James	Jon Hassler	978-0-8294-2430-0	$12.95
The Devil's Advocate	Morris L. West	978-0-8294-2156-9	$12.95
Do Black Patent Leather Shoes Really Reflect Up?	John R. Powers	978-0-8294-2143-9	$12.95
The Edge of Sadness	Edwin O'Connor	978-0-8294-2123-1	$13.95
Five for Sorrow, Ten for Joy	Rumer Godden	978-0-8294-2473-7	$13.95
Helena	Evelyn Waugh	978-0-8294-2122-4	$12.95
In This House of Brede	Rumer Godden	978-0-8294-2128-6	$13.95
The Keys of the Kingdom	A. J. Cronin	978-0-8294-2334-1	$13.95
The Last Catholic in America	John R. Powers	978-0-8294-2130-9	$12.95
The Man on a Donkey, Part 1	H. F. M. Prescott	978-0-8294-2639-7	$13.95
The Man on a Donkey, Part 2	H. F. M. Prescott	978-0-8294-2731-8	$13.95
Mr. Blue	Myles Connolly	978-0-8294-2131-6	$11.95
North of Hope	Jon Hassler	978-0-8294-2357-0	$13.95
Saint Francis	Nikos Kazantzakis	978-0-8294-2129-3	$13.95
The Silver Chalice	Thomas Costain	978-0-8294-2350-1	$13.95
Son of Dust	H. F. M. Prescott	978-0-8294-2352-5	$13.95
Things As They Are	Paul Horgan	978-0-8294-2332-7	$12.95
The Unoriginal Sinner and the Ice-Cream God	John R. Powers	978-0-8294-2429-4	$12.95
Vipers' Tangle	François Mauriac	978-0-8294-2211-5	$12.95

Available at your local bookstore, or visit
www.loyolapress.com/loyola-classics or call **800.621.1008** to order.